Foreword

Content warnings

This story does have a happily ever after, but please be aware it does contain some very sensitive topics that some readers may find upsetting. It's important to look after your own mental health and be aware of what you are reading. This story mentions alcohol abuse, adultery, absent parent, sexual assault, domestic violence and losing a loved one in the line of duty.

Please make sure you are comfortable with the above before reading.

I hope you enjoy their story.

Playlist

Prologue
Enough for you – Olivia Rodrigo
Bust your windows – Jazmine Sullivan
Heard it all before – Sunshine Anderson
Just a Mess – Tones and I

Chapter One
I can do it with a broken heart -Taylor Swift

Chapter Two
So long, London – Taylor Swift

Chapter Three
Grown Woman – Beyonce
Pink Friday Girls – Nicki Minaj

Chapter Four
Lovin' on me – Jack Harlow

Chapter Five
Where the party at – Jagged Edge
Only Girl in the world – Rhianna

Chapter Six
What's your fantasy – Ludacris
We found love – Rihanna
Higher Love – Kygo/Whitney Houston
Chapter Seven
SOS – Rhianna
Chapter Eight
Unwritten – Natasha Bedingfield
As if – Blaque
Chapter Nine
Caught Up – usher
Chapter Ten
Almost – Hozier
Waves – Miguel
Chapter eleven
The shoop shoop song – Cher
Chapter Twelve
Broken and it's beautiful – Kelly Clarkson
Chapter Thirteen
Little Bitty Pretty One – Thurston
Let's get Married – Jagged edge
Peaches and cream -112
Chapter Fourteen
Can I be him – James Arthur
Chapter Fifteen
Fantasy – Mariah Carey
Chapter Sixteen
Miss Independent - Neyo
Chapter Seventeen
He's Mine – Accelerate
Temptation – Destiny Child

The other side – Jason Derulo
Chapter Eighteen
I feel it coming – The Weekend
Chapter Nineteen
Never say never - The Fray
Run to you – Whitney Houston
Take me Home – Jess Glynne
Chapter Twenty
Soldier – Gavin De Graw
Act II Sugar plum fairy -Pyotr
Hop little bunnies – Toddler fun
Chapter Twenty One
The one that got away – Katy Perry
One touch – Jess Glynne
Chapter Twenty Two
Hotline – Pretty Ricky
Kiss me through the phone – Soulja Boy
Chapter Twenty Three
Give me everything tonight – Neyo
Chapter Twenty Four
Baby by me – 50 cent, Neyo
Love lifts us up- Jo Cocker
Broken – Jess Glynne
Chapter Twenty Five
Dive – Luke Coombs
Kiss me – Ed Sheeran
Chapter Twenty Six
Velvet – Mackenzie
Chapter Twenty Seven
Wrap your arms around me – Gareth Dunlop
Chapter Twenty Eight

The Bones – Maren Morris
Chapter Twenty Nine
Never fully dressed without a smile - Sia
Chapter Thirty
Birds of a feather – Billie Elish
Chapter Thirty One
Just like a pill - Pink
I'd rather Overdose – Honestav
Chapter Thirty Two
Piece by piece – Kelly Clarkson
I'll look after you – The Fray
Chapter Thirty Three
That's how strong my love is – Otis Redding
Chapter Thirty Four
Sunshine (my girl) _ Wuki
Chapter Thirty Five
Slow Grind – Pretty Ricky
Apologize – One republic
Chapter Thirty Six
Love me for the both of us – CJ Fam
Not a bad thing – Just Timberlake
Loved By You - Kirby
Chapter Thirty Seven
You are my sunshine – Jasmine Thompson
Chapter Thirty Eight
Can't help falling in love with you – Kina Grannis
Chapter Thirty Nine
The way you look tonight – Frank Sinatra
LOVE – Joss Stone
Chapter Forty
You don't own me – SAYGRACE

Happier than ever – Kelly Clarkson
Chapter Forty One
Try a little tenderness – Otis Redding
Chapter Forty Two
Neighbors know my name – Trey
Photograph – Ed Sheeran
From the Jump – James Arthur
A thousand Years – James Arthur
Chapter Forty Three
XO – Beyonce
You should be sad – Halsey
Chapter Forty Four
Rescue – Lauren Daigle
Chapter Forty Five
Rise up – Andra Day
Chapter Forty six
I knew I loved you – Savage Garden
Latch – Acoustic
Chapter Forty seven
Came here for love – Siagala
Chapter Forty Eight
There will be time – Mumford and Sons
Chapter Forty Nine
Until I found you - Stephen Sanchez
All my life – Kaci and JoJo
Epilogue
High – Lighthouse family

To Véronique

Dedication

To the girl reading this, who may question her worth. I hope this makes you believe that you deserve the type of love that doesn't make you question a thing.

*All my love
N. L'Amore
XO ♡*

Prologue

Ria

You know that question they ask you in high school? *'Where do you see yourself in ten years time?'* And of course, you say all the things you think you're meant to; Have a successful career, a loving, devoted husband, 2.4 kids, and a golden retriever. Well, I have all that.

I've got the husband, the kids, and the family. Eighteen-year-old me would be happy with the life I have; Twenty-eight-year-old me is faced with a reality that is not as idyllic as I imagined.

I stare at my husband's shirt, which is stained with red lipstick on the collar, feeling like I'm about to lose my mind because all I can think about is how I need to get this stain off. I can't look at the evidence of his wandering eyes anymore. My hand trembles as I reach for the stain remover. My heart races as I pour it onto the fabric. I scrub... and I scrub. but all I can do is watch as the stain grows, ruining the shirt forever. I can barely breathe, my body thrumming from the exertion. I pause the assault on the shirt, the smell of the stain remover tickling the back of my throat, my eyes burning with the threat of tears as I look down at the ruined fabric. I can't save the shirt. I can't fucking save the shirt. I've tried, but I can't. A lump lodges in my throat, thick and unwelcome.

An invisible weight drags my body to the floor as I grip the now wet material to my chest. Memories of all the other times I've ignored the stains on his shirts flood my brain. All the times I replaced them without question. But tonight, I needed to save the shirt. I know I can't keep replacing them. I can't keep pretending. A sob fights its way into my throat, but I stifle it and try to focus on anything that will ground me. The cool floor against my legs, the washer-dryer pressing against my back. It's enough to stop me falling apart.

How did it come to this? When did he decide I was no longer enough? When did he fall out of love with me? Was he ever in love with me?

I knew I didn't have the best example of what love was growing up. My childhood home was a burning one, fueled by chaos and drama, and after spending a brief time in foster care, I swore that wouldn't be my life. I'd get out, I'd do better. I thought I'd won the life lottery meeting Alex. Handsome, kind, from a good family and he showered me with love and affection, but maybe I was blinded by what I thought love was. Maybe, I am no better than my mother.

Have I spent my marriage being a blind fool?

Anger bubbles up inside me. This won't be my life. I refuse. My girls won't grow up like I did. I stare down at the shirt, the red stain still bleeding out and I know what I need to do.

I rise to my feet, throwing the shirt on the counter. Wiping my eyes with the back of my hand, I let out a long breath, sighing. I know what I need to do.

I grab trash bags from the cupboard and stride out of the laundry room and down the hall to our bedroom. I stand in front of his neatly hung suits and shirts in our walk-in closet; ones I've spent hours making sure were freshly laundered and ready when he needed them, and rip them down, one by one.

Tears flowing, my pulse racing, I shove it all into the trash bags. Every tug of his clothing pushes my anger levels higher until I'm shaking with unexpressed rage.

Dragging the trash bags through our bedroom, I open the window, tossing the lot out onto the manicured lawn below. The thought of removing every trace of Alex consumes me.

Taking the stairs two at a time, thankful that the girls are sleeping over at Alex's parents' house and not here to witness this. I want to hit him right where it hurts. Heading outside and opening up the garage door, I frantically look around for his most prized possession.

Bingo

I swear I'm having an out-of-body experience. I don't think about my actions, I just do it. Pulling his favorite club from the bag, I lift it above my head, and drive it as hard as I can into the garage wall, screaming every time metal meets brick.

Each strike is for every lipstick stain I've found on a shirt, every time he's climbed into bed smelling of another woman's perfume, the nights he's left me alone to tend to our girls and been God knows where, and for always feeling like an afterthought and never his priority. If I had a cent for every time he's made me feel worthless, I'd be worth something by now. I know we could have been happy, and that's the hardest part to accept, but I just wasn't enough. I hit again and again with every club till they are all bent and broken, just like he's left my heart.

Then, throwing the last club to the ground, chest heaving, I swipe my hair away from my sweat-soaked face, thinking of what I can get rid of next.

As I go back into the house, I try not to glance at the family photos that line the walls of the staircase. A reminder of the lie we've been living. I grip the handrail on the way up the stairs, steadying myself as a wave of dizziness washes over me. I focus on my breathing, rubbing my free hand against my thumping chest, willing the panic attack that's fighting to take over my body to settle.

Breathe, Ria. You're okay. Just breathe.

I slow my steps as I head back to our bedroom, taking in the mess I've left on our plush cream carpet; a carpet I chose for what was meant to be our forever home. My safe space from the chaos I was running from, but all I appear to have done is run from one burning building to the other.

The panic attack now almost suffocates me. I need to get out. I need him out. I search through the rest of the closet, grabbing as much of Alex's stuff as my hands will hold. As I throw his belongings like they are hand grenades ready to detonate, I hear the front door open and slam shut. Seconds later Alex roars, "Ria, what the fuck?" My body's stills. *Perfect.* He must have seen his clothes on the lawn. His footsteps echo against the wooden staircase as he climbs them quickly.

"Have you lost your mind, woman?" he yells, his eyes widening as he looks around the room. "Why are my clothes everywhere and why are my new clubs bent as fuck in the garage? Do you know how much they cost me?"

"I'm just helping you pack," I reply with no emotion in my tone.

"Why? Where am I going?" he barks, rubbing his forehead.

"I don't really know or care. A hotel, your office, or your latest fuck buddy. Go bump uglies till your dick falls off, but you no longer live here," I say breathlessly, whilst waving my arms around at all his stuff.

"I beg your fucking pardon. Where has this come from? Are you having one of your *episodes*?"

I turn on my heel and head back into the closet, Alex hot on my heels. "No, you self absorbed prick. I am not having one of my '*episodes*'," I say, using my fingers to make air quotes. "I found a stain on your shirt from your work dinner last night."

His face drops when the realization hits him. I can almost see the cogs in his pea-sized brain trying to conjure up another shit excuse. I push past him, carrying more shirts which I dump on the bedroom floor.

He turns to face me. "Ria, this isn't..." he stutters.

"Save your excuses for someone who gives a shit, Alex. I'm done. I should have left your pathetic ass the day I found the first shirt, but I didn't because of our girls. I wanted to try, and God, have I tried, but I'm done. I can't do this anymore." My eyes burn with tears that threaten to fall, but I refuse to let them. Relief floods my body at saying the words I've tried to say for so long, but I've been too terrified to let out.

"Ria, please let's talk about this. It's really not what you think, it's—"

"Not what I think," I scream before he can finish his sentence. "What I think, Alex, is you, for whatever reason, can't seem to keep your dick in your pants, and rather than come home to me, you'd rather stick it in whoever's open and offering." I suck in a breath before I continue, "I deserve better. I can't spend another day wondering where you are or who you're with. It's killing me, piece by piece, Alex. I am done. Pick up your crap and leave." My voice cracks on the last word.

His eyebrows pinch, his face reddening with anger. "This is my fucking house, Ria. If you are done, you leave."

"I don't have a job and I have the girls to look after. Where am I supposed to go?" I say shakily, shocked that he's telling me to leave.

He steps closer, invading my personal space, the stench of bourbon filling my nostrils, a smug smile forming as he stands inches away from my face. "Well, you should have thought about that, shouldn't you? And probably before you started launching my shit across the front lawn in a tantrum. Maybe if you calmed the fuck down and stopped being a drama queen, you'd see just how fucking good you have it, shut your mouth, and get on with it. You're making this more than what it is."

"More than what it is, Alex," I shout, my earlier rage bubbling to the surface again. my muscles quivering and my heart pounding in my chest. "You've been sleeping with other women. We're married. That is not okay."

"For fuck's sake. Show me a man that hasn't dipped his dick in his secretary or a bar slut. Don't take it personally. We all do it."

My mouth gapes. I have no words. The man I fell in love with at nineteen, who saved me, who gave me the two most precious gifts—my darling girls—has just stood in front of me and brushed his affairs off as if they are normal; something every man does, something I just need to accept.

I'm not sure where the strength comes from, but the words leave my mouth before I have time to process them. "Fine, then me and the girls will leave."

"What?" he scoffs. "Where the hell do you think are you going to go? You have no one, Ria. Your car crash of a mother is off fucking anything with a pulse. Your daddy doesn't want you," he mocks. "And your brother pissed off and joined the Marines just to get the hell away from you and your mom."

"Oh, and..." he adds as he throws back his head and lets out a demonic laugh. "I fucked your friend from college. Granted, not the best sex of my life, but fuck me, that girl could ride a dick like I was her personal show pony."

My stomach lurches at the reminder of his affair with my college friend, bile threatening to escape. *Why is he trying to hurt me more than he already has?* He hasn't apologized or even tried to.

"So, Maria Kennedy. Where the fuck are you going to go?" A slow, unkind smile spreads across his face.

The use of my full name feels like a stab to my heart. *It won't be my full name anymore.* Realization of how different things are going to be hits me, knocking the air from my lungs.

I take in my husband of six years. His baby blue eyes, chiseled jaw, the little scar on the left side of his top lip he got playing soccer as a teenager. His sandy blonde hair with the patch at the front that's a touch lighter than the rest. The five o'clock shadow that I always found insanely attractive. I wonder at what point the man of my dreams turned into the man of my nightmares.

"I don't know, Alex, but as long as it's away from you, that's all I care about."

He looks me up and down like he can't stand the sight of me. "Yeah, well, all the best with that. You need to clean up this shit show before you go." And with that, he storms past me; out of our room and out of my life.

Chapter One

Ria

"I think that's everything off the van now. Anything else you need before we go?"

"No thanks, Gary. You've been great," I say with a smile.

"You take care and say hi to your mom when you see her," he chuckles.

"I will," I tell him with an eye roll. Gary is an old family friend who knows just how much of a hot mess my mother is. When he found out I was leaving Alex, he offered to help me move.

I stand in the small entrance hall of my new home feeling like I can finally breathe for the first time in a really long time. A sense of pride floods me as I look round the small space. *I've done this.* I hung the gold pendant light myself. I've built the white wooden entry table with my bare hands and a rusty screwdriver I found in the previous owner's tool box. It's full of moving boxes and bubble wrapped photographs of the girls that I wasn't prepared to leave. They lean against the wall, making it like an obstacle course in here.

I can do this, I did this, I tell myself as I close the front door and step further inside.

My phone vibrates in my back pocket, and I reach inside and pull it free, seeing two text messages.

Noah

> Hey, baby sis. I'm sorry I couldn't be there to help you move. I'm so proud of you. Off on deployment now. I don't know how long, but I'll call when I can. Look after those nieces of mine. Love you x

I exhale, trying to ignore the little knot of worry about him being deployed forming in my belly.

Ria

> Stay safe, big bro. We love you x

The next message I'm not so excited to read. I nervously click to open it, my thumb trembling.

Alex

> Ria, come home. This is stupid. We can sort this.

I don't respond. He's been blowing up my phone all week and I refuse to let him get into my head and ruin today for me. I close my eyes, take in a deep breath, and shove the phone back in my pocket.

"Gary left already?" Ali, one of my best friends, calls as she walks from the kitchen, carrying two iced coffees.

"Yeah, he had to get back to work."

"Damn. I wanted to say bye and hug that wall of muscle before he left," she declares, wiggling her eyebrows.

"Ali, he's old enough to be your dad." I shudder.

"I know," she says with a smirk. "Just how I like them."

Shaking my head, I take my drink from her. "No, Ali. Just no."

"So, the kitchen is almost unpacked. Gabby is somewhere upstairs, losing a battle with a box of Lexi's and Elle's toys. She was almost buried alive by the boxes. I love your girls like they are my own but jeez, they have a lot of stuff,"

I nod my agreement, because I had to pack it all up. "Tell me about it. If I dare throw any of it away, Lexi will lose her damn mind, and honestly, I am at the point with her where I'm just picking my battles to make it to bedtime. Who knew four-year-old's were so brutal."

I take a sip of my iced coffee, welcoming the sugary taste and the cooling effect the ice has on the burning sensation that's been lodged in my throat since the night my marriage ended. Motherhood has been the hardest and most rewarding thing I have ever done, but the idea of doing this alone now makes me feel physically sick.

Every night I ask myself if I made the right decision... But remembering how unhappy I was, how every day was spent wondering where he was, who he was with, and then treading on eggshells on the rare occasions he was home, I know I've done the right thing. Me and the girls deserve more.

God, when I think about my girls, I know I need to make sure nothing and no one dampens the spark in them. I know all too well how that feels, and I'll be damned if that happens to them. A pain courses through my heart at the idea. Taking another sip of my coffee to help wash away the thoughts, I hear Gabby shouting.

"Ria, should we be concerned that some of Lexi's Barbie dolls have their heads missing and one looks like she's been tied up?"

I laugh. "No, it's all good. Apparently, it's normal for kids her age to do that."

"Ain't nothing normal about that girl and I mean that in the best way," Ali smiles, bumping her shoulder. I nod, agreeing.

"Okay, then... I'll put the decapitated Barbies in their Dreamhouse," her disembodied voice declares. Gabby is the final piece of our trio. We met at a therapy group for young teens called Teenhood. Gabby joined a couple of years after Ali and I and the three of us have been inseparable ever since. Nothing like some serious trauma to bond you all. None of us have had it easy, but they prove the hardest life battles can bring you the greatest rewards.

I point to Ali, signaling that I best go and rescue Gabby, and then I walk up the stairs to the girls' new room.

The soft pink walls glisten as the sunlight bounces off the crystal light shade that we brought with us from Lexi's old room, sending rainbows dancing across the space, entrancing me and making me smile.

My attention is pulled back to the present when the sight of Gabby catches my eye. She's surrounded by boxes and stuffed animals trying to build the Barbie Dreamhouse.

I really do have the best girlfriends. Not many friends would give up their Saturday to build kids' toys, clean your new house, and put together furniture.

"I'm gonna need an old lady nap before Nancy's bachelorette." Ali's petite frame appears in the doorway, rolling her eyes at the state of the room before she flops onto Lexi's still unmade bed, her blonde hair splaying all around her. "I'm dead on my feet."

"Oh, crap. I totally forgot about that. Ugh, I think I might bail. I miss the girls. All I want to do is FaceTime them before they go to bed and then soak in a hot bath with a glass of wine and have a cry whilst listening to *Whitney Houston*."

"Well, that's fucking depressing, Ri," Ali declares, pushing herself up to sit. "Nobody died. It's Saturday night. You're kid free and you are coming out. No sad girl Saturdays for you." Grabbing my shoulders, she gives me a shake.

"I know, I know. I'm just so tired."

"If I'm honest, I could do with missing Nancy's bachelorette too," Gabby groans, standing and stretching out her back. "Why are we invited, anyway? We haven't seen her in years."

She walks to the only free space in the room, tying her long blonde, wavy hair up in a messy bun. "It will just be the Nancy show and I could do without her waving that massive rock in my face and listening to her brag about how many orgasms her fiancé gives her on the daily."

"No one likes a Bitter Betty, Gabriella. Quit your whining. You're going." Ali points at Gabby, then swings her index finger to me. "And so are you."

She stands up, leaning on the boxes as if it's a podium and she's a lawyer about to deliver her closing argument. "We haven't had a girls' night out in forever. You've finally dumped that dickbag of a husband and you have the girls taken care of. Why would you want to stay in, crying in your granny pants, necking wine sobbing to *Celine Dion*, like you're Bridget fucking Jones."

"It's Whitney Houston actually," I interject.

"That's irrelevant, "she declares, waving her hands. "You are now entering your hot single girl era and we are going to put you in a sexy LBD and take you to the club to party like you don't have any worries. Got it?"

"Shit, Ri, she's gone all motivational speaker on us. We aren't getting out of this one," Gabby whispers, sitting next me, and pulling me in for a hug.

"Fine," I huff. "I'll go, but I'm going to see the girls at Alex's parents' house quickly before we get ready."

"Deal," Ali says, banging her hand against the box. "You go see the girls. Gabby can finish assigning heads to Barbies, because honestly, seeing those will give me nightmares." Her body shudders dramatically. "I'll order us a Chinese takeout and pick up some hot ass dresses from my apartment and we can head out around nine," she instructs, jumping about like an excited toddler.

"I am not doing shots. Am I clear?" I give her a harsh squint.

"Crystal," she sings songs with a thumbs up and a smirk.

I know that Ali smirk. I am going to be so hungover tomorrow.

Chapter Two

Ria

I leave Ali and Gabby at the house and make the short drive over to see my girls. Walking out to my driveway, I still forget that I changed my car. A blue Ford sits on my driveway, a little beaten and imperfect.

Like me.

But she's all mine, just like the house behind me.

Now I'm free, I can see that Alex spent most of our relationship controlling me. What I thought was Alex providing me with the dream lifestyle was actually him controlling every aspect of my life. He paid for everything. He didn't want me working, controlled the finances and gave me an allowance. He paid my phone bill, for my car and our house were solely in his name. He owned everything and made it extremely hard for me to leave. I know now I should have left when Lexi was a baby and I was aware of the first of his many affairs. My life didn't feel like my own. I was more of an asset than a partner. Everything I wanted or needed required his permission, his approval. Now I get to decide when I do things, how I do things and I honestly don't know how I spent so many years living like that. If it wasn't for Ali and Gabby taking me in and the support of Alex's parents, I never would have been able to get back on my feet.

I confused controlling and manipulative behavior with love and care. I wonder if this must be how a bird feels when it's freed from its cage.

I let out a long, deep breath, relaxing my shoulders, knowing I can breathe. I have space. I am free.

I pull into the driveway of Alex's parents' house. Pushing open my car door, my feet thud on the concrete as I walk towards the familiar front door of Alex's childhood home. This place holds so many memories, good and bad.

Flashbacks appear in my mind of the day I showed up on their doorstep to tell them I had left Alex, fearing they wouldn't want me in their life anymore and I'd lose the only stable parental figures in my life.

My body trembled as Anne held me in her arms while I sobbed. We sat on her doorstep for what felt like hours, my legs not letting me walk through the door. She stroked my hair and soothed me in that comforting way mothers do.

She promised me nothing would change between me and her. It was everything I needed in that moment and, because of her support, today I stand on her doorstep, my legs holding me up, feeling contentment and peace for the first time in a long time.

Knocking on the solid oak door, I instantly hear Lexis' voice in the distance. The front door flies open and tiny hands reach out to grab my legs. "Mommy!" Lexi screeches. "I've missed you. Grandpa is playing dress up with me, but he's doing the tea party all wrong. Can you tell him how to do it?" she pleads.

"Sure, sweetie." I pick her up, wrapping my arms around her little frame and squeezing her. "I missed you too." I move her long brown hair from her face, tucking it behind her ears. She immediately leans forward, her big blue eyes looking up at me as she rubs her nose against mine like we always do. My heart squeezes in my chest. Some days, I need their hugs way more than they need mine.

"Lexi, give your old grandpa a minute will you" I hear Alex's dad call, his voice getting closer with every word.

"Hey, Steve," I say when he appears, as I place Lexi down. Steve is tall, built like a house thanks to all the golfing and tennis he does. Ali loves to call him a silver fox.

"Thanks again for having them. I hope they haven't been too full on."

"Absolutely no trouble, and what have I told you about knocking? You have a key. We are still your family. Our door is always open for you and the girls, you hear me?" he says with a pointed look.

I smile shyly, as tears prick my eyes. I will never understand how I got such amazing in-laws. "I'm sorry. I'll use it next time, I promise." I reach out and hug him.

"Anne, Ria is here," he shouts down the hallway as he shuts the front door behind me. I hear her before I see her. The kitchen is at the end of a long hallway and just as I walk past the staircase, she's already hurtling towards me with open arms.

"Oh, my girl, come here. How has the move been? You settled in?" she asks as she tightly wraps her arms around me, rubbing my back. Alex's mum is a classic beauty. Even in her older years, she still looks flawless. Her shiny gray hair is styled into the perfect bob. She always has her pearls on, and the familiar scent of her lavender scent perfume surrounds her.

"It's getting there," I lie because we still have so much to do, but I don't want to worry them. "I've left Gabby and Ali unpacking and reattaching Barbie heads to their bodies." I side eye Lexi who's trying to hide behind my legs.

"Oh, we've had it here too, dear. Steve nearly had a heart attack when he found a headless one in the bathtub yesterday. I thought he was a goner, and I'd have to cash in his life insurance and buy that condo I've had my eye on." She winks.

"See?" Steve says pointing, "She's plotting my demise."

She leans in to give him a chaste kiss, and the look they pass between them is pure love. They have the kind of relationship I tried so hard to have with Alex, but some things are just not meant to be.

"Yuck," Lexi declares, sticking her tongue out. "I hate it when Grandma and Grandpa kiss. They're old. Old people don't kiss."

"I'll give you old, little lady," Steve laughs, scooping Lexi up in his arms and tickling her.

"Grandpa, stop," she squeals as he carries her off into the front room. I can't help but smile at their interaction. It's everything I've wanted for my girls. This home is so full of warmth and love.

I follow them into the front room, and what feels like a lifetime of memories come flooding back. The sofa we sat on every year for family photos at Christmas. The brick fireplace in the center of the room, the mantle above it which houses family photos from over the years. The bay window where Anne would place the perfectly decorated Christmas tree each year. A brief moment of sadness hits me. Christmas won't be the same this year. What will Christmas even look like for us? My thoughts are quickly halted by the sound of a screeching Elle.

"Look who's here," Anne coos. I turn my head to see Elle bouncing in her arms, looking straight at me, beaming from ear to ear, showing off her four little teeth, and reaching for me with her chubby little arms.

"Hello, baby. Have you been a good girl for Grandma and Grandpa?" I take hold of her and inhale her soft baby scent that settles something inside me.

"Oh, good as gold. Wasn't a fan of Grandma's porridge, no you weren't, little miss," Elle wriggles in my arms and giggles. "I think Nugget had most of it since she tipped in on the floor, so cleaning up his poop will be a real treat for Steve later." I chuckle to myself. Give a three-year-old the responsibility of naming a dog, expect them to name it after their favorite food.

I look down at our family dog, who has appeared to have joined our living room reunion. His cute little face looks up at me. "Poor Nugs. How do you ever put up with them?" I bend down to stroke his soft fur and Elle blows bubbles in my arms, cooing away.

"Are you sure it's okay to have the girls tonight, too? Honestly, I'm hoping you would be desperate to give the girls back and be my get out of jail free card so I don't have to go to this bachelorette party," I say with a hopeful laugh.

"Absolutely not," Anne replies. "You are going out, getting glam and slay. Is that what you young ones say?"

I smile. "Erm, yeah, sort of."

Although I don't feel like a 'young one' these days.

"Her friend Shirley from her book club got that app on her new phone. What's it called, love? The ticky tocky? Now Anne's got it.

She watches these videos and thinks she is down with the kids," Steve says, gesturing wildly.

I snort. "I know the app you mean."

"Oh, you have to follow me, Ri," she adds, excitedly. "I'm gardenlover60 and I've got twenty-five new followers on there since I posted a video of my rose bush this morning."

Steve and I look at each other wide-eyed, and I have to bite my lip, stifling a laugh.

Do not laugh about your mother-in-law's bush.

I swallow the laughter, managing to keep my face as neutral as possible. "Of course I will."

"Right, I'm going to get these princesses some dinner. You head off and enjoy your night. Don't worry about a thing and you come by tomorrow night and have dinner with us before you take the girls back. I'm cooking my meatloaf."

I reach out and hug her. "You know I love you so much, right? I don't know what I'd do without you."

"I love you too, my girl. Now go enjoy yourself."

Chapter Three

Ria

I adjust the spaghetti straps on my sparkly black dress and comb through my shoulder-length brown hair to give it a natural wave. I've never been one to go heavy on makeup, but I add a touch of lip gloss, mascara, and bronzer and thanks to the early spring sunshine my freckles have started to come out. I stare at my reflection in the bathroom mirror and don't recognize myself; for the first time in a long time, I feel good.

"You sexy bitch." I quickly turn to see Ali standing in the doorway. "Where have you been hiding that body?" she asks, looking me up and down. I smooth my hands down my dress, making sure it's not revealing too much.

"Does it look okay? Do I look a little slutty?" I ask her anxiously, biting down on my bottom lip.

"Yeah it is, but that's the point," she says honestly, just like I knew she would. "You aren't a married maid strapped to the kitchen sink anymore. It's your time to find yourself again, Ri. Spread your legs and fly girl," she declares dramatically, lifting one leg in the air.

I laugh at her ridiculous antics as I push past her to my bedroom next door, Ali following close behind.

"Don't you mean 'spread' your wings and fly?" Gabby quizzes, zipping up her black bodycon dress, a perplexed look on her face.

"No, I don't. I meant spread your legs."

"Dear God. it's going to be one of those nights with you, isn't it?" Her eyes roll as her head shakes.

"Yep," Ali says, popping the *P*. "Work has been a bitch this week and we all know what I do as a stress reliever," she teases.

Gabby and I burst into fits of laughter and together we all chant, "Spread those legs and ride a dick."

"Words to live by, ladies." Ali adjusts her little black sparkly shorts and matching crop top before doing a little wiggle.

"You look amazing." I look at her in awe. Ali has been to hell and back, and her confidence and resilience amaze me. She's our wild one, the one who can't be tamed, but we all need a little wild in our lives.

"Cab is here in five. Let's do a shot and get this shit show on the road," Ali calls as she heads out of the room.

Gabby huffs before saying quietly, "I'm just going to change real quick. I don't feel comfortable in this."

"Oh, no, you don't," Ali shouts, as she marches back into the room. She grabs Gabby's hand and drags her toward the mirror. "You look fucking hot. You have the body of a goddess." She spins gabby around to show her peachy bum in the mirror. "All those Pilates classes you do, that ass needs to be showcased,"

"It's a bit short and tight and not very me." Looking at her reflection, she tugs at the hem.

"Gabs, you look stunning," I reassure her.

"Look, it's got full sleeves, a high neck, and covers your ass. A nun would wear this," Ali says, pointing as we all look in the mirror at Gabby.

Shaking my head and squinting my eyes at her, I say, "What nuns do you know?"

"None, but that's beside the point. You look hot and the cab is nearly here. You aren't changing. Stop hiding under your clothes. You're twenty-four for fuck's sake and you dress like my eighty-five-year-old grandma... And she's dead."

I snort a laugh. *That's our Ali, as honest as a judge.*

"Okay, okay." Gabby lets out a defeated breath. "But I need two shots before we leave."

"That's the spirit," Ali shouts and slaps Gabby on the ass, making her yelp.

"If you don't feel comfortable, you can change," I whisper as we all walk downstairs to the kitchen.

She blows out a long breath. "No, Ali is right. I need to stop hiding. I shouldn't be ashamed of my body." She rolls her shoulders back as if she's trying to convince herself she can do this.

We enter the kitchen, where Ali is already pouring drinks. "No, Gabs, you shouldn't." I kiss her cheek, stroking her silky black hair that she pulled into a high ponytail.

"Right, down in one, ladies," Ali cries, holding three double shot glasses between her fingers. We each take one and clink the glasses together before downing in one.

The cab beeps outside and as I reach for my clutch from the kitchen counter, my hands begin to tremble. I haven't been out for years. I can't remember the last time I had a night out where Alex wasn't there.

"Ri, where's your head gone. Tell me," Ali asks, obviously sensing my nerves.

"This is my first night out as a single woman. I don't know how to be single. I don't know how to be without him." I admit, my voice a little unsteady.

"Ri, you don't—"

I don't let her finish. I know where this question is going. "No. God, no." My tone is firm. "I don't want him back. I don't miss him, I just don't know how to be just me, you know"? I feel my chest begin to tighten and I instinctively start to rub my hand over it to ease the burning sensation.

"Ri, chill, babes. You are wound tighter than a nun's cooch."

A deep belly laugh erupts from me. Ali always knows when I need to laugh and to get out of my head.

"What's with the nun comments today? Are you planning on joining a convent, and this is your way of telling us?" I eye her suspiciously,

"Pretty sure I'd go up in flames walking into a place like that." I nod in agreement.

"No, but seriously, we got you. You just need to be you. You look incredible and it's good to see you smiling again. I know it might not feel like it, but this heartbreak saved you Ri. It's gonna make you. It was never supposed to work with him. He wasn't your person, and he didn't get you. You would've just kept trying until he completely broke you. Remember, the egg doesn't swim to the sperm—never chase a man."

"I know you're right." I shake my hands and arms as if the motion will expel any negative thoughts from my body.

Pulling me in for a hug and squeezing me tight, she says, "Ri, this is the beginning of loving yourself again... welcome back."

The cab drops us outside the main entrance of the club. Stepping out onto the street, the crisp March evening air hits us and I shiver, wishing I brought my jacket.

"Of course she would choose Aurora's for her bachelorette. Is she aware that not everyone is married to a billionaire?" Ali mutters. "The drinks in here will cost more than my rent."

"The invite said it was a free bar," Gabby says, pulling the invitation out of her clutch.

"Fuck, yes. I knew we stayed friends with Nancy for a reason." Ali claps her hands, a big smile now on her face. "Let's go find my future husband." Gabby and I look at each other, shaking our heads with a knowing look. We head towards the entrance and show the doormen our invites. He gives us silver bracelets with a charm on that says our names.

"She's unreal. I bet she wipes her ass with cash after she takes a shit on her gold-plated toilet," Ali mumbles under her breath as she puts on her bracelet.

"This way please, ladies." The doorman points us toward a spiral staircase, spotlights guiding us up the dark space to a huge set of double doors at the top.

Inside can only be described as being as opulent as a wedding reception. The floor, walls, and ceiling are white marble. Enormous photos of Nancy and her fiancé, Chris, in various poses and places around the world. There is a six-tiered white cake with a photo of Nancy on the top and in the center of the room is a table that's filled with glasses of champagne. As well as pink and white balloons that cover the ceiling and pop up stands for permanent bracelets, temporary tattoos, a candy station and a photo booth.

"I see ass, ladies. I repeat, I see ass." Gabby gasps. Our eyes follow her line of sight to reveal deliciously toned, tanned ass cheeks that belong to a Butler in the Buff.

"What in the MTV Super Sweet Sixteen is this?" Ali says, as we all look around the room, trying to process the scene before us.

"I have no idea, but it's insane," I declare, my mouth falling open. I've never seen anything like it. My actual wedding wasn't even half as elaborate as this.

"It's incredible," Gabby whispers, mimicking the same expression as me.

"I'm gonna need to get drunk ASAP to cope with this circus," Ali states, waving over a butler and taking some cocktails from the silver tray he's carrying.

The pink, glittery liquid swirls in our glasses as we walk over to the velvet seating area. I can't help but look around and feel a pang of jealousy. As my marriage ends, Nancy's is about to start. My stomach knots and tears threaten to fall, but I blink them away.

"Maria, Gabriella, Alice." We turn to see Nancy glide over wearing skyscraper glitter heels and a tiny white strapless dress, her thick blonde hair in big bouncy curls, and wearing the brightest shade of pink lipstick I've ever seen.

"Nancy," we all cry in unison as we try to sound as excited as she is. She leans in to air kiss each of us, one by one.

"Aaah, my girls. Thank you for coming," she says, bouncing up and down.

"We wouldn't miss it," Gabby lies and from the corner of my eye, I watch Ali downing her drink so fast I'm worried I'm going to be carrying her out of here, fireman style, in about twenty minutes.

Turning my attention back to the glowing bride-to-be, I swallow any lingering jealousy. "You look incredible, Nance. Congratulations again. How are you feeling?"

"Oh, thank you," she practically purrs, flicking her hair and flashing her giant engagement ring, which I am pretty sure could buy every house on my new street.

"It's just crazy. So much to do, so many things to consider. Well, you know, don't you, Maria? I mean, you're married," she says casually, sipping her champagne.

I take a deep breath. She knows I left Alex, but this is typical Nancy, and the real reason I didn't want to come.

"Actually, we split a couple of months ago," I tell her with a tight jaw, tracing my index finger over the indented spot where my own engagement ring and wedding band sat for so many years.

"Oh, my God. I forgot. I'm so sorry. What with all the wedding stress, it must have slipped my mind." She puts on a fake smile and I don't believe a word of it. "You'll find someone, don't you worry, I'll introduce you to Chris' friends," she says with a patronizing tap on my shoulder and I smile weakly.

I'd rather be raked over hot coals than date a man like your fiancé, thanks.

"I know our little librarian here doesn't have anyone." She points at Gabby, who clamps her mouth into a forced smile. "So what about you, Alice? Settled down yet? Found a man that can stop you partying like you're a freshman in college?" She chuckles into her glass before she takes a sip of her drink.

Seriously, Nancy read the room.

"Oh, no. Not yet, Nancy. I hear it's all downhill after you say *I do*, and the sex turns to shit, so I'm going to hang on to my singledom and mind blowing orgasms for a little while longer." She gives Nancy a shrug of her shoulders.

An awkward silence falls around us and I don't know what to do other than sip my cocktail and pray someone breaks it.

"Yes, well, that might be the case for some, but not me and my Chris. The man's built like a god and has got the stamina of a racehorse." She winks.

"You'll meet him later," she informs us, waving her hand around again to blind us with her ring.

"He's coming to your bachelorette party?" Ali asks, wrinkling her nose, looking between me and Gabby.

"Yes, he owns this club and his new business partners have joined him this evening."

"Of course he does," Ali mumbles with a sarcastic laugh.

"Anyway, enjoy the drinks and food. We are going to head to the main room soon to play some games, so get ready for some fun."

"Yipee," Ali mocks, but Nancy doesn't seem to notice. She's already clocked someone across the room and is walking away.

"God, she's a piece of work. Someone needs to put her in her place. Thinks she's better than us. Remind me again why we came?" Ali asks, taking a drink from a passing bulter, gulping the entire thing.

"For the free drinks and to find your future husband?" I stare at her, cocking an eyebrow.

"Ah yes." She snaps her fingers before pointing between me and Gabby. "Let's down as many drinks as we can and go find me my billionaire."

I tilt my head back and drain the remaining liquid, saying a silent prayer. *Dear God, give me the strength to make it through the evening.*

Chapter Four

Jack

The music vibrates through the room and the distinct smell of high-end liquor fills the air. Women in tight gold dresses, dolled up to the nines, meander through the VIP area holding trays of champagne and tumblers of whisky.

Aurora's is a cosy club in Manhattan, full of New York's elite. It's not my usual vibe, but I can see why it's popular.

We've done it. We signed on the dotted line and partnered with one of the biggest club owners in New York and Miami. When Christopher Stone approached us last year after hearing about our successful opening of The Champagne Lounge in Miami, he wanted in on the business, but after months of back and forth negotiating, we decided to start a new business venture with him.

The Boardroom is an exclusive cocktail lounge and club with a gentleman's club attached for elite members here in New York, and tonight we are out celebrating. This is new territory for myself, Brad and Harry, my business partners, but we are confident it's the right move. We have come a long way since our days in the Marine Corps.

"To the start of a beautiful friendship and the beginning of a successful new venture. Cheers." Chris raises his glass of whiskey. The three of us follow suit and swallow down the drink in one.

Chris places a hand on my shoulder and gives it a tight squeeze. "I can't wait for you to meet my Nancy. She'll be down in a minute."

"She's here?" I question, searching the room, wondering why he would bring her to a business meeting.

"Yeah, she's having her bachelorette in the suite upstairs. I told her to bring the girls down to the main room for a dance. Knowing Nancy's maid of honor, she will have planned some crazy shit for them to do, and I want a front seat to it."

"What do you mean?" My interest peaks. "You'll see. Tara is wild," he says, tapping me on the shoulder before walking away.

"How much longer do we have to stay here? I've heard there is a strip club round the corner and I wanna see what the fuss is all about. I heard the girls lick whipped cream off you," Harry says, licking his lips.

Harry, one of my best friends, is ridiculously good looking, but God, does he know it. He's got the whole tall, dark, handsome with a cheeky grin, thing going on; a different girl every day, he refuses to settle down and act his age.

"We can't leave now. Chris wants us to meet 'his Nancy'," I say in a mocking tone.

"Fuck, I need another drink," Brad says with a grunt, taking two large whiskeys from a passing waitress and downing them one after the other. "I'm sitting down. Let me know when we can leave."

"Don't worry, sunshine, we'll let you know when you can go home and snuggle up with your *Colleen Hoover* novel," Harry shouts over to him.

Brad sticks up a middle finger. "It was one book, one time, you fucker and my mom sent it to me," he grumbles.

"Still read it, though," Harry laughs.

Brad gets up, storming off. He's a miserable fucker. I don't blame him. We served two tours together and the things he's been through would keep the strongest man awake at night. 6ft 2, dark hair, covered in tattoos and built like a house. The man looks like he would snap you in half. He's a man of few words, but I couldn't do life without him by my side.

"Dude, I know Brad is a miserable fuck, but when can we get out of here? It's been an age since I got my dick wet."

"It's been two days, Haz," I say bluntly.

He tilts his head as if he's thinking something through. "Actually, four once you consider the time difference, so yeah, we've got a situation over here. It's so bad I've even started eyeing you up."

"I'm honored to be considered for your roster," I deadpan.

"As you should." He nods. "Only the elite make it on that list."

I shake my head, laughing, running a hand through my hair.

"Good, let's get outta here," Harry says, scanning the bar for Brad.

Someone taps me on my back and when I glance over my shoulder, I see Chris.

"There she is," he shouts over the music, nodding to the staircase.

We all turn to look in the direction he's facing to see a woman who resembles a life-size doll, followed by an entourage of women dressed in variations of little black dresses.

"Change of plan, we're staying," Harry yells, with a shit-eating grin.

Fuck's sake, he's going to ruin this business deal for us. If he fucks one of Nancy's mates and never calls. Chris might regret going into business with us.

Chris strides over to Nancy, picking her up and swinging her round in his arms, making her friends clap and swoon for the bride and groom-to-be.

Harry and I follow, so we can introduce ourselves, and even Brad drags his ass up off the sofa he'd retreated to.

Chris introduces us, his eyes greedily fixed on Nancy, his feelings for her clear to see. "Oh, you have to meet my girls. You'll love them," Nancy says excitedly.

"Ri, Ali, Gabs, get your hot asses here and say hi."

Ri. God, I haven't heard that name in years. The only Ri I have ever known was Maria Jones in high school, and I would be lying if I said she didn't enter my head more times than she should. She was the kind of girl that left a lasting impression and one who was always way out of my reach. I cared for her too much to risk pursuing her and I knew one moment with her could have ended my friendship with her brother. We joined the Marines, and she met someone and I had to accept we were just never going to be, and it's been a few years since I last saw her.

I scan the sea of women waiting for these girls to appear.

"Jack?" a stunned voice says.

I turn my head sharply to the left and there she is, looking as stunning as I remember.

Maria Jones.

Chapter Five

Ria

"Oh, my God." I lunge forward, throwing my arms around him, his muscular arms tightening around me.

"Hey, Ri," he whispers into my ear, sending a warm feeling through my body. Bergamot and pepper invade my nostrils and the smell has my eyes fluttering closed.

Realizing I've probably clung to him longer than is appropriate. I release him, stepping back and adjusting my dress, craning my neck to look up at him. I forgot how much taller he is than me, which isn't hard as I stand at a tiny 5ft 2, but he is as gorgeous and strong as the last time I saw him when he returned from Afghanistan five years ago with my brother. Jack had the sense to leave the military, but Noah was still running from our past and wasn't ready to come home.

I let my eyes graze over him from head to toe, taking in his light brown hair, dark blue eyes, and broad shoulders. He has an air of confidence as he stands in front of me. God, has he always been so... gorgeous? Of course he has, he's Jack Lawson. The boy I grew up with. I was just his friend's little sister though, so he never looked at me the way I wanted him to. Nothing ever happened between us, so why am I nervous? It's just Jack. He spent every weekend and some weeknights hanging out at our house throughout high school.

"How the hell are you? It's been a few years." My eyes roam over his black suit pants and a crisp white shirt with sleeves rolled up to his elbows and I can see a touch of the tattoo I know he has coming down his left arm. *Jesus, he looks good.*

"Last time I heard you were still living in Miami with Harry and Brad and opening up clubs?" I say, trying to act like I don't check his Instagram.

A deep throaty chuckle erupts from him and I didn't know a laugh could be a turn on till this very moment. "We've moved back and opened up a new place with Chris." He gestures over to Chris, who is practically eating Nancy's face off.

I curl my lips in disgust and look at Jack, who makes a gagging expression.

He turns his attention back to me and a moment passes between us, charged and heated as his blue eyes bore into mine, holding me hostage. His throat bobs slowly as he swallows, and I track the movement staring at the strong column of his neck. My pulse spikes as I swipe my tongue across my lower lip, wondering what the hell is happening to me. Why is it suddenly roasting in here?

"So you are staying for a while"? I force out, trying not to sound too hopeful.

He nods thoughtfully. "Yeah, I think so, at least until the new club is up and running and we will see from there. If I find a reason to stay, I could be convinced." Excitement blooms in my stomach and my cheeks heat at the idea of Jack staying in New York.

"Sounds great. So you're keeping well? You're looking good, you feeling good?" I stare at the ground, willing it to open up and swallow me whole. "Uhh, I mean—"

He interrupts me, tucking my hair behind my ear that's fallen in front of my face during my ramble. I look up to see his eyes creasing up at the corners in what I presume is amusement. "Yeah, I'm feeling good, Ri."

A desire to flee washes over me and I frantically look around for my girls to take the heat off me. "Gabs, Ali, come here." I wave them over and as Brad and Harry appear, standing next to Jack, both looking excited to see me.

"It's been ages, Ri. How are you? How's Noah?" Harry asks after hugging me, and I notice the touch of concern in his voice.

"He's good. He is about to be deployed again. Should be home by Christmas. He misses you guys."

"I swear to fucking God, Ri. If I have to look at her eat his face like that any more, I'm going to gouge my eyes out and ram them down her throat," Ali slurs, making me wonder how many drinks she's managed to down tonight.

"Well, who's this little pocket rocket?" Harry shouts over the music, as he moves to get closer to Ali and holds out his hand.

"And your name is?" she barks back, crossing her arms, looking him up and down.

"The one you'll be screaming tonight."

I clamp a hand over my mouth, stifling a laugh. *Oh, she's going to have fun with this one.*

"It's Harry," he leans in so she can clearly hear him.

"Ali, but you can call me Alice." She extends her hand.

"Alice, who the fuck is Alice?" he sings

Ali stares at him deadpan, not a hint of amusement on her delicate features.

"The song," he explains, taking her hand in his.

She's still staring at him like he's an idiot.

"Smokie?" he says, trying to get her to understand the joke *Fuck, this is awkward and funny.*

We all start snickering into our glasses, passing glances between us, but I notice that Jack's eyes are locked on me. My cheeks heat from the attention, my ego getting a boost from the way he's looking at me.

"I liked the look of you and then you opened your mouth and now I have the ick," Ali says as she pulls her hand out of his and wipes it down her shorts before she heads towards the bar.

"Marry me," Harry shouts after her as he chases after her.

"Oh, he's going to love her," Jack grins. "He's used to women falling at his feet."

"Ali takes no prisoners. Hope he can handle her," I tell him as I look away from Ali and Harry's exchange and look directly at him for a beat longer than I should and I feel *something*, something I haven't felt in a long time.

Brad interrupts whatever I'm feeling when he takes Gabby's hand in his and kisses the back. "Brad," he says with a nod.

"Gabriella," she replies softly, her cheeks flushing. He might look like he's from an episode of *Prison Break,* but underneath all those tattoos I know he's a gentle giant.

"That's a beautiful name. Can I get you another drink?" He gestures towards her empty glass.

"Don't be long. Tara is coming round with the dare cards in a minute," I remind her.

She nods and they vanish into the crowd, leaving Jack and I alone.

"What are dare cards"? Jack asks, his eyes focused back on me. More specifically, my lips. I trap my bottom lip between my teeth, forgetting all about the question he just asked me and instead imagining what it might be like to really embrace that single life I talked about earlier.

"Ria?" The way he says my name is so smooth and deep that I suppress a shiver.

"Yeah?" I say breathlessly.

"Dare cards?" He smirks.

I shake my head, regaining my focus. "Right. Dare cards." I repeat. "It's a game where we randomly pull a card out and we have to do what it says. Could be anything from taking a shot or dancing naked on the bar..."

"Well, I'm glad I've got a front row seat for this game." He places his hand to my lower back, encouraging me to sit at a nearby table, sending a bolt of electricity zapping through me. I slide into the leather booth and I expect him to sit opposite but he sits next to me, so close our thighs almost touching.

The way his arm flexes and the veins pop when he rubs his hand over his five o'clock shadow has me salivating while we sit reminiscing for what feels like hours, reminding me how easy he always was to talk to.

"It's been a weird adjustment. It took some time, but leaving the corps was the right decision," he tells me when I ask about him leaving the Marines.

"And your mom and dad? I bet they were happy you left." I smile at the memory of his mom's chicken pot pie she would send over with Jack. Everyone knew what our mom was like, and those little gestures of kindness meant everything to me and Noah growing up.

"Yeah, my mom especially. She never wanted me to join. My dad encouraged it, said it was 'character building'." He does a great impression of his dad.

"I'm proud of what I did, but it's not what I wanted anymore."

"And now you are this big fancy club owner?"

"Yeah, something like that," he chuckles. "I get to work with those clowns daily, so I can't complain." Averting his eyes to the bar area, he looks over to where Harry and Brad are mingling with the group of people.

"But enough about me," he says leaning in a little closer, steepling his index fingers and pointing at me. "How are you, Maria Jones? How's life? You've got two girls now, right?"

Smiling at the thought of my girls, I nod. "Well technically I am Maria Kennedy now, but yeah, Lexi is four now and Elle is nearly seven months"

His face falls and he lowers his hands to the table. "Of course, I forgot you got married. I hope your husband knows how lucky he is."

I nervously twirl the stem of my cocktail glass,

"So how is Alex?" he says with a clipped tone. "Still traveling a lot?"

"Erm, actually we separated a couple of months ago," I say awkwardly, avoiding his gaze.

"Oh... I'm sorry to hear that." There is a distinct change in his tone. He doesn't sound sorry at all.

"Really"? I knew deep down my brother and Jack didn't approve of Alex when I introduced them to him. I should have known then it wasn't going to work.

Shaking his head. "Not really," he smirks and drops his gaze to my lips and I can't help but do the same to him, drawn like a magnet as he leans closer, overwhelming my senses with his spicy scent. I have to grip the table to stop the dizziness that being so close to him has caused. "He's a fool if he lets you go, Ria."

I think I'm going to combust, my heart racing from his proximity. *Is he flirting with me? Or am I that sexually frustrated?* I even thought the mailman was trying to flirt when he said he had a big package waiting for me to unwrap in the back of his van. Turns out he had an actual package for me, which was my new vacuum. Who am I kidding? No one is going to want an unemployed single mother of two.

I'm destined to spend my days alone with Nugget and maybe with one of those battery operated boyfriends Ali raves about.

Get a grip of yourself, Ria

I am dragged away from my pitiful thoughts by Tara, Nancy's chief bridesmaid, who glides over, looking like a Victoria's Secret model. Her gaze rakes over at Jack like he's going to be her next meal and I can't help but frown at her blatant perusal.

"Games are starting, Ria," she tells me before she turns towards Jack and purrs, "And I'm coming back for you later."

My pulse races and irritation prickles my skin at the thought of Tara getting her perfectly manicured claws into him. But then I remember that he's my friend and I don't have any claim on him.

I stand and place my hand on his shoulder, shuddering as I feel his muscles beneath my palm. "If I have to do something gross that involves a man, then I'm coming to you, Harry or Brad. I've seen some of the men in here and not a chance in hell am I asking *Mr. Burns* over there for his boxers."

We both turn our attention to a creepy little man who looks the type who is going home to get off with his hand and a bottle of lotion to the photos he's clearly taking on his phone of the girls in here. I shudder at the thought.

Jack stands, closing the space between us until his hand wraps around my forearm, holding me in place. His head dips to my ear, his words dusting my skin. "Pick me."

"W-what?" I stutter, confused, my brows furrowing.

"Pick me for your games, use me... in any way you need tonight."

Holy shit. My pulse spikes, and my knees almost buckle.

"Well, that's an offer a girl can't refuse. Just don't leave, okay?" I straighten up and do my best to walk away with some sort of grace. Please, don't let me fall down these stairs.

"I wouldn't dream of it, sweetheart," he calls after me.

I can feel his eyes on me as I head toward the girls, and I can't stop the grin that spreads across my face. *What am I doing? He doesn't want me. He's just entertaining me. Don't read too much into it, Ria, but God, does it feel good.* Even if it's just a bit of harmless fun for one night, I'm going with it.

The dares have started by the time I reach the group. "My turn," Tara squeals as she pulls a card from the pack one of the other girls is holding. "Remove your bra without getting undressed and swing above your head in victory," she reads out loud.

Giggling like a schoolgirl and biting her bottom lip, she confesses, "Sorry ladies, I'm not wearing a bra so I pass my dare too…" Scanning the group, she points to Ali.

Letting out a disgruntled moan, Ali stands and climbs up on her chair. She fiddles under her crop top for a few seconds before pulling her bra free effortlessly and whipping it around above her head.

The crowd cheers and Ali dances in victory. "Yes, girl. Get it off," Harry bellows from across the VIP area where him, Jack and their friends are sitting. Ali, like the classy bitch she is, launches her bra across the room at him before giving him the middle finger. Keeping his eyes locked on Ali, he stands and saunters toward it. Then he picks it up and sniffs it, making us all groan as he shoves it into his back pocket, his stare telling us all what he wants to do to her later.

"Ria, it's your turn, pick a card," Tara announces, fanning out the pack of hot pink cards. I choose one from the middle and turn it over.

> **Do a tequila shot off a man's body.**

Oh, shit.

"Girls, can one of you do this?" My voice is shaky. "I am a mother, for Christ's sake, and still legally married," I whisper to my friends, hoping they'll understand.

"No," Ali says sternly. "You are separated, and being a mom is irrelevant. You're allowed to have fun. That doesn't stop when you have kids."

"Come on, Ri, have some fun. You deserve it and what happens on the bachelorette stays on the bachelorette," Gabby reassures me, putting her arm around my waist.

I let out a big huff. "Okay, fine, let's do it."

"Atta, girl," Ali cries, slapping me on the back. "Oh, Jaaaaccckkkk Your body is required."

I turn and glare at her while I panic about whether I can do this. With Jack.

"Oh, come on, the man hasn't stopped looking at you all night. He's game," Ali says, reading my mind.

I open my mouth, but it closes just as fast when I'm spun around to find Jack standing in front of me.

He slowly unbuttons his shirt, eyes locked on mine as they sparkle in a devilish way. I track the movement of each finger, as he reveals, inch by inch, every perfect muscle and part of his tattoo that I know runs from his chest down his arm.

My chest heaves faster the lower he gets, until finally, he's shrugging the shirt off his broad shoulders and suddenly I can't swallow.

My entire body hums to life at the Adonis in front of me and I have to lick him... *Jesus, how do I get myself into these situations?*

"Where do you want me?" he purrs, the deep timbre of his voice giving me goosebumps.

I feel my body temperature skyrocket. I gulp.

Oh, fuck.

Chapter Six

Jack

I can't help but revel in the look of sheer panic on Ria's face, but it's mixed with interest too, I think. She didn't think I'd offer, but there's not a chance I am watching her lick another man's body.

"You don't have to do this," she says to me with a shaky breath. "I'll make Ali do it."

"You are doing it, Ri," I say, pinning her with a determined stare. "Now, like I said..." I pause, waiting for her ocean-blue eyes to meet mine again. "Where do you want me?"

She scans the room, looking for the best spot and pointing to the corner of the VIP area. Ria walks beside me, like a deer in the headlights, and I reach for her hand, linking my fingers with hers. When I give her hand a reassuring squeeze, a tingling sensation floods my body at the feel of her skin.

We make our way over to the largest Table Ali can find and rally the bachelorettes to clear the glasses.

"Okay, action man, lay here," Ali says, tapping the table.

Unable to take my eyes off Ria, I don't miss the way she keeps glancing over at my torso like she wants to explore it—or maybe that's just wishful thinking, but it gives my ego a little boost. Her cheeks pink when she realizes I've seen her checking me out, and I give her a playful wink.

Tara appears with a shot of tequila, a salt shaker, and a slice of lime. "Okay, Ri, you need to lick the salt of these rock hard abs," she instructs as she glides her hands over me, my body unaffected by her touch.

"Then, only using your mouth, take the shot of tequila from his belly button and take the slice of lime from his mouth and suck, but no hands, okay?"

Ria just stares at Tara and nods.

The entire bachelorette party and the boys gather around the table. I can feel the buzz of excitement over the music. My senses heightened, my pulse quickening, abs tightening at the thought of what's about to happen. Ria's eyes dart round the room like she's looking for the nearest exit.

I make eye contact with her and mouth, "you can do this" and she gives a weak smile, nodding.

I lay back against the hard wooden table and Tara sprinkles salt in a line over my abdomen and hands me the slice of lime.

Ria steps forward, gathering her hair to hold it back. Bending down, she edges her mouth towards me and, I don't care about the people standing around us, clapping and cheering, all I can focus on is her.

Eyes closed, her warm tongue peaks from her mouth and swipes expertly over my abs, licking up every tiny grain of salt. She opens her eyes and looks up at me and, fuck, I've never seen anything hotter. Her eyes don't leave mine as she licks her lips clean. Tara then places a large shot of tequila on my stomach, the cool glass sizzling against my hot skin.

She wraps her plump lips over the rim of the shot glass and tilts her head back, draining the clear liquid from the glass, her neck muscles flexing as she swallows.

Freeing her hair, she takes the shot glass from her mouth, making eye contact with me again. I swear, I stop fucking breathing. Her blue eyes become heavier and I can tell something has changed between us.

Fuck, I want her, consequences be damned. I place the slice of lime in my mouth, leaving just enough of it peaking out for her to get to, but I know her lips will be forced to touch mine.

She leans in and sucks the juice from the slice, her soft lips covering mine. I hum softly as I taste her for the first time, my heart hammering in my chest and my already heated skin turning into an inferno. I grip the slice of lime firmer, so she's forced to press her lips harder against mine. My hands twitch at my sides, desperate to bury themselves in her hair so I can deepen this kiss and taste her properly.

She pulls away, bringing a perfectly manicured hand to her lips as if she can't believe our mouths touched. I'm not looking at Noah's little sister right now. I am looking at the sexiest woman I have ever laid my eyes on, and all I can think about is taking her home and making her mine.

I'm ripped away from my daydreaming by cheering and hollering and Harry dragging me up from the table.

"Jesus Christ, I thought I was gonna blow my load right in my pants watching you two," he laughs. "That was hot as fuck. If you don't take her home, I will."

I turn and glare at him. "Don't you fucking dare."

"Dude I'm joking. I've got my eye on little Ali cat over there." He smirks looking over to the far corner where I see her and Gabby hugging and laughing with Ria, who has her hands over her face shaking her head, probably in disbelief at what she's just done.

"I can already tell she won't put up with your bullshit," Brad mumbles from where he stands next to Harry.

I put my shirt back on that Harry hands me, button it back up, and head over to Ria. Looking flustered, she rambles, "Erm, thanks for doing that."

Running my tongue over my bottom lip, remembering how her lips felt on mine, I lean closer and whisper, "Believe me when I say it was my pleasure."

I can think of more places I'd like you to lick too.

We spend the next few hours chatting, drinking, discussing business ideas, but I can't help but stare at Ria all night. I'm not even being subtle about it, and I don't even care. I watch as she sways her hips from side to side to a *Rihanna* song, dragging her hands up and down her body and into her hair, as Gabby and Ali dance around her. A flush of warmth makes my dick twitch at the thought of my hands doing just the same to her body.

A long time ago, I promised her brother I'd look out for her but she had Alex so I backed off and buried the feelings I had for her, but tonight hearing she's single again stirs up those feelings all over again. The want I had for her flickers inside me like a dormant fire waiting for her to fan the flames. I know it's a risk; she's going through a break up and her brother happens to be one of my best friends and is fiercely protective of her, but I can't help but feel that maybe the universe has pushed us together for a reason and if there was ever a woman worth risking it all for, it would be her.

I watch her leave the dance floor, a *Whitney Houston* track coming to an end. She sways as she heads over to where I'm sitting. Flopping down in the booth next to me, it's clear she's drunk.

"How's it hanging, Jack Jack?" She giggles.

"Please don't ever call me that again," I deadpan when she quotes the line from the movie, *The Incredibles*.

She laughs, giving me a playful tap on my thigh, sending a signal to my dick that now is apparently the time to stand to attention. I rearrange myself as discreetly as I can, clearing my throat.

"Sorry, my Lexi loves that movie. If it's not that on at home it's *Minnie Mouse* or Princesses... ugh, I miss them," she sighs, sounding sad.

"Are they with Alex tonight?" *Thinking about that prick will definitely make my dick go down.*

"Ha, you've got to be kidding," she says in a sarcastic tone. "He's 'on a business trip'," she adds, making air quotes with her fingers. "Which is code for fucking his secretary or whatever poor soul he's convinced to open up for him."

I wince at how bitter she sounds. "Shit... I'm sorry Ri, you deserve so much better."

"Thank you," she huffs, her eyes getting heavy and fluttering closed. "I just wasn't what he wanted anymore." Her words becoming a mumble as her head rests on my shoulder.

I reach down and tuck away the stray hairs that have fallen over her face and I can't resist pressing a soft kiss to her forehead. *How could he cheat on her? How could you not want Ria?* If she were mine, I'd spend every day making sure she knew she was everything to me. Whispering, I tell her, "I think it's time we get you home." I glance around, looking for Ali and Gabby and spot Ali on the dance floor where she's been most of the night with some of the girls from the bachelorette. I catch her attention, gesturing down at Ria and then pointing to the exit.

Ali appears a moment later, looking way more sober than Ria. "Come on, you lightweight. Let's find Gabby and get you outta here." She drags an uncooperative Ria up from her seat and I instantly miss the warmth of her body leaning against mine.

"Use our driver, I insist, standing and pulling out my phone to call him.

"Oooh, you hear that, Ri? He's got a driver," Ali mocks.

"No, no, we can get an uuuu-Uber," Ria slurs then hiccups.

"I'm gonna text him right now" I fire a quick text to Graham and then wrap my arms around Ria's waist, taking her weight as she leans into me.

"You don't look like an Incredible actually..."

"No?" I ask, a playful tone in my voice.

Her hands drag over my shirt as she traces the outlines of my pecs and abs, making it hard to focus on what she's saying. "Like *Christian Hougue* or like an action man... yeah Ali's right, you do look like an action man. I could do with a bit of action, man." She giggles to herself like she's proud of her little joke, even though she's not making any sense to me.

I lean in, my mouth pressed close to her ear. "Sweetheart, I'll be your action man any day of the week." She leans on me more, pressing her chest to mine, her heart thumping as she lets me hold her, which makes my already aching cock even more needy. "But you need to get home and get some sleep first."

I look behind me, wondering where Ali disappeared to and I see her pulling a reluctant Gabby behind her, away from the bar where she was was standing with Brad.

"Sorry, had to tear this one away from the cocktail menu," Ali says when she reappears.

"Ugh, I'm not ready to leave. I didn't get to try the Bloody Mary," Gabby groans.

"We've got to get this drunk home." Ali gestures to Ria.

My phone beeps and I know it will be the driver, so I walk the girls out, practically carrying Ria and help her into the car.

"Can I give you my number so you can let me know you got home safe?" I ask Ria as I lean into the car, making sure she has her seatbelt on. Despite how drunk she'd seemed, the icy air seems to have sobered up slightly and she rifles around in her purse, finding her phone, unlocks it and hands it to me.

I save my number and send a text from her phone to mine before I hand it back to her. "Let me know when you get in, okay?" I lean in to kiss her cheek, but as I do, she turns to look at me and our lips crash together. We freeze, our lips pressed together, neither of us moving. Her vanilla scent wraps around me, and I swear she lets out a little moan.

Fuck, I wanna climb in this car with her and take her home.

She eventually breaks the kiss, looking embarrassed, tucking her hair behind her ear and clearing her throat. "Sure, ugh, thanks for tonight and the car. Next time I drink tequila I'll think of you.".

"You better, sweetheart." I wink. "Graham, get my girl home safe. Okay?"

My girl? Why the fuck did I say that?

"Sure thing. Sir," Graham assures me. I shut the car door, tapping the roof, Graham taking that as his signal to pull away from the curb into the New York traffic. A feeling of emptiness creeps over me as I watch the Black SUV drive off.

Letting out a slow, deep breath, I feel Brad and Harry walk up next to me.

"Fuck, you're in trouble," Harry declares, slapping my back.

And I know I am. Ria is back in my life, and this time I'm not letting her go.

Chapter Seven

Ria

I open my eyes, my head feeling groggy. I swallow. The stale taste of tequila making me heave.

Water, I need water and Advil.

I reach out my hand to find the bottle of water I always leave next to my bed, my hand knocking my phone to the floor as I move.

Groaning as I try to retrieve it, squinting one eye open, I feel a shooting pain in my head.

Tequila is the devil's drink.

My phone lights up. 10.08 am. Shit, I can't remember the last time I slept in this late.

When I manage to focus on my phone, I have a couple of messages from Anne saying she hopes I had a great night and a photo of her making cupcakes with Lexi, while Elle is in the high chair covered in yogurt. The girls are so lucky to have them, and so am I.

Then I notice a message from 'Jack'. I bolt upright and my stomach rolls. A groan comes from under the duvet and I look over to see Ali and Gabby are also in my bed, spooning.

"Don't make sudden movements, Ri. It hurts my head," Ali mumbles.

"Excuse me. Why do I have Jack's number, and why does he appear to have mine?" I say, louder than necessary. My heart races and my head thumps in time with each other.

Shit, shit. Did I embarrass myself last night?

"You gave him your phone, and he added it and then you kissed," Gabby tells me, barely moving her mouth.

"Sorry, what?" I shriek, leaping out of bed. "We kissed?" I press my hand against the wall to steady myself, the room spinning because of this killer hangover.

Ali sits up and rubs her eyes, hair everywhere and squinting to look at me.

"If you are going to be this hysterical, this early in the morning, I'm gonna need a Starbucks. Who wants?"

"Me," Gabby mumbles, sticking a hand in the air. Ali reaches for her phone and I know she's about to DoorDash our order.

Nerves flutter in my stomach as I open our message history and sink to the floor, my back resting against my bedroom wall as I read through them.

Ria

> Home, thank you for your fancy driver, duck he's cute ail thinks he's a daddy

> **Jack:** LOL I will let Graham know. Glad you got home safe. I hope the hangover isn't too bad in the morning, DRINK WATER please.
>
> **Ria:** Okay daddy!! I don't want to brush my teeth. I want to keep the taste of tequila and you in my mouth forever.
>
> **Jack:** Careful calling me that, sweetheart *winking emoji* *laughing emoji* Happy to give you another taste. Just say a time and a place.
>
> **Ria:** My house tomorrow, bring a bottle *winking emoji* *eggplant emoji*
>
> **Jack:** It's a date sweetheart winking emoji

"Fuck my fucking life. I told him I didn't want to brush my teeth because I wanted to keep the taste of him and tequila in my mouth and sent him an eggplant emoji. Oh, and I called him Daddy. Fuck!" I groan, getting up off the floor, stumbling to the bed and flopping face-first onto it.

"Smooth, honey, real smooth," Ali says, laughing

I look up, my untamed hair falling over my face. Ali is sitting up in bed wearing big black sunglasses, rubbing her temples with her fingertips.

"Look." I pass her the phone. "And I invited him over for more tequila. Oh God, my first night out as a single woman, and I'm offering myself up on a plate. Why am I like this? Why didn't you stop me?"

Ali lifts her glasses while she replies, looking at me with her bloodshot eyes. "Don't blame me, boozy. You know what you get like on the tequila and you had three more after that body shot."

The memory of licking salt from Jack's body floods my mind and I feel like I'm going to be sick. "Fuck" I shout. "I can't see him again. I'm such an embarrassment." I cover my face with my hands, shaking my head and groaning as I get up off the bed.

"A shower. I need a shower. I need to wash away the memories of last night. Do you reckon if you scrub hard enough you can wash away regret?" I'm speaking so fast, I sound like I've been put on x3 speed.

I'm spiraling

"Ri, indoor voices," Gabby mumbles from under covers.

"Gabs, I'm having a crisis here. Jack now likely thinks I'm an alcoholic who doesn't brush her teeth." I begin pacing the room. My stomach rolls. *Shit, I need to eat something to soak up this alcohol.*

"I'm sure he doesn't think that. Just text him back and say you don't remember anything and that drunk Ria and sober Ria are very different people," Gabby says as she sits up, rubbing her eyes.

"Yes, good plan." I take my phone back from Ali, and just as I start to type a text, my doorbell chimes.

"Wow, that DoorDash was quick," I declare as I head for my bedroom door.

"I haven't ordered yet," Ali replies, sounding confused.

I walk down the stairs, stumbling as I trip over something sharp. Looking down, I notice the heels I was wearing last night.

"Damn shoe," I mutter, kicking it down the stairs. Heading for the front door, weaving in and out of moving boxes, I haven't unpacked, I open it to be greeted by a man holding three large Starbucks bags and a tray of what smells like vanilla lattes.

"Ria is it?" The driver asks with a smile far too big for this time of the morning.

"Yes, but I haven't ordered anything," I mumble.

"There's a note in the bag. Enjoy your breakfast," the driver says, handing me the bags.

I kick the door shut and head for the kitchen, placing everything on the white countertop of the breakfast bar before I dig around to find the note.

Pastries, muffins, fruit pots, granola, and hot bacon rolls fill the bags, and my stomach rumbles in response to the delicious smells. *I am starving.*

"Oh, my God, who sent all this?" Gabbys asks as she strolls into the kitchen and takes a seat at the breakfast bar, followed by a very hungover-looking Ali. "It smells incredible. Gimme."

I find a note at the bottom of one of the bags and pull it out.

Ria, I thought you might need a little pick me up after all that tequila. Thanks for making my night. Tequila is my new favorite drink. Don't be a stranger... Jack a.k.a your action man.

"Oh my fucking God, is he for real?" Ali screeches. "Marry him."

"Little problem, babe. I'm still married," I deadpan.

"Well, pull your finger out your ass and sort that divorce, then invite action man over for another round of body shots," she says with a grin.

The girls dive into the bags and start attacking the food like feral animals.

This is the most thoughtful and sweetest thing anyone has ever done for me. I pick up my phone to send him a text.

> Ria
>
> Morning, I am so sorry about my texts last night *emoji with hands over the face* our Starbucks just arrived. You really are the sweetest. Thank you. Xx

Within minutes a message bounces back.

> Jack
>
> You're welcome, sweetheart, and no need to apologize. It made my night. I wish I could have hand delivered it but I'm stuck in meetings *snoring emoji* I mean it, don't be a stranger x

> Ria
>
> Thank you *blowing kiss emoji* Hope your meetings go ok.

> Jack
>
> Thank you, sweetheart. Have a good Sunday x

I flop down onto the stool next to Gabby and reach for a breakfast roll before I take a sip of my latte, unable to hide the biggest grin from my face. I don't know how or why Jack Lawson has suddenly come back into my life, but I am not mad about it.

Chapter Eight

Ria

1 month later

I sit in my car, taking in a shaky breath and looking into my rearview mirror.

You can do this Ria, get yourself together and get out of the car.

I am in the parking lot of my new job. My first ever real job working at a new club as a barmaid. I went to a local community college and studied music and psychology. I learned to play the piano during my time in foster care and at the youth trauma group I went to. Music was the only thing I grasped quickly, and it became an outlet for my trauma; my escape from what was going on at home. I wanted to become a youth group leader and help teens like myself through music and talking therapy, but life, or rather Alex, got in the way of my plans. But I've made a promise to myself to pursue my dreams once the girls are a little older, and we are settled. So, for now, this job will support us and pay the bills.

I take the lipstick out of my handbag and coat my lips before fluffing my hair with my hands.

Okay, let's do this, I say to my reflection.

I step out of my car, smoothing down my tight-fitting black dress, remove my sneakers, and slip into my black heeled pumps, because who can drive in heels? We have to wear a uniform at this club and I'll be working the bar and VIP areas. After a couple of sessions of training, I am about as ready as I'll ever be for my first shift.

I reach the staff entrance, swipe my ID card, and enter through the heavy door. I smile at the doormen who are getting ready for opening night.

Walking through the narrow hallway painted in a mocha brown with wall lights guiding my way, I enter the ladies' staff room.

Hair spray and perfume cloud the air as I meander through the groups of women applying lipstick and the finishing touches to their hair before our shift starts. I smile nervously at a few of the girls I recognize from our training days, and I suddenly have the urge to throw up. My nerves are trying to take over my body.

Breathe, Ri, you are okay. You can do this.

I put my bag and jacket away in my locker, putting my phone in the pocket of my dress. Wanting to keep it close in case Anne calls about the girls. It vibrates and I pull it out.

Alex

> Why won't you respond to my texts and calls? Come on, we can sort this. Why are you breaking up our family? Come back home x

Anger pulses through me. Is he serious right now? Why am I breaking up our family? I don't have time for this. I squeeze the phone in the palm of my hand and inhale a deep breath before releasing it slowly, trying to focus my thoughts on my new job, and not my ex. I'm suddenly distracted by a familiar voice shouting my name.

I look around and notice a petite redhead bouncing up and down excitedly, waving her arms.

"Harley," I all but squeal as a wave of relief washes over me. We did our training together, and she was the one person I really clicked with, along with a girl called Kate.

"How are you girl?" she says in her strong New York accent

"Nervous. I don't think I'm cut out for this." I swallow, a nervous ache in the pit of my stomach making me rub my hand over my belly.

"Girl, stop stressing. You will be fine and if anyone gives you shit, just call me over," she says, pointing at herself. "Actually, call Kate. I'm all talk," she adds, poking her tongue out.

We both burst into a fit of anxious laughter. I'm grateful she's working with me on my first shift.

"Did you get your little cuties dropped off okay?" she asks, adjusting her blouse.

"Yeah. I'm not used to spending nights away from them. It's going to be hard not seeing them till Sunday," I admit, staring down at my phone screen at a photo of Lexi holding Elle on my bed not long after we moved in, and they both have the biggest smiles on their faces. On the days I find it hard or if I am missing them, I use this image to remind me that those faces are the reason I'm doing this.

A tall woman in a tight black dress and a short sharp black bob appears, adjusting the headset she's wearing while looking down at a clipboard in her hand before shouting over the crowd of staff in the room.

"Okay ladies, we open in forty-five minutes. The owners are here and want to speak to you all before we open up. There will be press and media here tonight and some VIP guests, so I need you all to be on your A-game. You all know where you need to be and what to do, so don't let me or yourselves down. I'll expect you all in the main room in five minutes."

Standing at the bottom of the sprawling gold staircase, I can't stop my mouth from gaping. I saw this place during the day when we were training, but at night it comes alive. The dance floor sparkles like the night sky, echoed by the chandelier hanging above us. I scan the room, taking it all in.

We each take a seat at the tables that surround the black marble bar, and I can't help but search around to see who the new owners are.

Harley bumps my shoulder. "How about meeting the owners on the first night, hmm?"

I nod, goosebumps scattering my body at the idea of meeting them. "Yeah, do you think they're here much?"

"I have no idea, but—" She's cut off by the sound of footsteps across the dancefloor.

I turn my head to find three men walking slowly towards us. The low lighting in here makes it hard to make them out. But as they edge closer, their faces come into view and I swear my stomach nearly falls out my ass.

Brad, Harry, and Jack step up in front of us and glance around the room at the staff waiting patiently to meet their new employers.

Dressed in black button up shirts and matching suit pants, they look like they could be on the cover of a magazine.

This has got to be some kind of joke, right?

"Holy shit," Harley mumbles under her breath.

I match her wide-eyed expression, unable to speak, my mouth feeling like it's full of cotton balls.

Harry steps forward, his deep voice booming. "Welcome everyone. We'd like to thank you all for being here and for all your hard work preparing for tonight..."

I can see Jack smiling at his new employees. I keep my head down, praying he doesn't notice me.

I can avoid him forever, right?

Memories of the last time I saw him hit me like a freight train and my heart all but stops in my chest.

Oh fuck, I need a new job. I cannot let anyone know I licked my boss!

Jack's voice fills the room next and my stomach flutters with a herd of butterflies. *That voice.* His presence does things to me. I lift my head a little, checking to see if I can sneak out without him seeing, but no such luck.

The second I look up, dark blue eyes lock with mine and I swallow...hard. I don't hear the first part of what he says. I'm too busy trying to regulate my breathing.

I know he's addressing everyone in the room, but the way he's looking at me, he may as well be giving me a personal introduction. I shake my head, forcing myself to focus on what he's saying, but I only catch his final words.

"...I'm so happy you're here." A slow, sexy smile forms on his face as he continues to stare directly at me.

Chapter Nine

Jack

"...I'm so happy you are here." A spike of adrenaline pulses through me. *She's here*. Ria is here and working for me? This is both the best and worst news. It's been a month since I saw her. I wanted to pick up the phone and text her or show up at her door so many times, but I know she's going through a lot right now and I want to respect that.

She looks as stunning as ever. Ria is a natural beauty and even under the dim light of the club, her blue eyes are hypnotizing. It's only when Harry gives me a nudge that I realize I've stopped talking and I'm just staring.

I clear my throat. "All of you, I mean. We are so pleased all of you are here and together we can make this a fantastic opening. As Harry said, we want to thank you for your hard work and dedication thus far. We have every faith this will be a successful opening and we look forward to the future of The Boardroom."

The room erupts into whooping and clapping and I glance out to see Ria still looking stunned. As happy as I am to see her, this has just complicated things. She's now my employee, I am her boss. We can't blur those lines. I have one rule... don't date employees. Been there, done that and it always ends messy.

But she's not *just* an employee, she's Ria. The woman I haven't been able to stop thinking about for the last month... who am I kidding? I've had a thing for Ria since high school. Her lips on mine, her tongue on my body, the way I heated at her touch, how her eyes sparkle when she laughs...

Jesus Christ, I am simping hard.

The staff disperses and our front-of-house manager, Annabelle, comes over to take us to the VIP area. Tonight we will be experiencing the club from a guest and members' perspective as well as doing interviews and photo ops for the press and entertaining our VIP guests.

"Bro, did you see who's working for us?" Harry asks, slapping me on the back, grinning like he is truly enjoying my obvious discomfort.

"Ugh, yeah I did," I say, pulling my phone from my pocket, pretending I'm not bothered.

"So, what are you gonna do? It's going to be awkward knowing your staff sucked a slice of lime out of your mouth."

"Fuck off, Haz. And if that gets out and you embarrass Ria, I swear to God, you will regret it." I'm shocked at my tone towards Harry, but the wave of protectiveness for Ri is far greater than my guilt for snapping at my best friend.

"Woah, easy now. He was joking. What the fuck is wrong?" Brad steps between us.

I let out an exasperated breath. "Shit." I rub my hands down my face, a tornado of emotion shuddering through me. I like her, I've spent many years liking her, and now? Now she's here, working for me, and it's complicated, in more ways than one.

When we were kids, she was always Noah's little sister. We hung out on weekends and I always enjoyed her company. Noah never knew, but when I stayed over, I'd sneak out of his room when he was sleeping if I heard Ria up. We'd stay up till the early hours and talk about everything and anything around her kitchen table. She would make pancakes with whipped cream and M&M's. No one made them like she did.

I went off to college, and when I came back one summer, I knew my feelings for her were more than friends. I started to look at her differently. Wished she was mine, that I was the one holding her, making her laugh, and taking her away from her shitty life. Noah and Ria had it bad with their mom. I can't relate, thankfully. My parents were the greatest growing up and even now, if I needed anything, they would be there for me.

Noah and I eventually joined the Marine Corps. I only lasted a few years, like Brad and Harry. I only joined for the simple reason that I wanted to follow in my dad's footsteps; to make him proud, but I couldn't handle the long tours and when we lost a friend on tour in Afghanistan, that was my wake up call to leave. I came back to the news that Ria was marrying Alex. I was devastated.

But I had no right to be. Can you really feel that deeply for someone who was never really yours?

Believing her life was everything she dreamed of—the husband, kids, the house—I didn't interfere. I packed up and moved to Miami, and I've only seen her twice since. Had I known what was going on, I would have dropped everything and come back; saved her, told her how I felt, and hoped she felt the same.

Now she's single, back in my life, and working for me. The possibility of exploring my feelings for her is now within my reach, but can I really have her the way I want her... the way I've always wanted her? And not to mention, how do I have that conversation with Noah? How do I tell him I've had a thing for his sister all this time?

What a fucking head spin.

Harry slings an arm around my shoulder, silently telling me that he forgives my outburst. "But if you like her, that's okay, you know. You can't fake that insane sexual tension and chemistry you two had at the bachelorette party"

I nod, biting down on my bottom lip. *He's right.*

"Figure it out," he demands, tapping the back of my head before walking off towards the bar.

It's 3 am, and the club has closed. The last of the guests head out of the door, while the staff are getting ready to leave. Brad left a few hours ago saying he was going to do some work from home—whatever that means—and Harry left with a blonde woman about an hour ago. I could leave, I should leave, but I need to talk to Ria.

I head downstairs to the staff rooms, praying she hasn't left already, and find her in the corridor, head down, rifling through her handbag. Before I can say her name, she slams into me, dropping her keys.

"Shit, I'm so sorry. I wasn't looking." Panic laces her voice.

We both bend down at the same time, both reaching for them, our fingers touching. She slowly looks up, her eyes locking with mine.

"Jack," she whispers breathlessly, swallowing hard.

"Hey." I smile, feeling pleased with the effect I've obviously had on her. I reach out and help her up and she plays with her hair, tucking some behind her ear as if she's nervous.

"I, erm... didn't know you owned this place. If it's weird, I can leave and find something else. It was just the first thing I found that worked with the girls and..." She's rambling.

"Ri, breathe."

She lets out a long breath. "Sorry, I ramble when I'm nervous. It's been an evening."

"I know, and you've been amazing tonight. I don't want to lose you. Why would I want you to leave?"

She worries her bottom lip. "What happened at Nancy's bachelorette party. I swear I'm not normally like that. I'd had tequila, and it was my first night out and it all got out of hand. I'm so sorry for what I said after it was so inappropriate of me and..."

"Ria, you're rambling again."

She lets out an amused huff. "I am, aren't I?"

Our eyes meet, a beat of tension pulsing between us and all I can think about is biting down on that lip.

I take a step closer, her warm vanilla scent filling my nostrils, and I take in a deep breath, committing it to memory.

"Ri, believe me when I say you have nothing to apologize for, I was a very willing participant."

Her cheeks flush, and I have to fight the urge to touch her.

This is quite a drive for you. Why are you working out here?" I question why she's working nearly an hour from home.

"Erm," she stammers, fiddling with the keys in her hands. "Alex's parents are helping with the girls so I can work. I'm working weekends and then I have the week with them."

I nod, understanding.

"It's late. You can't drive all the way home now."

"No, Gabby and Ali live twenty minutes from here. I'll crash at theirs tonight."

"Well, you always have a place at mine if you need one." Her eyes widen at my comment and I realize what I've just offered may not have been my best idea.

"Thanks, but I don't think that would be appropriate. Would it? Sleeping at my boss's house. What would people say?" Her tone is dramatic as she holds her hand to her chest.

I let out a small laugh. "I'm your friend first and your boss second. You need anything, I'm here." *Let me be here for you, Ri.*

She smiles the most genuine smile and looks at me like I am the first person to truly want to help her. I don't understand why Alex didn't see what I see when I look at her.

"Thank you."

"Let me walk you out to your car." I press my hand to her lower back, guiding her towards the exit.

We walk in silence to her car, which is alone in the middle of the parking lot. The rusting old, blue Ford doesn't look like it will start, let alone get her home.

"Will that thing get you—"

"Home? Yeah, she will. She's not much, but it's all I could afford. Alex kept my car so..."

"What a dick," I mutter.

"Yep," she replies, clamping her lips in a tight line, avoiding my gaze, and fiddling with her keys.

I lift her chin so she has to face me. "You're doing great, Ri. I can't imagine how hard things are right now. You need *anything*, you call me, okay?" My thumb brushes her jawline and her eyelids flutter closed.

God, I want to kiss her.

"Thanks, Jack." She leans in to hug me, her hands wrapping around my waist, her head reaching just under my chin. I hold on longer than I know I should and she lets me. I get the feeling she needs this hug just as much as I want to give it. I run my hand down her back and kiss the top of her head, feeling her let out a breath and sinking into me.

As if remembering where she is, she steps back, breaking our embrace and tucking her hair behind her ear. "Thanks for walking me to my car," she says awkwardly before opening the car door. "I had better get some sleep. I'm back in 12 hours."

Hmmm, good to know she's working tomorrow.

"Drive safe and let me know when you are back home, okay?"

"Okay." Smiling, she closes the car door and turns the engine on. The car lights up and she pulls out of the parking lot. The minute her headlights disappear, I have this sudden urge to jump into my car and follow her. *Fuck, I'm screwed.* How can I be around her and not touch her. Her scent, the way she felt in my arms. No woman has ever had this effect on me. I know I said I have no issues with her working here and I was telling the truth, but that was before I'd touched her.

I walk back inside and head to our office. Picking up a bottle of our finest whiskey that's housed in a crystal bottle and pouring in the matching tumbler. I take off my suit jacket before I take a swig and sit back in my leather office chair, opening my phone so I can check our social media pages and the tags from tonight's opening. As I'm flicking through, thinking what a success it's been, Ria's name appears in a message notification. I'm surprised to see she's sent a selfie. She looks stunning. Makeup free, under white sheets, she's pulling a silly face with her thumb up.

> **Ria**
> Proof of life. I made it to Ali & Gabby's safe and sound. Thank you for walking me to my car.

I would give anything to be laying there with her and I want to tell her that but I settle with...

> **Jack**
> Anytime Ri. I wish I was in bed. This is my view… I send a photo of my laptop and the whisky tumbler.

> **Ria**
> Jack, it's nearly 4am. Get yourself to bed!

I take a moment. *Do I simply agree and end the conversation or test the waters?* I type my reply before I can change my mind.

> **Jack**
> Is that you offering up your bed to me, sweetheart? *Winky face emoji*

A couple of minutes pass. I can see that she's read the message but there's no response and I start to panic that I've gone too far. I sag with relief when her name appears on my screen.

> **Ria:** What would you say if I said it was...

Fuck, she wants to play.

> **Jack:** I'd say make some room, sweetheart. I'll be round in 20 *winking face emoji*

> **Ria:** I forgot to say it's a twin bed. I don't think it would fit someone of your size, action man. We'd be pretty squished together. It might get a bit hot and sweaty in these sheets.

I let out a groan. Fuck me she's killing me. She always was a little tease, even when she's not meaning to be. The thought of her soft, naked skin against mine, our bodies tangled in the sheets, has my cock hardening.

> **Jack:** Damn, Ri. You can't go round saying things like that. I'm off for a cold shower now.

> **Ria:** *Laughing emoji* *winking emoji* Night Jack *blowing kiss emoji*

> **Jack:** Night, sweetheart. Sweet dreams *blowing kiss emoji*

I know I am playing with fire, but I need her in my life in any way she is willing to let me have her. Consequences be damned.

Chapter Ten

Ria

I can smell coffee and feel a body next to me before I even open my eyes.

"Hmmm, coffee. Gabs, you are the best."

I open my eyes, turning my head to the side. She's dressed in a black sports bra and matching shorts. Knowing Gabby, she's already been on a run and done Pilates. I stretch out my arms and reach out for my phone.

"It's not from me, babe. Action man has outdone himself again."

"What, he sent Starbucks again?"

"Uh huh."

Okay, that is ridiculously sweet.

I open my phone to check my messages and thank him for the Starbucks.

> **Ria**
> Good morning. Thank you for the Starbucks. it was a lovely surprise to wake up to. I won't ask you how you knew Ali and Gabby's address *laughing emoji*

Within seconds, he replies.

> **Jack**
> Good morning, sweetheart. It's the least I could do after keeping you at the club. Ha, I know a guy who knows a guy.

> **Ria**
> Well, my employee feedback form will have a glowing report. 'Boss is very attentive and caring and will go above and beyond for his staff'.

> **Jack**
> Only for my best staff *winky face emoji*
> See you later, Ri.

Later? Will he be at the club? A flutter of excitement bursts in my stomach. *God, I hope so.*

Scrolling down, I see there is also a message from Anne.

Anne

> Good morning, my darling. The girls slept great and they are out walking Nugget with Grandpa, and this afternoon we are taking them to the park that has the sandbox. Lexi has plans to build a Barbie dream sand castle. Call anytime, but we are fine and you make sure you get some rest. I hope your first shift went well. We are so proud of you, love you, Anne x

Tears prick in my eyes at her words and my mind drifts to thoughts of my own mom, who I haven't heard from once since leaving Alex. She hasn't checked in or told me she's proud. *I'd give anything to hear those words from her.*

I sip my coffee and fire a text back, telling her my shift went great and I will FaceTime before I start my shift.

"So how was work?" Gabby asks as she sits crossed legend at the end of the bed.

"You'll never guess who my new bosses are..." She stares at me blankly, shrugging her shoulders and sipping her coffee. "Brad, Harry, and Jack."

She lowers her mug and her mouth falls open. "Shut the fuck up. I need all the details." She yells at the top of her voice, "Ali, get in here. Ria has gossip."

Once Ali has come in and made herself comfy on the bed as well, I tell everything, including how his hand on my back made me feel.

"I don't know what this thing is between us—if it's even a thing—but he makes me feel good, you know, like I'm worth looking at. He makes me laugh and I like how I feel when I'm around him"

"Ri, you're beaming... look at you," Gabby squeals, reaching and squeezing my hand.

"But is it too soon to be enjoying another man's attention?" I question, picking at the light pink nail polish on my thumbnail.

"Ri, there is no set time after a breakup, and he's not some random guy you met online. It's Jack. He's a good one," Ali reassures me.

"I know, but I'm not ready for any of that yet. I don't want a relationship. I just... I don't know. It feels good to have fun."

"It's your life, babe. You get to control what happens, what you do and who you let in. You wanna walk up the aisle with Jack tomorrow? We'll support you and if you just wanna ride him like a rodeo pony, then we'll support you too."

She scoots over and nudges my arm with her elbow and I rest my head on her shoulder.

"And we're gonna need all the details because if that man fucks as good as he looks, holy hell, Ri. Do not deprive yourself, you've gone far too long without some quality meat," she says, laughing.

I laugh so hard with her that tears roll down my cheeks and my sides ache. It's the laugh I didn't know I needed. I know I overthink, over analyze and question everything, but the idea and the reality of letting myself let go and moving on are two very different things.

Night two is just as busy. The club is heaving, so we've had to re-stock the bar twice. The rich sure can drink. To my surprise, Jack is here again. I didn't think he would be around so much, but I'd be lying if a small part of me isn't hoping he is here to see me.

I'm pouring a whiskey on the rocks in the VIP area when I feel eyes on me. I glance up and see Jack standing next to another man who is talking to him, but Jack's not paying him any attention as he's looking at me. I give him a small smile, and the one he gives back makes me feel giddy.

Get a grip, Ria. You're twenty-nine, not nineteen.

Jack's wearing his usual black suit pants with a crisp white shirt with the sleeves rolled up. His light brown hair has that messed up look but like it was intentional. His jawline looks like it has been hand-crafted by the people who built the pyramids. He hasn't shaved today and honestly, it only adds to his sex appeal. I imagine how good it would feel to run my tongue along his jawline. He looks edible.

I am snapped away from my daydream by one of the girls shouting my name over the thumping music.

"Ria, babes, we are running low on vodka and tequila. Can you go to the stockroom and grab a couple of bottles?"

"Sure thing," I shout back as she throws the key card in my direction and I catch it.

"Take the radio too, just in case we need anything else, I'll buzz ya." She points to the radio next to the cash register.

I escape the loud VIP area of the club and head down the back stairs to the stockroom, swiping the key card and opening the door.

It's a lot quieter down here and a bit chilly. Rubbing my hands over the tops of my arms to warm myself up, I scan the room for what I need. The music from the main room faintly plays through a small speaker in the corner. I hum along as I search the shelves of liquor. I spot the bottle of vodka I need and lean up to reach it, stretching on my tiptoes, my fingers only just touching it.

The sound of the door opening and slamming closed again makes me jump, the force of my movement, knocking the bottle off the shelf. It falls to the floor, shattering against the concrete.

'Shit,' I mutter, bending to pick up the larger bits of glass.

"Ri, no, leave." A deep voice echoes in the room.

Jack?

I look up and find his familiar blue eyes on me.

"What are you doing down here?" I ask, stepping over the broken glass to move closer to him.

"I saw you on the security camera heading down here. You shouldn't come down here alone. Always come in twos, okay?" There is concern in his voice.

"Sure. Sorry. It's busy and we need some more vodka. We've got some thirsty guests tonight." I giggle nervously at his proximity.

He smiles, his eyes, like always, never leaving mine. The intensity of his gaze leaves me a little breathless.

"Let me clear this up and I'll pay for the bottle. I'm sorry, you just made me jump."

"Don't apologize. It was my fault for startling you."

He reaches out his hand, helping me up on my feet. "Even so, I'm sorry." He takes my hand in his and his thumb caresses the palm of my hand, sending a warm feeling through my body.

"What else did you need? Let me get it for you."

I release my hand and turn to face the unit that houses the alcohol. "That one up there." Pointing to the top shelf where I can now see the tequila and the vodka I need, he steps behind me, his chest to my back. I gasp at the contact, his solid body like a wall of muscle.

"Turn around." There is a deep husk to his voice. I turn so we are chest to chest, closing my eyes because I'm not sure I can cope with him this close to me.

"Is this what you want?" I'm not sure if he's talking about the bottles or being pressed up against him, so I give my head a tiny shake.

He leans in and his nose brushes the shell of my ear, his lips grazing my neck gently.

Jesus.

My thighs squeeze together on their own accord, trying to ease the thumping arousal gathering there, causing my body weight to shift from one foot to the other.

"Ria," he whispers. "Tell me to stop."

I don't say anything.

"The thing is, sweetheart, the memory of you taking that shot off me and the feel of your lips on mine has been replaying over and over in my mind."

My mouth feels dry. *Holy shit, what do I say to that?* But he continues before I even find the words. "If you don't tell me to stop, I might have to have another taste of you."

His lips lightly dust my collarbone and I let out a whimper.

Dear God, Ri. Keep your cool.

"Tell me to stop," he rasps, snaking his arms around my waist and tugging my hips towards him. I lean my head to one side, giving him more access to my neck. He groans against my skin before he places feather-light kisses all the way up to my neck and my jaw.

"Tell me to stop Ri," he says with a little more force as he lifts his eyes to mine. They are hooded and full of want. I've never had a man look at me this way. Like he's fighting every urge not to devour me and I can feel his hard length against my thigh.

"Don't stop," I whisper. As the last word leaves my mouth, he crashes his lips to mine and we become frantic. My hands are in his hair as he grabs my ass with one hand and the other grips the back of my neck, deepening the kiss.

I let out another embarrassing whimper. I kiss him like he is my oxygen supply. His hand drifts down to my thigh and he slowly pulls up the hem of my skirt. I release another moan, moving my hands down his back, reaching for the base of his shirt—A buzzing sound fills the stockroom.

"Ria, are you okay? We need that alcohol, babes." Kate's voice crackles through the radio.

Jack and I both stop dead, trying to regulate our breathing. The reality of what almost just happened seems to hit us both.

He steps away from our embrace, running his hands through his hair as I smooth out and tug down my skirt. Reaching for the radio on the shelf behind me, I press the button to reply. "Yeah, I'm okay, Kate. Sorry, a bottle smashed. I'm just cleaning up. I won't be long," I tell her, trying to not make it obvious I was just kissing my boss, and he was seconds away from having my panties off.

"Okay, babe," she radios back.

I drop the radio back onto the shelf and turn away from Jack. Closing my eyes and covering my mouth with my hands, I let out a sigh.

What the hell just happened? How could I have let myself get carried away like that? This isn't me. Shit, I've just ruined everything. All because my horny ass couldn't keep herself together. I run my fingers through my hair, panic building in my chest, making my breaths shallow.

Jack puts his hands on my shoulders. "Ri, that—"

"Was a mistake," I interrupt. "And it shouldn't have happened, I'm sorry, I had a moment of weakness, I should have..."

He spins me around, cupping my face with his hand.

"No, it was wrong of me," he tells me. "I'm the one that should have stopped it. I got caught up and forgot my place. I'm so sorry, Ri... if I made you uncomfortable." His expression is full of regret.

"You didn't, you didn't do anything I didn't want, Jack," I reassure him, stepping out of his hold and taking the bottles of alcohol off the shelf. "But what I want and what is right are two different things." My voice is shaky.

"I don't have the luxury of making mistakes and putting my wants first. I've got my girls to think of, and I really need this job. What I want doesn't matter right now," I say, fighting back the tears that threaten to fall.

"Ria, what you want does matter."

"Jack, please," I say with a sniff. "This didn't happen, okay? Can we just forget it happened... please," I beg.

"Whatever you want, Ri" His gaze drifts to the floor, his voice sounding dejected.

I hurry past him, needing to put some space between us before I get lost in the feelings I have when he's around me." I need to get these up to Kate."

I walk as quickly as my shaky legs will carry me and fight back the tears that are trying to escape. I can't fall apart now. I don't have time. I've spent my whole life burying my feelings and my wants. What's another evening? I take a deep breath and swing open the club door. The music thumps and the smell of sweat and alcohol fills the air.

I see Kate and she waves me over. I take an order for four spicy margaritas, acting as if that moment with Jack didn't just happen. A moment I know I will replay in my mind like an old movie because for the first time in my life, I got a taste of what it was like to act on my wants, and God did it feel good.

Chapter Eleven

Jack

Two days. It's been two days since I saw her, two days since I felt her lips on mine, and it's all I can think about. I know we took it too far. I know she's not ready for anything right now, but I lose my head when I'm near her. I know she wanted it as much as me, but, for whatever reason, she just can't let herself give in to what she wants. I suspect that prick, Alex, is the root cause. How he's treated her and made her feel makes me feral. I want to find him and make him regret everything he has ever said or done to her.

Despite knowing I shouldn't, I've somehow ended up outside her house. I need to see her, to reassure her. To be her friend. Because I need her in my life. In any way, she's willing to let me in. She doesn't need another asshole making her feel like shit. She needs someone she can trust and rely on and I want to be that for her.

I'm sitting outside the blue and white house with flower boxes that decorate the porch. It's small but cute and has Ria written all over it.

I step out of my black Audi, walk up the small brick-paved driveway, and pass her car. *Fuck, she needs a new one.* I can't believe she drives around in that or more importantly that Alex lets the mother of his children drive around in that.

I didn't want to turn up as Jack, her boss. I want to be Jack, her friend, so I'm in a pair of tennis shoes, dark jeans, and a plain black tee. Does it show off my muscles? Maybe. Did I pick it out on purpose for that very reason? Also, maybe. I want her to see me as a friend, but I'd be lying if I didn't admit that I hope that, over time, she will see me as more.

I knock on the door and a dog barks on the other side—if you can call it that. It's more of an annoying yap. No one comes to answer, so I go to knock again just as the door opens. My eyes drop to where a little brunette, who is the image of Ria, stands. She's dressed in a pink princess dress, holding a little white dog, who is still yapping.

This must be Lexi.

"Hello, who are you?" she asks in the sweetest voice.

I am just about to introduce myself when the dog leaps out of her little arms and tries to jump up at me

"Nugget, nooooo," she shouts.

Nugget? The dog's called Nugget?

I scoop the dog up and stroke it till it starts to calm. I bend down so I am at eye level with Lexi. I don't know much about kids, but a friend of mine has a toddler and I know he likes it when I get down on his level.

"Hi, I'm Jack. I'm friends with your mommy. Is she here?"

In the distance I can hear Ria shouting as she comes towards the door "Lexi, what have I told you about opening the door? I was just getting your sister in the highchair..." She stops, eyes wide. "Jack? What are you doing here?"

I rise up, still holding the tiny dog, and smile. "I just wanted to check in and see how you were." I hesitate, wondering if I've done the right thing. "Is now a bad time?"

Before she can answer, Lexi speaks, "No, it's a great time. We are going to watch *Cinderella*. Mommy got popcorn and M&M's and she never lets me have M&M's, but she's got me some today. Do you want some?" She rambles without taking a breath. Looking up at me with big ocean blue eyes that are just like Ria's, there's no way I can say no to her.

"Sure, if that's okay with your mom." My eyes avert to Ria, who is worrying her bottom lip in that adorable way she does when she's thinking.

"Erm, sure, come in." She runs a hand across her forehead. "Please excuse the mess."

I smile, stepping into her narrow hall, shutting the door before I kick my shoes off and set Nugget down. He follows Lexi into a room and I follow Ria.

We round a corner into the kitchen. Farmhouse-style cabinets give the small space a cozy, homely vibe. I notice a vase of yellow roses in the window, her favorite flower if I remember correctly, and a fruity scent fills the air. I hear a little squeal and turn my head to a baby in a highchair, clapping her hands as Ria smiles at her.

"Sorry, I'm just giving Elle a snack before she has a nap. I'll feed her and then get you a coffee." She takes out a pink bowl from the microwave, stirring and blowing on the food. It smells like apples and berries. Elle's eyes light up, waving her chubby little arms around and licking her lips.

"It's too hot, baby. One sec," Ria says gently.

She pulls up a stool in front of the highchair and checks the temperature of the food before giving it to Elle. I can't help but scan her body and notice the way her black leggings hug her petite legs as she leans over to spoon-feed Elle. This is a side of Ria I haven't seen. Ria as a mom. Her hair is in a messy bun, with stray hairs falling, framing her delicate features. She's make-up free, but she has never looked more beautiful and I can't help but look at her and smile.

An unfamiliar feeling erupts in my stomach, taking me off guard. *Are those butterflies?*

"I can make the coffee, just show me where everything is," I tell her. She looks surprised by my offer but points to her coffee machine and the drawer underneath.

I find what I need and work out how the machine works to make us both a caramel latte and by the time I've placed them on the kitchen counter, Elle has finished her bowl of whatever mashed food Ria fed her and is now nibbling away on a rice cake.

"Thanks." She yawns, taking the coffee from my hand. "Sorry, the girls had me up early today. I'm gonna need another three of these to make it to bedtime."

"No problem." I pause, unsure how to explain why I'm here. "I'm sorry for just turning up, but I figured after what happened, you would find a reason not to let me come over if I asked."

"Yeah, maybe," she says with a smirk as she sips her coffee.

I pull up a stool so I'm on the opposite side of her small kitchen island and set down my cup. Nerves flood my body as I prepare to say what I came here to say. "Ri, I don't want to make things weird between us. I know you have a ton of stuff going on right now, so I understand your priority is all of this and your girls." I gesture with my hands around the room.

She gives me a small smile.

"So maybe, for now, we could be friends. Just friends. I want to be there for you, Ri, in any way you'll let me. You need milk, you call me. You got a flat tire, I'll come change it. You want takeout and a game of Scrabble, I'm your guy." I point to my chest.

She laughs, tilting her head. "You play Scrabble?"

"I do. As a matter of fact, I'll have you know that on our tour of Afghanistan in 2011, I was the Scrabble champion of Camp Bastion." Folding my arms across my chest, making my arm muscles flex, I don't miss how she tracks the movement. I might be agreeing to just be friends, but that doesn't mean we can't have a little fun too; still be playful like we have always been.

"So, do we have a deal? What happened at the club is forgotten?"

Should you ever want to explore whatever that was that happened back there, you let me know, is what I want to say, but, instead I tell her, "I'm your friend before anything else, okay?"

She looks at me like I've just said everything she needs to hear. "Deal." She nods, reaching out to clink her coffee mug with mine, and the way her entire face lights up has me transfixed.

The moment of silence is broken by Lexi shouting. "Mommy, can we watch the movie?"

"No rest for the wicked," she sighs. "Yes, baby, but I need to put Elle down for her nap then we can, okay?"

"Ugh, okay." Lexi's disappointment is apparent, despite her being in another room.

Ri laughs, getting up to pick Elle out of her highchair, kissing the top of her head. "You're welcome to stay and watch the movie with us, but I get it if that's not your thing—"

Without hesitation, I answer, "Yeah, I'd love to stay," because truthfully, I'd watch all the princess movies if it meant spending time with her.

"I need to put her down. Do you mind hanging with Lexi? If she asks for M&M's tell her she has to wait."

I chuckle. "Okay, I think I can handle that."

As I walk into the front room, Lexi tips one of the many toy boxes I can see dotted around the space, onto the wooden floor. An array of dolls and tiny accessories flood the floor and she looks at me with wide eyes. "Oopsie."

I sit on the floor next to Lexi. "What are you playing?"

Lexi eyes me, then her gaze drops to the floor. "You're not mad I made a mess?" I shake my head as my brow furrows slightly.

"No, why would I be mad?"

She shrugs, swirling her hand into the pile of toys. "My daddy always gets mad." My heart squeezes for her, for Ria and what they've been through. I can't focus on Alex right now though, Lexi is more important.

"Sometimes adults get mad, but it's not your fault." She nods. "Come on, show me your favorite toy."

"This one," she beams excitedly. "Barbie, do you like Barbie?"

"Yeah, sure," I reply, never having had an opinion about Barbie until now.

"Mommy only lets me play with Barbies if I don't take the heads off."

I tilt my head, looking at the mini Ria in front of me. "Why do you take the heads off?" *Probably a loaded question, but here we are.*

She picks up the doll, waving it in front of my face. "To swap them, duh."

"Of course," I say, tapping my forehead. "Silly me."

"But Nugget ate one of the heads and went to the doggie hospital, so now I don't swap them."

I laugh. *Kids are so funny.*

"Did you pick his name?"

She nods. "Chicken nuggets are my favorite food ever. They are soooo good."

"They sure are."

She stands up and drops the Barbie to the floor. "Do you like Cher?"

"Cher. the singer?"

"Yeah," she says excitedly, running over to the record player and pulling out a vinyl. "It's Mommy's favorite song and my song. Do you want to watch me sing?"

Oh, I can't wait to tease Ri about this.

"I think your mommy is getting Elle to take a nap. It might be too loud, sweetie."

"No, it won't," she says adamantly.

"Okay, sure." Who am I to tell her no?

Her little hands place the record on the player, and she walks over to me and gives me a remote. "This one's a fancy one. When I say hit it, you need to press the red button, okay?"

"Got it."

She drags over a little pink plastic microphone that's connected to a pink stand, full of confidence and determination, and gives me a thumbs up. I give her one back with a smile.

Shit, she's cute.

She turns around, so her back is to me and points her little finger in the air.

"Hit it."

I let out a little chuckle and hit the button and get the shock of my life when "It's in His Kiss" booms from the speaker. Jumping, I fumble in a blind panic, trying to find the volume button on the remote.

I don't move for two and a half minutes, watching this little four-year-old spin around and give the performance of her life.

Pointing her finger and doing a little scoop and sway to the "Shoop Shoop" part.

Just as Lexi is belting out the final bars, Ria opens the living room door.

"Yessssss, well done. Encore encore," I whisper shout, as I give her a standing ovation, clapping softly, conscious the baby is asleep.

Lexi takes a bow. "Okay, hit it again."

"Noooo," Ria shouts over us. "No encore, Lex. What have I told you about that song?"

"But you play it, Mommy. I like the Shoop Shoop bit." Lexi starts swaying again and I have to press my lips together to prevent a laugh from escaping.

"Okay, that's enough," Ria announces, rubbing her hands over her face in exasperation. "Lex, go get your stuffies and blanket and I'll get the movie on."

Lexi huffs and sulks out of the room.

Ria laughs, pinching the bridge of her nose. "Dear God, what is wrong with her? I'm sorry. She likes to perform but refuses to sing along to anything age-appropriate."

"Don't apologize, smile. She's great and a lot like someone else I know." I wink, making her cheeks pinken. "So Cher?" I say with a smirk. "Didn't have you down as a fan."

She bends down and starts picking up the dolls and placing them in the box.

"She's my guilty pleasure along with a few others,"

I kneel down to give her a hand.

"Why doesn't that surprise me? Me and Noah used to hear you wailing and moaning along to your record player in your room when you were a kid."

"Shut up," she squeals, giving me a playful tap to the chest. My body tingles at the contact. "I did not moan."

I lean in a little closer, focusing my eyes on hers and lowering my voice. "Oh, you did, but don't be embarrassed, sweetheart, I enjoyed hearing your moans."

She smirks, avoiding my eyes and she looks down at the floor. My dick twitches at the sight of her tongue running along her bottom lip and the idea of her moaning my name.

Yeah, this whole 'let's be friends' thing is going well.

She heads out towards the kitchen, and I follow. Stopping at the bottom of the staircase, she calls softly "Lex, movie time."

She turns, not expecting me to be so close behind, and her chest bumps with mine. She clears her throat, squaring her shoulders and looking up at me.

"Well, I hope you are in the mood for Cinderella."

"Always," I say with a grin.

I help Ria pop some corn and put some M&M's into a bowl and we make our way back to the front room. Lexi is already set up with her blanket and her pink bunny on the couch. She wasn't joking about Lexi and M&M's; she inhaled them in under ten seconds and she looked like a hamster who had overfilled its cheeks.

"Hey, leave some of those for Mommy, they are mine too," Ria whines.

Lexi shakes her head from side to side, unable to speak.

"Lexi, spit them out now you will choke," Ria demands, taking a bowl and squeezing her cheeks until out fly half-eaten sweets.

I clearly didn't hide the horrified look on my face well because Ria snorts a laugh. "You still sure you want to stay?"

"Oh yeah, absolutely. Just no M&M's for me... ever again." I wrinkle my nose.

We settle down on the couch, Lexi in the middle of Ria and I while we watch Cinderella, and by watch, I mean Lexi talked through about three-quarters of it. She was either asking me questions about my favorite princess or telling me what was about to happen and then, just as the prince was placing the glass slipper on Cinderella's foot, she crashed out with her head in Ria's lap.

"Wine?" Ria mouths and gestures a drinking motion with her hand.

"Absolutely," I mouth back.

Ria gestures for me to pass the gray scatter cushion that's next to me. I pass it as she slowly gets up and gently places Lexi's head on the cushion, pressing a light kiss to her cheek, and then heads out in search of wine. I can't help but stare at Lexi snoring away and smile.

Warmth fills my chest. I've never had the burning desire to have kids. Sure, I like them, but I've always been okay if I had them or not. I'm an only child, so I never grew up with siblings, but looking down at little Lexi and watching Ria with her girls, I think I could see them in my future.

I'm taken away from my thoughts by Ria handing me a glass of red. That first sip goes down so smoothly, the perfect mixture of acidity and fruit. I let out a slow breath, leaning back and resting my head against the couch.

"Isn't it too early for wine? It's like 4 pm?"

She manages to squeeze herself on the end of the couch next to Lexi, careful not to wake her. Raising her glass. "Well, it's 5 o'clock somewhere, right?" she laughs.

"Can't disagree with that," I say, clinking my glass with hers and taking another sip. "Do they usually nap this late in the day?"

"They should have woken up an hour ago," she sighs. "We had a rough night last night. Lexi peed the bed and Elle was teething so it was musical beds. They can sleep a little longer."

I look at her in awe. "How do you do it... do this?" I gesture at Lexi and around the living room full of toys.

"I don't know, I just do. I don't have a choice, but even if I did, I'd still want to do it. It's hard work, but they are amazing, and being a mom is the best thing I've ever done." She looks down at Lexi stroking her hair, a smile spreading across her face.

Watching her, I get it. Why she reacted the way she did to our kiss, why she panicked about losing her job. These girls are her world and she wants to be able to take care of them on her own.

"You're a great mom, Ri. They are lucky to have you."

"Thank you," she says with genuine appreciation, because I get the feeling Alex never told her.

We talk until we hear Elle wake on the monitor and Lexi wakes asking for more M&M's.

"I should probably get going. I've intruded on your day enough."

"No, stay," Lexi mutters sleepily, grabbing hold of my hand.

"Mommy is getting us pizza from the pizza shop. Do you like pizza?"

"I love pizza. What's your favorite topping?"

"Pepperoni," she says proudly, raising her hands in the air. She really is the cutest kid I've ever met.

I give a dramatic gasp. "Mine too."

She giggles and her little face beams with excitement.

"Can he stay, Mommy?" she pleads.

"Of course he can, but Jack is very busy, so he might not be able to."

My eyes find hers, never breaking contact because I need to know she hears what I'm saying. "I'm never too busy for you, Ri."

Chapter Twelve

Ria

We have been in our new house for a couple of months now. Work is going great, and the girls are thriving. We've found a ballet class for Lexi and I've met a couple of 'mom friends'. We go for coffee after ballet and we've found a cute little library with a park that is within walking distance of our house. Dare I say it, but we've fallen into a nice little routine and for the first time in a long time, I'm starting to feel a little more like myself. Don't get me wrong, I'm exhausted. I'm pretty sure I am running on eighty percent iced coffee and twenty percent prayer, but I am doing it.

Thankfully, I have only seen Alex a couple of times to hand the girls over. We do the exchanges with his parents and they supervise the visits. I expressed my concerns to my lawyer about his drinking and how he's never really had the girls alone, so until he proves he can manage, he will see the girls at his parents' house.

Alex keeps asking where we live, and I just don't want to tell him. Yes, you could argue that as their dad he has a right to know, because if the shoe was on the other foot I'd expect to know, but I know him. He doesn't want to know out of safety or concern; he wants control. He would have something to say about the house I've chosen, the area, how I've decorated and I just don't need that negativity in my life. I've come too far to let him back into my headspace.

He has asked me back numerous times, tells me he regrets what he did, begging for another chance. He tells me he's changed. All the usual bullshit. I admire his parents for remaining neutral throughout all this. Not once have they asked me to forgive their son or shared their opinion on the situation. I know they don't approve of what he's done and how he's treated me and the girls, and I know it breaks them watching me hand the girls over and driving away, and truthfully, I feel like I leave a piece of my heart every time I drop them off. There are no more Sunday dinners at their house, no more family weekends at the lake. All of that stopped because he couldn't keep his dick in his pants and treated me like I was an option rather than a priority. We all have a breaking point and four months ago, I reached mine.

The sun beams down on my face as I push Elle on a swing. "Wheeeee!" Lexi squeals as she bombs down the slide, landing on her butt with a laugh. I shake my head. These girls are crazy. Or maybe I'm the crazy one? I couldn't say no to Lexi when she saw the ice cream truck earlier, which is probably why she's so full of energy right now. I live for days like these. Me and my girls.

"Mommy, can I go on the swing too?" Lexi asks.

"Sure, baby." She skips over to the free swing and I lift her in and begin to push.

"When is Jack coming to our house? I like Jack, Mommy and so does Nugget."

I let out a little laugh. "Soon, sweetie. He's very busy with work."

Jack has been over a couple of times since he turned up that day and to be honest, I'm surprised he's come around after Lexi's performance and the M&M's moment.

True to his word, he has been there for me and kept our relationship completely platonic, and I know it's messed up, but there is a part of me that is disappointed. Why is he so perfect and respectful? He's at the club most weekends and the amount of times my mind drifts off when I look at him, thinking about the way his lips felt on mine and his firm grip on my ass as he pulled me into him.

But I can't be mad. He's doing exactly what I said I wanted. I wanted a friend, not a relationship, but after our encounter, I didn't realize how much I missed that kind of affection and intimacy and now I'm craving it.

Mine and Alex's sex life was anything but passionate. In the early days, sure it was fun, but after we got married, it became one-sided. My pleasure was never a priority. If he wanted it, and I didn't, he would make me feel guilty and grind me down till I gave in. Sometimes it was easier just to sleep with him than turn him down. I can't remember the last time I had an orgasm. I am a twenty-nine-year-old, single mom of two and I can't remember the last time I climaxed.

Well, shit, that's just depressed the hell out of me.

My pity party is interrupted by my phone ringing in my diaper bag. I rifle through, trying to find it before it rings out. I can't help but smile when I find it and see Jack's name on the phone.

"Hello," I answer.

"Ri, it's Jack."

I giggle. "I know. Everything okay?"

"Ermm, yeah, kinda. We've had a few of the girls call in sick tonight. They went out to a seafood restaurant, and it seems they got food poisoning."

Thank God I didn't go out with them in the end.

"Me and Harry will be working behind the bar tonight. I know you have the girls, and I wouldn't ask unless we were desperate, but is there any chance you could come in tonight?"

"Oh, Jack. I really wanna help, but Anne and Steve are out of town. I guess I could see if Ali or Gabs could have them."

Do I want to work tonight? Not really, but do I want to spend the evening with Jack? Absolutely. A flutter in my belly forms at the thought of being around him.

"I'll pay you double time for the inconvenience."

"Well, now, you're talking." I laugh. "Let me speak to the girls and I'll call you back."

"Thanks, sweetheart." He sighs, ending the call.

I type a text out to the girls in our group chat asking if either of them are free tonight to babysit.

Ali replies straight away, telling me she can, and gets off work at six.

"Lexi, how do you fancy seeing Auntie Ali tonight?"

"Yaaaayyyy," she squeals as I push her a little higher.

I call Jack back and he answers after two rings.

"Ria, baby, please tell me you have good news because Harley has just called in as well, and she's quote, 'shitting through the eye of a needle'. We'll have to close if we don't have enough staff. Brad's coming in too, but we have two bookings for the VIP area and..."

I've never heard him sound so stressed.

"Jack, you're rambling."

He lets out a long breath. "Shit, I am, aren't I."

"Yeah, you are, and yes, I can come in. Ali is going to have them but can't get there till six. Is it okay if I start a little later?"

I can hear him banging around, likely preparing the bar for opening. "Bring them," he says casually.

"Bring them? To work?" I ask, surprised by his suggestion.

"Yeah, if you can get here as early as you can, we can juggle the girls between us. We don't open till nine, but we are six staff down, so there is a lot to do."

"Erm, sure. I guess I can bring Elle's pack and play and put her in that," I say, mentally calculating everything I need to do and pack.

"I don't know what one of those is, sweetheart, but if it gets you here as soon as possible, bring all the stuff you need."

I look at my phone. It's 3 pm now.

"Okay, give me a couple of hours. We're in the park. I'll go home now, get the girls packed, and then drive up."

I hear him let out a sigh of relief. "God, I could kiss you right now," He declares.

Sorry, what?

"I mean, I'm grateful for you. I-I didn't mean, I'm not..."

I laugh. Rambling Jack might be my favorite.

"Drive safe, Ri," he tells me before he hangs up.

"Lex, change of plans. Do you want to come to work with Mommy?"

Her little face lights up. "Yeah! Will Jack be there?"

"He will," I tell her with a smile.

"Let's gooooo." I lift her out of the swing and do the same with Elle, putting her in her stroller as Lexi starts to run in the direction of our house. It seems she's just as excited as I am about seeing him.

Chapter Thirteen

Ria

Two hours later we are pulling into the parking lot of The Boardroom and as I step out of the car, I see Jack exit the staff entrance and stroll towards my car like he's been waiting for me to arrive.

I can tell by the tension in his jaw and the way his shoulders hunch, he's stressed, but he still looks like he's walked off the set of a GQ magazine shoot.

His black dress shirt bunches at his elbow, revealing the tattoo on his left arm. I watch with awe as he raises it to run the hand through his messed up hair. God, looking stressed has never been sexier.

His long strides reach me in no time, those thighs flexing with each step in his black pants.

Ria, honey, you're drooling.

"Ri, you're a life saver."

I step out of the car, and without hesitating, he pulls me into his arms and something inside me settles. His heart thumps beneath my cheek as he splays his hands over my back, the warmth of him seeping into my bones. My arms slowly return the hug and I whisper, "It's no problem." He releases me with a kiss to the forehead and I'm already missing his closeness. I'd stay in his arms all day if I could.

But he's your friend, Ri. That wouldn't be appropriate, would it?

I visibly shake my head to get rid of the thoughts spinning in there. I'll unpack that later.

He opens the backdoor and Lexi calls his name.

"How are my favorite girls?" he beams, reaching in to unclip Lexi as I walk round to get Elle from her carseat.

"Do you have M&M's," Lexi whispers with her little hand over her mouth so she thinks I can't hear.

Jack throws his head back and a deep laugh comes from him.

"Lex," I scold. "What did I tell you? No asking for candy."

I see Jack whisper something in Lexi's ear, and she nods.

We unpack the car and Jack helps me with all the stuff. It's honestly embarrassing how much crap I have with me, but kids don't travel light. I have Elle in the baby carrier strapped to my chest, her diaper bag in one hand, and a large tote with blankets, stuffies, a change of clothes, an iPad and enough snacks to last 2 days.

Jack is carrying Elle's pack and play and the mattress for it along with the diaper bag. I needed to be prepared in case Ali is late and Elle wants to sleep. He's wedged the rest of the stuff under his strong arms. My eyes drift to his forearms and the way his veins pop and his muscles flex as he adjusts the bag that's in his grip and all I think about is how I wish I was that pack and play under his arm so he could handle me like that.

I have to shake my head again to quit staring before he notices, but that only welcomes in new thoughts as I watch him effortlessly help carry things and talk to Lexi like he's known her for her whole life. This warmth flooding my chest and this calmness I feel when I'm around him is unfamiliar yet welcomed.

Lexi is dragging her little suitcase behind her, walking next to Jack as we head for the club and make our way to the main room. I have no idea what she's got in it. I told her to pack some things to keep her busy, so God only knows what's in there.

"We can set this up in front of the bar, we need to get the tables cleaned and the liquor fully stocked before we open," Jack says, dropping the pack and play on the floor and the way he's looking at it and all the stuff I put beside it I fear he might be regretting allowing me to bring the girls.

"I'm sorry about all this. The girls don't travel light." Feeling a little awkward at all the baby gear I've had to bring along to my place of work.

"Don't apologize. You are saving our asses tonight. Least we can do is have the girls here."

I give him a genuine smile. He always knows how to reassure me when I feel like I am being an inconvenience or a burden. Something I'm not used to.

"Ria, thank you for saving the day," Harry hollers from behind the bar.

"It's no problem. Sorry about all this," I gesture to Elle, who is still strapped to me, all our stuff on the club floor, and Lexi, who is unpacking the suitcase which is full of Barbies and coloring.

"They won't be here long. Ali is picking them up around six."

The biggest grin spreads across Harry's face and he claps his hands and rubs them together. "Oooh, the pocket rocket. It's been a while since I've seen her." He walks out from behind the bar and over to us.

Lexi looks up at him. "What's a pocket rocket?"

"Someone who is really fun," he laughs.

"And what's your name?" he tugs at his trousers, bending down so he's eye-level with Lexi.

"Lexi and that's my baby sister, Elle. We have a dog called Nugget, but Mommy said we couldn't bring him."

Harry looks at me and then Jack, his brows furrowed. "Nugget?"

"Best you don't ask," Jack mutters.

I chuckle and sway back and forth as Elle starts to fidget in the carrier.

"Well, it's very lovely to meet you both," he says to Lexi before getting up off the ground.

"And I have a lot of questions about Nugget." He bops Elle on the nose and she giggles. "Shit, your girls are cute, Ri."

"Language," Jack barks.

Harry clamps his hand over his mouth, forgetting he's in the presence of little ears.

"Oh, fuck. Shit, sorry, Ri," he stammers.

I can't help but laugh. "It's fine. She's heard worse. From her dad's mouth." Jack is glaring at him and Harry just looks down at the floor at the pack and play.

"Want some help?" he asks.

"Yeah, as long as you don't open that mouth again," Jack says sternly.

They both get on the floor and open up the pack and play. I lift Elle out of the carrier and start to get some things out of the bag ready. I look over and see them struggling, and it takes everything within me not to burst out laughing.

Harry is holding one side and Jack the other. I know that they need to flatten the base first, but I'm going to keep that bit of information to myself for now.

"Right, this side has clicked, now you click your bit," Jack shouts to Harry.

"I'm doing it and it won't click," Harry says, sounding frustrated.

"Pull it."

"I'm pulling," Harry grits.

"Are you pulling it right?" Jack says, clearly exasperated, his eyes narrowing as he leans back, like he's trying to work out what's going wrong.

"How many ways are there to pull?" Harry huffs. He stands up and lets go of the side he was holding and so does Jack and the pack and play collapses in a heap.

"Shit's broken," Harry concludes.

I snort a laugh and walk over to them. "Here, hold her." I pass Elle to Jack and he takes hold of her like she's a family heirloom and will break if he moves her. I pick it up, push the base down, and pull up the sides in two clicks.

"There, done," I say, a little too smugly.

Jack and Harry just stare at the now erected pack and play like they have just witnessed someone complete the Rubik's Cube in under thirty seconds.

"Well, that's embarrassing," Harry mumbles. "I'm gonna go back over there where I clearly left my common sense and my balls."

"Aww, don't be embarrassed, Haz," I mock. "I won't tell Ali you couldn't pop up a pack and play." He flips me the middle finger as he walks towards the bar.

"That was incredible," Jack says in awe, holding Elle to his chest. She squeals and slaps him across the cheek in excitement, causing him to jolt.

My hands fly up to come to my mouth, stifling a laugh as he stands there blinking rapidly, like he's trying to register what just happened.

"It really wasn't. It's the easiest bit of equipment to put together once you know how."

"You're always surprising me, sweetheart. What other skills are you hiding," he asks, quirking a brow.

I fold my arms across my chest. "Well, now, that would be telling, wouldn't it? I prefer to surprise people with my talents."

He moves closer and I open up my arms, thinking he will pass me Elle, but he doesn't. His free hand wraps around my waist and lightly tugs me towards him. "I look forward to discovering your talents." His tone is suggestive and I have no doubt he noticed the tremor that rolled through my body.

Oh, crap, it's going to be a long night.

Jack goes back behind the bar and continues setting up whilst I quickly feed Elle and get Lexi set up and then the three of us work our asses off over the next hour, polishing glasses and restocking the bars. Brad joined us, bringing up more glasses from the stock room.

"Mommy, I'm thirsty. All my juice is gone," Lexi calls, waving her sippy cup at me.

"What can I get you, little lady?" Brad calls over to her.

"Juice, pweese."

I pick her up and carry her over to the bar, placing her on top and hand Brad her cup. He pours some juice in but doesn't attach the lid. Instead, adds a straw and a little umbrella.

"Wow, look, mommy, a brella."

I give Brad a thankful smile and he gives a nod back.

"What do you say, Lex?" I prompt her.

"Thank yoouuu." She sips the straw.

"You are very welcome, princess."

"Why do you have drawings on your arms and on your neck and on your hands?"

She leans out her little hand and touches some of his tattoos and he lets her. Lexi has no fear and would talk to anyone, a quality I love, but also puts the fear of God in me. But I trust these guys.

"I liked them, so I got someone to draw them on me," he says softly, which is such a contrast to his usual deep, gravelly tone.

"Do they wash off when you go in the bathtub?"

He laughs. "No, they stay forever."

Her little face lights up. "Mommy, can I get drawings that don't wash off?"

"Absolutely not, miss." I pick her up and lift her down off the bar. "Go back over and pack up your stuff. Auntie Ali will be here soon."

Turning my head back to look at Brad, I say, "Thank you, you are really good with her.". He nods and offers me a small smile.

"My sisters got a kid a bit older than her, so I know I need to dial down the scary Brad round kids." I give him a thankful nod.

As I'm packing up the girls' stuff, I hear Ali before I see her. "Auntie Ali has come to rescue you girls."

"Ali," Lexi cheers, jumping up, running over, and throwing herself at her. Ali picks her up and swings her round. "Did you bring me candy?"

"Of course," she whispers, rubbing noses with Lexi. "But you have to wait till we get home and don't tell Mommy, okay?"

"Deal."

"Okay, let's get your stuff." As she bends to start packing up the piles of their things, Harry calls from the bar.

"You got one of those nose kisses for me, Ali cat?" He wiggles his eyebrows, as he edges towards her.

She doesn't even give him eye contact as she responds, raising her hand. "You wish, honey."

I don't miss the way his eyes drift to her ass, that I have no doubt is looking peachy, biting his lip, as he stares.

I laugh. "Are you ever gonna give that guy a chance?"

"Probably not." She shrugs.

I don't bother to ask her to explain why. Not right now, anyway. That conversation is going to need time and probably alcohol. "Thanks for this. We are so understaffed tonight, it's going to be crazy. I'm not sure what time I'll be home but you can stay in my bed."

"Shush yourself. I'm happy too. You know it's never any trouble. Now where is my baby?"

Reaching for Elle, she cradles her in her arms, kissing the top of her head.

I let out a slow breath and prepare myself for what I know will be a crazy night.

***

It's 1 am, and the club is still packed. Jack, Harry, and Brad have worked the bar with me and Kate all night. We've had two bachelorette parties and a hockey team in the VIP area. I feel for the girls working those areas. It's all table service, and they have been fully booked tonight. One hour to push and we can start closing down.

I'm making cosmopolitans for a couple of women who have propped up the bar all night. From the little I've overheard, one of them has left her cheating husband and my heart breaks for her so I've slipped her some free drinks when I can, the woman needs it. Solidarity, sister.

"How you doing, sweetheart?" Jack shouts over the music. Thursday nights are RnB nights. The DJ is playing a remix I haven't heard before and I can't help but sway my hips. When I haven't been mixing drinks, I've stolen glances at Jack every chance I get. He moves so effortlessly and could mix cocktails with his eyes shut. Watching his shirt tighten across his biceps and chest as he shakes the mixers has my body heating.

The sound of women cheering erupts over the music. I turn to see the bachelorette party fawning over Harry, who is mixing cocktails like a pro.

He's been on top form all night, even dancing on top of the bar and pouring shots into people's mouths. I think he's caught the attention of lots of the women and there are two in particular, I'm pretty certain he will be going home with tonight.

Jesus, I feel like I'm behind the bar with the cast of *Magic Mike* here. I'm starting to see why their other club was so popular if this is how they worked it. Looking at them, you wouldn't think they were multi-business owners with so much responsibility. They look like normal guys having fun, working a shift.

I've also noted the continuous line of women that Jack has had on his side of the bar all night. Can't say I blame them, but I'd be lying if I said it didn't bother me. *But he's not yours, Ria.*

I watch as he pours a cocktail from the shaker over the ice in the glass. He then takes a handful of cherries to add and pops one into his mouth, sucking it off its stem. I almost combust right there and then. He must notice my little perving session because the grin and the wink he gives me has me gulping like I've been holding my breath too long.

I clear my throat, realizing I hadn't answered his question. "I lost feeling in my feet about an hour ago and I'll be dreaming about sex on the beach for the next week," I shout back. A cocktail I'd never heard of, but Harry swears is really popular in England and the women in here tonight have gone crazy for them.

He puckers his lips and blows out a breath like he's having an internal battle with himself. I knew what I was doing there. I purposely didn't say I was talking about the cocktail, and his reaction was exactly what I was hoping for.

He takes payment for the drinks and then glides over to me, pressing himself against my back and lowering his mouth to my ear. "I'll make a deal. You, me, some sex on the beach and a foot rub once we close. "

I.

Stop.

Breathing.

He rocks his hips in time to the music and from somewhere I find the confidence to grind my ass ever so slightly, pressing his very obvious erection into the crack of my ass. I'm so turned on I've forgotten what I'm even supposed to be making.

He twists up to the top shelf, pushing his cock harder against me, making my breath hitch as I feel the length of it. He then hands me a bottle of vanilla vodka, as if that moment never even happened.

"You forgot the vodka," he whispers in my ear.

Two can play that game.

I tilt my head, so our lips are almost touching. "You've got yourself a deal, action man."

The look he gives me sends a rush of moisture in between my legs. Maybe it's the vibrations from the music, but I swear he lets out a groan, like he's trying so hard not to come undone.

For someone who wanted to just be friends, I'm not doing a very good job of proving it, because clearly, I can't control my thoughts, let alone my body when I'm around him. I never craved attention until I tasted his and now I'm desperate.

Chapter Fourteen

Jack

Fuck... I can't turn around with my dick straining against my pants. But being this close to her, her vanilla scent surrounding me and her ass grinding against me like that, how could it not affect me?

This whole 'let's just be friends' thing is getting harder and harder, *no pun intended*, but clearly I like to torture myself because keeping my distance isn't an option I'm willing to choose. Watching her work the bar, moving her hips to the music, tucking her hair behind her ear, and laughing with the guests makes me want to pin her against the wall and claim her. Let every fucker that's been staring at her all night know she's mine.

But she isn't yours.

I've tried not to make it obvious that I've been watching her all night. Not even the crowds of beautiful women that would usually be my type could stop me focusing on her because, these days, I only want to look at a pretty brunette with eyes like the ocean.

Somehow, despite being severely understaffed, tonight was one of our most successful nights since opening. The girls worked their asses off and I don't think Ria or Kate moved from behind the bar.

Exhausted, everyone went home as soon as we closed, except Brad, Harry, Ria and I. She kicked off her heels and swapped them for some flip flops from her bag and perched on a bar stool resting her head on the bar.

"Who wants a drink?" Harry calls, raising a bottle of tequila and holding shot glasses in the other hand. Ria doesn't even lift her head, she just shoots an arm up in the air and Harry slides a shot down to her.

"Just the one though. I need to drive home," she says.

"Tonight felt like the old days, boys. Mixing the drinks, dancing on the bar. Fuck, I miss it. I wasn't built for the corporate side of things," Harry declares, sounding jaded.

"Speak for yourself. I can barely move now," Brad replies, falling onto a stool next to Ria and picking up a filled shot glass.

"Oh, poor baby. Do you need a back rub?" Harry mocks.

"Yeah? You offering? Because I've got this part right down here that needs a good rub." Brad rubs his hand over his crotch.

We all laugh except Harry, who just downs a double shot.

Conversation flows until Ria yawns and glances at her watch. "Shit. I need to get going. It's gone 3 am. My girls will be up in a few hours.

"Damn, Ri. That's not a lot of sleep. You sure you'll be okay? Maybe you should take tomorrow night off?

She looks at me deadpan. "Clearly you don't know my kids because they don't let me have 'days off'." She raises up off her stool and gives Brad and Harry a hug goodbye and I jump up, ready to follow her.

She pushes through the door marked staff only and heads down the stairs and I'm hot on her heels.

"At least let me drive you home. I didn't even give you the foot rub I promised."

God, could I sound any more desperate? This is embarrassing.

She stops and turns around at the entrance of the staff room. "Jack, don't be ridiculous. It's late, we both have work tomorrow and it would be like a 2-hour round trip for you. I'm fine."

An unfamiliar feeling hits me, my chest tightening. *Why don't I want her to leave?*

She walks through to the staff room door and I am hot on her heels. She reaches for her purse and I grab it and hold it behind my back.

"Jack, give me the purse."

"No." I sound like a petulant child.

"Jack, it's late. I'm tired. Give me my purse please," she huffs.

"No, let me drive you."

She lunges forward to grab the purse. I take hold of her arm, pushing her back to pin her against the locker, still keeping her purse out of her reach.

"What are we? Twelve? Give me the fucking purse."

Ooohh, I haven't seen this side of her. I like feisty Ria

"Now, now, we are getting a little feisty, aren't we, sweetheart," I reply with a playful tone in my voice.

"Oh, you've seen nothing yet, action man," she mutters, giving me a challenging stare.

A spark passes between us and I have to remember not to take it too far again like I did in the stockroom. Stepping back, I run my hand through my hair, still gripping onto her purse.

"Jack, why do you want to drive me home so badly?"

"Because that thing should be illegal to drive and you saved us tonight, and I can't, in good faith, send you home in that death trap. It's late, you're tired and I want to make sure you get home safe or..." I pause, trying to decide if my next words are a good idea, but I say them anyway. "...You could stay at my apartment. Those are your choices."

The way she looks at me is like a punch to the gut. I get the feeling no one has ever fought for her safety or wellbeing the way I am. That she's been left to fend for herself too many times to count and that breaks me in a way I didn't know was possible. I want to take her, make her mine and show her what it's like to have someone who isn't okay with losing her. Because I'm not. Not even a little bit.

"Okay," she whispers, and I smile as an unfamiliar feeling of relief washes over me.

As soon as we leave the parking lot, Ria falls asleep. When we stop at a red light, I lean into the back seat for my suit jacket and cover her with it, before brushing her hair away from her face. She looks so peaceful. Like all her life stresses have left her, just for a moment. I don't know how she does it. She really is a real life superwoman. I've never met anyone like her.

The women I usually date are simple. No strings, no kids, no chaos, and truthfully, boring and easy. Ria is anything but easy. She is full of baggage and chaos and so much trauma it would take me years to unpack. I know the easy thing would be to back off, let her do her thing. Getting involved with a woman who has kids and in the middle of what sounds like a messy separation should be the furthest thing from my mind.

But it's Ria. She's never been a possibility until now. And while the timing might not be perfect at the moment, if I don't act, one day someone will love her the way she deserves to be loved and won't make her fight for it, and I want that someone to be me. But for now, she needs a friend, and as much as it's killing me not to reach over to kiss her, to touch her warm silk skin, and soak up her scent I need to put her needs before mine because I know that no one has ever done that for her.

I pull up outside her house, which is in complete darkness, aside from a tiny light that is glowing through her front door window. I look over to the passenger seat and find her still sleeping. She must be exhausted. It's nearly 4 am and I know her day will be starting soon with the girls. She shouldn't be busting her ass like this. But I get why she's doing it and it only makes me admire her more.

I lean over and stroke the back of my hand over her cheek and she stirs.

"Ria, sweetheart, you're home," I whisper, not wanting to scare her awake.

She slowly raises her head, looking round the car, blinking repeatedly.

"Oh my God, did I sleep the entire way?"

"Yeah, you did, sleeping beauty." I chuckle.

"Don't ever invite me on a road trip. I can never stay awake in the car unless I'm driving." She rubs her eyes and then smoothes out her hair.

"Noted," I say, staring at her, taking in just how beautiful she is. I am having to fight my instinct to lean in and kiss her. I wonder if she can sense this moment, this tension that's swirling between us.

Her throat bobs as she swallows and clears her throat.

"Erm, thanks for the lift home. You didn't have to. I would have driven myself," she stammers as she reaches for her purse to find her keys.

"I told you it was no trouble. I wanted to make sure you got home okay after helping us out. I'll pick you up for work tomorrow."

"You can't drive back now. It's such a long drive."

"I'll be fine. I'm trained to have minimal sleep, remember? Years on the front line will do that."

"Stay with me," she whispers so softly I almost miss it.

My eyes widen in surprise and she must see the look on my face as she tries to play down her offer. "I ugh.. I mean, on my couch. You can stay on my couch, please. I would never forgive myself if something happened because you drove me home."

I don't even have to think about my answer. I would share a bed with Nugget if it meant more time with her. That thought alone makes me realize how hard and fast I'm falling for this woman and that I need to get my feelings in check before I fuck this up and have her running scared.

We exit the car and walk up to her house in the silence of the chilly night. She opens the front door as quietly as she can and we both tiptoe into the house.

She drops her keys in a small bowl on a side table and flicks on a lamp that lights up her narrow hallway and I watch her reflection in the mirror as she slips off her shoes and reaches round to rub her neck.

I'm moving towards her before I realize it, my hands reaching for her shoulders without thinking. "Here, let me," I murmur.

She doesn't speak, doesn't nod, but the look she gives as we stare at each other in the mirror tells me it's okay to touch her. I slowly gather her hair in my hands and move it to one side, giving me access to her shoulders, and I start to massage them. She tilts her head to the side and lets out a soft moan that causes my dick to harden.

Fuck's sake, not now.

"You're so tight," I tell her, my voice husky, and then I mentally slap myself. *That didn't sound suggestive at all, you dick.*

"Uh huh." She moans, closing her eyes, relaxing under my touch. I lean in closer and even after a 10-hour shift, she still smells like warm vanilla.

"Oh my God, that feels so good," she mutters.

The soft noises of appreciation she makes have my dick weeping in my suit pants and I am either going to have to stop rubbing her shoulders or find a way to fill her mouth. That thought doesn't help the situation.

"Ria, baby, you've got to stop moaning like that. Those noises do things to a man."

My words seem to break our moment, and she moves away from me, clearing her throat. "Let me get you some blankets and pillows."

I watch her as she takes the stairs, her ass swaying in her work skirt, and it takes all my strength not to follow her. Instead, I head into the darkened front room and strip out of everything but my boxers, folding them and placing them on the edge of the couch.

Ria appears in the doorway holding a pile of blankets and a pillow. She stops dead in her tracks as her eyes blatantly rake over my body.

I work hard to take care of my body and the way Ria is staring at my muscles makes it all worth it. The heat in her eyes damn near makes me explode.

"Ri?"

"Yeah," she answers, not fully paying attention, still staring.

"Eyes up here, sweetheart," I say with a little laugh.

She jolts, raising her eyes to meet mine. A thrill runs through me at the way her cheeks flush and she flaps around trying to hand me the blankets whilst avoiding any more eye contact.

But I go further on my quest to get her all twisted up. I reach for her hand and pull her into me, then I place my hands on either side of her face. I can feel her breathing quicken. She wants this as much as me. But instead of crashing my lips to hers like I want to, I plant a kiss on her forehead.

"Night, sweetheart. Sleep tight."

She steps back, her eyes blown, looking disappointed.

"Night, Jack," she says in barely a whisper and she's gone. I lay down on the couch, pull the blankets over me, and close my eyes. I drift off, thinking how badly I want to follow her up those stairs and show her how I truly feel about her.

I sense someone standing over me before I even open my eyes. The smell of coffee fills the air and something warm and wet touches my foot. A giggle sounds, and it doesn't sound like a grown woman's giggle. *What the...*

My eyes pop open and I'm met with a pair of eyes that look just like Ria's, except they aren't Ria's. It's a miniature version of her. Standing next to her, about a foot smaller, is another, slightly balder version of Lexi, holding a pink rubber ring and babbling.

Thwack.

She smacks the rubber ring against my nose and then proceeds to suck on it, drooling all over it.

"What are you doing on the couch? Did you and Mommy have a sleepover?" Lexi asks, still staring intently at me. It's like she's trying to see into my soul, and I'm a little freaked out.

"Erm, yeah, sort of," I say, rubbing my eyes, trying to take in my surroundings. Yep, I'm on Ria's couch and that warm wet tongue is Nugget licking me.

Damn, Nugget.

"My daddy tried to have a sleepover with a girl at Grandma's house but Grandpa got mad and told them to leave," she says innocently.

I bet he did, the selfish son of a bitch.

Thwack.

Elle is clearly waiting for me to acknowledge her. "Well, good morning, Miss Elle. How are we today?" She squeals, waving her rubber ring in the air.

I reach out for my suit pants. I don't feel overly comfortable sitting here in just my briefs with the girls here. I slide them on under the blanket and then get up off the couch. Elle falls back on her bottom and starts to cry and my instincts kick in, picking her up.

I cuddle her and sway a little, which seems to calm her, and holding to hold her this time feels a little more natural.

Lexi then jumps on the couch and leaps onto my back. "Pick me up too, Jack," she giggles. I just about catch her with my spare hand, pulling Elle tighter to my chest at the same time.

"Lexi, pancakes," I hear a voice calling from the kitchen.

I make my way to the sound with the girls still attached to me. Entering the kitchen, the sweet smell of maple syrup fills my nose and I find Ali leaning against the kitchen counter in what I assume are her work clothes, sipping on a mug of coffee. Ria is standing at the stove beside her, spatula in hand, flipping pancakes, wearing the tiniest pair of baby blue pajamas shorts, showing off her toned legs, and an oversized t-shirt, hair in a messy bun on the top of her head, looking absolutely fuckable.

"Well, holy shit, who knew a man with a baby could be so hot?" Ali mutters behind her coffee mug. Ria whips her head up, and as her eyes lock on my body, the spatula falls out of her hand, clanging against the frying pan, but she doesn't react. Her eyes roam up my body, glancing at the girls and then meeting my eyes.

I give her a knowing smile.

Yeah, she likes me more than a friend. No fucking doubt about it.

Chapter Fifteen

Ria

Holy shit. How can a man look *that* hot first thing in the morning? He's only wearing his suit pants and Lexi is hanging on to his neck for dear life. Can't say I blame the girl. I'd like to hang off his neck like that too. Elle is in his arms, resting on his hip, and sweet baby Jesus, if it's not the hottest thing I have ever seen. There is something about a man with a baby and it's got my ovaries twitching.

"Ri, the spatula" Ali mutters under her breath, snapping me from my pervy daydream.

"Who wants pancakes?" I say slightly flustered, bending down to retrieve it.

"I'd love some pancakes, Ri" I glance up, and he gives the biggest pantie-melting smile there ever was. *Fucker.* He knows I was staring, just like I was staring last night. *I really need to get it together.*

Ali places her coffee mug down on the counter. "Not for me, babe. I need to get going. My boss needs me to go find a Birkin bag for today's shoot. I'll call you later."

"Thank you for last night." I squeeze her before she walks over to Lexi and Elle, and kisses them both on the nose, reminding them to be good for me.

"Have fun everyone, especially you two." She points between me and Jack before she backs out of the room. Both Jack and I awkwardly laugh, my belly doing a weird flutter at the idea of having fun with him.

"What about you girls? Do you want pancakes?" Jack asks in an animated voice, spinning them around. The sound of their giggles fills the kitchen and warms my heart.

"Me, me," Lexi demands as Jack sits her down on a stool and places Elle in her highchair.

Watching him, looking like a Greek god helping the girls with their sippy cups and making them giggle as he pulls silly faces, I'm starting to wonder why I am pushing this 'let's be friends' narrative. I know he wants me, or at least I think he does, and I know I want him, so why am I depriving us both?

The little looks, the way he massaged me last night, the way he kissed my forehead, and the undeniable bulge in his briefs when I walked in last night to hand him the blankets. He surely feels the same, right?

But why would he want me? He could have any woman he wanted. I'm covered in scars, both physically from having my girls and mentally from my childhood and my marriage. My life is chaos. But I've never felt like this before and I feel like I am stuck at a crossroads. Do I deny myself what I want? Take the road that is safe and has no risk of me getting hurt again? Or do I take a chance and lean into these feelings I have for Jack and explore that road with him and hope he feels the same way?

Where's the creepy old lady from the carnival with her crystal ball when you need her to tell you your future?

"Okay, pancakes for everyone," I declare, trying to distract myself from my thoughts.

Once the pancakes are plated up and the coffee poured, we all sit eat together and it's the most normal and relaxed I have felt in ages. This is what I always wanted. Mundane chat around the breakfast table, the girls giggling and making a mess with their pancakes, sharing the day's plans.

I look at my girls smiling as Jack shows Lexi how to make a pancake sandwich with three pancakes, Nutella, and strawberries. The fact he's got her to eat strawberries in any form has me shocked. He's a natural round kids, and watching him with them makes my heart happy and body warm in that way that lets you know that you are safe and that maybe, everything will be okay.

After breakfast, Jack and I clean up the kitchen together, which is a novelty in itself; not only having a man present at breakfast, but one who also helps wash the dishes. Seriously, Jack Lawson is ticking all the goddamn boxes, and he probably doesn't even realize it.

"Thanks for cleaning up. You didn't need to do that."

"Don't be silly, Ri. I ate so I can help. Besides, I like helping you."

Okay, why is he so perfect?

I watch his shirtless body as he dries the remainder of the plates. "Well, I appreciate it. I need to repay the favor for the ride last night and for helping this morning."

"Repay the favor you say?" He reaches past me to put the pile of plates away, his chest brushing dangerously close to me. When he leans back, he braces his hands on both sides of the kitchen counter, caging me in with a glint in his eye.

"Yep." I try to sound normal, but his proximity makes speaking feel impossible. "Name it. What do you want?"

I am treading on thin ice here and I know it, but I don't care.

His mouth grazes my ear, sending a shiver through me.

"Now that is an open-ended question, Ria, with so many possibilities."

"Anything you want. Just name it," I whisper.

He leans back slightly, and we lock eyes. Without blinking, he says, "You."

"W-w-what?" I stammer, not sure I believe he really wants me.

"I want you."

Heat races through my body, my chest rising and falling in quick succession. *Holy shit, breathe, Ria, breathe.*

His eyes are full of so much want and longing. He tilts his face down and I rise on my toes to try and meet his lips, desperate to feel them against mine. Just as I think he's about to kiss me, the moment is interrupted by a loud crash from the front room, and Lexi wails, "Mommy, something fell down."

I fall into his chest and we both let out a sigh. He leans his chin on top of my head and wraps his arms around me.

I clear my throat and pull away from his embrace. "Duty calls."

Jack stayed for the rest of the day. We walked to the park with the girls and got ice cream, played Barbies, and Lexi put on a show with her microphone. When Elle went down for her afternoon nap, we watched *Tangled* and when Lexi fell asleep on Jack's lap, we took a much needed nap next to her.

When I wake, I find Lexi still curled up, cuddling Jack next to me. I smile, seeing her little hand in his hand as she lays against his chest, his hand protectively placed on her back. But I can't help the pain in my chest when I realize I don't think I ever saw Alex cuddle Lexi like this, or sit down and play with her like Jack did earlier.

Jack is proving to me, day by day, that good men do exist, and I think I'd be a fool to not act on whatever this is between us.

If we explore whatever this thing is, I need to take it slow. I can't risk getting my heart broken again, but most importantly, I have to protect my girls.

Thankfully, Alex's parents picked the girls up this afternoon for me, since I didn't have my car. The stars aligned because Jack had gone out to pick up takeout when they turned up. I know I'm not doing anything wrong, and I know Anne and Steve wouldn't judge me, but I don't even know what we are, so until I have a clear idea, I need to keep that separate.

I get myself ready for work while I have the chance, washing and styling my hair in loose waves, before I apply my makeup and a ton of setting spray, because I sweat my ass off working in that club.

I slip on my uniform and pair it with some black heeled pumps, which thankfully are comfy. I grab my purse and throw in my gloss and powder to touch up later and spray my go-to vanilla-scented perfume and head downstairs to find Jack in the kitchen, leaning against the breakfast bar on a call and, holy shit, does he look good.

He's changed into the spare clothes he keeps in his car and knowing he was naked in my shower was the biggest test of my restraint to date. He turns round and his dark navy suit pants showcase his perfectly perked ass, making me want to walk over there and squeeze it.

Calm down, Ria, you horny bitch.

Jack clears his throat and I know I've been caught. The smirk on his face is entirely satisfied and smug. My face blazes with heat as I smooth my hands down my dress, trying desperately to ignore the fact that he saw me ogling him... again. "Ready to go?" I ask, praying my cheeks cool down soon.

"Absolutely," he says with that smile. The smile that makes me go weak at the knees. Honestly, I have never been so turned on by someone without them touching me, or even speaking. Jack Lawson only has to glance in my direction and I am a puddle who would do absolutely anything he wanted, and that both excites and terrifies me in equal measure.

Chapter Sixteen

Jack

Friday was just as busy as Thursday. Thankfully, when Saturday night rolled around, we were back to being fully staffed. I have now banned all staff from eating seafood for the foreseeable future. I didn't *'need'* to work Saturday night behind the bar, but if it allows me to be around Ria, fuck it, I was doing it.

I watched her work the bar with such ease and confidence. It's like this whole other side of her comes out at work. She's not a mom or someone going through a shitty breakup, she's just Ria. There are so many versions of her and with every version she allows me to see, she has me more enamored with her. The staff love her and so do the patrons, some a little too much. The past hour I've watched the same guy only go to Ria at the bar or call her over to his table, causing my jaw to clench every time I look at the prick.

I watch him wave his empty glass at her as she strolls around the VIP area, collecting glasses. I can't tear myself away from their exchange. He gestures for her to come closer, and she bends slightly so he can whisper in her ear. I don't like the look on her face, unease etched all over it. She shakes her head and smiles politely but the dick obviously doesn't listen as he snakes an arm around her waist and pulls her into his lap.

Rage courses through me at the sight of his hands on her. I'm striding over there, fists clenched, before I give myself time to think.

"Jack, I'm fine. He was just—" She tries to wriggle from his hold and I don't wait for her to finish her sentence. I pull Ria up gently, trying to keep my cool and tuck her behind my back to protect her from this sleaze.

"Out," I growl.

"What? Ah, man, it's all good. I was just talking to the pretty girl. No harm," he slurs, hands up in defeat.

"I don't care. You touch my staff, you're out," I shout. "Now leave, before I have security throw you out." My pulse hammers loudly in my ears, my jaw clenched so tight I'm surprised I haven't cracked a tooth.

The drunk staggers from his seat, taking his jacket and heading for the exit. I don't give a shit that he's a member. He touches Ria, he's gone.

I close my eyes and mentally count to five, trying to calm my ragged breathing before I turn. Forgetting where I am, I place my hands on either side of her face. "Are you okay, sweetheart? Did he hurt you?"

She places her hands over mine, squeezing them, reassuring me for a change. "Jack, it's fine. I'm alright." I check her over still, panic gripping my throat at how differently that could've gone.

"Listen, I don't need you to go all caveman on me every time a guy flirts with me. I'm a big girl, I can handle it. And besides, we're at work. You can't throw me over your shoulder and carry me out of here."

Yes, I can, is my first thought. My second is that she's right. God, I know she's capable. I just saw red. I drop my hands from her face and let out a long sigh.

"I don't like them touching you," I admit quietly, but I know she hears me. Her ocean-blue eyes assess me and soften at my admission.

"Jack, I promise, I'll be careful, okay?"

I nod, knowing she'll keep her word. But just in case, I stay out on the floor for the rest of the night.

I spend the evening keeping a watchful eye on Ria. The club has been packed all night and only in the last hour has it started to die down. Our bar manager, Annabelle, places a drink in front of me. It breaks my attention for a second and I gratefully accept the whiskey on ice. "Thanks," I mutter, keeping half an eye on Ria.

The whiskey slips down easily. Annabelle knows my favorite drink. She and I aren't exactly strangers, but we're definitely not more than a one-time thing either. The guys weren't happy when I told them what happened between us in Miami, but it's not happened since. And it won't again.

"Jack?" I turn to face Annabelle, not realizing she was still standing there.

"What's up?" I ask cooly.

"Can we go through next weekend's events? There are a few big name clients in the VIP book and I want to run some things by you," she says seductively, licking her bright red lips. When she leans over the bar, pushing her cleavage my way, I know exactly what she's getting at. "I thought maybe we should talk in your office tonight?" I place my drink down between us, purposefully creating a barrier.

"I think here is fine. I want to stay on the floor tonight."

It's a brush off she needs to hear because right now. All I see is Maria Kennedy. I don't want anyone else.

Chapter Seventeen

Ria

"God, it's packed in here," Harley shouts over the music as we work the VIP area. I nod in agreement.

I'm exhausted. I've worked the past three nights and I am dead on my feet. I miss the girls and all I want to do is go home and get to bed.

Jack has been here again, and it seems if I'm on shift, then he's here. His eyes are on me like a hawk and my ego gets a little boost every time I notice him staring like he's drinking me in.

I've never had a man act protective over me and the way he came to my rescue earlier did things to me. I wanted to kiss him, thank him for defending me, but when he walked back to the bar, Annabelle was glaring at me like I'd just stolen her favorite pair of Jimmy Choos.

I haven't asked, I've not wanted to know the answer, but I get the sense there is some history between Jack and Annabelle and it bothers me more than it should. I have no claim to him. He can do what he likes with whoever he likes, but it does bother me. However, I need this job, and pissing her off is not high on my to-do list, so I keep my head down and do what I need to do so I can get home.

I head back to the bar, trays full of empty shot glasses and champagne flutes ready for the glass washer. I'm mindlessly stacking them, when I spot Jack and Annabelle have moved over to the booth towards the back of the room. A sensation I have no business feeling creeps over my skin, making me sweat. It's probably business talk. Right?

That's all it is.

Then why are you still staring?

Slowing my stacking, I take just a little extra time to spy on them, but people keep getting in the way.

For fuck's sake, move.

"Ri, you okay, honey? You're bobbing your head about like you're stalking your prey," Harley shouts over the music from next to me, while polishing glasses.

That's exactly what I'm doing.

I let out a fake laugh. "I'm good. I thought I saw a friend, but it isn't her." I need to get it together and calm down. I inhale a deep breath and slowly release it, grabbing a dishcloth from the side and begin to mop up the mess on the bar top.

He isn't mine. I can't be mad that he's talking to another woman.

Finally, the crowd breaks and I have a full view of them. I watch as Annabelle slides closer to Jack, whispering something in his ear. Credit to Jack, he leans away, looking like he would rather be anywhere else than sitting with her.

Her tacky red nails drag over his exposed forearm and I watch, clutching the cloth in my hands until my fingers ache. I'm not sure

I'm breathing either because, when Jack removes his arm from her reach, I let out a deep breath.
Get it together.
Jack points at the papers in front of them, but Annabelle seems to have absolutely no interest in them at all. I watch, unable to think straight, as her hand slips under the table and everything in Jack's body tenses. That's when I snap, throwing the cloth down. My feet storm towards them without a forethought.

I don't know what I'm doing or what I'm going to say, but my feet move on their own accord, and before I know it, I'm standing in front of them, hands on hips, chest heaving.

"Ri, you okay?" Jack asks with concern.
Think, Ria, think.
"Yeah, erm..." I mumble, flitting my eyes between him and Annabelle, fury still bubbling in my chest.
Jesus, Ria, words, use your words.
A slow, knowing smirk spreads across Jack's face, his eyes narrowing.
Busted.
"I.. err... I need the key for the, erm the safe for closing. Kate asked me to get it from you."

"Sure, it's in my office. Come with me." He flicks his gaze to Annabelle, briefly dismissing her. "We'll catch up tomorrow, Annabelle." Her eyes narrow, as a snarl curls her red lips.

Back off, bitch. I give her a sarcastic smile and turn to follow Jack back to his office. I feel myself begin to panic, my palms sweating. I don't need the key, I never get the key. I'm such an idiot. I'm a jealous idiot who doesn't know what the hell she wants.

We enter the office, which I haven't been in yet. Everything in here is leather or dark wood and screams luxury.

He opens the top drawer of his desk and takes out the key as I hover by the door that I've closed behind me. Rubbing my arms up and down to comfort myself, I will him to hurry up, so I can get back out there and away from him and this ridiculous situation I've created.

"Here," he says, walking towards me, dangling the key from his finger. I take it and stuff it into the pocket of my skirt.

"Ugh, thanks. I'll go back now," I rush, keeping my eyes anywhere but on him. I can't let him see how flustered I feel.

"Ri," he says, his tone playful.

"Yeah," I mumble.

"Look at me."

I reluctantly lift my eyes to meet his, as my heart rate picks up.

Get me out of here.

"You didn't need the key, did you?" he smirks.

Clearing my throat and standing tall, I say as confidently as I am able. "Yes, I did."

"No, you didn't... I think you were a little bothered by Anabelle."

I let out the most un lady-like scoff and shake my head "What, don't be ridiculous. She doesn't bother me."

"Oh, really," he says, quirking an eyebrow as he steps towards me and I step back, my back hitting the door, causing me to gasp. He leans in, placing one hand above my head, leaning against the door, trapping me. He's so close our lips are almost touching and I hold my breath.

Is he going to kiss me again?

"Does it bother you when another woman touches me?"

My eyes flutter shut for a brief moment, my body heating, and my heart feels like it's about to break out of my chest. "I... erm..."

"Because watching that man put his hands on you earlier made me insanely jealous. The thought of him touching you, being that close to you, drove me wild."

"Jack, I..." My breathing is erratic. I need him to kiss me, touch me. I can't pretend anymore.

"Tell me to stop, Ri." His voice is low and gravelly, making me ache for him. He lightly brushes his lips with mine. It's not quite a kiss, but it leaves me needing more.

"If you don't tell me to stop, sweetheart, I might have to have another taste of you..."

He swallows, his throat bobbing "... and this time, I don't think I'll be able to stop," he says, his voice barely a whisper.

I lick my lips, my tongue grazing his lips, and he lets out a groan. His jaw flexes and his eyes close, as if he's having an internal battle *Kiss me,* I silently beg.

"Fuck it," he growls, as his free hand grabs the back of my neck in a possessive grip, crashing our lips together and devouring me. I've never been kissed like this. With so much want.

His hips grind into mine and my body moves on its own, rocking into him as my hands fist his hair. It's a sensory overload; his scent, the taste of whisky, his touch.

He breaks away, locking eyes with mine. I don't know how long we've been kissing, but my lips feel swollen, my chest heaving.

"You have no idea how badly I want you."

I want the chance to feel what it might be like to be his. "Please, don't stop," I beg.

Chapter Eighteen

Jack

The way she begs me not to stop has me desperately clinging onto my control. I want her, but I need to slow things down. I don't want to rush this. I can't, not with her. She's not a meaningless hook up I fuck in my office. She's Ria. But I've been fighting the urge to make a move for months and now she's given me permission, I'm not wasting another second questioning it. I want to savor everything about her.

Leaning down, my nose brushes against hers just as she lets out a perfect little gasp that makes me even harder. God, this woman drives me wild. My mouth is back on hers in an instant and with every swipe of her tongue, I begin to unravel.

I trail my hands down her sides, bunching her skirt up until her soft skin meets my palms as I grab her ass to lift her, her legs wrapping around my hips. I align us right where we both need friction and push into her center. Pulling back to look at her face, her swollen lips, hooded lust-filled eyes that are staring at me, my heart skips a beat. "Do you know how long I've wanted to kiss you like this?" My kisses trail back up her neck, along her jawline. Biting down on her lower lip, I tug and she rewards me with another moan.

We kiss like we're starved. It doesn't feel enough. The need for her is so strong, I tighten my grip on her hips, as she weaves her hands in my hair and whimpers against my mouth.

Spinning us around, I carry her to the couch, laying her down, my body hovering over hers. I press open-mouth kisses down her neck, but she doesn't let me go and something possessive streaks into my chest. She said she wants it, but now she's showing me with her body.

"Jack... please." Her voice, laced with need, is barely a whisper. I know in this very moment I'd give her everything. Anything she wanted, it's hers. I grin against her skin. Dusting feather light kisses down her neck, torn between wanting to drag this out or let my restraint snap and devour her.

My senses become heightened; the music from the main floor, the sounds of her breathy moans, her vanilla scent making my head spin. My hand glides higher till my fingertips are touching the lace of her underwear. She lets out a low moan and her head leans back off the arm of the couch, chest heaving. She looks so fucking beautiful right now; I am completely enamored by her. I'd spend all night doing whatever is needed to make her look the way she does right now.

My fingers slip under her panties and I run my fingers through her folds, feeling how slick she is already.

She wants this, and fuck, am I going to give it to her. Needing more, I pull away from her and her eyes widen, looking at me in disappointment.

"Don't worry, sweetheart. I haven't even started with you yet."

I tug down her lace underwear slowly. She rolls her hips, widening her legs, and I press my fingertips to her clit, rubbing small circles over her swollen nub. Her breathing becomes faster, heavier. My own quickening as the realization hits me that this is finally happening between us. The months of fighting this undeniable chemistry and mutual desire for one another that we've tried desperately to resist has now become too strong to ignore. It's all unraveling and we are both too far gone to question it.

My hands begin to ache with the need to touch and explore her body further. A flush of warmth spreads to my groin as her darkened eyes full of lust lock with mine.

I push two fingers inside and her tight walls clench around them. Her eyelids flutter shut. My gaze falls to her lips as she hisses, "Oh, fuck, yes"

"You like that, sweetheart?" I murmur against her lips. Seeing her like this turns me on in a way I never could have anticipated, my dick now straining against the fabric of my boxers.

"Yes, oh my God."

I pick up the pace, pumping my fingers in and out as my thumb continues to circle her clit.

"So fucking perfect," I groan. My mouth sucks on that sensitive part just between her neck and collarbone. Her hand grips the nape of my neck, making my skin tingle, her body begins to tremble and I know she's close. Her back arches off the couch as her walls tighten, her arousal coating my fingers. I watch her come a part as she rides the waves of pleasure pulsing through her body, the sight of her making me shiver with desire. I've played this out in my head, over and over again, what it would be like to have her come apart under my touch and the reality far outweighs the fantasy. Her other hand clamps around my bicep, my shirt rumpling and I wish I had taken it off so I could feel her touch. The adrenaline pumps through me as her nails dig into the cotton. I crash my lips to hers and she moans, writhing beneath me, making my cock swell.

I slow my movements as her vice-like grip on my fingers eases and her breathing starts to slow. I break away from her lips, pressing soft kisses along her jaw and down her neck, inhaling her sweet scent, feeling her body shudder beneath me.

I lift my head to find that Ria, post-orgasm, has to be one of the sexiest sights I've ever seen. Hooded eyes, flushed cheeks, and swollen lips. I want to devour this woman and never come up for air. I bring my fingers to my mouth and suck and groan as her sweet taste explodes on my tongue. "I can't wait to taste you properly."

Her breathing hitches, her gaze focusing on my lips.

"I think watching you come undone for me is my new favorite thing."

"And I think you making me might be my new favorite thing," she laughs softly.

I roll on my side, pulling her in towards me and pressing my lips to her forehead. I hold her whilst she catches her breath, keeping her close, never wanting to let go.

Fuck, I don't want to go back to being just friends with her.
She's... everything.

Chapter Nineteen

Ria

A woody musk scent overwhelms me as I take a deep breath in before opening my eyes and stretching... But I can't move, my body is held tightly by strong muscular arms and I am pleasantly surprised to look up to see Jack sleeping peacefully next to me.

Shit, what time is it?

I panic, realizing we are still in his office and I try to roll free from his embrace, but his arms tighten around me.

"You aren't leaving." he mumbles, his head pressed into the back of my neck, pressing his warm mouth to my skin, making it tingle.

"Jack, I need to pee, like really bad."

"I guess I'll let you up then," he mutters before letting me up. Just as I sit, I hear my phone buzzing on the floor and the realization hits me.

No one knows where I am.

Jack's office is windowless, so I have no idea what time it is. Reaching over, I scoop it up off the floor.

"Shit, it's 9.38 am." I leap up and remember that I'm not wearing any underwear. *Where the hell is it?* I turn to see it crumpled on the floor next to the couch by his shirt.

When did he take his shirt off?

Then it all comes flooding back to me. The kiss, the way I rode his fingers, the orgasm I thought was going to send me into another dimension. My cheeks heat at the memory. Seriously, I have never had an orgasm like it. He's got magic fingers.

"Oh, shit," I whisper.

"Everything alright?" Jack asks, stretching out on the sofa, rubbing his eyes.

"Ermm, not exactly," I reply, scrolling the notifications on my phone.

I have missed calls from Ali and Gabby, about a hundred and thirty-seven text notifications from our girls' chat, and a message from Anne. I go to open the message from Anne but another message comes in from the group chat.

Ali – 3:15 am

> Have you finished riding his dick yet? *GIF of a woman riding a mechanical bull in a bar*

What the fuck?

I scroll up through the endless messages.

Ali – 3.23 am

> Hey, Ri, hope tonight went okay. Just let me know me know when you are leaving. x

> Gabby – 3.58 am
>
> Hey Ri, have you left the club?

> Ali – 4.04 am
>
> Ri, I've tried calling you, answer the phone, where are you??

> Gabby – 4.10 am
>
> Ri, we are starting to panic now. We don't want to worry Anne by calling her. Just let us know if you have gone there to stay with the girls. We love you. xx

> Gabby – 4.13 am
>
> Ri, I'm really worrying now, please answer your phone!! xxxx

> Ali – 4.20 am
>
> Bitch, answer your phone!!!! I am this close to filing a missing persons report, me and Gabs are freaking out. ANSWER YOUR PHONE

God, I am the worst friend ever. Whilst I am getting the best orgasm of my life my friends are freaking out thinking I've been abducted.

Ali – 4.46 am

> BITCH I AM SO HAPPY FOR YOU AND MAD AT YOU. I called Nancy to try and get Brad and Harry's number. I called Jack and no answer. Harry thought I was calling him for a booty call WTF!! He wishes. He said he's got an opening on his roster, whatever the fuck that means. The guy is a prick, BUT he told me he's checked the club security and you are still at the club with Jack * winking emoji* GET IT GIRL!!!!!

Ali – 4.49 am

> p.s still pissed you made us worry and that Harry now has my number. He's already texted me AGAIN telling me he's free for a booty call. YOU OWE ME GIRL. Now I need a new number.

Gabby – 4.50 am

> Ri, we've been so worried but get it girl!!! Need all the details in the morning and don't lie. Ali, we all know you want to join Harry's roster.

I cover my face with my hands, not wanting to think about what Harry saw. "There's a camera?" I shout, spinning round to look at Jack, who sat up scrolling his phone and rubbing a hand down his face.

"Uhh, yeah. Don't worry, he couldn't see anything. Haz told me Ali called him looking for you and for a 4 am booty call."

I laugh. "He wishes."

I open the message from Anne.

> Anne – 8.54 am
>
> Good morning, my girl. I hope your shift went well. Lexi slept in till 8, which was much appreciated. Poor Elle was suffering with her teeth in the night. She's woken up a little warm, so I have given her some Tylenol and she seems to be feeling better. I hope it's not another ear infection brewing for the poor baby. No rush to pick them up, they are in safe hands. See you later, Anne xxx

Anxiety floods my body, my stomach churning with worry. Shit, I'm a terrible person. My friends have been worried, my poor baby is sick, and I've been curled up with Jack getting finger banged on his couch.

I should have had more willpower to resist him. I should have driven to Ali and Gabby's and then gone to Anne's first thing to be with my girls. I don't get to be selfish. I'm a mom. I need to be with my kids, not getting off on my boss's couch. I throw my phone into my purse and search for my underwear.

"I need to go," I snap without looking at him.

He rises from the couch and walks towards me. "Hey, what's wrong? Aren't we gonna talk about what happened?" His eyes scan my face.

"No, Jack. I don't have time right now. I have places to be." My tone is sterner than I meant it to be.

"Wait, Ri, just take a breath and sit down." Knowing Jack, he can sense my panic and my growing anxiety, but my head is spinning. I need to get out of here and get to my girls. Last night shouldn't have happened, I know it shouldn't, but the way he looked at me, the way he touched me, is the way all women want a man to look at them, isn't it? Even the strongest woman would have snapped.

"Elle, she's sick. I need to get to her," I say, pulling on my underwear so fast I'm surprised I don't rip it. "Where the hell are my shoes?" I groan, looking round the room, avoiding eye contact with him. I don't get to be selfish and carefree. My girls are my number one priority. It's bad enough their dad doesn't put them first. I'll be damned if they ever feel like second best because of how I choose to live my life.

"Shit, Ri, I hope she's alright. They are over there." He points to my shoes by the door. "Let me get them."

"No, let me get it... please." I brush past him, but he takes hold of my arm and pulls me into him.

"Look at me." His tone is pleading.

I don't. Instead, I stare down at my bare feet that are sinking into the dark plush rug in his office.

"Maria, look at me." His words are firmer.

I slowly raise my head to meet his gaze, preparing myself for him to be mad, but his eyes are soft and full of understanding. He reaches out to hold my face in his palms and I sink into his warm touch.

"I know you're feeling guilty and blaming yourself, but you deserve to take a moment for yourself, Ri. That doesn't make you a bad mom. Please don't regret what happened here, because I don't, not a second of it."

I don't say anything, but I rise up onto my tiptoes and place a soft kiss on his lips, and then I whisper, "I'll call you later." I pull out of his touch and it kills me. Jack deserves better, deserves more than I can give him. I want nothing more than to stay here with him, to have him hold me and reassure me that everything is okay, and maybe explore what went on last night and continue further, but I have to leave.

I race to Anne and Steve's, dash from the car, and for the first time in ages, use my door key, relieved when I hear faint voices.

I find them sitting around the kitchen table having what looks like a late breakfast. Lexi is showing Steve how to make a pancake sandwich and Anne is feeding Elle some porridge. Both girls are smiling and look happy, and a smidge of the mom guilt leaves my body.

"Morning, Ri. Busy night at work?" Steve says, looking at my work uniform that I'm still wearing and it's looking creased as hell.

Oh shit.

"Uh, yeah, busy busy. I crashed out in my clothes and headed straight here when I woke and saw Anne's message. I'm so sorry I didn't see it earlier. How are you are you, baby girl?" I walk over to Elle in her highchair, stroking her hair and kissing the top of her head.

"She's fine, love. Been a bit fussy in the night and running a low-grade fever, but she's okay. Just keep an eye on her today."

I smile at Anne, giving her a little nod in appreciation.

"You work too hard, my girl, pull up a chair and get some food in you. Steve, get the girl a coffee," she demands in her bossy tone.

"On it, love," he says, edging out of his seat and shuffling over to the coffee machine.

Lexi has been so busy eating her pancake sandwich and watching her iPad she hasn't even acknowledged me. I sit in the chair beside her. "Morning, Lexi girl, I missed you." I give her a kiss.

She turns to look at me, her face full of Nutella, and gives me the biggest grin. "Hi, Mommy. I missed you too. Grandma made pancakes, and I made them just like Jack showed me!"

And suddenly my heart is full and the last bit of mom guilt leaves my body, for now anyway.

We spent the rest of the morning with Anne and Steve. I was told to go have a bubble bath and relax. Is it weird that I hang out with my ex's parents and bathe in their home? Probably to most people, yes, but Anne and Steve are the most amazing people I have ever met and I couldn't do life without them.

Drying off with a soft towel, I grab my work bag and change into my spare clothes I keep in there, when I catch Jack's scent. Damn, I need to text him.

Ria

I don't regret last night. I just need time x

We make it home mid-afternoon and have a quiet day. Sofa snuggles, building Lego, watching *Mickey Mouse Clubhouse* on repeat, and eating all our favorite snacks. It was the quiet afternoon I needed.

When bedtime finally rolls around, Lexi requests a disco bath where I put glow sticks in the tub and turn on the bubble machine, blasting our favorite songs from my phone.

"Mommy, look." Lexi giggles, lifting the bubbles in between her little hands and blowing them over Elle, who's sitting in her little bath chair. When they land on her, she kicks her chubby little legs and waves her arms around, sending water splashing everywhere, including over me.

"Girls, girls," I squeal, trying to shield myself with a towel. Seeing them happy and carefree makes my heart feel full. This is all I've ever wanted for them. There are very few memories I have of my childhood that are full of fun and laughter. Most of mine are of me being alone, or my mum drinking, or her bringing another random man to the house and being sent to my room with a can of Diet Coke and a bag of Cheetos.

I want to go back and hug younger Ria, just to tell her she will be okay and that in a few short years, she will meet girls who become her family and life will be so different. Raising my own girls is healing my inner child in ways I can't even describe. They will have the childhood I never got, even if I have to sacrifice all my personal wants, because ultimately my biggest want is their happiness.

I dry them off and get them into their matching white with pink heart covered pjs. They won't fit them for much longer and I'm sure Lexi won't let me match her with her baby sister forever, so I will make the most of it while I can.

"Who wants a sleepover in Mommy's bed?" I ask.

"Meeee," Lexi squeals, leaping into my arms and nearly knocking me flat on my back. *God, my girl is growing up and getting big.*

"Okay, go get your stuff."

I quickly change into an oversized white tee and a pair of gray shorts, pick up Elle, and climb into bed. I can't help but sniff the top of her head, not believing that she turns one soon. It's been the quickest and most stressful year of my life. I feel like I blinked, and she's almost a toddler. She's almost lost that baby smell, the one that smells of milk and baby powder. I'd bottle it if I could.

Lexi wanders in from her bedroom, dragging her blankie, pink bunny, and her baby doll. "Move up, Mommy. All my friends need to fit."

"Okay, baby."

I scoot over and Lexi settles in next to me and I wrap my arms around them both. I lean over to switch off the bedroom lamp and turn on Elle's white noise machine. It only takes a few minutes for the girls to drift off into a peaceful sleep.

They are my nightlights, my comfort, all I need when life feels out of control and I need to feel safe, to feel wanted. I know they need me but I need them so much more than they will ever know. Tonight my chest feels heavy and thoughts of last night run through my mind like a herd of wild stallions.

The taste of his kiss and the heat of his touch. I wonder if there will ever be a way I can have it all without feeling this immense sense of guilt. *Will there be a day where I believe that I am enough?* A warm tear rolls down my cheek. I don't let myself cry. It was a pointless emotion, my mom would say. Crying got me nowhere. I lay staring at my bedroom ceiling, cradling my girls with the sounds of waves crashing on Elle's sound machine. It brings me a sense of comfort as I drift off to sleep and dream of a man that I don't feel worthy of having but desperately want to be mine.

Chapter Twenty

Jack

Ria didn't call like she said she would, but I get it. I know she would have been busy tending to the girls. She sent a message saying she didn't regret the other night and thank God, because it's all I've thought about. Now I've had a taste of her—for real this time—I need more. Visions of her coming apart beneath me invaded my dreams and provided me with a visual for my morning jerk off in the shower.

However, my morning of work doesn't allow much time for daydreaming about Maria Kennedy. I'm stuck in back to back meetings with our investors and accountant, making plans for the festive season. Before our next meeting starts, I need to check she's doing okay. Rising from my seat, I swipe my phone from the table and head for the door.

"Where you off to, lover boy? Is the wifey waiting for you in the office for a cheeky hook up?" Harry grins, leaning back in his chair.

"Fuck you," I mutter back, trying not to let him get a rise out of me.

"Don't forget your hand stretches. Wouldn't want you to get cramp, in those fingers." He laughs, making Jazz hands.

Brad lets out a low chuckle.

"You know, I'm starting to see why Ali can't stand you. No wonder you're single," I bite back

"Nah, she loves me. She just doesn't know it yet," he says with a shit-eating grin.

"You keep telling yourself that," I deadpan. "I'll be back in five. Can you start the meeting if they get here early?" I ask, directing my question at Brad, who replies with a nod.

I've left the other side of the club to Brad. I've been reluctant to dive into that side of things, but he was adamant it's the way forward and extremely lucrative. You only have to show Harry a dollar sign and the man will sign on the dotted line. Chris suggested we have a private gentleman's lounge with dancers during our initial meeting and knowing he and some of his associates are on their way to discuss the opening of the lounge, I use that as my opportunity to sneak out.

I never thought I would be involved with a woman who has kids, but those little girls have found a way into my heart. I think about them every day; *What are they up to? Is Lexi causing havoc? Has Elle taken her first steps on her own yet?* I know Ria has said she's so close to walking and for some reason, I really hope I get to witness one of her firsts.

I slip into my office, take off my suit jacket, and hang it on the back of the door. I add a pod to my coffee machine, welcoming the rich aroma filling my office. Taking my steaming mug of coffee with a dash of creamer, I sit on the couch and memories of Saturday night come flooding back. Ria writhing beneath me, my fingers buried inside her, her sweet taste.

Fuck, I want her again, need to have her again.

I pull my phone from my pants pocket and swipe to find Ria's number.

It rings and rings, and just when I think it will go to voicemail, she answers. "Hey, Jack. Now's not a great time. Can I call you later?" she rushes.

I can hear Elle wailing in the background. She doesn't sound happy at all.

"Ri, is everything okay?" I'm concerned that she's managing all this on her own because I know for sure fuck face Alex isn't there helping her with *his* daughters. In the time since Ria has come back into my life, I can count on one hand the times Alex has seen his girls. I've spent more time with them lately than he has. Why would he not want to be with his girls, all of his girls? He truly fucked it, and the sad part is, I don't even think he realizes it or cares. If they were mine I'd never let them go.

"Ugh... yeah... ssshhh, baby, it's okay. It's okay," I hear her soothe Elle, who's still wailing in the background.

"Elle woke with a fever so I took her to the doctor. She's got another ear infection. I picked up her prescription but forgot to get more Tylenol for the pain and her fever, so—yes, Lex, wear whatever shoes you want, sweetie, just put something on."

I don't know how she multi-tasks like that. It's like she's having three conversions at once.

"... so, I need to go back to the pharmacy and get some, but Elle is screaming and Lexi won't put shoes on and..."

I'm up on my feet, walking towards the cupboard to grab a change of clothes before she finishes her sentence.

"Ri, stay where you are. I'm going to get the Tylenol and bring it over." Wedging the phone under my chin, I unbutton my shirt to change into some gray joggers, a black tee, and some tennis shoes. I learned from my last visit not to wear my expensive suits when seeing the girls.

"Jack, don't be ridiculous. You're at work, and I'm just getting the girls in the car now. I'm fine."

"Ri, let me help you... Please," I reply, my tone pleading.

There's a pause, as if she is contemplating my offer. As if on cue, Elle lets out a shrill cry and I can hear Lexi in the background saying she can't find her sparkly shoes.

"Uh, okay... okay, if you're sure."

"Yes I'm sure. Text me what you need and I'll swing by the pharmacy."

"You're a lifesaver... thank you."

"Anything for you, sweetheart."

I pull up at CVS and head inside, armed with the list Ria texted me.

Baby Tylenol, teething powder, and size 4 diapers.

I head to the aisle that has a sign saying 'baby'.

What the hell?

There are about five different brands of diapers. I can't even find the teething powder, and the Tylenol comes in two flavors. Bending down and narrowing my eyes at all the different boxes, rubbing my forehead, I feel my heart rate begin to rise, anxiety settling in.

I don't want to mess this up and let her down.

It must look like I don't know what the fuck I'm doing and clearly a fish out of water because an older lady in a white pharmacist coat comes over and offers to help me.

I tell her what I need and she shows me.

"What brand does your baby wear, dear?" I don't want to appear like an idiot or tell this random lady that I'm not buying for my baby, and I'm buying for my friend's little sister, who is currently going through a divorce, and I have feelings for her and am desperate to spend time with her, so I'm here trying to decide if I should buy Huggies, Pampers or some brand with a creepy looking baby on it.

"Ooohhhh, ermmmmm, well, we are in between brands, so I'll get one of each."

The lady gives me a knowing smile. She knows I'm full of shit and pats me on the shoulder. "Don't worry, dear. Lots of dads don't know the brands of the diapers their baby wears."

I smile back, not correcting her that Elle isn't my baby.

Is it weird that a part of me wishes she was? That they were both mine... all three of them?

I pay for the items plus a bunch of other stuff the woman suggested to help Elle. I head out of CVS and next door is a Starbucks. I know damn well Ria hasn't eaten today because she wouldn't have thought to put herself first, so I grab her favorite vanilla latte, a breakfast bagel for each of us, and of course, cake pops for Lexi.

I head out and place it all on the passenger seat of my Audi. The sun has finally peaked through the clouds and I reach into the back seat and grab my black baseball cap. I glance at myself in my rearview mirror; I forgot to shave this morning. I run my hand over the five o'clock shadow across my jawline and take a deep breath. Mentally preparing myself to see Ria, a mixture of nerves and excitement.

Less than ten minutes later, I'm pulling into the driveway of her house. Exiting the car I give her neighbor, who is tending to her front lawn, a little wave. Opening the passenger door and reaching in to grab the Starbucks bag and the three bags from CVS.

Jeez, bought a lot of shit.

I step onto Ria's white wooden porch and before I take a second step, Lexi comes flying out the front door and runs towards me.

" Jaaaaccckkkkkk."

"Careful, Lexi girl, I've got hot coffee for your mommy."

"Did you get me anything?" she asks with a smile that is impossible to say no to.

"Maybe." She turns to skip in the house and I hear Elle crying before I even enter.

I kick the door shut as I have no free hands and head for the kitchen. I place all the bags on the kitchen counter and go in search of Ria and Elle.

Ria is in the front room with Elle in some sort of sheet wrapped around her front, swaying her from side to side. Ria looks exhausted, but still just as beautiful. She could never be anything but beautiful to me, but it's clear she hasn't had a minute and has barely slept.

She turns to face me and her eyes light up, like my being here has suddenly made everything okay, and my heart does a weird flutter.

"My hero," she says on an exhale, walking towards me, I open up my arms and she leans against my chest.

"Hey, sweetheart," I say softly. I press a kiss to Elle's forehead. It feels so hot you could fry an egg on her. "Hey, baby girl. You're not feeling good, huh?" Her little face is bright red from all the crying and she is tugging at her right ear.

"She hasn't stopped crying since around four this morning. She's got a bad infection in her ear. I've given her the antibiotic the doctor gave her, but it won't kick in till tomorrow. Thank you for running errands for me."

"It's no trouble," I tell her honestly before taking her hand and leading her to the kitchen to show her everything I got. She stops in the doorway, looking at her kitchen counter covered in the bags.

"Did you do a full grocery shop?" she laughs. "I only needed three things."

"Yeah, I went a bit overboard. I wasn't sure what brands you use and Carol in CVS clearly saw me coming because she sold me every brand of diaper and teething powder going. She even threw in…" I reach in the bag and pull out the items, placing them on the white marble effect kitchen counter. "Ear drops, bath salts, a rubber duck, bath crayons, a fun sponge that changes color when it gets wet, wipes, diaper rash cream, baby shampoo, and princess bubble bath. Soooo, yeah, I think you are set for the next six months."

Ria bursts out laughing and it's the sweetest sound. I'd do anything to hear her laugh like that every day. Elle seems to finally calmed a little and Ria stands there swaying slowly side to side looking between all the items I got.

"Wow, Carol had your pants down, didn't she, convincing you to buy all this?"

"If she had offered me stocks and shares in the cattle market, I'd have signed up if I thought it would help you."

She stills, staring mouth slightly agape, looking at me so intently, as if the idea of someone wanting to help her is a foreign concept.

"If I ever go into sales, I'm hiring Carol. She's a force." I lean in over the kitchen counter towards Ria, lowering my voice. "But there's only one woman I'd let have my pants down." A pink blush hits her cheeks, and she bites down on her plump lower lip.

Yeah, I think we are okay.

I open up the Starbucks bag and start taking everything out. "And because I know you probably haven't eaten, I got you a vanilla latte and a breakfast bagel... oh and a cake pop for Lexi because, well, it's Lexi... I'd buy that girl a whole candy store if she asked."

."Jack... you... erm." She blows out a slow breath. Titling her head to the ceiling, her eyes fill with tears and I just want to hold her. To me, this is just the basics, the least I can do. I get the feeling Alex never did anything for her and she would have had to wade this storm on her own.

I walk to stand behind her, pressing my front to her back and bring my arms around her to hug not only her but Elle too, inhaling Ria's sweet scent, letting her know, without speaking, that I am here for her, for all three of them.

"Thank you," she whispers, swiping her fingertips under her eyes.

"Anything for you, Ri," I murmur, pressing a feather-light kiss to the side of her head.

I release her from my hold and we both start to unpack away the insane amount of crap I bought, whilst Ria gives Elle some Tylenol and eats her bagel, and drinks her coffee. Just as I finish my own, Lexi comes into the kitchen in a pink tutu and waving a wand. "Come on, Mommy, let's goooooo," she says, spinning.

"Oh, crap," Ria mutters under her breath, closing her eyes. She opens them and looks down at Elle, still wrapped in this weird sheet thing.

Note to self, find out what that is called.

She's finally fallen asleep and, according to Ria, her fever has started to go down.

"Lex, I'm so sorry. We're gonna have to miss ballet today. Elle is too sick. We'll go next week, baby, I promise."

The little look on Lexi's face breaks me. Her mouth turns down and her bottom lip pokes out before she hangs her head. I'd do anything to take that look off her face so without even thinking about what I'm offering, the words leave my mouth. "I'll take her."

Ria whips her head around. "You'll take her?" There's surprise in her voice.

"Yeah." I shrug.

"To ballet?" she repeats, still sounding confused.

"Yeah," I say like it's no big deal.

"*You* will take Lexi to her ballet class?" she says again, like she can't quite believe what I'm offering.

"Why not? You can stay here with Elle. I've cleared my schedule for the day. What do ya say, Lex? Want me to take you?"

"Yeeeeaaaaahhhhhh," she cries, spinning on the spot.

I laugh. "Okay, go get your shoes. Let's go."

"Jack, are you sure?"

"Of course, as long as you're okay with it. I'll keep her safe and I won't let her out of my sight," I reassure her, worrying I've overstepped.

"I know you will. I trust you completely."

Oh, thank fuck.

Warm pride fills my chest. She trusts me.

"Alex would never take her, no matter how much she asked." And that statement right there is like a sledgehammer to the heart. How could he not want to take his own daughter to her activities? He really is the biggest prick going and doesn't deserve to be their dad.

"She's the coolest kid I know, Ri. I love hanging out with her." I lean over the counter and place a chaste kiss to Ria's lips. Then I freeze, realizing what I'm doing, but she doesn't pull back. It felt so natural and right to kiss her goodbye and I hope there is a day I get to kiss her hello and goodbye forever.

I pick up my baseball cap and put it on before I grab my keys. "But I'm taking her in my car. Not a chance I'm driving your death trap."

I turn towards the doorway, "Okay, Princess... Let's go," I call.

I've never driven a kid in my car. I drive so slowly I wonder if we are actually moving, but I have precious cargo, so there's not a chance I'm taking any risks.

When we pull up outside the ballet studio, I get out and walk to the back of the car and get Lexi out. Thankfully unbuckling her seems a hell of a lot easier than buckling her in the damn thing. I swear my assault pack I wore in Afghanistan had less straps and belts than this carseat.

I lift her out and place her on the ground where she does a little twirl. She's dressed in a pink tutu and matching ballet slippers. Ria has put her hair up in a bun on the top of her head and finished it with a pink bow. *Shit, she looks cute.* She reaches up and holds my hand and leads me towards the dance studio.

I open the door to a smaller waiting area to find at least twenty little girls huddled together. Lexi lets go of my hand and skips over to them.

The room falls silent and all eyes are on me. I feel like a prized pig at the county fair. On show for everyone to have a good look at and decide how much I'm worth before they place their bets. I glance round the room to find I'm the only male.

Well, this is awkward.

One woman stands and walks over to me. She's blonde, a bit taller than Ria, caked in makeup, looking like the *Lululemon* store threw up on her.

"Hey, I'm Ria's friend, Margot. You must be Jack." She extends her arm and reaches for my hand with her perfectly polished fingernails and the giant rock on her wedding finger catches my eye.

I shake her hand and reply hesitantly wondering how the heck she knows who I am.

"Errm, yeah, I'm Jack, nice to meet you."

"I hear poor Elle is sick. Ri texted me to say you would be bringing Lexi so she couldn't make our coffee date. Lexi plays with my daughter, Emery. She's over there." She points to a little blonde girl who is talking to Lexi and I smile.

"And this is Shannon, Maddie, Britney and Paige. We're the ballet moms." She points out the women one by one who look like carbon copies of her. Ria doesn't fit in with these women at all, but they seem nice enough. The only one who breaks the mold is Paige, who looks like she can still move her face, unlike Margot here, who I can't work out if she's twenty-eight or forty-eight due to all the Botox.

"You can sit with us." She grins, and the way she strokes my arm makes me uneasy.

Just as I go to take a seat, the dance teacher appears in the doorway, ushering the girls to form an orderly line and enter the studio.

"Parents, if you want to line up behind the girls we can then head on in and get the class started," she shouts in order to be heard over the chaos in the room.

Line up? Where are we going?

"I thought we waited out here?" I asked Margot.

"Oh we do usually, but, it's parent participation week."

I look at her wide eyed. "Come again, it's what now?"

"Parent participation week," she says like I am supposed to know what the fuck that is. "Once a semester the parents join in with the class. Did Ria not tell you?"

I just stare at Margot, regretting all my life choices. "No, must have slipped her mind."

"Oh, well, it's lots of fun. You can sit with me."

I follow the moms into the studio. I can't back out now. Lexi can't be the only kid in class without an adult with her, so I suck it up, pull up my big boy pants, take off my tennis shoes and pray to God I can make it through this class without embarrasing myself or Lexi.

Twenty minutes later I'm sitting on the studio floor cross-legged wearing a plastic crown on my head and holding a pink wand. I catch a glimpse of myself in the mirror that lines the back wall and wonder how I got here. How did I go from living in Miami, spending my days running our bar to here, living my best life, participating in a pre-schoolers ballet class.

Because you are falling hard for her mom, the voice in my head whispers and I don't deny it.

Lexi appears out of nowhere, holding her hand behind her back with a mischevious look on her face.

"What have you got there Lex?"

"I'm going to make you a fairy"

"Oh yeah, how are you going to do that?"

"Surprise!" She giggles, as she throws a handful of glitter, but I'm not quick enough and the entire thing lands in my eye.

"And sprinkle the magic, sprinkle," Miss Susan chants as she circles us, and with that, Lexi launches another handful of glitter into the air. I duck, covering my face with my hands in preperation for her next attack.

Jesus this stuff stings.

"Are you having fun, Jack? I'm having so much fun. The next song is my favourite" Lexi says, practically vibrating with excitement. I don't know if I want to know what this next song is. I'm still recovering from our performance of the Nutcracker.

"Yeah, so much fun Lex," I tell her, whilst picking silver glitter out of my eye. I'll be billing Miss Susan for the laser eye surgery I'll be needing to regain my vision.

Miss Susan stands in the middle of the circle and claps her hands. "Okay, my little bunnies, it's time to hop hop hop up on to your feet."

Bunnies? Hop?

Margot leans over and whispers, "You might wanna hold on to your bunny for this next part," she mutters, gesturing to my dick with a wink.

What the hell?

A song I've never heard before blasts through the speakers. Miss Susan shows everyone how to put their hands in front of their face like little bunny paws and she starts to jump up and down.

I feel like an absolute idiot holding my hands like this, but it's for Lexi so I can't not do it.

And as I start jumping I instantly understand what Margot was talking about. I definitely need to hold on to my 'bunny' somehow. My gray sweatpants give everything away, unfortunately. In my defense, I didn't anticipate hopping around with a bunch of kids today.

"Jump, Jack, jump!" Lexi yells and I automatically obey and yep, my bunny is trying to escape the hutch. I try to half jump, but Lexi isn't having any of it. She stomps over and points at my feet. "Feet off the floor like me." She jumps high and raises her eyebrows for me to copy. So I take a deep breath and hop... *my poor bunny.*

If Harry and Brad could see me now they would have a field day and never let me live this down.

I strategically place my hands lower to cover my crotch in the hopes that no one notices my leaping dick as I jump around, trying to keep my back to everyone. I'd rather shield innocent eyes here. The less damage we all leave with, the better.

The song begins to slow and the girls all fall to the floor and I thank whoever's listening that it's all over except I'm wrong, so fucking wrong. The beat comes back again and so do the hops. Everyone leaps to their feet again. Sweat beads over my brow as I alternate one hand covering my junk and the other perched beneath my chin, smiling like a sweet little bunny. *Jesus, Lord above, kill me right fucking now.*

Ria owes me big time and I can think of a few ways she can make it up to me.

Chapter Twenty-One

Ria

I managed to get Elle down for a nap in her crib and take a much needed shower. I change into some leggings and an oversized sweatshirt, grab the baby monitor where I can see Elle sleeping soundly. It breaks my heart seeing my girls sick. I would trade places with them every time. I always feel so helpless when they are in pain, but she's settled and I take the opportunity to tidy up the toys in the front room and make myself a coffee.

Finally, taking a seat on the couch, I put my feet up and let myself sink into the plush cushions. This is such a strange feeling. I don't think I have spent any time on my own with just Elle since she was a newborn. Alex never took Lexi out on her own. It was always his parents. And the one time my hot mess of a mother did show up, she created more problems than solutions.

That familiar tightness in my chest when I think about my mom hits me. Rubbing my hand across my chest, willing the feeling to leave, it dawns on me that I haven't heard from her in nearly six months. What kind of mother doesn't call her daughter when she knows she's going through a divorce? I have spent years calling and chasing her. Begging for her love and attention and I don't think I can put myself through it anymore. I spent my entire marriage begging to be loved, to be a priority, and if being around Jack has taught me anything, it's that if people wanted to, they would.

I mindlessly scroll my phone and reply to the girls to make plans for a night out that is way overdue, according to Ali. I get two incoming messages. One from Margot, one of the moms from ballet, and one from Jack. I look at the time. 12.13. The ballet class must be over.

I open up the message from Margot first.

Margot

> Missed you today at ballet, but thank you for the treat you sent us *fire emoji* I think I speak for the entire class when I say we all appreciated his efforts during the hop little bunnies routine *eggplant emoji*

What the hell?

And then it hit me. It was parent participation week. *Oh shit! Poor Jack.* I hesitantly open his message.

> **Jack**
> Taking Lexi and myself for a well deserved slushie. I have three words for you Ri…

> Parent
> Participation
> Week

And he sends a gif of the weird kid who just stares with a WTF expression on his face.

> Be back soon x

I snort a laugh, covering my mouth with my free hand. Oh, my God.
I text him back.

> **Ria**
> I am so sorry. I completely forgot! Thank you again for taking her. I promise I will make it up to you xxx

Less than a minute later, a message from him comes through.

> **Jack**
> Oh yes you can, sweetheart *winking emoji with tongue stuck out* And I have a list of ways you can do it xxx

My body heats and my hands tingle. Just a few simple words turn me into a walking hormone. I have never been so affected by a man. Even during the good years with Alex, he never affected me the way Jack does.

I should have known back then how deep-rooted my feelings were for him. But I was Noah's annoying little sister. What would he see in me? I wonder if he ever noticed the way I would stare at him from behind the books I pretended to read when he was playing Xbox with my brother. Or how I would linger on the landing of our family home when I knew he was staying over in the hopes I would bump into him on the way to the bathroom.

The nights we spent in my kitchen eating pancakes are some of my most cherished memories. I smile and a little flutters stir in my belly, thinking how we would talk about the most mundane things and the way he would make me laugh. It was one of the few times I was truly happy.

When he left with my brother to join the Marines, my little teenage heart broke into tiny pieces. I never felt I could tell him how I felt about him. I knew it was wrong and living with my feelings felt far easier than living with the embarrassment of him rejecting me. I lived for the weekends. He would come home to visit me with my brother. I would send them both care packages when they were posted abroad and write them letters. Jack would write me back sometimes and I still have some of those letters stashed away.

One weekend, he came home, and I overheard him talking to Noah and Harry about a girl he hooked up with. I sat at the top of the stairs and it felt like my heart was being shredded bit by bit with every word that left his lips. I don't think he ever knew how I felt about him, and it's something I swore I would take to the grave. I knew Noah wouldn't approve and Jack respected my brother too much to ever hurt him or their friendship, so I didn't see any point in acting on my teenage lust. But now I wonder if Noah would feel differently.

When I met Alex at the age of nineteen, he seemed like my ticket out of my daily hell and so I threw myself into that relationship, and whilst I don't regret it for a single second because I wouldn't have my beautiful girls, I know he was the wrong guy at the right time and I will have to live with those choices I made for the rest of my life. They say the hardest boy to get over is the one you never had, and sadly, I know that to be true.

My trip down memory lane is interrupted by the sound of a car pulling up outside. I fold back my blanket and head for the front door, opening it before Lexi can bang on it and wake Elle.

Lexi is jumping around and running her mouth a mile a minute. Hello, sugar rush. Jack follows behind, looking like a shell of his former self. I watch as he lets out a long breath, rubbing a hand over his face.

Oh shit, was it that bad?

"Mommy, Jack got me candy and slushies and he got me the blue one, Mommy. The blue one," she cries, speeding past me.

"Lex, Elle is asleep, indoor voices please, sweetie," I say quietly, knowing damn well she didn't hear any of that.

I turn to face Jack, who slowly walks up the porch steps, stopping at the top step and looks at me deadpan. I stifle a laugh. "Jack, I'm so sorry. It completely slipped my mind"

He doesn't move, still staring at me dead in the eyes. I don't know if he's going to cry, laugh, or strangle me to death right here on my front porch.

"I'm gonna need some sort of therapy to get over that, Ri. I feel violated," he mutters, still staring at me. I don't even think he's blinked.

I cover my mouth with my hands and laugh. "Come in and tell me all about it. Do you want a coffee?"

"No, I want a whiskey... neat," he replies, walking past me and heading for the kitchen.

I follow him in and peek my head round the door of the front room, checking on Lexi. She's bouncing on the couch, watching the Disney Channel.

"Lexi," I whisper. "Sit down."

"Okay, Mommy," she whispers back and sits. I walk into the kitchen to the sound of running water.

I thought he wanted whiskey?

Jack is bent over the kitchen sink at an awkward angle with his face under the faucet, and from the look of it, rinsing his eyes out.

What the hell is he doing? Was it that traumatic?

I tiptoe over to my kitchen stools and sit down, leaning my chin on my hands to watch him. He stays like that for what feels like minutes, rubbing his eyes, lifting his head up to blink and then going back under the faucet.

"What are you doing?" I ask, narrowing my eyes.

He turns off the faucet and reaches for the paper towels and pats his eye. "I'm getting all the glitter out of my eye that Lexi threw at me. I'm surprised we made it home in one piece. I haven't been able to see a solid shape out of my left eye for nearly two hours. Who the heck gives little kids glitter to throw around?" he says so quickly, I almost miss it.

I don't speak, sensing he's about to offload his ordeal and the least I can do is listen.

"And that's just the tip of the iceberg. First, we arrive and I'm the only one with a dick in the room. The women in there looked like they hadn't seen a male with a pulse in years," he says, pointing to himself.

He starts pacing up and down, waving his hands about in a theatrical manner. I've never seen him like this, but it's the funniest thing I've ever witnessed.

"And let me tell you, Ri, I've seen some things in my life. I've fought on the front line, and those women were scarier than any enemy I've encountered." He stares at me, not blinking as if he is reliving it in his head. I have to clamp my lips together to stop a laugh escaping.

"Also, can we talk about Margot for a second? Her face. It never moved. No wrinkles, no lines, no emotion. I was terrified. And then she kept trying to grab me, which I hated. Consent, Margot, it's a real thing!"

I can feel myself visibly shaking as I try my best to suppress my laughter.

"Oh, and Daphne! What the fuck's her issue? She looked at me like she hadn't eaten in weeks and has been living nil by mouth… licked her lips and everything." Visibly shivering, he looks like he's been shook to his very core.

Oh God, I really did send him into the lion's den.

"Then, as if that wasn't terrifying enough, Miss Susan comes in to announce I need to partake in the class and gives me a plastic crown. I wasn't gonna let Lexi be the only one without a parent, so I did what any self-respecting man would do; I put that crown on my head, flexed my toes and danced." He's spiraling now. I can tell by the way his face is flushed, and he's panting.

And it's with that line my laughter fades and my heart melts. Knowing he did all this for Lexi, just so she wouldn't feel left out, makes me want to cry with happiness. No one has ever shown up for her like that.

"Then the glitter came, and I wondered if I'd ever see out of this eye again." He points at his left eye. "No amount of blinking or rubbing would get the shit out. Pretty sure Miss Susan thinks I was winking and flirting with her, so be prepared for that conversation at your next class."

And I'm back to laughing.

"And then..." he cries loudly, throwing his arms in the air. "Just when I thought it couldn't get any worse, the ballet gods had a real good laugh at my expense and they played hop little bunnies..." Lowering his voice, he whispers, "And let me tell you, sweetheart, my bunny was hopping."

I press my lips together and let out the most unlady-like snort. My body vibrating as I silently laugh.

He rolls his eyes at my reaction. "Well, I'm glad you find it funny. I'm surprised I wasn't arrested for indecent exposure." He's so serious that it makes me laugh, harder.

"Jack... I'm..." I can't get my words out. Tears are rolling down my cheeks. God, I haven't laughed like this in months. I close my eyes and take a moment to pull myself together. When I open them again, he's staring at me, wearing a wry smile.

"What's that look for?" I ask, wiping my eyes with my fingertips, questioning what's got him looking at me like I am the best part of his day.

"I love to see you laugh like that." And there he goes again. Melting my heart.

I get up from the kitchen stool and walk towards him, slinking my arms around his waist, pressing myself against him. He's so much taller than me that I have to crane my neck to meet his gaze. I inhale his manly musk scent and press my nose into his chest.

"Thank you... thank you for doing that for Lexi." And without realizing I place a light kiss to his chest.

"Ri, I know I'm ranting but the truth is... I'd do anything for you and your girls. Glitter, bunny hopping, anything." I lift my head to look at him. We don't say anything, we don't move, and I don't even think either of us is breathing. The air shifts between us and no words are needed. We are saying everything without saying anything, which seems to be how me and Jack communicate when we want to admit how we feel about each other.

I wet my lips and my top teeth sink into my bottom lip. Jack clears his throat. The tension between us is suffocating. I close my eyes as if it will help me find the words or give me the ability to move. And then I feel it; his lips meeting mine. It's soft and gentle. Not like our previous kisses.

I open my mouth, inviting his tongue to meet mine. Our tongues intertwine and his hands come up to the back of my head and gently fist a handful of my hair, pulling me closer, deepening our kiss.

Sparks of pleasure shoot up and down my spine under his touch and my hands move on their own accord, stroking up and down his broad back and then up to his hair. His free hand travels to my ass, squeezing it ever so gently. His touch causes flutters in my chest.

I pull back ever so gently, planting one chaste kiss before I break the kiss completely. His hands find their way to my cheeks as his thumbs smooth over my bottom lip and he kisses my forehead.

We stand like that for what feels like hours. Not speaking, not looking at one another, just standing there in each other's arms, trying to process what that kiss meant. That wasn't just a kiss. It was *the* kiss. The kiss that radiates through your entire body and makes your toes tingle. The one that gives you that fluttering feeling in the pit of your stomach. It wasn't rushed, it wasn't frantic. It was slow, soft and full of passion and so much meaning. I'm scared as hell to want him like this but yet here I am, wanting him anyway.

"I really don't want to go away for work next week," he says, pressing his forehead to mine.

"You're going away?" A knot tightens in my stomach at the idea of not seeing him.

"Yeah, back to Miami. We've got stuff to sort at the club. I've been meaning to tell you, but I didn't want you to think I was leaving you."

"No, Jack, I totally understand. It's for work. I get it"

"I'm going to hate being away from you."

"Me too." I really am going to miss him.

Chapter Twenty-Two

Jack

It's been weeks since the ballet class from hell and I think I've only just got all the glitter out of my eye. If you want to see a grown man physically roll around on the floor and nearly piss his pants laughing, just tell Harry you had to partake in a four-year-olds ballet class and everyone saw your dick swinging in your pants and one of the horny moms nearly mounted you in the parking lot.

"Bro, you must know that gray sweats are like crack to women," he howls.

"No... believe it or not, I didn't, but I won't be wearing them again unless it's in front of Ria."

"Dude, you got it bad if you are taking ballet," he taunts.

I don't comment. Just swirl the golden liquid in my tumbler and smile. Thinking of her.

I told them about the kiss with Ria and we unanimously agreed I am indeed pussy whipped. I need to tell Ria how I feel but I need to find the perfect time and way to tell her. The timing isn't right though. I need to be home and see her, be with her, because I think she feels the same way, and I want to see the look on her face when I tell her and make sure she knows she's allowed to grab her own happiness.

Knowing Ria for as long as I have, she's always been the most selfless person. She's always put her brother, her mom, her dick bag husband before herself. The thought of her suffering makes my chest ache. How can I convince her that putting herself first every now and then is good for her.

We've been back in Miami for three weeks now, working and then Chris had his bachelor party last night. I spent it talking about or thinking about Ria and truly embarrassed myself when I kept texting her, telling her I missed her like some horny prepubescent boy.

Usually, we would tear up the strip, and party till we passed out, but things have changed. I'd rather be in my hotel room talking to Ria. We are back at the weekend as it's Nancy and Chris' wedding shower, whatever the heck that is. But Ria will be there and it's the only thing getting me through the week.

We wrap up another dinner meeting and Harry and Brad head off to the bars to get in a few hours of partying. I'd usually join them, but my head and my heart are back in New York with a pretty brunette with eyes like the ocean.

It's nearly midnight and I head up to my hotel room to shower. I don't bother putting on boxers and just climb in under the crisp white hotel sheets, switch off the bedside light and open up my phone to do my nightly scroll of my photo album. A photo of her and the girls, photos I've taken with the girls the last time I went over, and the only photo I have of me and Ria together. It's a little blurry, but it's my favorite. It's us dancing in her front room next to the record player. Lexi took it after putting on one of her performances. I jokingly asked Ria to dance with me to the old country music that was playing after I had finished twirling Lexi around. The girls were giggling watching us and it's one of my favorite days I've spent with them. My chest aches, wishing I was back there with them now.

I know it's late and she will be sleeping but I send a short text.

> **Jack**
> I miss you beautiful. 3 days till I see you. It can't come soon enough xxx

I'm surprised when I get a reply back straight away.

> **Ria**
> I know. It's been too long! I think all future business trips should be cancelled, just come and see me instead.

> **Jack**
> Suggestion approved! All future business trips are cancelled. Are you alone in bed?

> **Ria**
> Yeah, why?

I switch the call to FaceTime, and Ria's sleepy face fills my screen.

"Hey, you," she says in a soft voice.

"I miss your smile," I tell her.

"I miss your face too."

I groan at the sight of her, at the thought that she's in bed and I am too.

"God, sweetheart. I wish I could touch you right now."

She hides her face with her bedsheet. "I think I'd like that too. I don't know if I can wait that long. I couldn't stop thinking about you earlier. I had to..." She stops.

"Are you gonna finish that sentence?" I eye her curiously through the screen. "You had to do what?"

She bites down on her bottom lip and tugs it between her teeth in that way that always makes my dick twitch.

"Maria Kennedy, are you telling me you think of me when you touch yourself?" I say suggestively.

"Maybe... Do you think of me?"

I let out a low moan and reach down to palm my now throbbing cock under the sheets. "Sweetheart, you are the only thing I think about. I don't think you understand what you do to me."

We don't say anything, we just stare at each other through the phone and even though we are thousands of miles apart, the tension between us is palpable.

"Show me," she eventually whispers, so quietly I almost miss it.

I love that she's feeling confident enough around me to let this side of her finally come out. That she feels like she can be in control and take what she wants.

I pull back the sheet and reach down to take hold of my hard cock, and gently tug, letting out a low groan. Precum dripping on my fingers.

I lower the camera just for a brief second so she can see what I'm doing and how she's affecting me. She lets out a gasp. We've gone too far now, we can't go back. I'm all in and I think she is too. I lift the camera back up to my face, still stroking my hard length and my breathing becomes heavier. "Your turn," I moan, my voice low and gravelly.

Her cheeks pinken and her eyes become heavier. She hesitates for the briefest second and then pulls back her bed sheet, moving the camera down her body to reveal a pair of white lace underwear, and fuck... she's not wearing a top. Ria's perfectly shaped breasts are on full display and I'd give anything to be there right now, and put one of her hardened nipples in my mouth and suck on it to make her moan.

"God, baby, I want you. Show me how you touch yourself."

Using her free hand, she strokes down her body, over her breasts and her stomach, until she slips her hand into the top of her underwear. I know when she's found her clit because her breathing hitches and the moan that escapes her sends a jolt to my already painfully hard dick.

Her hooded eyes stare back at me through the phone. Ria, looking flustered and turned on, is something I never want to forget.

"Fuck, baby. I'm gonna come if you keep looking like that."

She bites down on her bottom lip, closing her eyes, arching her back and letting out a sexy little moan.

Shit, is this really happening? We are having phone sex. I'm having phone sex with Ria. Her breasts rise and fall in quick succession, and she moans again. I remember that sound; she's close.

"Shit." I hiss, feeling that familiar build up heating in my core.

"Are you close, sweetheart? I want you to come with me," I pant.

She nods, too lost to her pleasure to speak.

Increasing my pace, my balls tingle and draw up tight as I watch her face flush a deep shade of pink. She moves the camera down her body and I watch as the hand that's dipped inside her laced panties move in quick circles.

Fuck, I wish that was my hand.

"Jack..." She pants "I'm—"

"That's it, baby. Let go, come with me." The sounds that leaves her parted lips sets me off.

I come so hard I can't grip my dick tight enough to stop it exploding all over the sheets. My eyes are fixed on the screen as Ria falls apart, writhing around in her bed, her body trembling with pleasure.

We lay there, still on the line, staring at each other through the screen that separates us, waiting for our breathing patterns to even out. There's a silence between us. It's not an awkward one, it's a silence that has us processing and accepting that we've taken another step in our relationship that leaves us a little less like friends and a little more like lovers.

I end the silence by speaking. I need to reassure her that this only changes things for the better between us and hope she doesn't run again.

"Sweetheart, you are perfect. I wish I could be with you right now." and as I say that, the look of relief that washes over her face tells me that we are okay. That she's not going to panic, that she was just as ready as I was for this next progression in our confusing relationship.

"I wish you were here too. Just three more days." She smiles, followed by a little yawn.

"Get some sleep, sweetheart. Sweet dreams."

"Night Jack." Blowing me a kiss, she ends the call.

Chapter Twenty-Three

Ria

I feel like my body has been vibrating and running off adrenaline all day. I don't know if I'm anxious, excited, had too much caffeine, or if it's all of the above. Tonight I get to see Jack after more than three weeks. Our FaceTime call has been replaying over and over in my head. I couldn't believe how brave I was. I would never dream of doing that, but with him, it feels right. He makes me feel safe and wanted, and my belly does a little flip when I think about seeing him later.

Our schedules have been crazy. He's been traveling for work and I've been busy getting the house finished, and Lexi signed up for Pre-K. I'm moving forward with the divorce proceedings and finally the thought of divorce doesn't leave a bitter taste in my mouth. I feel relief and happiness; I am finally choosing me and what I want. Having this time away from Jack has made me realize just how much he means to me and how different I feel when I'm around him.

Dropping the girls to Alex's parents' house earlier was awkward as hell. He showed up and demanded to know my plans because his parents let it slip that I had the night off. The man's delusional thinking he has a right to know where I am and what I'm doing. It's none of his damn business. It's taken nine months to be in a head space where I feel strong enough to stand up for myself and ignore his demands.

I've had my everything shower and given myself a bouncy blow out. I rarely wear my hair like this but I want to go all out tonight. I want to feel like the woman I've always craved to be. Tonight I am not someone's mother, I'm not someone's wife. I'm not anyone's anything. I am me and it feels so fucking good to say that. I've gone with a smoky eye and a nude lipstick, adding some highlighter to my cheekbones and for the first time in a long time I like what I see staring back at me in the bathroom mirror. I don't see the broken Ria staring back at me with her haunted eyes and hollow cheeks; I don't see my limp and lifeless hair that was falling out by the handful due to the stress of the separation and I don't see dimness in my eyes. I see the new me. Dare I say it, but I feel like I've got my color back. I've still got a long way to go, but I can feel myself being loved back to life by the people I've chosen to surround myself with.

But I'd like to be something to Jack.

A knock at the door surprises me. Grabbing my robe, I throw it on and head for the front door. A man stands with a huge bouquet of lavender roses wrapped in white paper and tied with a matching ribbon.

"Maria Kennedy?" he asks.

"That's me." There is excitement in my voice. I thank him, closing the door and placing them on the entry table, bending down to inhale the sweet scent. I spot the card and open it,

Ri, I've missed you more than words can say, so here are two dozen roses, one for each day we've been apart. I can't wait to see you... Your Action Man x

I press the card to my chest, closing my eyes. My heart flutters in my chest. *How did I get so lucky?* I race upstairs to finish getting ready, excitement coursing through my body like hot lava.

I grab my clutch and quickly text the girls to let them know I'm about to leave. Staying on brand with this new Ria vibe I've got going, I treated myself to a little black dress for tonight's party that is so out of my comfort zone I boxed and unboxed the thing three times, unsure if I was going to keep it or return it, but now it's on, I love it. As I reach for the front door, my phone buzzes in my bag. Convinced it's Gabby checking I have indeed left, my heart does a little flutter when I see Jack's name on the screen.

> Jack
>
> You've been on my mind all day, sweetheart. Hurry that cute ass here. I've missed you. X

Tonight is going to be a good night.

We arrive at the hotel where the wedding shower is being hosted. Trust Nancy and Chris to be extra and have a joint wedding shower and host it at Manhattan's hottest rooftop bar.

I smooth my dress down and take out my compact to check my lipstick hasn't smudged. My stomach is full of butterflies that feel like they are fighting desperately to escape.

"Damn Girl you look hot." Gabby whistles, looking me up and down. I smile and do a little spin.

"Maria, Maria, Maria, you are going to make that man's head spin. He's not going to be able to keep his hands off you," Ali says, reaching for my hand and giving it a reassuring squeeze.

That's the plan.

"You've got your sparkle back, girl. You enjoy tonight."

We are shown to the rooftop area by a staff member who is dressed in black and holding an ipad. He checks our IDs and signs us in. As we open the glass doors and step into the party, my heart feels like it's about to beat out my chest at the idea of seeing Jack.

There is a giant swimming pool in the center of the rooftop, where the DJ is on a podium with the New York skyline as his backdrop. Strips of fairy lights stretch above our heads. Everyone is dressed in black and white cocktail attire and fire lanterns decorate the edges of the roof. Tables and chairs are placed around the pool and a dance floor sits between the DJ booth and the bar at the edge of the pool.

"Holy shit, she can throw a party." Ali whistles.

"Oh, my God. Is that *Neyo*?" Gabby screeches.

"Shut the fuck up! Where?" Ali shouts over the music.

Sure enough it is Neyo in the DJ booth, dancing with Nancy and two other girls, but I don't care as I scan the rooftop to find a certain someone.

A woman holding a tray of champagne flutes appears in front of us and hands us a glass each. Ali takes the lead and we follow, heading towards the pool and the table and chairs area. I don't miss how heads turn looking at her ass swaying in her little white strapless dress. Even Gabby has gone out of her comfort zone and Is wearing a little black dress that is tight fitting down to her ass and then flares a little and paired it with some sky high black pumps. She looks stunning and for the first time in a long time I feel worthy of standing next to them.

I feel him before I see him and I lock eyes with Jack across the pool. He's dressed in black suit pants and a black button up, the sleeves rolled to the elbow and his watch catches the light from the pool as he lifts his drink to his lips. It's as if he lights a fire in me when his gaze wanders up from my heels until he reaches my eyes. The grin on his lips and the way he licks them has me almost reaching for the closest person to me to keep me up right. My body is heated and I want, no need, to be near him.

"Over here." Ali gestures with her hand pointing at the table Jack, Harry and Brad are seated at. Jack places his drink down on the table as he sees us approaching and rises to his feet, reaching for me and tugging me against his hard body. He smells incredible, like spice and whiskey. He buries his face in my hair and I swear his body vibrates as he lets out a low moan, as if he's been waiting to inhale me as if I was his oxygen.

"You Look incredible," he whispers into my ear, just loud enough for me to hear. I pull back to look up at him and again without giving me a second to get my bearings, he plants a chaste kiss to my lips, leaving me speechless. I feel that heat and that tingling in my hands and feet again. *Why is my body so responsive to him?*

"Thank you for my roses. They are beautiful."

"Thank you for being someone worth missing." My heart somersaults. *Holy hell, I don't stand a chance with him.*

Taking my hand, he leads me towards the large chairs he was sitting on and we sit next to each other. Placing an arm around me, I reach up to hold the hand that hangs from my shoulder. I exhale, feeling all the adrenaline that has been pumping through my body all day in anticipation for this very moment leave my body as I lean into him. *This is where I want to be.*

We all fall into comfortable conversations, catching up on the last few weeks' events while Ali does everything she can to avoid talking to Harry for more than a minute.

"Oh my God, Carter's here," Ali says, placing her hands over her face.

"Who the fuck is Carter?" Harry huffs, looking around, trying to see who she's talking about.

"Oh, just one of my old buddies." She winks at Harry, who looks at her deadpan, knowing exactly what she is insinuating.

"Is he the one?" Gabby asks, using her hands to gesture the size of his dick.

"Yeah, dick so big you could land a plane on it. Shame he didn't know how to use it." Rolling her eyes, Ali takes a sip of her champagne.

"Well, Ali cat, if you need someone who knows what they're doing, look no further." Harry holds out his arms, looking down at his crotch.

Ali's face is priceless. She looks like she's smelled something that passed its expiration date. "That's really bold of you, but you strike me as someone that gets nervous cracking an egg, so to save us both the embarrassment, I'm gonna have to give it a miss." She leans in toward him and pats his chest. "But we love a confident king, so you keep trying." And with that, she gets up and sashays off toward the bar.

Laughter erupts around the table as Harry sits there, looking like a kid who's just been told Santa isn't real. "She's so fucking mean," he mutters, and I actually feel bad for the guy.

"If you can't handle it, baby, just say, we can take it slow," he shouts as he stands and follows her to the bar. I get the feeling he can handle Ali and she may have finally met her match.

The evening passes by in a blur of shots, champagne, and dancing, with one girl stripping off and jumping in the pool and having to be escorted out. Jack has had a possessive hold on me the entire time. His hands on my thigh, rubbing it absentmindedly, sending a rush of moisture in between my legs. Searing every touch into my skin.

We are now the only ones at the table; Ali and Gabby are tearing up the dancefloor with some guy who looks old enough to be their dad. Brad and Harry have been propping up the bar for the past hour and Harry has been looking at Ali like he wants to either throw her in the pool or fuck her into next week and she glares straight back at him in the same way.

Lips graze my ear, Jack's gravelly voice whispering, "Have I told you how incredible you look tonight?"

"You have, but I don't mind hearing it again." I turn to face him, my body tingling from his gaze, and my hands instinctively reach out to touch his face.

"You are pretty hot yourself. The women in here haven't kept their eyes off you."

"I wouldn't know. I've only been looking at you, sweetheart."

And with those words, I melt.

He leans in, our lips almost touching. "I really wanna kiss you, but the problem is, if I did, I don't think I'd be able to just stop there…"

I graze the shell of his ear with my teeth, feeling brave. "And why would you think I'd want you to stop?"

"Oh, will you two just fuck already? I'm gonna combust just watching you two. The sexual tension is killing me," Ali says dramatically, flopping down on the chair and then lying back as if she's fainted.

I let out a squeal as I am suddenly dragged to my feet and flung over Jack's shoulder. I let out a yelp when he smacks my ass, keeping his hand there to stop my dress riding up.

"Yessss, atta boy," Ali cheers.

Thankfully, it's got to that part in the evening where everyone is drunk and doesn't notice Jack hauling my practically bare ass across the rooftop bar towards a door at the edge of the building.

He opens the door and we enter into a stairwell.

"Jack, put me down," I giggle, whilst I try and fail to smack his ass.

"No chance," he laughs, spanking my ass and I'd be lying if that didn't reach my core and give me a flutter.

New kink unlocked.

He walks down a few flights of stairs and then opens a door.

The room is dark and dimly lit by a fire exit sign. I am gently placed on my feet and I straighten out my dress and flatten my hair. Jack drags a chair in front of the door, wedging it under the handle.

"What is this pla—" My sentence is cut short by Jack crashing his lips to mine. His hands cup my ass and he lifts me so my legs instinctively wrap around his waist. He walks us backward until my back meets a cold brick wall and I let out a whimper.

"Fuck, I missed you," he murmurs against my lips.

Our kiss is frantic. Like starved animals fighting desperately for every bite. We are panting, our breathing ragged. Our tongues intertwine and fall into a perfect rhythm as another rush of moisture floods my underwear. My body has a mind of its own as I start to grind against him, desperate for the friction to give me some release.

"Do you need some help with that, sweetheart?" His hand leaves the back of my neck and traces down the front of my body, brushing over my swollen breasts and settling in between legs, under my dress and finding my clit.

"God, don't stop." My voice sounds strangled.

"I don't plan to, sweetheart."

His fingers push aside my underwear and slide between my folds. "Fuck, you are so wet. I've been thinking of this pussy ever since our call."

I dig my nails into his shoulders and arch my back. I am so close and he's barely touched me.

"I need to taste you," he demands, his voice gravelly and strained, and he runs his tongue along my bottom lip, making me whimper in pleasure

I don't overthink it. I unwrap my legs from his waist and he places me down on my feet, pinning me against the wall. He bends down, pushing up my dress and dragging my soaked underwear down my legs. I step out of them and watch him as he brings them to his face, inhaling my scent. "Mmm, so fucking sweet," he moans.

Jack on his knees in front of me may be the hottest thing I have ever seen. I feel so empowered, knowing this man is at my feet, wanting to put my pleasure ahead of his.

His hooded eyes meet mine, and my ragged breathing starts to slow. I bite down on my lower lip and give him a slow nod; the permission I know he's waiting for.

"I'm going to need you to open up those legs for me, sweetheart."

Dear God, did he just say that?

I part my legs slowly, watching as his eyes stare at me intently, his jaw flexing, showcasing that perfect jawline of his. He lets out a low moan, and holy hell, if it isn't the hottest sound, my nipples pebble against the fabric of my dress at the sight of him between my open legs. I'm exposed, but my want for him, for his touch, outweighs any insecurities I have in this moment.

"Do you know how long I've waited to taste you?"

I close my eyes, my chest heaving and the throbbing between my legs becoming unbearable.

And then I feel it. His mouth clamps down on my clit and I almost explode on the spot.

"Jack... oh, my God," I gasp.

His warm tongue licks through my folds and back up to my clit. The sound he lets out almost has me coming on the spot and it only spurs me on. I feel another rush of moisture and I know he feels it too when he moans again.

"Fuck, you taste so good, sweetheart," he murmurs, face still in between my legs.

"Please," I beg. I Need more.

He lifts one leg, placing it over his shoulder, opening me up for him, then he slides two fingers inside me.

My back arches away from the wall as his expert fingers curl inside me, hitting that spot he seems to find so easily.

Sucking on my clit and plunging his fingers inside at a pace that has me teetering on the edge of euphoria. I have never felt pleasure like it. My hands grip the back of his head as I grind against his mouth.

"Jack," I rasp. "I'm gonna come. I'm gonna cu—" I don't finish that last word, as an orgasm a hundred times more powerful than the first one he gave me rips through me and I wonder how I am still standing or even conscious at the end of it. He continues to lick and thrust his fingers through my release, slowing the pace as I free fall back down to earth.

A sheen of sweat runs in between my breasts, my breathing still erratic my eyes feel so heavy I struggle to keep them open and focus on Jack. I do my best and look down at the hottest man I've ever laid eyes on kneeling before me. His dark sandy hair has that just fucked look, thanks to my hands clawing at him as I rode his face. He is still panting too and we just stay like that, staring at each other. We know it's there; we know how we both feel about one another, but still not finding a way to actually say it and admit it. I know we need to talk and figure out what this is. I can't run again. I don't even want to. I want him and I need to tell him because I fear if I don't, I could lose him for a second time and I don't think my heart could handle that.

Chapter Twenty-Four

Jack

Rising to my feet, licking the remnants of Ria's arousal off my lips, I press my body against hers. I can feel the thump, thump of her heart through her chest matching mine.

Fuck, I want to be inside her, but I want our first time to be special. She deserves more than a quickie up against the janitor's closet wall. I should have resisted tonight, restrained myself, but the way she looked in that dress and the feel of her in my arms, I snapped. I had to taste her, be close to her. I know she wanted it to too but I hope to God I haven't scared her and fucked this up. I press my lips to hers and hear her whimper as she tastes herself on me. I need to know we are okay. Need to know she's not getting ready to run again.

I feel her hands at the waistband of my pants and the tug of my button coming undone. The kiss turns frantic again and I start to lose myself in her. She reaches inside my pants and pulls free my hard cock; the tip dripping with precum. She swipes her thumb over the end, smearing my arousal over me before she rubs her hand up and down my shaft.

"Fuck, Ri," I groan, not breaking the kiss. I am seconds away from coming and I need to try and make this last. I reach in between her legs again as a way to distract me from my own building pleasure, but she pauses. Looking at me through her thick lashes, her crystal blue eyes glistening under the fire exit light, she licks her lips. The air crackles between us and I can't fight this anymore. I want her, I need her.

"You are so beautiful," I pant, fighting the urge to blow my load there and then. She sinks to her knees.

"My turn for a taste," she whispers.

"Ri, baby you don't have t-t—" My sentence is cut short by the sensation of her hot lips wrapping around the end of my length and her tongue licking my pre cum.

She moans around my dick and I have to plant my hands against the wall to steady myself and she goes to work on my dick.

"Jesus, fuck, you keep doing that sweetheart and I'm gonna come," I say on a strangled breath. But that just spurs her on.

She looks fucking incredible on her knees before me. She must sense my eyes on her and she looks up at me, her eyes watering slightly, her now swollen lips wrapped around my dick, and it may be the hottest sight I've ever seen.

My dick is throbbing, my heart racing, my breathing heavy as that wave of white-hot pleasure builds. "Ri, baby, I'm close," I warn.

But in true Ria style, she surprises me, taking me deeper, her head bobbing and her hand comes up to cup and massage my balls, pushing me over the edge. Cumming with force, I explode in her mouth and she drinks it down, sucking me dry before she uses her tongue to lap up the last drop, looking at me as her throat works, swallowing it down.

My knees go weak and I have to brace my hands on the wall to steady myself. She releases my cock from her mouth with an audible *pop* and wipes the corner of her mouth with her fingertips.

"That was... fucking incredible," I pant as I help her up. "You on your knees like that... fuck." Pressing my lips to hers, tasting my arousal, her arms wrap around my waist.

She breaks the kiss, pressing our foreheads together and we stay like that, losing all sense of time.

"People might wonder where we are," she whispers eventually.

"Good, let them," I reply. "Stay with me tonight?"

"I'd love that, but I think we need to talk about... this," she says hesitantly, gesturing between us.

"I know, but I don't wanna push you, Ri. We go at your pace, whenever you are ready, whatever you want." A relieved look washes over her face.

"Okay," she sighs, "but not tonight, okay? Let's talk tomorrow morning.

I just want to have fun tonight and just be with you."

"Sounds perfect to me."

We straighten ourselves up and I reluctantly give Ria her underwear back. I'd love the thought of her bare under that dress, but the idea of someone seeing her that exposed builds a rage inside me.

We head back towards the party, and I've lost all sense of time. God knows how long we've been gone, but it must have been some time because Ali is actually giving Harry the time of day and dancing with him, while Gabby is talking with Brad at our table.

It's clear everyone has been taking advantage of the free bar in our absence, and on route to the table, I take two glasses of champagne from a waiter walking past us.

"And what have you two been up to?" Gabby asks knowingly, looking back and forth between us with a smirk. They've moved to a low table surrounded by couches near the bar.

"Ermm, Jack just had to show me something," Ri mumbles, avoiding eye contact.

"Oh really, like his dick?" she slurs drunkenly.

Brad snorts, choking on his drink.

"Gabriella," Ria scolds.

Gabby falls back against Brad's chest and they both erupt into laughter. I swear, I've never seen the man laugh like that. It's good to see him relax and enjoy himself.

Ali heads over to us, walking like Bambi on ice with Harry hot on her heels. "Well, you're looking mighty relaxed, both of you." She winks at us. "I just don't know if I can forgive you for leaving me with this whiny ass." She points to Harry as he approaches us.

"I don't whine," Harry shouts over the music, sounding as pissed as Ali looks.

"Ali, why are you so mean to me? Ali, why don't you wanna fuck me? Ali, why won't you reply to my texts?" she mocks.

Harry glares at her, looking like someone has pissed in his cereal. "Have you taken some extra bitch pills today?"

"I have. They were doing a two for one special, so I stocked up when I knew I had to spend the evening with you."

He gives her the middle finger and walks off towards the bar. Ali falls back onto the couch, cackling like a witch.

"Are you gonna put that man out of his misery?" I ask, my eyes pinned on her.

"Now that wouldn't be fun, would it, Jack?" she says, laughing as she pokes her tongue out. I shake my head and roll my eyes, taking a sip from my glass. I think taunting him has become a sport for her.

I let out an exhale and sink further into the couch and look up at New York's night sky. Not a star in the sky can be seen, just the twinkling of lights from surrounding buildings and a plane flying overhead. I love New York. I dreamed of moving to the Big Apple my entire military career. It was the only thing that kept me going during deployments. The idea of getting out and moving to New York apartment with views of the city and having someone to share it with... with her.

"I just need to make a quick call," she announces, freeing herself from my hold and pulling the phone from her bag. She gives me a chaste kiss and heads over to the corner of the rooftop to make a call. I can't take my eyes off her. The sway of her hips as she walks, her long toned legs showcased thanks to the killer heels she's wearing and I have to adjust myself in my pants at the memory of her leg over my shoulder and my head buried in her pussy not too long ago.

I watch as she talks to someone on the phone and I don't miss how her body stiffens and her head swings round, scanning the rooftop. She turns her back to me so I can't see what she's saying, but her body language tells me everything her words aren't. Her shoulders are hunched, and she is visibly shaking. My gut instinct is to go to her rescue, but I know I have to let her handle whatever she is dealing with. I have to tread very carefully when it comes to her girls but I'll be here with open arms when she's done and will do what I can to ease the stress.

She ends the call and rubs her forehead, looking frustrated. I watch as she strides towards the bar and signals two fingers to the bartender. He slides two shots of something toward Ria and she necks one after the other.

Oh, fuck, this can't be good.

She then asks for two more and that has me out of my seat and walking toward her. "Ri, what's wrong?" I demand.

She throws back another shot before wiping her mouth with the back of her hand.

She turns to face me and plasters a fake smile on her face. "Nothing," she bites.

"Really?" I question, unsure of what to make of her obvious lie.

"Really. Now let's go dance." Taking my hand, she drags me to the dance floor.

It's clear she doesn't want to talk and wants to lose herself in the music, in me. We move in sync, her ass grinding against my dick, my hands on her hips. She reaches behind to hold the back of my neck, turning her head, and pulling my face towards hers, kissing me. I don't know what's going on with her, but if this is what she needs right now, I'll give it to her.

My erection thickens as Ria rotates her hips. It's clear the shots have hit. Her balance is slightly off and her eyes are hooded.

She turns. "I want you. Let's get out of here."

It takes a second for me to register how forward she's being. I love it but I can't help but feel there's something going on with her and she isn't acting herself. I don't want to question her here, so I simply nod and take her hand.

I let Gabby and Ali know I'm taking Ria back to mine and Ali warns that she will cut my dick off if I don't look after her. To be honest, I'm more concerned about her cutting Harry's dick off. I warn the guys to get the girls home safe, and while they may be a pair of party boys, I'd trust them with my life and the safety of any woman.

We exit the rooftop and I wave down a cab, not wanting to bother our driver as it's only a short drive to my apartment. Ria is visibly intoxicated and, by the time we reach my apartment building, she can barely stand. She stumbles out of the cab and falls on the curb, erupting into a fit of giggles.

"Come here, boozy. Let's get you upstairs," I tell her, helping her up on her feet.

We head for the door, but she stumbles again, dropping her purse and bursting into another fit of laughter.

"Okay, sweetheart, I'm gonna have to carry you." I scoop her up like a groom carrying his bride over the threshold and she lets out a gasp.

"Oh, Mr. Lawson, my hero. I feel like Paula in *An Officer and a Gentleman*." She throws her head back, waving her arm in the air, and starts to sing the theme tune, *"Love Lifts Us Up, Where We Belong"*.

I walk through the foyer of my building, giving a nod to the doormen as he walks over to the elevator, pressing my floor. "Evening, Frank. Thanks."

"My pleasure, sir. Have a good evening. Please call down if you need anything."

We enter the elevator and go to my floor, Ria's eyes taking in the environment.

"Shit, are you rich, or rich rich?" She whistles, looking around the elevator that has mirrors throughout with a gold and wood ceiling.

We exit the elevator, and thankfully, my apartment is opposite. I place her down on her feet and reach in my back pocket for my wallet, pulling out the keycard for my apartment. I tap the card on my door panel and open the door. We walk through to the entryway and I hear Ria gasp.

"Holy shit, you are rich, rich, rich."

I smile, knowing exactly what has her gasping like that, and it's the very reason I bought this apartment. The entire back wall of my apartment is glass, looking out at the New York skyline.

"Can I get you a drink?" I ask, heading toward the open plan kitchen, but she's too entranced by the view to answer me.

Taking two bottles of water from the fridge, I watch as she runs a hand along the back of my dark leather couches, taking in the room.

"What's down there?" she asks, pointing down the hall.

"Bedrooms and the bathrooms."

"And that way?" She points to the opposite side of the apartment where another hallway is.

"My office and home gym."

"Oooh fancy," she mocks, kicking off her shoes, stumbling slightly as she walks towards me.

"I'll take a tequila slammer, please, action man." She giggles.

"I was thinking a water or a tea," I deadpan.

"Sorry, Daddy, didn't realize I wasn't allowed to drink," she mocks.

I don't miss the way my dick twitches when she calls me daddy, but now is not the time to unpack that.

"You will thank me in the morning if you take the water," I say, handing her a cold bottle.

"I'd be thanking you a whole lot more if you gave me a tequila and a screaming orgasm," she replies, slightly slurring while leaning over the island, causing her breasts to push together creating a cleavage I would very much like to bury my face in. But I will be a gentleman. I'm not sleeping with her when she's this intoxicated, no matter how badly I want her.

"I will happily treat you to all the orgasms you want... after the water and some sleep. I circle round the kitchen island and come toe to toe with her. She reaches out to grab my shirt and pulls me towards her.

"Come on," she slurs. "I'll suck your dick again." She fumbles at my buttons. I place my hands over hers, stalling her.

"Tell me what's going on in that head of yours, sweetheart." Anxiety is brewing in my stomach. I know something is wrong.

"Are you telling me you don't wanna fuck me?" She stares at me with no emotion on her face.

This isn't my Ria.

"I very much want to fuck you, more than you know, but not like this, Ri. You're drunk and that's not how I want our first time to be. You need to sleep it off." I stroke her cheek, but she yanks my wrist away before storming away.

"Why does everyone think they have a right to tell me what to fucking do, or what I need? I'm a grown woman. I can do what the hell I want, when I want," she rages, as she collapses onto my count, cradling her head in her lap.

I walk over and sit beside her, placing a light hand to her lower back. "Ri... Who's upset you? Tell me. Let me help." My chest constricts at the idea of her hurting like this. She lets out an exhale, swiping her hair away from her face and wiping her eyes. Tears I didn't realize were falling stain her cheeks. She looks so fragile and broken.

She closes her eyes as if it's too painful to look at me while she speaks. "It was Alex. One of his asshole work buddies was at the party tonight an clearly didn't know we are getting divorced, as he called him to tell him that his 'wife' was all over some guy."

My stomach sinks, guilt hitting me. Not because what we did was wrong, but for Ria.

"He texted me to call him immediately, made it sound like the girls were sick or something, but when he answered he just went off at me, told me to act like a mother and not a slut, that I was an embarrassment and to hurry up and get this life crisis I am having over with and come home where I belong. He said I am still his wife and I should behave like it." I can hear the disgust in her voice and feel her body tremble, visibly angry.

"That piece of shit I'm gonna fucking rip him apart," I spit. I wrap my arm around her and press my lips to her temple, hoping my touch will comfort her.

"He's not worth it, but I am so angry. He's never going to let me go, never going to let me live my life. I spent so long being the good wife and doing as I was told, but tonight I just thought no, screw him. I'm not listening. I wanted to block out the noise. Forget his words and do what I wanted to do, not what I was told to do. So I had those shots and just wanted to get lost in it... to get lost in you." She sniffs back her emotions, and I just want to fix everything for her. Take away all her pain.

"Ri, sweetheart, you should've told me."

"Why?" she asks. "So you can pity me. Poor Ria. Can't get her life together. Poor Ria, too weak to take care of herself."

"Stop that, stop that shit. You are the strongest woman I know. Don't you dare talk about yourself like that." It comes out angrier than I intend, but it cuts me deep hearing her talk about herself like that.

"Oh, my God and then I come here and expect you to have sex with me." She laughs manically. "I really am an embarrassment. I need to go" She goes to get up from the couch and I pull her back, pressing our foreheads together.

"Listen to me," I demand. "I'm not letting you run. You have no idea how much I want you, all of you, every fucking inch of you in my bed right now, but this isn't how I want it to be. You deserve more than a drunk fuck and I wanna know that, when it happens, it's happening because you want it, and not to get back at your shit bag ex. Because once I have you Ri, I know I'm not gonna be able to let you go."

I see my words register, but her eyes still look haunted. "Jack," my name barely a whisper from her lips. "I'm sorry. I just—" Her words break into a gut-wrenching sob.

I hold her so tightly I think I might squeeze the air from her. "I know, baby. I'm sorry too."

We stay like that for what feels like a lifetime as she draws circles on my chest with her index finger and I nuzzle my nose into her hair.

"Am I hard to love?" she whispers eventually.

Her words hurt my heart. "No, sweetheart, of course you're not. You just chose the wrong person to love you."

"I really want to be happy, but every time I start to feel it, something inside me tells me that I don't deserve it, so I panic and..." Another sob escapes her lips.

"Ri, you deserve all the happiness in this world. You just got to believe that and let people in... let me in."

"I'm scared to lose you if I let you in fully. I don't think I'd ever recover if I lost you," she sniffs.

Her confession hits me square in the chest. Knowing that she may feel just as deeply for me as I do for her.

"Sweetheart, you are well and truly buried in my heart to ever lose me. You deserve someone who isn't okay with losing you, someone who will love you the way you deserve to be loved, and you won't have to question it or fight for it."

Her breathing slows, her body feeling heavier against my chest. I tighten my hold on her, letting her know I've got her.

"And if you let me, I want to be the one to show you." It's barely a whisper and I don't know if she heard me, but when she doesn't speak, I lift my head ever so slightly to find her sleeping peacefully in my arms.

Chapter Twenty-Five

Ria

I have done just about everything I can to keep my mind busy and not think about last night—how I completely embarrassed myself in front of Jack. Threw myself at him and then acted like I did when he rejected me.

Don't be dramatic, Ria, he didn't reject you.

I get it, even respect him for it. I was intoxicated and he didn't want to take advantage, but now I fear I have not only ruined any chance for us, but our friendship too. I've texted him to apologize but had no response. He was sleeping when I snuck out of his apartment this morning. I left a note promising I wasn't running, but that I needed to get home and clear my head.

Anne and Steve still have the girls this weekend and even though I'm off, and they told me to relax. *What's relaxing?* I've been batch cooking, cleaning, and randomly started labeling my spice jars, because what else does one do when they're low-key freaking out about life?

After a long shower, I'm in my comfiest clothes, "Luke Coombs" is singing to me over the speaker system and I am on the sofa, eyeballing the Chinese takeout menu just when there is a knock at the door.

I make my way there and open it to find Jack dressed in gray sweatpants and a white t-shirt that shows his biceps off to perfection. He's got a backward cap and is holding a bag of takeout in one hand and scrabble in the other.

Fuck me sideways. Why does the universe hate me?

"Jack, you're here?"

He smiles, and my heart jumps at the sight.

"I am. I bought Chinese food and Scrabble. Hope you're ready to lose a game or two."

I grin, nodding as he pushes past me like he's comfortable enough to do that. Maybe I didn't make that much of an idiot out of myself last night after all.

I follow him into the kitchen, watching as he unloads the food while he tells me he ordered one of everything, which is a lot.

"Jack, about last night. I'm sor—"

"Please don't apologize, Ri. You had a lot to deal with."

"Yeah, I guess you're right." His finger lifts my chin so I'm forced to face him.

"Is that all that's on your mind?"

I blink. "What you said last night, about wanting to be there for me, be the one to show me how I should be treated... Did you mean it? Because I think I'd like that..." I say quietly.

"I meant every word Ri."

Two games of Scrabble in and a whole lot of Chinese food and wine later, I'm losing. We are sat on a blanket on the floor in front of the couch, music echoes around us, as we laugh and try to score points with the most ridiculous words. Jack looks so happy, so at ease as he smiles at me and my chest expands, watching him, the soft glow of the lamps making him look even more handsome.

I know I wanted to take things slow, but something has shifted. He allows me to be me. I don't feel nervous around him. I'm not scared to say how I feel or what I want, and what I want is him.

It's Jack's turn and I watch as he meticulously places down the letters K-I-S-S. As soon as the word registers, my eyes snap to his and track him, licking his lips. Suddenly, the game of Scrabble feels like the last thing I want to be doing.

There's a shift between us. It's like all my senses become heightened. The taste of red wine in my mouth becomes fruiter, my heart thumping in my ears and the heat between my legs almost burns. My hands tingle, itching to touch him. But I can't, not after last night. My pride won't let me. If he wants me, he needs to make the move.

"Ri," he says in a throaty gasp.

"Yeah," I reply, my voice barely a whisper.

He moves closer and we are almost nose to nose. Eyes closed, I can feel his breath on my lips.

"Well, what do you say, sweetheart? Do I get a kiss?"

I nod; it's all I can manage. I want this, I want him, on me, in me. I want all of him. We've fought this long enough.

"Use your words, Ri."

The air crackles between us and my mind, body and soul knows this is going to be the time we finally cross that line and go all the way. I've craved this for too long.

I open my eyes to find his biceps bulging as he removes his hat and tugs his t-shirt over his head, throwing it onto the couch. I bite my tongue to stop the whimper I'm desperate to release at the sight of his tanned body and six-pack.

I sink my teeth into my lower lip and shrug my cardigan off, revealing my zipped yoga bra. His eyes scan my face, my lips, my breasts, my stomach and back up again, and the strain in his sweats does not go unnoticed. He wants this just as much as me and I'd be lying if seeing him like this isn't the biggest confidence boost. He lifts me onto his lap, so I'm straddling him.

I stroke my hands through his messy hair and I take a moment to study his face. I stare into his piercing blue eyes and trace my finger along his strong jawline, enjoying the way his stubble feels against my skin. I want to remember this moment; commit the way he's looking at me right now to memory. My words are breathless as I say, "I want you, Jack…"

Chapter Twenty-Six

Jack

"I want you, Jack."

Her words are my undoing and my restraint snaps. The years of fighting the need to be with her. My hands fist into her hair as I crash our lips together.

We are panting between kisses as she devours me. I need to slow this down; I want to enjoy every inch of Ria. I break the kiss, reaching up and taking the zipper on her bra between my thumb and pointer finger. Our breathing uneven, as we both watch the agonizingly slow pace I pull it down, her breasts bursting out. Our eyes lock, and I know there's no going back now. She's mine.

"Fuck, baby, you are perfect." My voice is husky, full of want. I tilt her back slightly, taking one of her nipples into my mouth and sucking, earning a hiss of pleasure from her as she grinds herself against my hard length, spurring me on. I move my attention to her other nipple and the sounds she makes causes my dick to strain harder against my sweatpants.

Taking her mouth again, I slide my tongue between her full lips and it's the kiss that could speak a thousand words. We both know what's going to happen next, and it only intensifies the moment.

"I need you," I tell her honestly.

"I need you, need your mouth on me," she pants, her chest heaving.

I want her to know she's in control, that she can tell me what she wants and how she wants it. She's spent too many years doing as she's told and pleasing others. As much as this moment is about us, taking our relationship to the next level, it's also about her.

I lay her down on her back on the blankets and cushions we've had on the floor. Rising, I crawl over her and trail kisses down her neck, watching as goosebumps scatter over her skin. My mouth reaches her stomach, and she tries to cover herself with her hands.

"What's wrong?" I ask, halting my movement.

She worries her bottom lip, avoiding my eyes. "I... erm... I don't like my stomach... having the girls has made it look different and I just—"

I cut her off. "Look at me." She does. "Ri, you are perfect, every part of you. Don't hide from me." She gives a little nod. I hook my fingers into the waistband of her yoga shorts, pulling them over the curve of her hips and down her toned legs. I press open mouth kisses along her stomach and trail down her body, rubbing my nose against her clit, inhaling her intoxicating scent, groaning in pleasure as I lick through her wet folds, making her back arch as she lets out the sexist little moan.

I continue licking her slowly and working my way up till I clamp down on her clit and suck. She starts to writhe beneath me. Nothing tastes sweeter than Ria. I could do this all night long if she let me.

"Don't stop, don't stop," she pants. I slide two fingers inside her, pumping slow deep thrusts and curve my fingers round to find that sweet spot.

My free hand trails up to her stomach, caressing the skin she was so conscious about, but she's truly beautiful to me in every way. I keep moving my fingers but replace my tongue with my thumb so I can watch her. A rush of color flushes her cheeks and chest just as her body starts shuddering.,

"I'm coming. Oh God..." I don't stop. I want to wring every ounce of pleasure out of her perfect body because seeing Ria come undone for me will never get old.

"You look so beautiful like this," I murmur, slowing the pace as her body softens.

"One second, sweetheart. I'm not done with you yet," I tell her as I ease my fingers out of her, loving how her arousal spills from her already. I stand, stripping out of my sweatpants and pulling my wallet from the pocket.

I find the condom and hold the foil packet up between my fingers. She bites down on her lower lip and nods. She moves to kneel and curves her fingers into the band of my boxers, her touch searing into my skin. She eases them down in one smooth motion, my hard cock springing free, causing her breath to hitch.

I rip open the foil packet and roll the condom over my hard length.

We both lay back down, my throbbing cock begging for some attention.

I lay over her, nestling myself between the apex of her thighs, bracing my forearms on either side of her and cradling her face, lightly stroking her flushed cheeks as she looks at me, her eyes searching for something.

"Jack..." vulnerability shines in her eyes and it hits me. She's scared. She needs to know I won't hurt her, not physically, but emotionally. She needs reassurance that I won't break her.

"I won't hurt you, Ri...I promise."

The very idea is unfathomable to me. Looking at her now I can't believe someone thought she wasn't enough, because this beautiful, selfless woman is more than enough, she's it for me.

"I'll never hurt you" I brush my nose against hers, pressing my forehead to hers, just taking a moment before everything changes between us.

I know in this very moment I'd give her everything, anything she wanted, it's hers. Her body relaxes and softens beneath me. She widens her hips, arching in invitation and I line up, ready to push in.

Her eyes drift closed, but I need to see her.

"Baby, look at me."

She does. I press my chest to hers, feeling her heartbeat as erratically as mine in anticipation of what's to come. The line we both know we are about to cross.

I push against her entrance, sliding in slowly, and fuck, does she feel incredible. She feels like heaven. She gasps, never breaking eye contact with me, and I groan at the sensation of our bodies becoming one. She looks up at me, lust swirling in her ocean-blue eyes.

I start with slow deep thrusts and I look at her beneath me. The look that passes between us, is one that will change me. I've never had a woman look at me the way she is and I know damn sure I've never looked at a woman the way I'm looking at her. Like she's my everything.

Her arms wrap around my shoulders, her leg tightening around my waist, her body surrounding me like warm velvet, and I'm lost, almost drowning in her scent and the feel of her.

She weaves her fingers in my hair and pulls me down to kiss her. I thrust, slow and deep, taking my time with her. The music that is playing in the background fades. All I can hear is the sound of our bodies becoming one and Ria's sexy little moans. Her body trembles in that way I know means she is close, and thank fuck, because I'm right there with her.

"Fuck, baby, you feel so good." Her walls tighten around me and I am torn between wanting to feel her come apart and not wanting this to end because I haven't had enough of her. But when it comes to Ria, it will never feel enough. I will forever want more with her. Her body stiffens and then shudders as she finds her release and it's my undoing. I crash my lips to hers, swallowing our moans as my release rips through me. I swear I blackout for a second, as wave after wave of pleasure hits.

I collapse on top of her and we are a breathless, sweaty, tangled mess.

"That was…" I try to say, trying to catch my breath.

"Incredible," she sighs.

After tonight, I know for certain I want to dive all the way in with Maria Kennedy. I don't care how complicated it gets; I need her.

Chapter Twenty-Seven

Ria

I spent the entire night in Jack's arms. He gave me three more earth-shattering orgasms. Once again on the living room floor and then he carried me upstairs to the bedroom, where he kissed and touched every part of my body. I have never been with a man who truly worshipped me and made me feel like I was the source of his oxygen—that if he didn't have me, he might die.

There's no doubt Jack and I have a connection that's rare to find in this life. Emotions fleet in and out of my mind as I think about us. About him. I want to be his, to belong to him. But I know I need to be free of Alex's clutches fully first, because that's what Jack deserves. He deserves all of me, not just the broken parts and the little slices I can give him at the moment. I just pray he is willing to wait for me. I'm not naïve. Jack could have any woman he wanted. He's smart, charismatic, generous, has a body that looks like it's been carved by the Greek gods, and a mouth that should come with a warning. Because one taste of Jack and you won't ever recover.

I lay with my arm draped over his chest and our legs tangled together in the sheets. His breathing is slow and watching his chest rise and fall helps my own breathing pattern to even out. I am full of so many thoughts and worries, but I need to learn to enjoy the present and stop worrying about the future.

My room fills with the morning light peeking through the curtains that we didn't fully close. I trace a finger over his tattoos. They run down his left arm, across his chest and down his torso. I focus on his bicep that has a military map on it and notice a scar, unable to stop myself edging my middle finger over it, feeling the slightly raised skin.

Jack moves and begins to wake next to me. He stretches his arms above his head, rubbing his eyes, before he looks down at me with a look of confusion for the briefest of moments before breaking into a panty-melting smile when he realizes where he is.

"Morning, sweetheart," he says, his voice laced with sleep.

"Good morning, you." I smile back.

He looks down at my finger where I am still tracing over his scar.

"How did you get this?" I ask softly. He tenses and swallows hard, making me worry I have overstepped.

"I, err, got shot," he mumbles.

I lift my head quickly. "You got shot?" I gasp.

How did I not know he got shot?

"Hey, hey," he reassures me. "It was just a graze."

"That feels more than a graze."

His hold on me tightens, my face pressed against his chest so hard I can feel his heart hammering.

"Do you want to talk about it?" I ask cautiously, worried I've unlocked a memory he's fought hard to bury. I know all too well how that feels. He stares at the ceiling for a few beats before letting out a slow breath.

"It was our last tour of Afghanistan. We were out on a patrol. Noah was in command and we cleared the area. It was safe. There was no way of knowing we would be ambushed. They opened fire on us and a bullet grazed my arm, but..."

He stops, clearing his throat and closing his eyes. I nuzzle into him, trying to show I'm here for him.

"We called for back-up. It was the five of us. Harry, Brad and I took on one side and Noah and Scotty the other, but Scotty got shot and..." His eyes glaze over as if he is replaying the event in his mind.

"Jack, I'm so sorry you had to go through that." My voice cracks. I can't begin to imagine the things he's witnessed and the stuff he's had to do to survive. My chest tightens at the thought of him and Noah being in that situation.

"It's part of the job. We know not everyone comes back, but it always hits harder when it's someone who is like a brother to you," he replies as he absentmindedly brushes the back of his knuckles up and down my back, causing me to melt into his touch.

"Noah dragged Scotty to the building to try to bring him back, while the rest of us stayed out to give them cover until back up came, but it was too late for Scotty. After that I couldn't face another tour, so Harry, Brad, and me started to make plans to leave and move to Miami. We tried to get Noah to come, but you know him..."

"Stubborn as a mule," I agree.

"Yeah." He laughs, but it's empty.

"I think you are pretty incredible, Jack Lawson. You really are a real life action man."

Chapter Twenty-Eight

Ria

"Okay, sweetie, hold the board up." Fighting the tears that threaten to form, I take another photo. My baby girl has her first day of Pre-K and I've gone all Pinterest mom with the first day of Pre-K board and a cute outfit.

"Cheese." Lexi beams, holding up her board, looking every bit the cheeky little girl she is. The bow I ordered is almost the size of her head, but hey, if you can't wear a bow as big as your head when you are four, when can you?

"Okay, a couple more photos and we can go inside and make pancakes," I say, sensing she's reaching her limit.

I turn, hearing a car pull into my driveway and beam when I notice who it belongs to. My friends have never missed an important moment in mine or my girls' lives and it looks like today is no different.

"Where's our big Pre-k girl?" Ali calls as she steps out in a little pink sundress, her blonde hair blowing in the gentle breeze.

"Yeah, where is she?" Gabby calls as she walks up the path to my porch. Holding a pink gift bag, she's dressed in a dark blue maxi dress and her hair is in a sleek ponytail. It's a beautiful warm September day even at 8 am.

"Auntie Ali, Auntie Gabby, look at my bow." Lexi smiles, twirling round, showing off her outfit.

"Thank you for coming." I hug Ali, while Gabby has already headed over to Elle, who has been sitting patiently in her stroller on the porch.

"Babe, our girl is starting Pre-K. We wouldn't miss waving her off. This is a big day."

I am so grateful for these girls. "Dare I ask if he who shall not be named has been in touch?"

I know she means Alex, and I shake my head. He knew today was her first day and there have been no calls or texts, nothing to wish her good luck.

"Well, she's got us and—" Her words are cut short by Lexi screeching "Jack," at the top of her lungs and running past us to the front lawn.

In synchronization, the three of us whip our heads around to see a suit-clad Jack striding toward the house, balloons and a gift bag in one hand and a box of what looks like donuts from Lexi's favorite bakery in the other.

"Ria, sweetie, close your mouth, you're drooling," Gabby whisper-hisses out the side of her. Noticing the way the tailored suit clings to his muscles has me feeling like I've lost the ability to swallow.

"We'll give you a minute," Gabby says, tugging Ali towards the front door, taking Elle's stroller with her.

"Will we? I wanna watch her—" Ali starts.

"Ssshhh, inside you," Gabby instructs, and then they vanish.

Jack bends down, giving Lexi a hug and hands her the balloons and gift bag. My heart flutters and tears prick my eyes.

He remembered.

"Mommy, look, Jack got me a present." Lexi beams. "Auntie Ali, Auntie Gabby, look," she shouts, running past me to follow them into the house.

Never has a man made my heart and panties melt at the same time. I want to jump on him, wrap my legs around him and show him how grateful I am, but I remember it's 8 am on a Monday and Doris, next door, is out watering her pansies and doesn't need the early morning show.

"You remembered?" I say softly.

"Of course I remembered. This is a big day, and I wasn't going to miss it. She should have her favorite donuts with sprinkles today."

"You spoil her." I chuckle.

"She's worth spoiling... all of you are," he replies, his tone low.

My cheeks heat. *God, this man.*

He gives me a soft kiss that sends tingles right to my toes.

"Thank you for showing up." My voice sounds a little shaky. "This means a lot to her, to... to me."

"Always, Ri."

My heart swoons. He is the biggest plot twist in my life, but they say that some of the best things in life are the things that happen unexpectedly, and God, does that feel true.

I bite down on my lower lip, anxious to ask him my next question, not because I think he would say no, but because this is a big step. "It's Elle's birthday next weekend. Would you like to come? I'm having a little get together here Saturday afternoon. Just a few friends and family, Brad and Harry are welcome to come too. Tell Harry the pocket rocket will be there."

"Is your crazy friend from ballet coming? I might have to decline the offer for my safety if she is." He shivers, clearly relieving the ballet class in his head.

"She is, but I'll protect you, action man, don't worry," I promise. "So, would you like to come?"

"Of course I'll be there."

And just like that, I think I fall for Jack just a little bit more.

Chapter Twenty-Nine

Ria

"Left a bit... no, right... no, a bit higher," I shout at Ali and Gabby, who are standing on my kitchen bar stools, trying to hang the bunting on the fence in the backyard.

"Girl, I love you, but I am this close to choking you out with this damn bunting," Ali grumbles.

"Sorry, sorry, I just need it to be perfect," I sigh.

"Aaannd, it's perfect," Gabby announces as she climbs off the stool.

It's not, but I can't make them do it again.

Ali appears next to me. "Ri, it's perfect. You've done an amazing job."

I look around the backyard and it does look pretty good. I've set up a blanket area for the babies, hired a bouncy house, and made a table where the kids can do some crafts. This party is my first big celebration as a single mom. I just want it to be perfect for her.

"Thanks, I just feel on edge. Jack's coming and so are Alex's parents and God only knows if my mom will show and I don't know if I made enough food and what if the bouncy house deflates with the kids in it and what if someone gets sick? Maybe I should have done a gluten-free cakes, and wha—"

"Ri, you're spiraling, honey. Take a breath." Ali mimes a deep breath in and out, waiting until I do the same.

"The bouncy house will be fine, we have enough food to feed a small army, and thank fuck you didn't get a gluten-free cakes, because those things taste like shit."

I nod because I know she's right.

"I know you're nervous, but the party will be great. We've got you, girl."

I give her a small smile, grateful for my girls.

We finished setting up the backyard. Thankfully, the summer doesn't seem to have left the outskirts of New York just yet. Everything is pink and Minnie Mouse themed. I know Elle won't remember this, but I will, and I just want it to be a day filled with love.

The sound of tires crunching tell me that a car is pulling up on my driveway and Nugget starts barking. I wince, knowing Elle is taking her nap and I'm not ready for her to wake just yet.

"Jaaaaccckkk," Lexi squeal from inside the house. I head back indoors, breaking into a slight jog to open the front door, but Lexi is beating me to it.

She's dressed in a pink and white Minnie Mouse dress with matching ears and pink, glittery heels. Before I can stop her and grab Nugget, she flings the door open and runs down the porch steps towards Jack's car.

Jack, Harry and Brad exit his black Audi, and holy shit… they are a sea of muscles, Ray-Ban sunglasses, and t-shirts that hug in all the right places and I think I may have to physically lift my jaw off the floor.

Lexi launches herself at Jack and he picks her up, his bicep muscles flexing as he swings her round, throwing her up into the air, catching her so effortlessly. Her giggles and squeals fill the air, and he brings her in for a hug and my heart flutters.

"Hello, princess. Are you excited for the party?"

"Uh huh. Did you bring me a present?"

"Of course I did," he says as he rubs his nose against hers. If I wasn't already melting into a puddle, that right there did it.

Brad and Harry say hi to Lexi as Jack sets her on her feet and heads to the trunk of the car, taking out a big pink gift bag. Her big blue eyes go wide with excitement. He bends down, and she takes the bag, leaning in and kissing him on his cheek.

My heart is now ready to burst. I can tell how much that meant to Jack by the big smile on his face and the way he's looking at her. She turns, clutching her bag with her little hands, running back towards the house as Jack reaches back into the trunk of the car pulling out a large box.

"Mommy, Jack got me a present." She doesn't stop, running into the house. I swear that girl never stops running.

"What do we say to Jack?" I call.

"Thank yooouuuuu," she shouts, her voice fading as she heads to the backyard, no doubt showing Ali and Gabby her present. I turn back around to see the three men walking towards me. Brad and Harry greet me first and I direct them towards the backyard.

Then it's just us. I haven't seen him all week and those familiar flutters in my stomach and tingles in my fingers work their way into my body and I can't help but look at him and smile.

He takes a step towards me and sets the gift down on the porch, removing his sunglasses before hooking them into the collar of his shirt. Cupping my face, he presses his lips to mine, and I melt into his touch.

Breaking our kiss, he licks his lips and doesn't take his eyes off mine. "Hey, sweetheart. I've missed you."

And suddenly everything I was worrying about felt so insignificant. He's here, he showed up, he came, and that was all I needed.

"You didn't need to get them gifts. You being here is enough. What did you buy her?" I gesture to the box that has Elle's name on it, which is almost as big as me.

"Not a chance I was turning up at my baby girl's birthday party and not getting her a gift."

My baby girl. My heart flutters at the idea of her, of us being his.

"I asked the assistant to help me pick something for a one-year-girl who loved Minnie Mouse, so now Elle is the proud owner of her very own Minnie Mouse Club House."

My mouth falls open. "A what? You got her a playhouse?"

"Yeah." He shrugs like it is no big deal.

"Jack, those things are like hundreds of dollars. That's too much, she—" He presses his index finger to my lips to stop my talking and I still.

"It's not too much, and I'd buy her five of them if it made her smile."

I peak my tongue out and lick the pad of his finger, not sure how else to react to his generosity.

Heat flashing in his eyes. "Fuck," he groans under his breath before he adjusts himself in his pants and swipes a hand through his hair.

"I've got plans for that tongue later, sweetheart," he whispers against the shell of my ear.

"Can't wait," I whisper back, excitement coursing through me.

We head to the backyard, and I see Gabby and Brad sitting with Lexi, helping her build her princess castle Jack brought her. God, he really has spoiled them. Brad furrows his brow as he reads the instructions, as Gabby helps Lexi click together what looks like the towers of the castle.

I glance over to find Harry and Ali blowing up pink and white balloons at the end of the yard. I can't quite hear what they are saying, but Harry deflates the balloon he was blowing up in Ali's face and she smacks him with her inflated balloon. It bursts with a loud bang, making everyone jump.

"That's his fault," she shouts, pointing at Harry and I roll my eyes.

I'm not getting involved.

"Guess who's here?" I turn to find Alex's parents standing by my back gate.

"Grandma, Grandpa," Lexi squeals, heading towards them, jumping into Steve's waiting arms.

"Thank you for coming" I greet them both with a hug, relaxing a little when I feel their familiar warmth wrap around me. They are the best people I know. This will be fine.

I let out a breath. "Steve, Anne, this is my friend, Jack," I say, anxiously wringing my hands together as they meet Jack, who is hovering close behind me.

"It's lovely to meet you, Jack." Anne smiles, before giving him a hug. It seems to take Jack by surprise, but he returns the hug.

"It's lovely to meet you both," he says, extending a hand to Steve, who takes it with a friendly grip.

"Pleasure to meet you too, Jack. Any friend of Ria's is a friend of ours."

"Jack is really fun, Grandpa. He plays Barbies with me, and does ballet and makes pancakes, and he sleepover on our couch," Lexi rambles.

Oh, dear God.

An awkward silence falls over us and I have never been more grateful for Jack when he says, "Can I get anyone a drink?"

"That would be lovely, dear. Thank you. I'll take an iced tea, please. Steve will take one too."

Jack nods, giving my shoulder a squeeze before heading to the house.

"Well, Jack sounds like a good man," Steve says. I give him a small smile and a nod, and he does the same. And that right there means everything to me. To have the approval, I didn't realize I so desperately needed.

Chapter Thirty

Ria

The rest of the guests arrive, and the party is a success. The kids blew bubbles, bounced till they were soaked in sweat, and ate cake till they were ready to puke. Elle was blessed with too many gifts to count. Watching Jack avoid Margot all afternoon was my favorite part of the day. He physically recoiled when she brushed past him and asked him if he would be joining next week's class.

"I've got back-to-back meetings I'm afraid, maybe another time," I hear him say before he mouths "help me," and I have to stifle a laugh.

We sang happy birthday with everyone around Elle as she sat in her highchair, decked out with a pink *"I am one"* banner and wearing a party crown. She clapped along as we sang. As Lexi and I helped her blow out her candle, I couldn't help but make a wish of my very own.

Happiness with Jack.

The party guests started to leave one by one, all thanking me for a great party, and I can't help but feel proud of what I have achieved despite my own mom not turning up. I shove those feelings to the back of my head. It was stupid of me to hope she would come. She hasn't seen us since I left Alex, she's likely too busy with her latest lover boy and admitting she needed to go to her granddaughter's birthday party would have revealed the lie she had likely told him: that she was young and carefree with no family. That's what she always told them. Once I had to tell a guy she was dating that I was her niece.

"Oh, my girl, you did a fantastic job," Anne says, pulling me in for one of her hugs. "Now tell me if I am overstepping here, but I like Jack and I know he likes you too. I don't want to make this weird for either of us, but I just want you to know that I think he's good for you and the girls. I saw how he was with you all today, and it warms my heart. I'm just sorry that..." Her voice breaks and tears form in her eyes.

"I am just sorry my son couldn't be the man you and the girls deserved and the man I hoped he would be. Steve and I tried, oh we tried, but he has always been a stubborn one and I'm sorry that we failed him... failed you all." She sniffs.

"Anne, you didn't fail him. You and Steve are the best people I know. Sometimes, no matter how hard we try, people will choose their own path in life, no matter how hard we try to steer them on the right one."

Nodding, she reaches for my face and strokes my cheek. "I know, my girl, and I don't like to be harsh about your mom, but you too are proof that you can grow up on a bad track but steer yourself on to a good one. I'm sorry your mom didn't show up today, but I'm proud of you," She smiles tenderly, her voice gentle and comforting.

"You are the daughter I never had, the daughter I hoped and prayed for but never blessed with. But now I see it's because God had other plans for me. You were meant for me, and I want you to know you will always be my daughter no matter who you are with, you will always have a place in our family and there will always be a seat at our table for you and whoever you choose to share your life with."

"I love you," I whisper, scared how much my voice will break if I say it any louder.

"I love you too, my girl."

Two hours, five trash bags and three bottles of wine later, the party is almost cleared up. Anne and Steve took the girls back to theirs, so Alex could spend some of Elle's birthday with her. That's the part that sucks when you divorce. Shared holidays, shared weeks. I don't get to tuck my baby in on her birthday; I have to share her. I don't want to. He doesn't deserve that privilege, but I have to be the bigger person, put my feelings aside and do what is best for the girls, and as long as he's responsible and doesn't cause them harm, I have to give him space in their life.

"I think that's the last of it." Jack says, turning into the kitchen, carrying a tray of glasses.

"Thanks, I'm nearly done here," I reply, placing the plates I've been washing on the drainer.

"Harry looks like is enjoying himself" I nod my head, gesturing to my backyard where I can see him jumping in the bouncy house whilst Brad, Ali, and Gabby sit around my fire pit, drinking wine.

"I know. I'm going to need the number of the company you hired for his birthday."

He comes up behind me. Pressing his front to my back and reaching his arms around me, boxing me in. My hips press into the kitchen counter at the feel of his growing erection pressing against my ass. My head instinctively falls back on to his chest, tilting to the right and his warm mouth presses a kiss to my neck. My body tingles at his touch. This is what I've craved all day.

I moan in appreciation, and it only spurs him on. He begins to lick and suck on my neck, and my hips move on their own accord.

"Jack," I moan.

"Do you know how badly I've wanted to do this all day" he says in between kissing and licks.

My breathing quickens, my chest heaving as his hand disappears under my pink skater dress and grips my ass cheek. My legs part without hesitation. His strong fingers stroke my now wet pussy and my knees start to buckle as he inserts a finger inside me. I grip the edge of the sink to steady myself.

I don't care that one of our friends could come in and see us. I just need him, crave him. I have been on edge all day. I need a release. He groans, and it's the hottest sound. I grip the counter firmer as he inserts another finger and quickens the pace.

"Fuck, sweetheart, if I'd have known you were this ready for me I would've taken you upstairs hours ago."

"Let's go, now," I beg.

"Get that sweet ass upstairs now." His tone is low, full of want, as he eases his fingers out of me and smacks me on the ass. I've never moved so fast. Grabbing his hand and pulling him towards the stairs, he smacks my ass again and I will squeal with excitement, my body vibrating with anticipation.

As we take the stairs, there is a loud banging on my front door. We whip our heads round at the same time, and a figure fills the glass panel.

"Are you expecting anyone?" Jack asks.

"No, no one." I squeeze past him and head towards the door, opening it with a slight hesitation and stop dead in my tracks, staring at the older, blonder version of me.

"Mom?"

Chapter Thirty-One

Ria

"Surprise, baby. Give your momma a hug."

What the hell?

She flings her arms around me and it takes me a second to reciprocate. She smells of cheap perfume, cigarettes and booze. My mom's signature scent, reminding me of the worst parts of my life. I blow out a breath to stop the bile that's rising in my throat, as memories of my mom, drunk, random men, take over.

"What are you doing here?" I ask, stunned at the fact she's actually here. Late, in true Stella style, but she's here and I don't know what to feel first. *Confused, happy, upset, glad?*

"It's my grandbaby's birthday party. I wasn't goanna miss that now, was I?" she says in her southern accent. She's lived all over but never lost her twang.

"The party was this afternoon, Mom. It's 8 o'clock. Elle isn't even here. You should have called," I say, trying not to raise my voice.

"Oh... well, never mind. We were passing through anyway. Sid's taking me to New York for the weekend."

"Who the heck is Sid?" I fire back angrily, scrunching up my face.

"Oh, he's parking the car. He'll be in a minute."

I stand in the doorway, staring blankly at her. It's been nearly a year since I saw her, yet here she is, acting like everything is fine. Her bleached hair in need of a root touch up, her clothes are two sizes two small and her boob job, that she convinced some poor guy to pay for on full display. If it wasn't for the years of drinking and smoking, my mom was a stunning woman. But like everything in her life, booze, nicotine and men were her top priority. Consequences be damned.

"Aren't you going to let me come in properly? Offer me a beer?"

No, is my first thought. You missed it all, is my second, but something inside me softens slightly because I've never been able to say no to my mom.

"Sure, come in." I sigh, stepping aside.

"Well, hello, who is this gorgeous creature? Is this the upgrade?" She winks.

"Mom," I scold.

"What, I always told you, never downgrade, always upgrade, and your Alex was a catch, but I can see why you ditched him for this one," she says eyeing Jack up and down.

She reaches out her skinny arm, covered in bangles, and holds her hand out with her staple red nail polish like she expected him to kiss the back of her hand. "Stella Jones, it's a pleasure to meet ya,"

"It's nice to see you, Stella," he says, taking her hand and shaking it.

Looking at him like it's finally clicked that Jack spent most weekends at our house when we were teens. "I remember you; you hung around with my Noah back in high school. Damn, Maria, you did upgrade, girl." Leaning towards me, she whispers, "I bet he fucks damn good too." Clapping her hands together, she walks towards the kitchen. "I'll get us some beers."

I didn't need to say a word. Jack knew, he always knew. He wraps me in his arms, and I let out a shaky breath.

"I'm so sorry. My mom is, well, she's a lot."

"I remember, but I got you." His tone is reassuring. Knowing I have him in my corner will make this a little more bearable.

"Let's get this over with." I exhale, taking his hand and heading for the backyard where I can hear laughing.

Everyone is silent but my mother as we sit around the firepit. In true Stella style, she's talking about herself and not asking anyone else a damn thing. Sid, who we found out is called Simon, is a strange old guy, likely old enough to be her dad, but he screams money and midlife crisis. And I get the sense they haven't known each other very long or that their relationship will last past Monday. He's already fallen asleep in my lawn chair as my mom spins stories of her girls' weekend in Vegas.

"So, what are you going to do in New York?" Ali asks, thankfully ending Mom's story about how she and her girlfriend ended up on stage at the Magic Mike show.

"Bit of this, bit of that. Sid's gonna show me where he grew up, and he's booked us a penthouse." She grins and does a little wiggle, taking down the last of her beer. "I've never fucked in a penthouse, so I can't wait."

"Mom, seriously," I mutter under my breath, covering my face with my hands.

Why doesn't she have a filter?

"Oh, don't worry, honey, old Sid here can still get his disco stick up if you get my drift. A few pops of the blue pills and he can party all night long, can't you, baby?" she says, smacking him on the leg. He jolts awake and mumbles what I think is a "yeah baby."

I wince, looking at everyone's awkward stares at my mother.

"I bet you boys can make your disco sticks stay up all night long, am I right ladies?" she says staring at Gabby and Ali, who are too stunned to speak.

Dear God, kill me now.

"I need some air," I announce.

"But, baby, you're outside," my mom says, sounding confused.

I ignore her, heading for the house. Once inside, I stand in front of the sink, filling a glass of water, and gulp it down like I've just run a 10k. I can feel my chest tightening, an all too familiar sense of panic rising through my body.

Breathe, Ria, breathe, you're okay.

I take in a deep breath, feeling myself on the edge of a panic attack, something I haven't had for a long time. A mixture of hate, anger, and hurt swirling around my head. *How can she turn up and act like this? How can she not ask me how I am, how the girls are? How can she think it's okay to talk like that in front of my friends?*

Strong arms wrap around me from behind.

'Maria, baby, Momma's gotta make tracks. Sid wants to get to the Big Apple before midnight and he has to take his evening pill."

She stops in the doorway, a look of satisfaction on her face.

"Looks like I'm not gonna be the only one riding tonight. You have fun, my girl."

I can't help it, couldn't stop it if I wanted to. I feel it bubbling up inside me, like a pan at boiling point. Years of putting up with my mom's crap, years of feeling like an option and not a priority in her life, years of her skipping in and out of my life, and now my girl's life, putting men before me; it all breaks through the surface and I explode. Slamming the glass I was holding down with such force, it shatters into hundreds of tiny fragments, scattering across the floor, just like my heart. She's leaving me again.

"What the hell is wrong with you?" I bellow.

Her eyes widen, all the color draining from her face. I've never raised my voice to her, not once. But now I can't seem to care.

"Excuse me?" she asks, her tone low.

"How dare you show up at my daughter's birthday party and make it about *you*. You show up six hours late, no phone call, no text, with your new flavor of the week, and embarrass me in front of my friends."

I feel like I'm having an out-of-body experience. I'm watching myself finally say everything I have wanted to say to my mom for years. I can feel every limb trembling as I run my hands through my hair, tugging the strands, welcoming the burn of pain on my scalp. Squeezing my eyes closed and shaking my head, the words spill from me, my voice so loud it vibrates off the walls.

"In case you had forgotten, Mother, I've had one of the worst years of my life. I left my cheating asshole of a husband, and you haven't called, you haven't checked in. It's always about you. You only show up when you need a place to stay, money, or want to show off your new boyfriend. You—"

"How fucking dare you speak to me like that. I'm your mother. You will show me some respect." Her face contorts with rage like she is ready to lunge at me.

"Ha, *Mother*, that's a bit rich. You've never been a mother to me. You've always picked your boyfriends over me and Noah. Chose the bottle over us. Why the hell do you think he left us as soon as he turned eighteen? He wanted to get away from you!"

My body is shaking and I clench my fists so tight they go numb. "You've never been there for us, Mom, never. I really needed you this year. I called, I texted. I even wrote a fucking card telling you my new address and asking you to visit. But you didn't, and then you show up on my daughter's birthday like this," I say, gesturing at her state of her.

Hot tears prick my eyes, my chest tightening. A wave of panic cursing through me. *Am I really saying all this?*

"I can't have you in my life anymore, Mom. You've done it this time. I've forgiven you for so much. I forgave you for all the times you forgot to pick me up from school, the times you left me for days on end with nothing more than a fridge full of leftovers." I feel my voice breaking; I close my eyes, mustering up all the strength I have to say the next part. "And I forgave you for what you let that disgusting bastard do to me. I forgave you when I got sent to foster care, but I wish…"

I stop, feeling my breathing becoming erratic. It's making me dizzy. I take in a breath and release it shakily.

"God, I fucking wish you never got me back. I wish you left me in that foster home. I had no home with you. You ruined it."

The look my mother gives me is like a knife to the heart. There's no love, just disgust. Her lip curls up and she sneers.

"You selfish, ungrateful little bitch. I did the best I could. I might not have been a perfect mother, but at least I didn't walk out on you like your deadbeat father," she spits.

I sniff, wiping the tears I hadn't realized were free falling down my face. "I wish you had, Mom. It would have saved me so much hurt. I just wished you loved me as much as you loved getting your highs."

We stand there, an unsettling silence surrounding us as we stare at each other, knowing this is it. Unless she truly changes, I can't have my mom in my life anymore. She brings out the worst feelings in me and I've spent too long healing for her to ruin it all.

I say a silent prayer that this will be the moment, the turning point in our relationship, where she will take me in her arms and hold me and be the mom I have longed for.

But she doesn't. Instead, she turns and without a word she leaves, walking out of my life for what will probably be the last time. I hear her shout for Sid and my backyard gate slam, and that's it, she's gone.

I can't let myself fall apart, not yet. Everyone enters the kitchen and Jack gives them a nod, letting them know they should go. Once we're alone, I give in and I crumple to the floor, landing on the shards of broken glass that cut into my legs, but I welcome the pain. I let out the sobs I had been fighting to keep in. Jack sits, holding me as I let out what feels like a lifetime of pain. I haven't let myself cry like this, and finally, I give in and let all my bottled tears flow. Tears for the mother-daughter relationship I'll never have, tears for my failed marriage, and tears for the younger me who only wanted to feel loved and wanted as the man I am falling for holds me so tightly, giving me hope, that maybe, not everyone leaves.

Chapter Thirty-Two

Jack

I don't know how long we stay on the kitchen floor. Seeing Ria fall apart like this has to be the most gut-wrenching thing I've ever witnessed. Even the things I experienced out at war don't compare to the pain of watching someone you love fall apart when there is nothing you can do but just stand by them.

Her breathing starts to even out and her body relaxes a little in my arms. I press a kiss to her forehead and slowly rock her. "I'm here, sweetheart. Just tell me what I can do to make it better," I whisper.

"This, just do this." I have so many questions. But I don't want to push her. I knew her childhood was messed up but, I didn't know everything. The idea of some asshole hurting my girl breaks me in two. I want to find him and tear him limb from limb. I was fortunate enough to have two loving parents who doted on me. The idea of a parent walking out on their kids or mistreating them is unimaginable.

We sit in silence with only the hum of the refrigerator filling the room. I almost miss her words. She's so quiet.

"She let him touch me."

I stiffen and I knew she wouldn't have missed it. Blood runs cold through my body.

I clear my throat. "Who?" I ask, trying to keep my tone as calm as possible.

"Her boyfriend, Greg. He started dating my mom when you and Noah left for the Marines. It started with some comments, a grope of my ass and I told her. I told her he made me feel uncomfortable, that he would rub up against me when he walked past me, would 'accidentally' walk in on me in the bathroom. But she told me I was being stupid. Why would he do that when he had her? So I didn't say anything again."

She wipes the tears that haven't stopped flowing down her cheeks.

"I used to sleep with my desk pushed up against my door. In case he tried to come in."

I grit my teeth so hard I'm surprised my teeth don't crack. But I say nothing. I just let her open up. This is hard to hear, but it's harder for her to share.

"He stayed over most nights and one night my mom was at a party with some girlfriends, I came out of my room to get a drink and he was drunk in front of the TV, he..." She stops, her voice breaking, and she starts to shake.

"It's okay. I'm here, you're safe."

"He tried to force himself on me, and my mom came home and found him on top of me, trying to unfasten my jeans She dragged him off me and I ran to my neighbor's house and called the cops. I got taken into foster care and mom kicked Greg out, but it took months till she got me back."

"And that's why Noah took leave after basic training finished?"

"Yeah, he tried to get custody of me so I didn't have to live with her, but the judge ruled in her favor;, she proved she was capable of looking after me and Greg went to prison for a few years and then got let out for good behavior," she scoffs "but with the agreement that he went to a rehab for his drinking"

"Fuck," I growled, my fists clenching. How the fuck is that justice?

"Baby, I am so sorry, I'm so fucking sorry that happened to you." I tighten my hold on her, letting her know I'm here. I'm not going anywhere.

"In a weird way, I'm not sorry it happened. If it hadn't, I wouldn't have been sent to my therapy group and I wouldn't have met Ali and Gabby."

I pull her face to mine, looking her straight in the eyes so she understands me. "Nothing like that will ever happen to you again. No one will ever hurt you again, I promise."

She buries her face into my neck, her body begins to relax into me. Leaning my cheek against the top of her head, she sniffs, wetness coating my neck as the last of her tears fall.

"You keep saving me," she mumbles, as if she can't believe my promise.

"Because you are worth saving, Ri."

I stayed the night and slept with Ria in my arms. I felt that this was where I was meant to be, where I wanted to be.

I've only had one woman in my life who I would consider a girlfriend. But it was never love. I've always been too busy in the military or starting up our clubs, and a relationship has never been a priority for me. But finally, I am holding the only woman I have ever truly wanted, spending my free time building Minnie Mouse playhouses, taking ballet classes and shopping for diapers and I've never been happier.

Fuck, this is what I want.

I want this life; I want Ria; I want her girls and all the pink shit that comes with them. But I'm scared to tell her. Scared I'll frighten her and come on too strong. She's said she's scared to let me in. That she'll lose me, but she won't. I know she's it for me. I just need to prove that to her.

I know her divorce isn't finalized, and it's early days, but truthfully, I'd have made her mine when we were teens. I was just too scared to act on it then.

She rolls out of our embrace and onto her side. Her hair fanned out on the pillow and her skin glowing in the morning sun, showcasing the dusting of freckles on her nose. God, she's perfect. I feel my morning wood pressing against the sheets, but I need to let her sleep. Last night wrecked her emotionally and I want to do something for her.

I slip out of bed, careful not to wake her, put on my boxers and head downstairs. Nugget greets me at the bottom of the stairs, and I let him into the backyard. I decide on coffee and pancakes for breakfast and raid her cupboards and fridge for the ingredients. I find a packet of M&M's and chuckle. Lexi and Ria's favorite. I mix the ingredients and start on the pancakes as the coffee brews.

I'm pretty impressed with my culinary skills as I plate them up and spray some whipped cream on them along with a few M&M's sprinkled on top. I take a fork and have a quick taste test.

It looks like Lexi made them, but I know Ria will appreciate the effort. I hunt for a tray and as I turn to place the breakfast on it ready to take up, I am greeted with her leaning against the kitchen doorway, only wearing my black t-shirt from the day before. She's all tousled hair and toned, tanned legs, and fuck me, she is the definition of sex on legs.

"Mmmm, whipped cream, my favorite," she hums.

Chapter Thirty-Three

Ria

I stalk towards him, drinking him in. His toned, naked chest, the tattoos that run from his chest down one of his arms. I want to run my tongue along them. Last night was heavy. So many emotions to deal with, but all I want to do right now is get lost in Jack.

He sets the tray down and reaches for me, tugging me so I land against his chest.

"Morning, beautiful."

"Morning, you."

I go on to my tiptoes and press a kiss to his soft lips, tasting the remnants of pancakes and whipped cream.

"You made us breakfast?" I ask quizzically.

"I did, but suddenly I'm in the mood to eat something else."

"Oh, really? And what's that?" I reply, trying not to smile.

I yelp as he lifts me onto the kitchen island.

"You," he says with a hunger in his eyes I've never seen before.

I swallow and my breathing starts to quicken, heat forming between my thighs, the cool kitchen counter pressing against my bare ass.

"But I do want you to try these first?" He brings a forkful of pancake to my lips, and I open up my mouth as he presses the fork to my waiting tongue. I close my eyes and hum a moan of appreciation. The pancakes are warm and fluffy, and the cold cream has started to melt.

"Keep moaning like that, sweetheart, and I won't be able to control myself." I open my mouth, waiting for another bite, and when he gives me another bite, I moan louder this time. I love seeing the effect I have on him.

"I want a taste," he groans. I think he's about to reach for a forkful of pancake, but instead, he lifts the can of whipped cream and begins to shake it, his arm muscles flexing with every shake.

"Where to taste first?"

I gulp.

Holy shit.

He lifts my hand and sprays a small amount of cream on my finger, bringing it to his mouth, closing his eyes, and sucking it clean.

A gasp escapes me as my gaze fixates on his lips.

Next, he sprays some cream on my forearm and licks it off in one effortless movement. He tips my head to the side, exposing my neck and sprays the cream along it, before his hot tongue licks up toward my earlobe.

He groans in approval and I squirm on the kitchen counter. A lump of cream drops on to his t-shirt and I get the sense he did that deliberately.

"Oh, dear. It seems I've made a mess. We better clean that up. Arms up, sweetheart" and like the submissive I clearly am, I raise my arms with the enthusiasm of an athlete at a competition.

A low chuckle vibrates through his chest.

"Someone's eager," he says as he pulls it up over my head in one smooth sweep. He takes a moment to scan my body up and down. I'm naked, on my kitchen counter, exposed and vulnerable, yet I've never felt more confident in my life.

Next, he squirts the cream across my breasts and nipples, my head rolling in pleasure at the feel of his warm tongue on my puckered skin. He licks it from my left nipple, causing my head to fall back on a moan.

He takes his time, sucking and swirling his tongue over my now erect nipple. Goosebumps prickle at my skin with every swipe of his warm tongue. He repeats the movement on the other side.

"Oh. My. God," I pant.

He frees my nipple from his mouth and moves closer, using his thighs to part my legs further. He sinks to his knees and sprays the cream on the insides of my thighs. I suck in a breath in anticipation of where I hope his mouth might go. He does agonizingly slow strokes with his tongue up and down the inside of my thighs. I spread my legs wider and lean back on to my forearms, encouraging him to move higher, but he doesn't.

"Jack, please," I moan as a rush of moisture pools in between my legs.

"Please," I plead again, wriggling around on the kitchen counter, desperate for some friction.

"Hearing you beg is such a fucking turn on," he growls.

"Please, I need you," I beg, and with that, his tongue presses against my clit.

I lay back against the kitchen counter as he tugs me towards him, so my ass is hanging dangerously to the edge and he places my legs over his shoulders.

He leisurely licks me, eliciting just the right amount of pressure to make me want to beg for more but just as I open my mouth, he latches around my clit and sucks hard, making my back arch off the counter, I palm my breast for something to grip on to and it only intensifies this wave of pleasure I'm riding.

He growls into my sex as my hips start to grind against his face. He breaks away from my clit for the briefest moment and moans, "you taste so sweet baby" and then he's back on my clit.

He inserts a finger, and he hits that sweet spot, and it is my undoing. My orgasm hits me and I practically levitate off the kitchen counter. I am too lost in my orgasm to realize he's pulled his fingers out of me and pulls me to a seated position, crashing our lips together. I can taste my arousal on his tongue. It's sweet and warm and intoxicating.

"I need to be inside you. Have you got a condom?" he pants against my lips.

"I'm clean, I got tested and I'm on the pill." The words leave my mouth before I can register what I've said. He breaks the kiss and looks at me.

"Are you sure? I'm clean. I've always used condoms."

I nod. "I'm sure."

And his lips are back on mine. I want this with him—nothing between us.

"Let me take you upstairs," he rasps and goes to lift me.

"No," I beg. "Here, take me here." I am too lost in this moment, lost in him to move. I hook my fingers into his boxers and push them down, watching them fall to the floor, licking my lips as his hard length glistens with pre cum.

I run my fingers down his six-pack and back up again, tracing the lines of his abs with my index finger, moving along to trace the outline of his military tattoo. I can see him battling with his decision. Does he carry me upstairs or does he fuck me right here?

"Jack." I lock eyes with him.

"Please, fuck me." I'm surprised at my own bravery, but my words seem to be his undoing.

He grabs my hips as if he's lost control. Lining up against my entrance, he looks down at me, his gaze heated, and then he slams into me. I let out a scream, but not one of pain; it's one of utter pleasure. He's never been this rough with me, but God, if it's not the best thing I've ever experienced.

"You like that, baby?"

"Yes, don't stop," I rasp

"Hold on then, sweetheart."

I grip the counter as he continues his deep thrusts and I think my eyes do a full roll in my head. The pleasure is out of this world. I didn't know it could feel this way. His punishing strokes causing my orgasm to build again. I grip my breast and tug at my nipples, needing the friction.

"You're so tight, baby. Fuck, you feel incredible."

How does sex feel this good? I am almost at the peak of my pleasure when Jack quickens the pace and reaches down and lightly flicks my clit and it's like a button to detonate my orgasm. I thrash around and moan.

His name falls from my lips like a prayer as he throws his head back, gripping my hips so tightly he'll mark me. His hot cum fills me and the sensation has me feeling breathless and dizzy. I have never felt so calm and yet on fire all at the same time, and I know deep in my bones that he is the one for me. He falls forward, his head on my chest as we both ride the waves of pleasure that pulses between us.

His sweat-sheened face lays against my sticky breasts. I lift my arms, which have a delicious ache to them, my body utterly spent and run my hands through his hair as we breathe in a synchronized rhythm.

He slowly rises, our skin peeling apart as he slides out of me, the loss making me wince. He wraps his arms underneath me and pulls me to a seated position, pressing his lips to mine.

I match his actions and kiss him back like my ability to breathe relied on his kiss alone. Kissing Jack always has my toes curling and my body humming, but after this, having no barrier between us has shifted things between us. I want to tell him how I truly feel about him, but I am so scared to want him like I do, to be happy. But as much as I want to believe I deserve this, I'd earned this happiness, I can't ignore the little voice in my head that tells me I don't. Because to be loved by Jack would be everything.

He breaks our kiss, pressing his forehead to mine I grip the back of his neck, needing to be close to him as we both fight to steady our breathing.

"Ri, I... I can't." He swallows hard, obviously struggling to find his words. What is he trying to say? Panic rises in my throat, but before I can speak, I hear him.

"I can't just be your friend anymore. I want more. I want you. I need you. I want you to be mine." He kisses me again. A flutter explodes in my chest at his admission, which works its way down to my core.

"I know it's messy and complicated, but I want you anyway, no matter what. I know you're gonna tell yourself you shouldn't, but Ri, I can't pretend I'm okay with just being your friend anymore."

I wet my lips and swallow, my throat suddenly feeling dry as I whisper, "I want more too, but it's so—" He breaks my rambling with a kiss.

"Stop, we'll figure it all. I just need you to know that I'm yours. I'm all in and I'm not going anywhere. We'll take it slow, but, sweetheart, I can't go another day without calling you mine."

My heart is free falling as I process his words.

Mine.

No man has ever said words to me with such meaning. I might be a little broken but maybe there is some beauty in that. A beauty that he sees. Last night proved to me that in my darkest hour, he didn't leave me. I didn't run, and he stayed and that's all I've ever wanted.

"I'm yours."

Chapter Thirty-Four

Jack

She's mine. Having Ria officially as mine has filled a void in my life that I didn't know was there. We've fallen into a comfortable routine of spending time at hers with the girls and nights at mine after work on the weekends when they are with Alex and his parents. I know she wants to take it slow and wait till she's officially divorced, and I respect that, but I'd be lying if I said that didn't bother me. I want to shout from the rooftops that Ria Kennedy is mine, but Ria begged me to keep things professional at work and I begrudgingly agreed.

Business has been booming and there is talk of us opening up another club, but deciding on a location is proving difficult. Do we stay stateside or take a real risk and go overseas? We have some meetings with potential investors and in order to get them to agree we need to make sure everything is above board, so today we have all staff in for various training, including Ria.

I finish my coffee as I sit at my desk surrounded by paperwork, trying to get my head around these potential locations when I hear a little tap at my office door.

"Come in," I call.

The door opens full force and in comes a bouncing Lexi, a slightly stressed looking Ria and smiley Elle on her hip, chewing on her hands and drooling.

"Hello ladies." I smile, standing from my chair to walk round my desk and greet them.

"Hey, are you sure about this? It's not too much?" Ria asks, sounding hesitant.

"Firstly, no, it isn't. I told you I'd watch the girls whilst you did the training. I'm just sorry it's in the middle of the day, and secondly..." I press a gentle kiss to her lips. "Hi, sweetheart."

She lets out a breath. "Hi."

I reach out and take Elle from her. "Go, go get a coffee and relax. You've got twenty minutes, me and miss Elle here are going to read through some contracts and Harry is coming to color with Lexi, and he might have some M&M's," I say looking down at her and the grin on her face makes my heart skip a beat.

"Yesssss." She claps.

"Okay, okay, everything you need is in this bag," she tells me, handing me a bag the size of a suitcase.

"What the heck is in this? I packed less for a deployment to Afghanistan."

She laughs. "Trust me, you're gonna need it."

"Be good, girls." She blows them a kiss and heads for the door, and I watch her ass sway in her uniform.

"Right, who wants to have a snack?"

"Meeeee," Lexi squeals, shooting her arm in the air.

Harry shows up with enough art supplies for Lexi to fill an art studio and they make a picture on the floor.

"Harry, no, that bit is pink, this bit is blue," she scolds when Harry apparently gets it wrong.

"Sorry, Lex," he grumbles. "I thought it looked good blue."

"It doesn't," she says so matter-of-factly.

"Getting put in your place by a four-year-old, Haz... priceless," I laugh.

Elle has been bouncing on my lap and dribbling over paperwork and in between kisses on her head and cuddling her and her using every gadget on my desk as a teething ring. I think I am handling this babysitting thing. It's then I realize I don't just want to babysit, I want this to be my life. I want my days spent with them.

The office door opens, and Brad enters making a gagging sound. "Jeez, what is that? It smells like ass in here," he says, covering his nose.

I lift Elle's butt to my face and sniff. I gag. "Fuck," I mutter under my breath. "That smells so bad."

"Do you know how to change a diaper?" Harry asks.

"I've watched Ria do it loads of times. Get the bag." I point at Harry. He opens it and starts pulling out various things.

"Jesus, what the hell is in here? It's like *Mary Poppin's* bag," Harry says.

"Pass me that." Grabbing the diaper-changing mat, I lay it on my office desk.

"You're doing it on there?" Brad asks, his face dropping.

"Where else am I meant to do it?"

"I don't know, man, but not on the oak desk," he replies, his tone horrified.

Fuck, I'm sweating. I don't know what I'm doing here, but if this is going to be my life, I need to figure it out.

"Shall I go get Ria?" Brad asks looking a little green. "Shit, it smells so bad. What's she feeding her?"

"No, no, we can do this."

"WE?" they both shout, staring at me.

I lay Elle down on the changing mat, take off my suit jacket, and start rolling up the sleeves of my shirt.

"Right, Haz, you get me the wet wipes and a new diaper. Brad, you get the trash can ready."

"Roger," they say in unison like we are back in the Marines.

I unbutton Elle's onesie and peel back the yellow sticky tabs on the diaper like I've seen Ria do. I pull it down and I'm met with the most toxic smell that makes my eyes water.

"Jesus Christ," I mutter.

"I'm gonna puke," Harry says, dry heaving. "Why the fuck are there no windows in here?" he mumbles, looking round the room for a way to escape.

"Man, that's toxic. How did that come out of someone so tiny?" Brad asks, holding my suit jacket over his mouth and nose.

Elle starts to roll and the most feminine screech I've ever made leaves my throat as I reach for her, terrified she's going to get shit all over my contracts.

"I told you not to do it on the desk, Jacqueline," Brad laughs.

"Harry, wipes, now." I hold out a hand, waiting for the wipes, but when I look up and he's lying on my couch still dry heaving.

"God, you are useless. How the hell did you cope at war?"

"War didn't smell like that, brother. I've seen some things, but that, that smell could end a war. Just drop one of Elle's diapers into enemy territory. They will be waving the white flag in no time."

"Pull yourself together and get me the wipes." He gets up and takes one of Elle's spare onesies, tying it round his face like a mask, only exposing his eyes as hands me the wipes.

Elle gurgles and squeals, kicking her legs and trying to roll as I wipe her. "Baby girl, hold still, please." Christ, it's like trying to baptize a cat.

"Right, I need a clean diaper and some butt cream, or powder. I can't remember."

"What's the difference," Brad asks. "Why would you put powder on a baby's butt?"

"I don't know. Something about a rash?" I rub my forehead, feeling a tension headache forming.

"Let me Google it," Harrys says, pulling out his phone.

"Lexi, what does mommy use? , does she use powder or cream?" I ask her.

Why the heck I am asking a four-year-old for diaper changing advice? Desperation, clearly.

"Erm, both."

"What goes first, the cream or the powder?" Harry asks holding up both items.

"I don't fucking know," I whisper shout so Lexi can't hear me swearing.

God, I feel myself teetering on the edge, sweat rolling down my back.

"It like the egg and the chicken debate. Who came first ?" Harry laughs.

"The egg," Brad blurts out.

"The what?" I ask, confused as hell at this conversation.

"The egg came first," Brad says confidently.

"No, it was the chicken," Harry confirms.

"How did the chicken get there then... from the egg."

"So how did the chicken get there then, dumbass? Tell me that. Did it just fall out the sky?"

"Will you two zip it? I don't give a hoot who came first, the chicken, the egg or the damn duck. Just someone pass me something before she pees all over these contracts," I say through gritted teeth. I can feel myself unraveling. How is it this hard to change one diaper?

"Here, use this."

Harry passes me the butt cream, and I put it on and then go in with the powder.

"Oh, noooo," I mutter.

"What?" Dumb and Dumber mutter in unison.

"It's made a paste; she looks like a rotisserie chicken ready for the oven," I say in horror.

Why would Ria want to be with me or have me around her girls, if I can't even change a damn diaper?

"Jack, look, look at my flower," Lexi calls waving around a piece of paper.

"Great job, princess. I'll take a look in a sec," I say back, lowering my tone, muttering, "Jack's just having a crisis at the minute."

How the hell does Ria do this? She's Superwoman.

"Yeah, you are meant to use butt cream or powder, not both, Google says," Harry tells me, looking at his phone.

I glare up at him.

"Where the hell was that information three minutes ago, huh? Quick, hand me a wet wipe."

"I can't. You used them all cleaning up the baby shi—uhhh, poop."

I wipe my hands down my face in frustration, forgetting they are covered in butt cream and powder.

"Bro, you got a little something right there." Harry gestures to my cheek.

I slowly turn my head and stare at him dead in the eyes, giving him a murderous look.

"Never mind, looks great." Shaking his head, I can see he's desperately trying to stifle a laugh.

"Why am I still holding this trash can?" Brad groans, looking round for somewhere to put it.

Our heads all turn at the sound of running water coming from my desk.

"Aaahhhh, the contracts," I shriek as I scoop Elle up. Harry dives for the contracts, flinging pee in mine and Brad's direction.

"Dude, what the hell?" Brad shrieks.

Game over, I lose it. Tears prick my eyes and I laugh. Looking round my office, it looks like the aftermath of *The Hangover*, we're just missing the tiger.

Clothes, toys, wet wipes, diapers, food and drinks scattered everywhere. Harry looks like he's about to go in to battle with his makeshift balaclava still round his face and Brad hasn't moved the suit jacket that's now covered in pee that he's been holding in front of his face for fear of breathing in the smell of baby poo.

I accept defeat and tape the new diaper together before I dress Elle. The poor baby has her onesie half undone and a very loose diaper hanging off her butt.

"I need a drink," I breathe out.

"One step ahead of you" Harry hands me a tumbler of whisky and one to Brad, removing his makeshift mask. "Cheers to surviving that shit show," he says, lifting his glass, clinking it with ours and downing in one.

"So, are we going to talk about what this means?" Brad asks giving Elle a pointed look.

"What do you mean? She took a poop, I changed her. What do you mean, what does it mean?"

"I don't know about you, but the only way I would be changing diapers and running Daddy Day Care out of my office for kids that weren't mine would be if I was in love with their mom," Brad says matter-of-factly.

"Agreed, or if she was a freak in the sheets," Harry adds, pouring another whiskey while chuckling to himself.

"Don't talk about her like that," I hiss, slapping him on the back of the head. "And no more drinking." I take the drink out of his hand.

"Oooh, look Brad. Daddy's spoken," he says mocking me.

"Do you use that tone with Ria? Is she into the daddy kink? Does she like a little spanking," he says, bending over my desk and giving his ass a shake.

Jesus Christ.

"I swear to God, you are lucky I am holding Elle right now. Don't talk about her like that," I whisper hiss, mindful Lexi is in the room but thankfully busy with her coloring to notice the chaos on this side of the room.

"Ha! see! You do, you love her, I know you. Nothing bothers you, nothing angers you, you only react like that when it's something or someone important to you. Admit it."

I wipe my free hand over my face, smearing more cream and powder over my cheeks in frustration.

Fuck, he's right.

"It's complicated with Ri. She's going through a divorce and I don't wanna make things harder. There's Noah to consider, and she wants to take things slow and... I don't know." I let out an exasperated breath.

"I see the way she looks at you, and the way you look at her. Aint no fucking way she doesn't feel the same way about you. You need to tell her," Brad says calmly, always observing this one.

Harry wanders over to the couch near Lexi and Brad sits himself against my filing cabinet, clutching his whiskey.

Harry looks at me like he's had a lightbulb moment. "It's her isn't it, Ria? She's the secret girl?"

"What?" I reply like I don't know what she's talking about.

"The girl, the girl you wouldn't talk about, the girl who would write to you, the reason why you haven't settled down. Whenever I asked you why you couldn't be together, you said it was complicated. It's Ria, isn't it?"

I can't find the words, so I just give him a knowing look and a small nod.

Harry looks back at me as if suddenly everything made sense. "I don't mean to get deep here and bring the mood down, but you know how short life is, more than most people, the stuff we've seen, the things we've done." Harry pauses.

"It's why we got out. You've changed since you've been around her. I've never seen you happier. So, if you love her, tell her, don't wait. Don't spend another ten years pinning for her."

"Well, shit, who knew Harry had it in him to talk sense?" Brad mutters.

He's right, I know he is.

"Who do you love?" Lexi asks, lifting her head up from the coloring she's been concentrating on.

Shit, how much has she heard?

Before I can think of a way to answer that question I am saved by the sound of my office door opening. I whip my head round to see Ria stood in their, mouth wide open, eyes bulging out her head, taking in the scene before her.

"Mommy, look I did a picture," Lexi shouts excitedly from the only corner of my office that's untouched from the diaper mission.

"What happened?"

"Your baby took a shiii—poop in her diaper," Harry says dryly.

261

Ria's hands fly up to her mouth and her body starts to vibrate with laughter.

"I don't know what you're feeding her, but it smelled so bad you should bottle that and send it to your enemies."

"Well, now you're back, I'm going outside to breathe in some fresh air and book myself a vasectomy, so I don't ever have to do that again," Brad says, getting up from his spot on the floor.

"Right behind ya, buddy," Harry says, following Brad out the door. Reaching the door, he mouths "Tell her", before closing it and leaving.

"I think I ruined her. I didn't know if you used cream or powder and Lexi said both, so I did both and it made a paste. Now she looks like she's been seasoned for the oven." I look down at Elle, and her little eyes look up at me and I give her a weak smile. "Sorry. Kiddo."

I wipe my brow. *Shit, I'm sweating again.*

She walks towards me, reaching out and affectionately stroking Elle's face, then looking up at me, she says, "Thank you."

"Thank you? For turning your baby into a rotisserie chicken?"

She laughs, falling into my side. The sound hits me right in the heart. I want to hear her laugh like that every day.

"Thank you for trying, thank you for looking after them. You did an amazing job."

"The state of my office and the sweat stains forming on my shirt respectfully disagree, but I appreciate the praise."

"You also have something here." She reaches out to my cheek and wipes away some paste with her thumb, before moving in closer and kissing me. I think she will pull away as our kisses in front of the girls are always brief, but she doesn't. She deepens the kiss ever so slightly and I wrap my free arm around her, pulling her into me.

I stink of baby poop and sweat, and I'm covered in powder, but I don't care, and I don't think she does either. I know I need to tell her, to show her how serious I am about us. I just want it to be perfect. This moment feels like another turning point in our relationship as we navigate this journey from friends to lovers, hopefully forever.

Chapter Thirty-Five

Ria

Saturday night shifts at the club are always busy, but tonight, thanks to a new DJ, the place is packed. We've made every cocktail going and restocked the shelves twice already. Kate and Harley are on shift, and the three of us work so well together. We've had some unwanted attention from a group of brokers in the VIP area, but Kate has been lapping up the attention and who can blame her, she's young and single and, as flattered as I am by the attention, no one catches my eye like Jack does.

It's been hard balancing my job, the girls and my new relationship, so the moments we can steal to be alone, we take them.

"Ri," Kate shouts over the thump of the music. "Jack needs to see you in his office."

"Okay," I call back, nodding, placing the tray of glasses down on the bar and heading out back to Jack's office.

As far as I know, no one at work knows about us. I've wanted to keep it quiet at work. I'd hate for people to think I got special treatment because I was sleeping with the boss. I hurry down the hall knowing we won't have long till someone comes looking for me. The clicking of my heels on the wooden floor echoes around me and I quickly smooth out my pencil skirt and fluff my hair before knocking.

"Come in," a deep voice booms from behind the door.

I open the door to find him sitting at his desk looking delicious in his signature white button up shirt with the sleeves rolled up just far enough for his tattoos to show.

"You wanted to see me," I say coyly.

His eyes rise from the paperwork he was reading and scan my body from my heels to face.

"I did. Lock the door," he demands, not breaking our eye contact.

I do as he asks and then lean back against the door, trying to calm the excitement that is running through my body.

"You've been here six months now and as your boss I have to review your performance and fill out this paperwork," he says, holding up a sheet of paper.

"Oh, really?" I reply, biting my bottom lip. "What can I do to ensure I get a glowing report?"

"I can think of a few things." He lifts his hand and gesture me over. "Come here."

Trying to appear cool, calm and collected—everything I am not—I slowly make my way over to him. He spins on his chair to face me and he reaches out for my hand and pulls me towards the desk.

"Sit." His tone is demanding."

I sit on his desk, opening my legs slightly.

He breathes in deeply. "Fuck I've missed you." Placing his hands on either side of my thighs, he smooths them up towards my waist.

"I've missed you too," I purr.

I feel my insides warm, and my heart rate pick up. I know we are at work and right now I should be on the main floor serving drinks, but all I can think about is having Jack between my legs and his name falling from my lips.

I surprise myself by standing up and pushing him back against his chair. I slowly pull up my fitted skirt and reach for my underwear, sliding it down my legs, letting the lace fabric fall to the floor as I sit back on the desk.

"Fuck," he moans, barely loud enough for me to hear.

"You were saying, about my performance," I say, tilting my head, looking him up and down, admiring the way his muscles strain against the cotton of his shirt and hoping it won't be long before I'm wrapped up in those arms.

He doesn't say anything, he just stares, likely shocked that I've just taken off my underwear in his office. I feel like a different person around him and I want to show him just how much I appreciate him.

"Do you know how many times I've fantasized about taking you on my desk, in this chair?"

"Well, let's make that fantasy a reality," I say, shocked at my own bravado.

He's out of his chair, and on me before I can say another word. Our lips meet and the kiss turns frantic. I unbutton his shirt and rip it open. He pulls my blouse up over my head, so I'm just left in my bra and skirt.

I fumble for the buckle on his belt and undo his pants, letting them fall to the floor. He's pulling up my skirt so it's bunched around my waist and he sits back down in his chair.

"Now…" gesturing to his lap. "sit."

We haven't done that yet. It's always Jack taking the lead. He's so big I don't even know if I could. But I don't overthink it. I lift myself up, straddling his lap, feeling the head of his hard cock pressing against my entrance. I sink down slowly, letting out a moan as I take him inch by inch.

"Fuck, baby, you're so tight," he groans.

I start to move up and down slowly, and he's hitting yet another new spot. The fullness and pleasure so intense I can feel my orgasm building already.

"Jack, I'm so close."

"Keep moving, sweetheart. Ride my cock. I wanna hear you moan."

He starts to thrust into me, matching my rhythm as we quicken the pace.

"Jack, oh my God, yessss."

I grip the back of his chair to steady myself, my heals tapping on his office floor as I ride him, his hard length going deeper than I thought possible with every thrust.

Out of nowhere, my orgasm rips through me and I moan so loudly I'm surprised the people in the bar can't hear me above the music. He grips my hips in a bruising touch and lifts me like I weigh nothing, putting those sculpted thighs to good use as he rises from the chair and lays me on his desk, never breaking our connection, then driving into me hard and fast.

My back arches in pleasure and I move my hands to grip the desk, knocking a glass as I do. We hear it shatter on the wood floor, but neither of us seem to care.

The room fills with the sounds of our bodies coming together, our moans and a low hum of music from the club above us. I run my hands up my body and over my breasts, tweaking my nipples through my lace bra as he continues to thrust into me.

With one expert flick of his wrist and skilled fingers, he unhooks the front clasp of my bra and my breasts spring free. He lets out a low growl.

He continues his punishing thrusts and I brace my hands above my head, gripping the edge of the desk to stop me sliding off.

"Do you know how fucking perfect you look right now?"

I bite down on my lower lip, closing my eyes, reveling in this euphoric feeling. My breasts bounce as he slams into me, my core tightening, the burning heat coursing through me.

"That's it, baby, come for me."

And I do, loudly and without a care. My orgasm hits, sending a tingling surge of euphoria through me. Jack follows, coming inside me with such force that it sends another pulse of pleasure through my body.

We are panting and sweating as he looks down at me with hooded eyes, the sexiest smile forming across his face.

"You... I... Fuck," he pants, fighting to catch his breath. He doesn't finish that sentence.

He pulls out of me, taking me with him, so I'm seated on his desk. God, I'm a mess. He reaches into his desk, passing me a box of tissues.

"I better get back to work, but how did I do?" I ask as I pepper kisses up his jawline.

"I think you'll need to come back to mine tonight so we can work on a few kinks before I give my full review."

I smack his chest. "You are something else, Mr. Lawson." I begrudgingly get up and pull down my skirt and look for my blouse. He gets himself sorted and I see him swipe my underwear and put it in his pocket.

"Erm, I need those."

"No, you don't. You'll get them back after your shift." He gives me a sexy wink that makes going back to work the last thing I want to be doing.

I return to the bar floor and thankfully no one questions where I've been or why my cheeks are flushed and my hair has some extra volume, thanks to Jack's roaming hands. I head up toward the VIP area to help clear tables as it's been extra busy tonight. Suddenly, an unwanted hand wraps around my arm and I twist my head.

"Alex?" My eyes widen. What the hell is he doing here?

"So, this is where you are working then?" he slurs.

"I thought you were with your parents and the girls. What are you doing here? Are they okay?"

"They're fine. We need to talk." He leans in and I can smell the alcohol on his breath.

"I'm working. We can talk tomorrow." I shrug free from his grip and turn to walk back towards the bar, but he grabs my arm and hauls me back so my back hits his front.

"I said, we need to talk and I'm not fucking leaving till we do," he grits. I don't want to cause a scene at work, and I don't want people knowing who Alex is, so I nod and gesture for him to follow me out back towards the fire exit.

"Okay, what is it?" Folding my arms, I wait for his response.

"When are you coming back?"

"Back where?" I say confused at his question.

"Back to me. Come on, Ri, this mental crisis you are having should be done by now. You've made your point. I've told Melanie and my secretary we can't fuck anymore and that I'm a married man."

"Oh, that's big of you, but you are about five years too late," I say bitterly.

"Look, I'm sorry. I know I fucked it but come back to me. I miss you."

The anger begins to rise in my body, burning me from the inside. "You put me through hell, Alex, and I thought that was love. Now I know what we had, what you felt for me wasn't love. I'm not coming back." I don't realize I'm shouting.

"I know and I'm sorry, babe, please, I miss you," His tone is pleading. Six months ago, this might have made me cave and give him another chance, but not anymore.

"You don't get to miss me. You had me, and you lost me because you treated me like I wasn't worth a damn thing."

"Fuck's sake, you can't be serious about this," he yells, driving a fist into the wall next to me and I jolt. Moving closer to my face, he spits, "I got the paperwork from the lawyer. If you think I'm signing, you are outta your mind." He taps my temple with his index finger.

I grit my teeth and my fists clench. Why is this so hard? Why can't he just let me move on? I know he doesn't want me; he just can't bear the thought of losing control.

"Alex, we've been done for ages. Please just let me move on now. You had me, and I tried. God, did I try, but you didn't and I can't do it anymore. Just be there for the girls, but you and me... we're done." It feels good to finally have my say.

I stare at him; his glassy eyes are filled with hatred and fueled by alcohol. Any feelings I had for this man have well and truly gone. I just feel hate now.

"I've gotta go back to work."

I push past him and head towards the door to the main room and he grabs my arm, slamming me against the wall, my head bouncing off it. In all our years together, Alex has done many things, but getting physical with me has never been one of them, until now. He presses himself up against me and puts his mouth close to my ear, cupping my jaw.

"Maybe I didn't make myself fucking clear. We are married, and if you think I am signing those divorce papers you must be fucking crazy like your mother, who by the way called me last week to say she was sorry to hear about the divorce and that you had shacked up with some fucker from high school, so who is he?"

"Alex, please, you are hurting me. Let me go." The fear is evident in my voice as I try to free myself from his firm grip.

"Alex, please," I plead, trying to push him off me, but his body is crushing me. Suddenly I feel like I can breathe as Alex is ripped off me and I see Jack with Harry and Brad behind him. He holds Alex by the back of his neck.

"Get your fucking hands off her," he growls.

Harry puts a protective arm around me as I begin to shake.

"Get the fuck off me, you asshole. She's my wife. We were talking."

He gets up close to his face.

"She's not your fucking wife anymore. You lost the privilege of calling her that the minute you disrespected her. You can either leave by yourself or I will throw you out," he yells, baring his teeth, his face reddening.

"Is this him? Is this the asshole you're fucking? Alex shouts.

"Alex please, just go," I beg, tears now falling from shame. Embarrassed that this was the man I married.

"Fuck you, Maria. I'm not going anywhere," he slurs.

Jack slams him into the wall, and his eyes dilate. "You're done. Get the fuck out."

"I'll take him," Brad calls from behind Jack and drags him to the back exit.

Jack is on me, wrapping me in his protective arms.

"I'll go help Brad," Harry states softly and leaves me and Jack alone in the corridor to process what just happened.

"Sweetheart, I'm sorry I didn't get here sooner. Are you okay?"

I cry into his chest. How can the night go from one extreme to the other? How did my life end up being this? Just when I start to feel like I've moved on and found some happiness, my past choices have to come back and screw it all up.

"How did you know I was here with him?"

"Harry and Brad were watching the CCTV and saw you both, and came and got me. Ri, please don't ever go anywhere alone with him again, okay? Please, promise me. I don't even wanna think about what he would've done to you if Harry hadn't seen."

"He didn't hurt me," I interrupt. "Just shocked me. He's never been like that with me." I'm lying. He hurt me. My head is throbbing, but I don't want to make Jack worry any more than he is.

"I don't care. He doesn't get to put his hands on you like that or speak to you like that," he replies, his breathing ragged.

I rub my hand in soothing strokes up and down his back. "Jack, I'm okay. I promise."

"You don't deserve to be treated like that, sweetheart."

I lean into his touch and enjoy the feeling of being protected. A feeling I had never experienced till Jack, and yet here he was again, saving me, again, and again and again and I hope he never stops wanting to save me, because here, in Jack's arms feels like the safest place on earth.

Chapter Thirty-Six

Ria

Jack didn't allow me to finish my shift. I'm in a daze, trying to process what's just happened. *How did my life become this? Where did I go wrong?* Part of me wishes I never met Alex, but then I wouldn't have my girls and if having them meant I had to do the past ten years over again, I would, because a life without them would be no life at all.

But how I wish things were different. That Alex could have been the man he claimed to be when I first met him. Or if I was being truthful, I wish it had been Jack from the very start and that the girls were his. That thought keeps me awake at night, but I am slowly accepting that life doesn't always end up how we thought it would, and sometimes that's for the best.

Jack might not biologically be the girls' dad, but for the past nine months, he has been there for them like a dad should be. I have this constant battle of feeling so angry and disappointed that Alex can't be the dad the girls deserve and thankful Jack has shown up for them, for me.

The drive back to his apartment is silent. I lay back against the leather seats of his Audi and look up at New York's night sky out of the passenger window. It's a mixture of twinkling lights and dark sky, and it comforts me. It's the city that brought Jack back into my life to the start of the most unexpected chapter.

Out of the car and safely inside, I walk through Jack's apartment, kick off my heels, and head to the kitchen for some water. I feel at home here now. I lean against the marble counter and soak in the view from his apartment. Next to his insane bathtub, the view is my favorite part of his apartment. His arms snake around me and pull me in towards him. His lips find the top of my head and I let out a breath and feel my body instantly relax.

"If you want to talk, talk, but if you don't, I'm here okay, I'm here."

How does this man just get me? He just knows me inside out.

"I have something to show you." I turn my head to look at him and see a glint of excitement in my eyes.

"We spend all our time with the girls at yours, which I love, but I want my home to feel like your home and the girls' home."

"W... what?" I'm lost for words.

He takes my hands and guides me to the kitchen cupboards; he opens them and to my complete shock, it's stocked with all the girls' favorite snacks and sippy cups.

"They have their goldfish, and of course M&M's for Lexi and here..." The excitement in his voice is bringing a lump to my throat. He takes me towards his guest bedroom. Opening the door, I'm met with a sea of pink. I cover my mouth with my hand, a tingling sensation flitting through my chest as realization hits me.

He's making space for us in his life.

The drapes have been changed to pink butterfly ones, with a matching comforter on the bed. There are two Minnie Mouse cuddly toys on the bed and beside the bed is a pack and play with pink sheets.

"Jack... I don't know what to say. This is... beautiful." I step further into the room, taking in all the details. So much thought and care has gone into this and every little piece shows how well he knows the girls.

"You got a pack and play?" I point with a hint of humor to my voice.

"Yeah, but I got my housekeeper to build it. Not a chance I was attempting to unpack one of those again."

I let out a laugh that's mixed with the onset of tears.

He did this for them... for me.

"We can change it if they don't like it and we can get Elle a proper crib, but I want them to know they have a home here... that I want them here. I want you all here."

"God, why are you so perfect?" I laugh through sobs, wiping the tears that won't stop flowing.

"Well, I try," he replies, bringing my face towards his.

"This is the sweetest thing anyone has ever done for us," I tell him, choking back another sob.

"I..." He clears his throat. "I know you have a lot of shit to sort, but, sweetheart, I'm crazy about you. I just need you to know that, okay?"

I swallow, finding the courage to say what I want to say, but I settle on repeating his own words. "I'm crazy for you too. Thank you. I can't explain how much this means to me... but I'd like to show you." My tone is low, full of need for this incredible man.

I press my lips to his and our kiss is slow and passionate and full of all the unspoken words we are yet to say. I spend the night getting lost in Jack with New York's night sky behind us, casting shadows over our naked skin as we make what feels like the closest thing to love I've ever experienced.

Tonight, we let our bodies say what we are too scared to say and prove that if two people are meant to be together, they will eventually find their way into each other's arms, no matter what, because the way we are when we are together, it's impossible to believe that we weren't meant to be.

Chapter Thirty-Seven

Jack

We collected the girls earlier this morning. Seeing their little faces light up at their room was everything. They wasted no time making themselves at home. Every hard surface in the apartment is covered in something pink and plastic. The sofa cushions are on the floor and Lexi's new obsession *Frozen* is on its second go on the TV and I have honestly never felt more content.

I smile from the couch, watching Ria hold Elle on her hip, a whisk in her free hand, using it as a microphone as she dances around the island as Lexi stands on top of it like a stage.

Watching Ria move and laugh with her girls is the most beautiful sight. She's dressed in gray sweat shorts and a white tee, her hair piled on top of her head and when she's like this, to me, she is the sexiest woman alive. Sure, she's stunning dressed up, but watching her smile, and glow, and just be herself is a different level of beauty.

This woman has been to hell and back and yet doesn't let the storms she's weathered damage her girls. I don't think she realizes how incredible she is. A flutter hits my chest and I know this is what I want all my Sundays to look like.

We order takeout for dinner and sit round the dinner table. When friends come over, we usually eat at my kitchen island, but this feels good. To see the girls all here, looking out over New York as the sun goes down, a warm feeling fills my chest; we feel like a proper family.

Ria places her chopsticks down on top of the takeout carton, dabbing her mouth with a paper napkin. "Okay, Miss Lexi, Miss Elle, it's time for bed."

"Noooo, Mommy, please can we stay up? I want to watch Frozen just one more time, pleaaassseeeee," Lexi begs, fluttering her eyelashes, trying to master the art of getting her own way at just four years old.

"No, Lex, it's late already. Let's get you cleaned up and changed for bed."

"No," she protests, crossing her arms and pouting her lips. I have to bite down on my lip and look out the window. She's a little madam but she's so funny too and it's hard not to laugh when she's challenging Ria.

"Lexi Marie Kennedy," Ria says sternly "It's time for bed."

"No. "Lexi shakes her head. "I want Jack to put me to bed."

Ria looks at me, obviously unsure how to answer. I sense she doesn't want to put me in a situation I might not be ready for. But I can do this.

"Of course I can put you to bed, Princess, and Elle too."

"W-what, are you sure?" Ria asks.

I get up and lift Elle out of her highchair.

"Of course. I don't know if you know this, but I am a bit of a pro now at changing diapers and managing kids. I've got this."

Ria looks at me like I'm so full of shit. It's as if she doesn't know if she should laugh or swoop in and save me.

"Go, take a shower, a bath, whatever you want. I can handle the girls," I say, waving her off.

"Okay, if you're sure. Good luck," she chuckles.

"Right," I say, looking at Elle and then down at Lexi. "Let's go girls."

After two diaper changes because I fucked it the first time by ripping the tab off, three story books, a pillow change because it was too fluffy, a bottle of milk and a sippy cup of water, Lexi and Elle are all tucked up. Elle fell asleep as soon as I laid her down, looking adorable, sucking on her little thumb.

"Night, Lexi. Sleep well, Princess," I whisper and kiss the top of her head.

She closes her eyes and I turn to leave. As I reach for the door, I hear a little whisper. "Jack, can I tell you a secret?"

I turn back, kneeling by her bedside. "Of course you can, Princess. You can tell me anything."

"I really like your house, and I really like my room."

I can't help but smile. "I'm glad. You can stay here whenever you like."

"Can I tell you another secret?"

"Of course," I say, smiling down at her, looking at her beautiful eyes that are just like Ria's.

"I don't think my daddy likes me. He doesn't do fun stuff with me or buy me M&M's like you do."

And my heart shatters for this little girl. I don't know what to say. How do I respond to a little girl who believes that her dad doesn't like her?

"Lexi, your daddy likes you a lot. I think he's just a bit busy with work right now, but he will do some fun stuff with you soon, I'm sure."

"Yeah, maybe." She sighs.

Just when I get up, she whispers, "Can I tell you one last secret?"

I smile. "Of course, Princess."

"I wish you were my daddy."

My heart stops.

I clear my throat and lean in a little closer. "Can I tell you a secret?" I whisper back.

She nods excitedly, her big blue eyes widening.

"I wish I was your daddy too."

Chapter Thirty-Eight

Ria

"Okay, which ones, black or silver?" Ali asks, holding up two different pairs of strappy heels against her pink silk dress.

"Silver," Gabby and I say in unison.

Ali gives a nod and walks back into the bedroom of our hotel room, leaving Gabby and I to finish our hair and make-up.

"I still can't believe Nancy is having her wedding in the New York Plaza. She's come a long way from that hot mess we met at "Teenhood". I'm happy for her... jealous as hell but happy," Gabby says, staring at her reflection in the mirror as she winds a strand of hair around the curling iron, creating loose curls.

"I know right, the girls done well," I say, finishing up the last of my make up. I've gone for a gold eyeshadow with some defined eyeliner to match the new golden blonde tones that run through my hair, framing my face in soft waves. I took a day for myself and got my hair, nails, and a wax knowing tonight I would get to spend the night with Jack in a gorgeous hotel room and I want it to be special. I want to look as good as he makes me feel. My body heats at the thought of Jack in his black tux I know he's wearing. I don't know how I am supposed to make it through the ceremony, dinner and evening without jumping on him.

Control yourself, Ria.

"Okay, I think I am ready," I announce, walking back into the bedroom, Gabby following behind me, still in her white hotel bathrobe.

"Fuck, Ri, you look hot. Jack isn't going to be able to keep his hands off you," Ali says, whistling.

I do a little twirl, the gold dress moving with my body. The back straps cross over and go all the way down to my waistline. I beam. I don't think I have ever felt this happy or content.

"That's the plan," I grin.

"It's so good to see you smile again, like really smile," Gabby says, squeezing me. Ali walks over and joins in with the hug.

"You've been through so much this year, and I know it's Nancy's night, but fuck it. Make it about you and Jack, okay? You deserve this happiness."

Tears prick at my eyes. "Girls, my make-up," I cry, pulling away from their embrace to dab underneath my eyes, careful so as not to smudge my makeup.

"Sorry, I don't wanna make you cry, but you do. We always said one day it will feel like we're not fighting anymore for that happy ending and Ri, your fight is over now. Enjoy it, and don't let yourself believe you don't deserve it, okay?"

I can see the tears forming in Ali's eyes, and that girl is made of steel. I think I have seen her cry twice in all the years I have known her.

I change the subject. "Okay, Gabs, what are you wearing?" I ask, clapping my hands together, needing to stop this emotional therapy session we seem to be having.

"You aren't allowed to dress like a nun," Ali says sternly. "Not tonight, Gabriella. There will be too many hot single men at this wedding and I will not have you looking like one of your mom's friends from bible study."

Gabby laughs, turning and walking over to her dress bag that is hanging on the back of the bathroom door. She unzips it, revealing an emerald green dress, satin by the look of it, floor length with a slit up one side and spaghetti straps. Very fitting for a December wedding.

"Yesssss, girl yesss," Ali cheers.

"It's stunning, Gabs," I say, smiling at her. I know wearing fitted clothing isn't her thing, but she has the most incredible figure, thanks to her Pilates classes. She shouldn't be ashamed of showing her body, but I know for Gabby, it runs deeper than that.

There's a knock at the door, and we turn our heads in unison.

"Are you expecting someone?" I ask confused about who would know our room number.

"Oooh, maybe it's Jack coming for a pre-wedding bang," Ali says in a suggestive tone, heading towards the door and opening it.

"I have a package for a Ria Kennedy," one of the hotel staff says from the doorway.

"That's me, thank you," I reply, taking a black gift bag with white ribbon on it from his hand and Ali takes the large white box from him. I close the door and walk over toward the table under the window of our hotel suite.

"Oh my God, open it," Ali screeches.

I untie the ribbon and reach inside and pull out a long black velvet box.

I open the box slowly and gasp. The most stunning platinum diamond tennis bracelet sparkles before me.

"Holy shit, that's gorgeous," Gabby gasps, leaning over me to take a glimpse.

My hand flies over my mouth and I can't decide if I am going to laugh or cry from shock. How did I get so lucky?

I pass the box to Ali, and she helps put the bracelet on. It is the most beautiful piece of jewelry I have ever worn. I can't stop looking at it.

"What's in there?" Gabby asks, pointing at the box on the table. In all the excitement of the bracelet, I forgot there was another gift. I take the lid off the large white circular box and inside are too many perfectly shaped red roses to count.

"Oh, my God!" I gasp, too stunned to speak.

I reach for the card, my shaky fingers fumbling to pull it free from the envelope.

I may never find the right words perfect enough to describe how much you mean to me, but I will spend my days searching for them because you, Ria, are worth every one.

Chapter Thirty-Nine

Jack

There she is, looking absolutely breathtaking as she walks towards me in her gold satin dress, her hair falling effortlessly around her face, a glint in her eyes and I spot the tennis bracelet I had sent to the girls' room sparkling on her delicate wrist, and it makes my heart skip a fucking beat.

No woman has affected me the way Ria does, never made me feel or think about things the way she does. Watching her now, walking towards me like she's walking on water, makes me think how good it would feel to watch her walk towards me in a white gown and become my wife.

A firm hand slaps against my back. "Breathe, buddy, breathe. You are no good to her passed out on the floor," Harry whispers.

And I let out a breath, long and slow.

"Fuck, you are so pussy whipped" he laughs, I smirk at him, not missing the way he's looking at a certain someone.

"Hey action man," she says with a smile that makes my heart do a weird flutter and my dick twitch all at the same time.

"Sweetheart, you look absolutely stunning." I slink an arm around her waist and pull her towards me, pressing my lips to hers, not giving a damn about where we are or who's around us. I push my tongue between her lips and let out a little moan when she opens up and her tongue entangles with mine.

"Get a room," Harry chants like a disgruntled teenage boy. Ria smiles against my lips before I break our kiss and turn to Harry, giving him a murderous look.

"Sorry, man, but some of us are single and don't need it rubbed in our faces."

"And whose fault is that?" Ali injects, never missing a moment to wind Harry up.

"And what's your excuse, Ali cat? I don't see you with a man. Maybe if you changed your attitude, you'd find one willing to take you on."

Ali lets out a shocked laugh. "I'd really love to give a fuck about your opinion of me, but it doesn't really go with my outfit," she declares, staring at him like she wants to claw his face.

"Oooh, who sprinkled the bitch dust when you were getting ready? The party's barely begun, babe, and you've given me your best lines already."

Ali steps closer to Harry, reaching for his face. Convinced she's about to slap the taste out of his mouth, we all hold our breath, but to our surprise, she strokes his cheek. "Oh, sweetie, why don't you leave the sarcasm and insults to the adults? Wouldn't want you to hurt yourself. Instead, why don't you go play in traffic with the other juveniles?" Tapping his face firmly, she then walks off like she's walking the runway at Fashion Week. Harry being Harry instantly follows her, no doubt hurling more insults at her.

"Those two are either going to fuck each other silly or kill each other," I say, looking down at Ria.

"I hope it's the latter," she giggles.

"Thank you for the gift. You didn't need to get me anything. It's not our wedding da—" She cuts the sentence short as if she realizes what she just said.

I bend down lower, grazing my lips with the tip of her ear, and whisper, "Not today it isn't, sweetheart... but one day it will be" And the gasp that leaves her mouth was the exact reaction I was hoping for.

The ceremony was everything you could expect from a couple like Nancy and Chris. The room was surrounded by large pillar candles and white flowers. Nancy looked beautiful in a white lace wedding dress and walked down the aisle being serenaded by a man singing "Will you marry me" accompanied by an orchestra.

Throughout the ceremony, my hand was either in Ria's hand or stroking her thigh and all I could think about was how I want to be stood up there, watching Ria walk towards me. I never thought I was the marriage type, but they say it only takes one person to change the entire trajectory of your life, and she's that person. I never imagined myself settling down and especially with someone with kids but it's all I seem to think about, the day I can call Ria my wife, raising the girls with her and if she allows, have more babies with her.

I am taken away from my thoughts by applause and cheers as the bride and groom are declared husband and wife. One by one, we are ushered from our seats and to the ballroom, where our evening meal will be served. It's another extravagant room full of fresh white flowers in oversized vases in the center of the tables. A large white dance floor sits in the middle of the room underneath a crystal chandelier. Ria and I sit at a table with a couple of guys we briefly met at the wedding shower, along with Brad, Harry, Gabby, and Ali, so this should be entertaining.

The next couple of hours are a blur of speeches, courses of mouth-watering food, and champagne on tap. Looking around the table, Gabby seems to have fallen into an effortless conversation with one of the guys next to her. Ali is sitting between the other guy and Harry while Brad looks like he wants to be anywhere else but here. The two guys leave the table to go mingle with some friends, and Ali is already swooning over the new man she's met.

"Oh my God, how fucking hot is Paxton?" she says, biting down on her lip and reaching for her glass of champagne.

"What kind of a name is Paxton? It sounds like the name of a fucking wardrobe from Ikea," Harry bites, clearly not happy about Ali's new found friendship.

Gabby laughs and then chokes on her drink, causing Brad to start smacking her on the back. I turn, raising an eyebrow at Ria after the most unladylike snort just escaped her.

"Sorry, but he's not wrong," she laughs.

Ali turns to face Harry and I almost feel like ordering popcorn and sitting back, ready for the showdown between them.

"And how long did it take you to come up with that remark?" she challenges him.

"You know, you sound better and look so much hotter with your mouth closed," Harry quips back.

"I'd agree with you, but then we'd both be wrong, wouldn't we?" she comes back quickly.

It's like watching a tennis match.

"You know what? You are the walking version of a migraine," he retorts. "When I'm around you, I get this throbbing pain right…" he says, pointing to his temple.

"Well, pop some aspirin, baby because it's about to get painful," Ali says, finishing the last of her drink.

"Please, save your breath, you'll probably need it to blow up your next date, or 'Paxton'," he mocks.

"I don't know what your problem is, but I'm guessing it's hard to pronounce for you," she bites back.

"Remember that time I said I liked you... I lied," Harry says, staring her dead in the eyes.

Ali gasps, pressing her hand to her chest. "What...are you saying you don't like me?" she says dramatically. "Please give me a few moments whilst I recover from this tragedy." She rolls her eyes.

"Fuck me, you are..." Harry spits, not finishing his sentence. Instead, turning away from her as he downs the remainder of his drink.

"You know, as tempting as that is, I don't know where that little dick of yours has been, so I—"

"Right, that's it you two, enough," Ria shouts, startling us all, but her shout is instantly followed by a laugh.

Oh, tipsy Ria has joined the party.

"You two are like a pair of children. Don't make me put you in a time-out in your rooms."

I lean in and whisper whilst she is mid-scold, "Feel free to put me in a time-out."

I feel a little shudder run through her. Excitement runs through me, knowing I have this effect on her.

She clears her throat as if she needs a second to find her words.

"Now then, this is a wedding. It's full of love and happiness and I love this song, so we are going to dance and you too are going to kiss and make up. Come on."

She's up on her feet, pulling me to mine and heading towards the dance floor, and to my shock, Harry and Ali are following us.

A female singer is singing "Love" with a live band and the carefree smile and laughter coming from Ria as I dip her and twirl her around the dance floor hits me right in the heart. This is it; this is what I want. Seeing her like this every day.

I glance over at Ali and Harry, who, to my surprise, are dancing together, both sporting sour expressions. I see one of the other guys from our table offer his hand to Gabby and she accepts, and they make their way over to us. Brad is being the boring bastard he usually is, drinking a whiskey on the rocks and scrolling his phone.

I lean down and whisper, "I need you. Let's break away for a minute. I know a little spot."

"Let me freshen up and then I'm all yours," she whispers back before pressing a kiss to my cheek, causing my dick to twitch again.

The effect she has on me. I nod and she walks away and heads for the bathroom, glancing over her shoulder and smiling at me as she exits the dance floor.

One thing I hate is Ria walking away from me, but God damn, does she look good doing it.

Chapter Forty

Ria

I look back at the woman in the mirror in the hotel bathroom as I touch up my lipstick. I feel giddy. I can't wait to spend the night with Jack. He booked us a suite, and if I'm being honest, I just want to ditch the rest of the wedding and ride him likes my own personal show pony, but I can't. I need to get through the next couple of hours, and then he's all mine.

With a quick powder of my nose and ruffle of my hair, I exit the bathroom and make my way down the hallway back to the man ballroom. My phone vibrates and I reach in my purse. I smile seeing Jack's name.

Jack

> Change of plan, get your fine ass up to suite 410

I change direction and head towards the elevators and hit the button to take me up to the suites.

I exit the elevator and walk down the lit corridor, taking in the detailing of the cream walls and the gold and gray carpet. I've never stayed anywhere so fancy before. I follow the signs to the suite when an all too familiar voice fills the hallway.

"I fucking knew it was him."

I freeze. The hairs on the back of my neck stand on end and it feels like a lead ball has dropped in my stomach. I turn slowly to see Alex leaning against the wall.

"What are you doing here?" I ask, shaking my head and blinking. *Is he really here? How?*

"I'm on a date," he answers. "I think you know her... Tara. Right little fire cracker." He has a smug look on his face.

"So, you are here with another woman, but you are going to give me shit for being here with someone else?" My blood is boiling. *How dare he?*

"Wow, someone's got fucking brave, haven't they? Remember your tone with me. We are still legally married, Maria Kennedy."

I grit my teeth. "Don't full name me, you prick. You've got days left to call me that. I haven't been your wife in a very long time now, so I suggest you build a bridge and get over I. I've moved on, you clearly have too, so why are you still making my life hell?" My nostrils flare.

He pushes away from the wall and stalks towards me. I turn, making quick steps to head to Jack, but Alex reaches for me, tugging my arm and pulling us down another corridor and pressing me to the wall. He's trying to intimidate me again, but it's not going to work.

"You will be my wife for as long as I say. I've applied for an extension on our divorce papers. I'll drag this fucking thing out for as long as possible. You could have just marched your perky little ass back home but no, you had to go and think you could do better than me and fall into bed with the first man to pay you a little attention," he sneers.

"Fuck you, you had me, and you lost me. I tried to make our marriage work, be the wife you needed, the wife you wanted, but you didn't try, you didn't try at all so don't you dare be mad at me now I'm giving someone everything I wanted to give to you." My voice is laced with anger.

"And Jack's the one you want to give it to? He's your brother's fucking friend. How twisted is that? He might be your new little fuck toy, but he will never play daddy to my girls. I'm going for custody."

The laugh that erupts from me comes from deep within as if I have kept it buried for so long. "That's a good one. There isn't a judge in the land that would give you custody of those girls. You couldn't even tell me Lexi's favorite color or Elle's favorite toy, but Jack... he could tell me all of it. He's a better dad than you will ever be." Pure venom is spilling from me. I'm done being scared, done keeping quiet.

"You fucking bitch, I'm gonna..." Before he can finish, a door creaks open and footsteps round the corner and there stands Jack. Suit jacket and tie off, looking angrier than I've ever seen him. Flared nostrils and a reddening face, he looks like a bull ready to charge.

"Get your fucking hands off her," he barks.

Alex releases me and lunges towards Jack. "Think you can play happy families with my wife and kids? You piece of shit." He lifts his fist to punch Jack but before he can, Jack grabs his hand, twists Alex's arm behind his back and slams him into the wall, face first.

"Now, Alex," Jack grits, "we can be gentlemen about this, or I won't hesitate to make you cry for your mommy and regret the day you were born. I've had the training to do so, it's up to you, but if I ever see you touch my girl or speak to the mother of your children like that again, you won't be given the choice. Do I make myself clear?"

"Fuck you, you prick. You can't tell me what to do with my wife or my girls. I'm their dad, so you can get fucked. This is between me and her," Alex mumbles against the wall.

"Maybe I'm not making myself clear. Ria is no longer your wife, and you may be the girls' father according to DNA, but you are a pathetic excuse for a dad. Where were you when Elle got sick? Where were you when Lexi started Pre-K? Where were you when Elle took her first steps? All those times Ria called you and you did nothing, no word, no answer, so don't you dare play the dad card because you also lost that privilege."

I watch as Alex struggles under Jack's hold, but Jack is barely breaking a sweat.

"I know you must be kicking yourself daily because losing a woman who is as beautiful and amazing as Ria must be a killer, but luckily for me, I plan to never find out because I will treat her with the respect she deserves. So, hear me when I say I will spend the rest of my days proving to her how a man should treat a woman. Now, I'll ask you again, are you going to walk away and leave Ria the hell alone or am I going to have to remove you myself and make you regret it."

"I'll leave," Alex spits.

"Good choice," Jack says, releasing him with a shove. Alex staggers, keeping himself upright. He walks past me, but before he leaves for the stairwell, he looks at me with cold eyes, causing a shudder to run through me.

"This isn't over. You'll be hearing from me." He disappears, and I let out a breath. My heart beats so fast I fear it's going to burst through my chest.

Jack doesn't say a word. Just takes my hand and pulls me into our suite. The door closes behind us and I feel the adrenaline rush hit me and I begin to shake.

Jack is on me, his muscular arms enveloping me, making me feel safe.

"Fuck, I wanted to kill that prick for touching you again. Are you okay, sweetheart?" I lean away from his embrace and stare up into his beautiful blue eyes and run my hands across his five o'clock shadow and smile.

"I'm fine," and I mean it. Because in Jack's arms, how could I not?

Chapter Forty-One

Jack

I feel like I have won the life lottery, waking up with Ria laid across my chest in this incredible suite, looking out the large windows, watching the snow fall over New York. We spent the morning dressed in white robes, eating room service brought to the room by the suite's butler. Every pastry, fruit and type of pancake was delivered along with some freshly brewed coffee and squeezed juices.

"Oh my God, can this just be life every day, please?" Ria moaned, taking another bite of her warm croissant.

"It can be for another couple of days if you like."

She stops mid-bite and stares at me. "What do you mean?"

"You and me are spending some time together. I'm taking you away and before you ask, I've got the girls taken care of."

"By who?" Concern is etched in her voice.

"Harry and Brad. They are diaper changing ninjas now. They can handle it," I say, taking a sip of coffee.

She drops the pastry to her plate, flakes falling to the table. She wipes her mouth with her napkin and swallows. "Dear God, please tell me you are joking. I love them, but Lexi will run rings around them. I'm not worried about Lexi and Elle. It's Brad and Harry I'm worried about."

I laugh, not able to keep this going any longer. "Don't worry, Ali and Gabby have it covered. They feel that you deserve a few nights off work and mom duties and I happen to agree, and selfishly, I want you all to myself for a couple of days." I reach for her hand and stroke my thumb over the back of her knuckles.

"I'd love that." She beams looking up at me.

"And then when we are back, I promised Lexi I'd do something fun with her so I figured we could go ice skating at Rockefeller Center, and I know Elle is too little for that so I'll take her to one of those indoor parks with all the slides and balls. Harry weirdly knows a good one. I didn't ask how." I stop my ramble as I notice tears well in Ria's eyes and I reach for her face and wipe the lone tear that falls from her cheek.

"What's wrong?"

"Nothing," she sniffs. "I'm just happy."

"Eat up because we have a little road trip ahead of us." I press a kiss to her forehead as I rise from my seat. "And if you wanna know how marble tiles feel against your back, then I suggest you take a shower with me, sweetheart," I say, heading towards the bathroom door. Before I reach it, Ria jumps on my back.

"Hell, yeah I do."

We get dressed and leave our suite and head for the elevator.

"Damn, it's not fair how hot you look dressed like that," she says, biting her lip, taking in my dark jeans, black sweater and dark gray jacket.

"Likewise, sweetheart," I reply, drinking in the way her knitted jumper dress clings to every curve of her body. The elevator stops a couple of levels down, the doors open and to our surprise, Ali steps in, still wearing last night's dress, shoes in hands and hair looking messy.

"Good night, Al?" I ask, trying to stifle a laugh. I have a feeling where she's coming from, but I keep that to myself.

She doesn't say anything, just nods and smiles.

"Oh, my God, are you doing the walk of shame?" Ria squeals. "Did you bang Paxton?"

"Who... oh yeah, yeah, wild night," Ali mumbles, rubbing her head.

"I need all the details when I get home. Are you sure you are okay to have the girls?"

"Absolutely. I'm driving over to Anne's later and picking them up with Gabby and we are going to have tons of fun. Go enjoy yourself and don't do anything I wouldn't," she teases.

We say goodbye to Ali and head down to reception to check out before we wait for the valet to bring round my car.

"That isn't your car," she says scrunching up her nose, looking confused as a black Audi SUV pulls up in front of us and the man driving it hands me the keys.

"No, it isn't because it's actually yours, well ours, but we can work that out later."

"Sorry?" she shakes her head like she's struggling to digest what's happening. "This is my car?"

"It is," I tell her, rubbing the back of my neck, suddenly aware that this was maybe too much. "Listen, I can't stand the thought of you driving your car and it breaking down again. Plus, this gives us more room with the girls."

She doesn't speak, her mouth slack as she stares at the vehicle. A plethora of emotions cross her face, but she finally looks at me, eyes shining.

"Jack, I don't know what to say. I don't know how I can repay you for this." I snake an arm around her waist. "You don't need to thank me. I wanted to do this for you, for us." I lower my mouth to her ear and whisper, "But I could think of a few ways you could thank me in that car."

She raises her eyebrows. "Oh, really?"

"Yeah, now let's get going. I've got another surprise for you."

Ria falls asleep on the drive to my next surprise. It's about two and a half hours away and it's given me time to think about how the last nine months have been and how my life has changed since Ria walked back in it. We finally drive into upstate New York, and I smile, a sense of calm washing over me as I pull into the driveway of a place that holds so many fond memories for me. A place I hope to make new memories with Ria and the girls. I lean across and stroke Ria's hair out of her face.

"Hey, baby, we're here. Wake up," I say softly.

She slowly opens her eyes and looks around the car and then at me. "Where are we?" she asks, yawning.

"Come on, I'll show you."

I get out of the car and head round to Ria's side to open the door for her. She gasps as she steps out and looks up at the house, wide eyed and mouth open like a child who's seen the Disneyland castle for the first time.

"This house is beautiful" She closes her eyes and takes in a deep breath; no doubt inhaling the fresh country air, and lets out a slow breath. "It's my dream to live in a house like this one day." She turns to look at me, eyes full of contentment.

"I know, I remember," I say, reaching for her hand.

"You remembered?"

"Yes, I remember you telling me that your dream was to live in a white house on the lake, surrounded by trees and a dock that you could sit on in your chair and watch the sun go down, I remember everything about you, Ri."

"I can't believe you remembered," she says in disbelief. "I only told you once."

She presses a kiss to my lips, and I deepen the kiss, wanting her in this moment. Hoping she knows I am all in, that she is it for me. I can't picture a life without her. During my deployments, I would dream of weekends spent in this lake house with Ria, but couldn't let myself wish for too long because she wasn't mine... I never thought she could be mine. She was someone else's, so I forced myself to think of a new dream, one that would help me on my toughest days. But now it finally feels like I can allow myself to dream of a future with her.

I break the kiss and brush my nose against hers. "Come on, let me show you inside."

Chapter Forty-Two

Ria

"Oh, my God, I am never leaving this place," I say, sinking lower into the bathtub, bubbles overflowing, and the scent of lavender and eucalyptus filling the bathroom from the bath oils and candles we've lit. The bathroom is a stunning off-white with gold hardware on the cabinets and has that luxury farmhouse vibe. This bath could happily house a family of four and I need to work out how to fit one of these in my bathroom at home.

We had the most incredible two days at his parents' lake house. We even FaceTimed them to catch up. I hadn't spoken to his parents since I was a teen, but Jayne and Andy were just as sweet and kind as I remember. My heart melted when they asked about the girls, and it was very clear from their questions that Jack had been updating them.

He massages the balls of my feet and I lean over to take the glass of champagne. The cold rim of the glass is a welcoming feeling against my hot mouth. I drink it down, the condensation from the champagne flute trickling down my fingers as I place it back down on the bath tray.

"That feels good," I hum, my eyes fluttering closed, as I rotate my foot in Jack's hands.

"I've got something else that would feel good," he murmurs in a low, husky voice. I open my eyes to his gaze is fixed on me. *I know that look.*

God, did it just get 100 degrees hotter in here?

"Come here," he says, his voice low, gesturing for me to sit in between his legs. I turn round in the bath, position myself between his legs, and lean back against his firm chest. My head falls slightly to the left, and he presses soft open mouth kisses to my neck, while his hands come up to my shoulders and massage my tight muscles.

"You are so tight, sweetheart," he says in between kisses.

My body tingles at his words. I press myself into him harder, his erection pressing into the small of my back.

His hands slide forward and begin kneading my breasts, filling his large hands. His expert fingers rub and tease my nipples and my body starts to writhe beneath his touch.

"Touch yourself," he whispers, and without a second thought, my fingers find my clit.

"Fuck," he grunts, tweaking my nipples a little harder, earning a gasp from me. I quicken the movement of my fingers on my clit as I rotate my hips.

Without warning, his hands leave my nipples, and in one quick motion, are on my hips, lifting me so I'm standing. He rises out of the tub, trickles of water rolling down his golden torso, his abs flexing as he wipes a hand over his face and through his wet hair. A wave of cold air hits my skin from the open window, a slight shiver rolling through me.

"On your knees," he growls. I lower myself back down into the tub. "Hands on the edge of the bath." His breathing is uneven as he settles behind me. Goosebumps scatter across my body, excitement surging through me.

I grip the edge of the bathtub, looking out the window, out across the lake to the neighboring house.

God, I hope they can't hear us.

"Good girl," he says and slaps my ass cheek. A jolt of pleasure pulses through me.

The water sloshes around as Jack adjusts his position in the bath. My breathing quickens as a hot flush creeps across my skin as I wait impatiently for his next move. I wiggle my hips in a silent plea for him to touch me. When it doesn't come, I turn my head just as he sips the glass of champagne, his throat working with a quick swallow. The clear liquid clings to his lips as his tongue slowly swipes across them and heat pools in my belly. My eyes scan down his muscular frame, watching the tiny beads of water roll down his toned abs down to his Adonis belt. He takes another gulp, draining the glass and my eyes meet his as he places it back down, giving me a wink.

His calloused hands grip my hips, tilting them, the cool air hitting my sex. Before I register what's happening, cold liquid trickles in the crack of my ass, rolling down my thighs and coating my folds just as cool lips press against my warm center. I gasp, the sensation from the steamy water beneath me and the champagne cooling my skin, makes me feel dizzy with pleasure. My body involuntarily rolls forward, seeking pressure, causing water to spill onto the tiled floor. He stills my hips with a firm grip and begins to suck and lick at my clit. I've never done this at this angle before and holy shit, it feels all kinds of dirty and hot.

The warmth of his tongue has my eyes rolling, and my hips grinding down onto his face.

"Holy shit," I gasp, and I can feel him smile against my entrance.

The fucker. He knows what he's doing to me. His tongue pushes inside me and his hand leaves my hip, sliding in between my thighs. It's a sensory overload. Firm fingers rubbing my clit, his expert tongue in and out of my pussy at a deliciously punishing pace. I grip the edge of the bathtub with white knuckle force as my orgasm builds.

"Jack, I'm almost there," I pant as his tongue swirls inside me, making my legs feel weak. I don't know how much longer I can hold this position. Just as my orgasm almost reaches its peak, he swipes his tongue over my asshole and I cry out in surprise at the move and at how good it felt. My ass has always been an off-limits area, but I think I'd explore that with Jack.

The water splashes again as he gets on his knees. His mouth presses kisses up my spine, making me shudder in pleasure. He reaches my shoulder and grips my chin, turning it to face him. Crashing his lips to mine, biting down on my lower lip, I groan. Breaking the kiss, I inhale sharply, like he's just sucked the air from my lungs.

"You are so fucking perfect, Ri." His voice is gravelly and low and I swear I could climax just from the sound. Before I can respond, he slams into me from behind and I jolt forward. The more we've had sex, Jack has got a little rougher with me and I am not mad about it. I don't want to be treated like I'm breakable. I want it like this and he's giving that to me.

My core tightens around him with every punishing thrust he gives me. My back arches as I throw my head back, screaming in pleasure, begging for more so loudly, I am sure the entire lake hears me.

"You like that, baby?" he teases.

"Oh, my God, Jack, they're gonna hear us." I sound hysterical, clearly teetering on the edge of pleasure or insanity. I can't decipher which.

"Good," he grunts. "I want them to know who you belong to. I wanna hear you scream my fucking name."

Holy shit, where did this Jack come from?

He reaches round, cupping my breast, tweaking my nipple and I go off. That familiar wave of pleasure crashes through me, but more intense than ever before. My vison blurs, my toes curl and it's more than I have ever experienced.

"Jack... Oh, fuck I'm..." My body shudders and firm hands grip my waist, keeping me from collapsing into the water as my orgasm surges through me. His firm chest presses against me, his mouth latching onto that sensitive spot on my neck as he finds his own release.

"Hearing you scream my name as you come is the sexiest sound," he purrs in my ear.

"What... the hell was that?" I pant.

"That sweetheart was me just letting the neighbors know who you belong to."

After our bathroom antics, we made our way back downstairs to cook; I say cook. I sat on the kitchen island drinking more champagne as Jack worked his way round the kitchen like a five-star Michelin chef, chopping vegetables like a pro, and then tossing them in the wok with such ease.

Seriously, is there anything this man can't do?

I wasn't expecting our little break away, so I didn't come prepared for the trip. I'm dressed in yoga pants and an oversized jumper. At the beginning of our relationship, I'd have been embarrassed to be seen like this, but I feel so relaxed around Jack I know he wouldn't care if I was sitting here wearing a trash bag.

An idea pops into my head. "Do you have Scrabble here?"

"I think so. You in the mood to get that sexy ass beat at a game?" he says, his tone low as he settles in between my legs, slowly grazing his hands up my thighs.

"No, I was thinking I would bring down the Scrabble champ."

He laughs. "I don't think so, sweetheart, but I'm going to enjoy watching you try, but yeah, I'm sure there's a board up in one of the boxes upstairs. I'll go look after dinner," he says, walking over to the stove to stir dinner, which smells incredible.

I jump down from the kitchen island. "It's okay. I'll go look."

"It's upstairs down the hall, third door on the left." I give him a little nod before I make my way upstairs. Photos adorn the walls up the staircase of Jack over the years as a little kid, playing in little league, high school football right till he enlisted.

He was a cute kid.

I stop and smile at a photo of Noah with Jack. The day they passed out of basic training. I remember this day so well. I was the proudest sister and friend, but memories of how my heart ached to be Jack's ,come flooding back.

I kiss the pads of my fingers and press it to the photo of Noah. I haven't spoken to my brother in so long. I move on up the stairs and make my way down the long hallway. This house is stunning. I can imagine my girls growing up somewhere like this, filling the rooms with their laughter and music and for the first time in a long time, that dream feels like it's within touching distance.

I open the door to the room and I'm met with a sea of boxes, all with Jack's name on suggesting this must have been his room once.

I turn to start opening boxes, most filled with clothes, sporting equipment, and board games, but no Scrabble.

I move to a box that's in the open closet. I reach in and pull out Jack's Marine Corps uniform. My thumb grazes over the patch where his surname is stitched.

I set it down on the floor next to me and look back inside to find a metal box, a little bigger than a shoe box. My curiosity gets the better of me and I open it.

Inside, I find his dog tags. I pick them up and hold them in my hand. Staring at his name and number engraved on the metal. I clutch them and bring them to my chest. Closing my eyes. Thanking my lucky stars that he is one of the lucky ones that came home.

A stack of photographs catches my eye. I pull them out, laughing at the photos of him, Noah, Brad, Harry, and Scotty. Various countries they visited and deployments they did. I only met Scotty once at Noah and Jack's passing out parade from basic training, but he was the type of guy who left a lasting impression.

I wipe a tear that's rolled down my cheek, continuing to flick through Jack's memories and I feel like I have got to know the side of him I didn't get to see when I was with Alex. I stop my flicking when my eyes land on a photo of me. I must be about eighteen or nineteen and I'm wearing a USMC t-shirt, one that, if my memory serves me, was Jack's. The one he gave me when my shirt got wet when we spent a bonfire on the beach.

The next photo is of me and Jack. His arm is draped over my shoulders as I laugh into the camera, eyes closed and happy. But it's the look on his face that stops me. He's staring at me with so much affection that I don't know how I ever missed it. The softness etched into his easy smile, the glisten of something in his eyes. The way he looked at me like I was his everything, just like he looks at me now.

I put the photos back into the box and find a stack of letters all addressed to Jack and every one written by me.

He kept them.

So many emotions run through my head. I flick through the letters—too many to count—when I come across one that's not marked with a stamp and is unopened. My heart stops, a lump forming in my throat when I read handwriting that's not mine.

My last letter, for Maria Jones

I place the remaining letters back in the box and slowly open the letter addressed to me.

NL AMORE

Afghanistan
Camp Bastion
March 28th 2011

Dear Ria,

If you are reading this letter, you already know what has happened and our story didn't end the way I hoped, but I will cherish and take with me those moments I did get with you. I wish you weren't reading this, but I promised myself I wouldn't leave this earth without letting you know how much you meant to me.

If the right person at the wrong time was a thing, then I truly believe that's what we were. So many times, I have wanted to find the courage to tell you how I felt about you, but it never seemed to be the right time. I know you are with someone now and I hope he is good to you, because a heart as pure as yours deserves the world. I just wish I could have been the one to give you the kind of life you dreamed of.
I held out so much hope that the universe would find a way to bring us together, but maybe in another life, our paths will cross, and it will be our time. I knew you were special the moment I met you. Stood in your kitchen dressed in a yellow dress and chucks eating a bag of M&M's.

I will never forget the way you smiled at me, and I knew then that I was in trouble. You had my heart right there and have kept it ever since. My one regret I will leave this earth with is that I wasn't brave enough to tell you how in love with you I am and wondering if you felt the same, because I know being loved by you would have been everything.
I need you to know that my heart has held you even when my arms couldn't. In another lifetime, I promise to be brave enough to love you out loud, because it's always been and will always be you, Ri. Until the next life.

All my love, Jack x

A tear hits the letter and smudges the ink on Jack's name. *He loved me, wanted me, the same way I wanted him.*

My chest feels heavy, my heart thumping so loudly it fills the room.

My brain is a tangled mess of thoughts. Every look, every touch, every smile, every kiss, flashes through my head like a photo book. *Were the signs there? Were we just naïve to what was in front of us all along?*

If we had both been brave enough to say something, our lives could have been so different, but maybe this is how it was meant to be. We had to fight our battles separately to find our way back to one another and eventually heal.

"Ri... you okay?" Jack's voice echoes from downstairs, but I can't respond. I'm trying to process all this. I rise to my feet, my hands still clutching the paper.

"Ri, did you find the—" He freezes in the doorway, his eyes scanning the room.

"You wrote me a letter," I choke out, barely above a whisper, but I know he heard me.

He looks down at the paper I'm holding and the look that flashes in his eyes he knows I'm not just holding a letter, I'm holding *the* letter; the one every soldier writes in case they don't make it home. Jack chose to write one for me.

"Yeah," he says, his voice quiet.

"And you kept the letters I wrote you?" I glance at the box of letters and then back to him. "Why?"

He takes slow, steady steps towards me, taking the letter from my hand and settling it down on top of the still-open box.

"You really wanna know why?" My eyes meet his.

He strokes my cheeks with the pads of his thumbs and I see his throat bob as he swallows like he is preparing to say something.

"Because I have been in love with you from the first day I met you. I'm so in love with you. I was just too scared to admit it. You were Noah's sister, and I didn't want to ruin anything, and maybe I was a little scared how you would react." He sighs, regret shining in his eyes.

"And then you met Alex, and I thought he was the better choice for you, that he was going to give you the life you deserved, but I wrote that letter because if I didn't find my way to you..." His voice cracks, my heart somersaulting behind my ribs. I reach up and stroke his face.

"...and it was my time to go, I couldn't have you go through life believing that you didn't mean anything to me, that I didn't love you."

He moves even closer. Our lips are almost touching. I can't imagine what he went through emotionally, writing that letter.

"Because, sweetheart, you were and still are everything to me."

My chest expands to its fullest. He loves me. He's always loved me. My lips tip upward into a smile as I stare at him, his eyes searching my face for something, anything. I kiss his lips briefly. "I love you too," I whisper.

He blinks with surprise. "You do?"

I nod. "You make me feel like I'm worth loving, and Jack, you are everything to me. I never want to lose you."

"God, Ri, I love you," he says in a whisper and then he crashes his lips to mine, and I kiss him back like he's the only thing keeping me alive. I have dreamed of being loved by Jack Lawson for as long as I can remember, and it is more than I ever could have imagined.

Chapter Forty-Three

Ria

"Lex, maybe put that one there," Jack suggests, pointing to a tree branch that doesn't have a Christmas ornament on it.

"Nope, I want it on this one," Lexi argues, completely ignoring Jack's suggestion, and I bite my bottom lip to stop a laugh escaping. Jack twitches and then scrunches his nose up at Lexi's decorating skills, while Elle bounces on his lap waving around an ornament she got out of the box.

We've been decorating the Christmas tree at my house and Jack has stayed every night since we got back from the lake house last month and I have no intentions of suggesting we spend a night apart. I like having him here. No, I love having him here and so do the girls. It's a welcome change to have help and support. We share the cooking and putting the girls to bed, and when they are sleeping, we play Scrabble, watch trash TV or sit and talk about our days. This is foreign to me. Spending so many years doing it alone and begging for help, Jack entered my life, and not once have I had to ask or beg for anything from him. He's just here, doing it, being here for me, for my girls. In all the ways we didn't know we needed him.

I stack the remaining empty Christmas decoration boxes in my hall closet as Jack tiptoes down the staircase above me. An empty pink baby bottle in one hand, and Lexi's Elsa doll in the other, gray sweats and a black t-shirt, his tanned tattooed arm flexing as he tucks the Elsa doll under his arm as he bends to pick up a baby blanket he's dropped on the floor, that familiar fluttery feeling in my chest whenever I look at him hits me.

"This daddy vibe you got going on suits you," I say, waving my hand in front of him.

He stalks towards me, eyeing me up and down. "Hm, Daddy, hey? I like the sound of that word."

"You do?" I say, acting coy.

"Yeah... I do." He stops in front of me. I crane my neck to look at him. His blue eyes meet mine and I smile. A sickeningly happy smile.

He presses a kiss to my forehead, and I wrap my arms around his waist and inhale his scent. He smells of the girl's strawberry cupcake bubble bath and a hint of his cologne.

"Thanks for getting the girls to sleep. Did Lexi give you a hard time" I ask, still wrapped around him. His arms encase me, his hands not quite touching me, still holding on to the girls' things.

"Oh, you know it. Three stories, two songs and now we added a song that involves us clapping our hands together to the bedtime mix." He chuckles. "But it's my favorite part of my day with them. Thank you for letting me do it."

"Thank you for wanting to do it."

"Now go take a bath, pour some wine and I'll go pick us up some takeout," he says, unraveling himself from me.

"Sounds perfect."

I check on the girls, who are sound asleep, looking like the most angelic angels. I add some essential oils to my bath and light some candles, hoping Jack might join me when he gets back. It will be a squeeze and not the same as our bath at the lake house, but I am sure we will find a way to make us both fit. I change out of my yoga pants, sweatshirt, and underwear before I slip into my white bathrobe and head downstairs to pour a glass of wine.

I hum a *Beyonce* song I've had in my head all day and as I turn to go through to the kitchen, I hear a knock on the front door. Jack has a key, but he's likely got his hands full of takeout and probably more. I practically skip to the front door, my stomach rumbling at the thought of spring rolls and sweet and sour chicken balls. I open the door without thinking.

"You didn't take long, I'm starv—" I freeze, my blood instantly cold as I try to register who is standing on my porch with a look of pure evil in their eye.

"Evening, Maria," he slurs. "I've come to get what's mine."

Panic floods me. I act on instinct and try to slam the door shut, but for someone who is clearly under the influence, his reflexes are quick, and he holds out an arm and wedges his foot in the doorway, stopping me from closing it. My breathing quickens, sensing the danger I'm in and that all too familiar feeling of pure fear rises in my body like the night I was assaulted by Greg. I try as hard as I can to close the door but he's bigger, stronger, and he pushes it open with such a force it sends me flying backwards hitting the console table in my entrance hall, knocking a framed photo of the girls, the glass smashing with a crash on the wooden floor.

"Y-y-ou need t-t-o leave," I stammer weakly.

He steps into my home, slamming the door behind him. His glazed eyes slowly rake over my body, venom oozing from him.

"Jack's going to be back any second you need to leave, now," my voice cracking on the last word.

"I don't give a shit," he scoffs, stumbling toward me again. I move backward, trying to scramble to my feet, but I'm stuck in fight or flight mode and my body freezes.

"Alex, please, you're drunk. You need to leave. The girls are sleeping. We can talk in the morning."

"We're gonna talk right fucking now, Maria," he spits. He lunges towards me, grabbing me by the arms and hauling me upright. I try to stifle my scream, but it's useless. The sound leaves my throat echoing in my hallway. He pins me to the wall, one hand around my throat and the other pushing my hips. A cold sweat breaks out all over me as my heart beats so fast and irregular it causes sharp pain to jolt through me. I try to focus on my breathing to stop myself from falling headfirst into the panic attack that's fighting to take over my body.

Fight it, Ria, fight it.

"Now… I already warned you that I wouldn't have you play happy fucking families with that asshole, but you didn't listen," he spits forcing my head against the wall with a punishing grip.

Tears prick my eyes and I silently plead for Jack to hurry home.

"Alex, we are getting divorced now, you can't control what I do or who I'm with," I say, staring at him dead in the eyes, willing myself to find the courage and strength to stand up for myself, to fight back. "I'm not yours anymore, you need to move on and let me go," I plead.

He lets out the most sadistic laugh and presses himself into me. Bile rises in my throat at his proximity.

"Is that what you fucking think?" he scoffs, and the alcohol from his breath assaults my nose.

"I can have you any time I want. Like right fucking now."

He loosens his hand around my neck slightly as I greedily suck in air. He moves his free hand slowly down my side until he gets to the slit in my robe and forces his way through the material, tarnishing my skin with his touch.

Flashbacks from Greg getting on top of me flood my brain, terror working its way through me, but I choose to fight. I lift my knee, trying to hit him in the balls. My hands claw at the hand that's slowly restricting my airway and I fight with all the strength I have to get him off me.

He catches my knee before it makes contact and chuckles darkly, an emptiness in his dark eyes. "Ooohhh, feisty, you like it rough now, do you?" His hand grips my thighs so hard I know it will leave bruises. I pull and claw at his arms as best I can and we fall slightly, knocking the lamp off the console table.

"Get off me," I hiss, bringing my knee up again to meet his balls and this time I manage to hit him hard. He groans and hunches over and I see that as my moment to break free and run upstairs to the girls. I'm almost at the staircase when he grabs me around the waist. I kick and flail my arms and legs around, making it hard for him to keep hold of me.

"Stop, you crazy bitch," he shouts, slamming me against the bannister face first, hitting my head so hard my vision blurs for a few seconds. A pressure in my chest builds, making it hard to breathe.

I slump to the ground, my hands bracing against the bottom step as I try to get my bearings. A sharp pain shoots through my head, making me whimper.

The unmistakable sound of a belt buckle makes my blood run cold, my limbs begin to tremble uncontrollably as he tugs at my robe, causing the burn of bile to return to my throat and my body to go numb. I will myself to move, but I'm frozen, fear taking over.

Come on Ria, fight.

I somehow find the strength to kick my leg out behind me, my foot meeting his shin making him growl in pain, and just as I try to free myself from his grip, a little voice rings out from the top of the staircase.

"Mommy?" A sleepy Lexi is silhouetted on the dark landing. Silence falls, Alex not moving.

"Go to bed, sweetie. Mommy and I are talking," Alex says sweetly.

"Why was Mommy screaming? Are you hurting her?"

I swallow hard, my tongue feeling like lead in my mouth. I try to speak, to reassure my baby girl that I'm okay, but he beats me to it.

"We were playing. Mommy was excited. We are just having a nice little chat about what we are going to do as a family tomorrow, so be a good girl and go to bed."

I glance up the stairs just in time to see Lexi mumble an 'okay' and walk back to her bedroom. The relief is instant that she's away from him, but I'm still stuck here.

"Alex, please, you need to go. You're gonna scare Lexi. Just let me go," I beg. He shoves me forward and releases me, so I slump onto the stairs.

"I don't want you anyway. You make me sick. I bet you've been fucking all those guys in that club. You can do what you want, but I'm taking my girls."

Alex steps over me and walks up the staircase, making his way to the girls' bedroom. My protective instinct kicks in and I run after him, lunging for him before he can reach them.

"You are not taking my babies," I growl as I fall into the wall, my shoulder hitting the concrete, but I don't feel any pain, adrenaline taking over my body.

"Fucking watch me," he barks. I pull his arm, tugging him back towards the stairs, fighting to get past him, but he shrugs me off, sending me careering backward, and I let out a scream.

The world goes into slow motion as my foot misses the top step and I fall. My last thought is a wish: that Jack gets back in time to save them.

Chapter Forty-Four

Jack

I drive back to Ria's, taking in the Christmas lights that cover the houses on her street. I love living in New York but there is something about this small town just outside the city that Ria found herself in that has that feel of home that I want. The smell of our Chinese takeout fills my car, our car. I love saying 'our'; this is it for me, Ria, and the girls and as much as I love her little home, I want to find somewhere that is ours, something we choose together.

I tap my fingers against the steering wheel to the radio when a bright light floods my car, so bright I have to squint and raise my hand to shield my eyes. The car is coming at me full speed and I pull the wheel with force to miss it as it speeds past.

"What an asshole," I shout, pressing my car horn.

I pull into the driveway and get the bags of takeout. I exit the car and walk up the steps to Ria's house but something feels off. It's the same feeling I would get when on the frontline in Afghanistan when the enemy was closing in, or before we entered a compound. I notice the front door is open and I drop the bags, racing up the porch steps.

My heart constricts when I see Ria laying in a heap under her white robe at the bottom of the staircase, a small pool of blood on the floor next to her head.

The air leaves my body and my knees buckle.

I find my bearings, stagger over to her and fall to my knees. "Ri, baby, can you hear me?" I rush, panic filling my voice. I press two fingers to her pulse point on her neck and lean my ear to her mouth to check her breathing. It's shallow, but it's there. I know I shouldn't move her. I've dealt with many casualties when on tour and I acted without a second thought, going through the motions, the relevant checks, and administering the first aid they needed. But this isn't a comrade, a brother in arms, or even a friend.

This is Ria, my Ria, the love of my life. Laying lifeless in front of me, blood dripping down her perfect face. My chest tightens at the thought of losing her. I stroke my hands over her head, trying to see if I can find the source of the blood loss.

"Ria, sweetheart, it's me. I need you to wake up for me okay, wake up, baby." I stroke the hair away from her face with one hand and fumble in my pocket for my phone.

I dial 911, my fingers shaking so much I have to redial the numbers several times to get it right.

The wetness on my fingers triggers something... a flashback of being shot back in Afghanistan, Scotty covered in blood, but I can't let myself go there, not now. I shake my head, a wave of dizziness taking over. I inhale a deep breath. Silently pleading for the operator to answer.

"911, what's your emergency?"

"My girlfriend, she's hit her head. I don't know if she fell or got hurt, but you need to send an ambulance, now," I say, fear clawing at my throat as I fight back tears. I need to keep it together. I can't let my fear take over. I need to save Ria.

I hang up from the operator once I know an ambulance is on the way, and that's when I hear crying from upstairs.

The girls.

"It's okay girls, I'm coming," I shout up the stairs.

Ria stirs and groans, trying to move her head as if she can hear them too.

"Sweetheart, don't move, okay? Help is coming. You're going to be okay, I got you."

"Alex... The girls," she mumbles.

"Alex?" I say, confused. "Did he do this? Where is he?" I ask, anger coursing through my body. "Ri, did Alex do this?" but she doesn't respond.

"Fuck," I roar with a guttural moan; one I hope I never make again. If he did this, if he takes her from me, from the girls, I'll—my thoughts are interrupted by loud cries again coming from upstairs. I'm so torn. I don't want to leave Ria, but I need to check the girls are safe.

I kiss Ria's forehead. "I'm coming back, baby. I'm getting our girls. I'm coming back, I'm not leaving you."

I stand on shaky legs and race up the stairs and head for the girl's room. I burst open the door to find Lexi crying in the corner of her room, curled in a ball, tiny hands over her ears, and Elle wailing in her crib.

"Lexi," I whisper, utter relief flooding my body at seeing the girls here, and safe. Lexi stands and runs to me. I open up my arms and scoop her up. Her little body trembles in my big arms and I feel the tears I've been fighting back free fall.

"Daddy hurt Mommy," she sobs.

"Daddy was here?" I check. She nods. "Mommy screamed and there was lots of banging and Daddy shouted."

"Okay, princess, you did good. Now I need you to sit here with Elle whilst I go help Mommy. Do not leave this room, okay?"

"Okay." She nods. I lift Elle and soothe her, giving her the pacifier and then I place Lexi in the crib with her. I turn on Elle's projector and music to hopefully drown out any noises that may come up here from downstairs. I don't want them to see Ria the way she is. I need to protect them.

"I'll be back in two minutes," I say, holding up two fingers. I edge out of the bedroom, my heart hammering in my chest.

Is he in the house? I feel myself go back to Afghanistan when we enter compounds to clear them, anticipating the enemy to jump out at us at any time. I check the bathroom. *Clear.* I then check Ria's bedroom—*clear*—and I am thankful the house is small.

As I reach the bottom of the stairs, the entryway is flooded with flashing lights as the ambulance pulls up in front of the house. Relief washes over me at the sight.

"They're here, baby. You're gonna be okay. Stay with me." I reach for her hand that is flopped lifelessly across her stomach and squeeze it. It feels cold and clammy, and I squeeze a little harder, willing the life back into her.

Paramedics charge inside with bags and equipment. and it's as if time slows and everything goes in slow motion.

"Sir, I'm gonna need you to stand back please so we can assess the patient." the paramedic says, bending over Ria. I nod, knowing I need to give them the space to work on her.

"We haven't had enough time. Please don't leave me," I beg, but all I can do is stand there and watch, feeling helpless as they try to save the love of my life.

Chapter Forty-Five

Ria

I have always considered myself to be a dreamer. I spent my childhood dreaming of having a happy home and a mom who chose her kids instead of men. I spent my late teens dreaming of finding the type of love you read in romance novels and secretly wishing it would be Jack. I spent my marriage to Alex dreaming of the day he would change and that he would choose me instead of random women, or a bottle of bourbon, and I'm someone who dreams every night of the life I want for my girls.

But right now, I sense I'm waking, but my mind is blank. Did I dream? I flutter my eyes open, but bright lights burn.

I begin to panic as a pain like no other shoots through my head. I swallow, my tongue feeling dry and stuck to the roof of my mouth. I blink and take in my surroundings. I'm hit with a sterile smell of chlorine and hand sanitizer. Everything is white, the faint beeping of a machine is in the distance. I look down to see a hospital band on my right wrist and a blue blanket covering me.

Where the hell am I?

I try to twist my head, another shooting pain goes through me. I lift my hand to touch my head but I can't because of the sling keeping my arm close to my body.

As my senses slowly come back to me one by one, I feel warm air blowing on my other hand. I avert my gaze to the other side of the room and see Jack, hunched over, head on the edge of the bed, holding my hand, resting it against his face.

I wiggle my fingers to see if I can move them, and he jolts awake.

Wide blue eyes with dark circles meet mine and I've never seen him look so broken, so tired.

"Hey, you," I rasp.

"Hey, sweetheart," he whispers back. Lifting my hand to his mouth, he presses a kiss to the back of it. He closes his eyes; a tear rolls down his cheek.

"I'm okay." I have no idea that I am. I don't even know what's happened to me, but I sense he needs to know I am okay.

"I thought I lost you when I saw you laying there..." he croaks. "It was like my world had ended, Ri."

"What happened?" My voice sounds a little clearer and louder now.

He lays my hand back down on the bed, holding on like he's never letting go. "You don't remember?" he asks.

I shake my head slowly, pain coursing through my head, and I wince.

"Be careful, you've got a broken collarbone and a nasty concussion and cut to the head."

I blink, trying to process his words.

"Lexi said Alex came over and he was shouting." He swallows hard, eyes glassy. "I found you when I came home, but he was gone." Then it all rushes back to me and my heart near stops.

"Jack, the girls where—" I try to sit up, moving my sheets so I can go to them, but Jack gestures for me to lie back down.

"The girls are safe. They're here. Nothing happened to them."

My breathing slows, the anxiety leaving my body at the sound of his words.

"I need to see them, Jack."

He nods and stands just as I think to ask another question first.

"Is Alex... I mean where is he?"

"He was found about a mile from the house. He's been arrested and he's being questioned. They are going to need to speak to you, but when you are ready, okay?"

I nod slowly, careful not to cause that shooting pain in my head.

"You're always saving me," I say shakily.

He smiles. "I told you, sweetheart, you're worth saving and if you let me, I'll spend the rest of my life proving that to you."

I sniff back the tears that have started falling down my cheeks. "I'd like that". He leans in and presses his lips to mine, it's tender and gentle and my body relaxes under his touch.

"There is a waiting room of people wanting to know you are okay and some doctors that need to check in on you. I'm gonna go get them okay?"

I smile, excited to see my girls. Jack opens the door and calls down the hospital corridor, "She's awake."

I hear the chaos before I see it. "Mommy," Lexi calls and my heart flutters. No words have sounded better. She runs through the door and Jack scoops her up into his arms, kissing the top of her head, and my heart melts.

"Mommy, are you feeling better? You got an ouchy on your head."

"I'm okay, baby. Come here." Raising my good arm, Jack sits her on the bed, and she snuggles into me. I nuzzle my nose into her hair and inhale her strawberry scent. The smell of my babies has always been my comfort. On my hardest days, I've taken them in my arms and simply breathed them in, knowing that as long as I have that smell surrounding me, I know that I'm okay.

I hear more of a commotion in the hall and Ali walks holding Elle, Harry carrying the diaper bag and toys followed by Brad and then Gabby, her usually clear porcelain skin-tinged red from crying.

Ali walks to the other side of my bed, puffy eyes and scratch marks mar her long neck, something she does when she's upset or anxious. She gives me a small smile, doing her best to keep it together. "Ri, if you ever do that to me again..." She sniffs, blinking fast, fighting back the tears.

"I know... I'm not going anywhere," I say gently, reassuring her I am not leaving her.

"Good, because I can't do life without you, you hear me," she says sternly, eyes glazed, clutching Elle tightly like a security blanket.

"I hear you, and I couldn't do it without you". We stare at one another, wrinkling our noses and blinking back tears. My sister from another mister, the one who held me up more times than I can count. She sits on the edge of the bed and brings Elle to my face so I can kiss her.

"Hey baby girl," I whisper.

"It's good to see you smiling, Ri. You okay, yeah?" Harry says, clearing his throat.

I give him a smile. "I'm okay. Better."

"Glad you're okay, Ri." Brad nods and I mouth, "Thank you."

"Ri... I... Ugh, I thought we were going to lose you," Gabby sobs, walking to my bed, wrapping an arm around me.

"Oh, Gabs, I'm okay, I promise."

I look round the hospital room at this mix of people who have come together for me without forcing it, without begging, without dreaming. They have become my family and while it may not have been the way I dreamed it as a child, this, right here, is far better than anything I could have wished for me and my girls.

Chapter Forty-Six

Ria

Four months later

I lean my head back and take a deep breath as the hot water from the showerhead beats down on my face, my body instantly relaxing. I run my hands through my hair, rinsing off the shampoo. It's the first time I've been able to wash my hair on my own since the incident. I broke not only my collarbone but injured my shoulder and elbow and after months of physical therapy, wearing a sling and Jack helping me wash my hair or treating me to visits at the salon, I finally can use my arm fully again.

It took a few weeks, but as the doctors predicted, my memory came back, and I remembered everything that happened that night. Alex was arrested and after a lengthy court case, not only did the judge sign off our divorce but sent Alex to jail for fifteen years for multiple charges, DUI, assault, attempted sexual assault, to name a few. It turns out Alex's issues were far deeper than I had realized. No punishment will be good enough in my eyes after what he did to us, but sadly that is our broken system. It's made me even more determined to fulfill my dream as a support worker, to work with women and children like us. I must believe that I have survived what I have in order to help others, to help make a change.

Even though my only goal as a mom was to give my children a childhood they didn't have to heal from, I know the bravest thing I ever did was run. We can't control what happens in life, only how we deal with what's thrown at us.

We got Lexi into an amazing therapy group, and it's really helping her understand her emotions and help her process what happened. It's the furthest thing I wanted for her, for both my girls to come from what society deems as a broken home. But it will only be broken if we let it.

We moved into Jack's apartment after I was discharged from the hospital. I couldn't face going back to that house, knowing what happened there, and Jack didn't want us out of his sight.

I haven't worked at the club since. I've instead spent my days focusing on getting better, but I hope to get back to normal soon, back to work, back to taking Lexi to her ballet classes, although I think Jack has secretly enjoyed that part of my recovery. He was born to be a girl dad. It comes so naturally to him, he's even learned to do braids, loose ones, but he's trying and that's more than I could wish for.

Elle is running rings round him and no matter how many times I tell him that she can give herself her bedtime bottle, he insists on rocking her to sleep and feeding her. Despite the trauma we have been working through, the past four months have also been the happiest.

I hear the bathroom door open and sense Jack's presence before I see him. I continue to face the tiled wall, the hot water beating down on me and suddenly a hard body presses against my back, arms wrapping round my waist and a kiss pressed to my shoulder.

"Hey, you." I smile. "Did the girls go down okay?"

Peppering kisses across my shoulder, he answers, "Elle did, but Lexi had fifty-four things on her to do list before she let me leave the room."

I let out a laugh. "Sounds like a standard bedtime".

"I've got the monitor, but I've locked the door," he breathes. A bolt of pleasure shoots through my body. We haven't been having sex due to my recovery. He's been so supportive throughout, but finally, I'm feeling more myself, and now I need him more than ever. I push my hips back, grinding into his erection and moan.

"Need something, sweetheart?"

I wrap my arms around his neck behind me.

"You."

"Hands on the wall and part those legs, sweetheart."

I do as I'm told at an embarrassing speed. He laughs, deep and gravelly. "So eager." His hand strokes down my ass cheek and reaches between my legs, brushing through my folds, and I know I'm wet. "... and so ready for me, baby."

I bite down on my lower lip, closing my eyes, the water still beating down my back. I circle my hips, encouraging him to push his fingers inside me, and when he does, I gasp.

"Yesss." I lean my head back against his hard chest.

He takes his free hand and kneads my breasts, tugging and twisting my nipples, his fingers thrusting into me and a delicious pace, hitting my front wall and my legs quiver.

"Jack, oh God."

"You feel so good. Tell me what you want, Ri."

"You inside me." He removes his fingers and I wince at the release and the emptiness I feel.

He grabs hold of my hips in that bruising way and I can't help the grin that takes over my face. This, this is what I want, what I need, what we need.

"Arch that sweet ass for me, Ri." I do as I'm told and feel the tip of his cock press against my entrance.

I groan in anticipation, waiting for him to push into me, but he doesn't. "Come on," I complain.

"So needy, sweetheart," he laughs, running his finger down my spine and stopping at my entrance. I shudder with excitement. It's almost painful how badly I need him.

"Jack please, fuck me...hard" I beg. I don't care that I'm begging. I promised I'd never beg a man for anything but in this instance I'll make an exception. I'll beg Jack to take me all night long.

Slamming into me with such force, taking me by surprise, I have to steady myself with my hands on the wall and dig my heels into the tiled floor and fuck me hard, he does.

One hand grips my good shoulder, the other on my hip as he bucks into me with such force I'm sure I see stars. The room fills with the sounds of our desperate moans and our wet bodies slapping together; the sound only spurs him on. The more I moan, the harder he thrusts.

Hitting that sweet spot, my legs start to shake in that telling way and I brace my hands further up the shower wall, readying myself for the waves of pleasure that are about to hit.

"That's it, good girl. Fuck, Ri. You feel so good."

"Jack." His name comes out on a scream as a powerful orgasm hits me, my body spasms. His hand finds its way to my clit, and he rubs circles as my body is flooded with pleasure. I feel the telling jerk of his cock inside me as finds his own release.

Gripping my hip harder and pulling me against his chest, our chests heaving, our breathing erratic. He eases out of me, turns my body and pins my body to the shower wall, and crashes his lips to mine.

Waves of pleasure still rock my body as our tongues intertwine and my hands find their way into his hair. His stubble feels rough against my chin, but I welcome it. I break our kiss and take a deep breath. Him; this is exactly what I needed.

I change into yoga pants and one of Jack's t-shirts. He throws on some gray joggers, leaving his broad chest and abs of steel on show and I mentally have to have a word with myself to not jump his bones again.

This is my favorite version of Jack. Whilst he looks utterly fuckable in his work pants and button ups, but casual Jack is something else. I've never been a flashy girl. Yes, fancy dinners, extravagant date nights at high-end restaurants, wearing a dress and heels is fun, but sitting here on the floor of our apartment, looking out over New York, playing Scrabble, eating takeout with a bottle of wine whilst the girls sleep soundly in bed is my favorite kind of date night.

"You are clearly cheating somehow," I say, throwing down my remaining Scrabble squares. I've got the worst letters ever.

"Aww, is my baby a sore loser?" he mocks and like the mature mother of two I am, I stick out my tongue. He laughs in that beautiful way that makes the laughter lines around his eyes show and his face glow.

"I've got something that will make you feel better," he says, standing and heading for the kitchen.

"Ooh, tell me more." My interest is peaked. He disappears and returns holding a tray with two shot glasses, a saltshaker, a bowl of limes, and a bottle of tequila.

"Tequila Are you joking?" My eyes are bugging out. "Me and tequila have a love-hate relationship," I remind him before pressing lips together.

He winks in that cheeky, yet insanely hot way "Oh I remember, but I also remembered it's a year today since you used me as a human shot glass and licked this stuff right off my body, so I thought we could take a trip down memory lane."

I stop in my tracks. Has it been a year? I go through my memory bank and realize he's right. One whole year ago, Jack unexpectedly showed up and walked back into my life, changing it and me as a person in a way I could never have predicted, and I have Nancy and a bottle of tequila to thank.

He passes me a glass full and takes my free hand, licking the back of it and sprinkling the salt on. He takes his own shot glass and raises it in the air. "To a year of us and all the years we have ahead."

I want to say something, but I lose all ability to speak. He's so incredibly thoughtful, he always remembers the little things, the moments most would forget about, but not Jack. They are the moments he absorbs and uses when I least expect, making me fall further in love with him. We clink our glasses, lick the salt from the back of our hands and suck in the lime slices.

"Fuck, that's strong." He winces. I just nod, unable to utter a response as I suppress the urge to gag.

"Okay Mr. Lawson, your turn," I say, clapping my hands together, turning our attention back to our game, mentally preparing to be beaten again. I reach for my glass of red wine, desperate to get the burning taste of tequila from my mouth.

Jack places his last Scrabble square down and spins the board round so the words are the right way up.

It takes me a second to notice he's removed some of the words I know I placed down. I search the board trying to find the new word and there, in the center, are the words MARRY ME.

"Jack, is this..." I can't finish my sentence, I'm being silly, it's a game, It's just words.

"Sweetheart, a year ago today you quite literally stumbled back into my life when I least expected it and bringing with you two little girls who have stolen my heart. I've fallen in love with them as if they were my own. I have spent too many years wishing I had told you sooner how much you meant to me. Wishing I had been the one to have all your firsts with, but I'm hoping there are still many firsts we can share together."

I exhale and wipe the tear falling down my cheek. This man and his words are my undoing. He takes my hands and pulls me towards him ever so slightly. His hands frame my face, and he strokes the tears that fall down my cheeks.

"I want to be your family, Ri. Let me be your safe space. You don't need to do this on your own anymore. I want it all with you. I want the lake house and the white picket fence, the Sunday morning pancakes topped with whipped cream and M&M's. I want a house full of pink tutus and Barbie Dream Houses, the ballet classes and I'll get better at diaper changes because I want all the babies you are willing to give me. I am so in love with you, and everything that comes with you."

He gets on one knee and my hands fly to cover my mouth.

Pulling a black velvet box from his pocket, he opens it up to reveal the most stunning platinum band ring with three large diamonds.

"These three diamonds represent us and our relationship. You are part of my past, you are my present, and I want you to be the biggest part of my future. Maria Kennedy. Will you marry me?"

"Yes." It comes out on a choked sob and a laugh.

He slides the ring on my finger and the diamonds sparkle under the light from the windows.

He rises to his feet, reaching for my hands, pulling me up and into his hard chest. I reach up on my tiptoes and crash my lips to his.

"I love you," I pant in between kisses to his soft lips.

"I love you too, Mrs. Maria Lawson-to-be."

"That has a nice ring to it," I hum.

"It sure does. Now, I'd like to explore my wife-to-be's body and show her just how much I love her."

And explore he did. We spent all night getting lost in one another and discovering new levels of pleasure we had not yet experienced. I don't ever want to come down from this high, knowing this man wants me, despite my chaos, despite all the crazy I bring to his life, he wants me. He came into our lives so unexpectedly, picking up all our broken pieces and put us back together in a way that made us unbreakable. He loved me even when I still tasted of heartbreak and fear and showed me what it's like to have someone walk into your life and never leave.

Chapter Forty-Seven

Ria

One year later

"Jesus, Ri, you're gonna ruin my make up," Ali says fanning her face, fighting back tears as she looks at me as Gabby fastens the last clasp on my wedding dress. I chose a simple satin, backless white gown. It hugs my curves in all the right places, and I know it will drive Jack crazy. I wanted elegant and classy, but also want to make my husband tear it off me later. My hair is pinned in loose waves at the base of my head with a veil clipped in.

My girls look utterly adorable in white flower girl dresses and satin bows in their hair.

"Mommy, you look like a princess," Lexi says, standing next to me, looking at our reflections in the mirror. I bend down, careful not to crease my dress and get down at her eye level. "And so do you, my girl. Are you ready to walk down the aisle? You know what to do?"

She nods her little head. "Uh huh, I take my basket and me and Elle will throw the petals everywhere."

"Perfect." I smile, bopping her on the nose. Elle stands next to Ali, holding her hand, a bit unsure of all the commotion. She's my little wall flower, quieter than her big sister, and I just hope she can manage today without feeling too overwhelmed.

"Ri, you look perfect," Gabby sniffs, smoothing her hand down my veil.

"Me? Look at you two beauties" They both twirl on the spot, looking like models in their satin sage bridesmaid dresses. Their hair in a similar style to mine. It's a spring wedding, and I wanted everything sage and white, plain and simple.

The flowers are a mix of white roses and calla lilies for our bouquets, and the same flowers will fill the ceremony hall and the tables at our reception. Jack told me no expense would be spared on our dream day and while that may be music to most bride's ears, I just wanted the day to be about us and our love and celebrating it with our nearest and dearest. It breaks my heart that I don't have parents to share this day with, but I have all the love I need around me. The one person I wish could be here is Noah. He's deployed again, and while I hoped he would be back to walk me down the aisle, he couldn't be released. I'm just grateful we got to spend this past Christmas with him.

"Okay, I think we need to leave. The car is waiting to take us to the church. Let's get this show on the road," Ali says, ushering the girls towards the door. I turn to look at myself one last time before I walk down the aisle and become Mrs. Lawson. I reach for my flowers just as a knock at the door startles us all.

"Quick, quick," Gabby panics. It's probably the driver. Ali opens the door and as I adjust my dress, I hear Noah's name . I whip my head round so fast I'm sure I give myself whiplash. But there he is, my big brother, all tanned, dressed in his military blues with his white cap, looking as handsome as ever.

Tears pool in my eyes and I blink away so they don't fall and ruin my makeup.

"Uncle Noah," the girls' screech. He bends to hug them both and now I'm really fighting back the tears.

"Okay, girls, let's get in the car," Ali instructs, giving me a nod, knowing I need a few minutes alone with my brother.

"You came," I say, my words shaky.

"Did you think I was going to miss walking my baby sister down the aisle on her wedding day to one of my best friends?"

We've FaceTimed countless times since me and Jack got together and I found out not long ago that Jack called Noah before he proposed to check it was okay; ask his permission or just give him a heads up I don't know, but the fact he did that meant everything to me. My brother, aside from Jack, has been the only man to be there for me. He's been my constant and even though his job makes him leave a lot, he never truly leaves me.

"I hoped you wouldn't," I reply, reaching to hug him and he squeezes me in that protective big brother way.

"You look beautiful. You look happy. It suits you."

"He makes me happy," I tell him.

"I know he does, and you, more than anyone, deserve all the happiness life has to offer and I couldn't think of a better man for you to be happy with."

Bending his arm and offering it to me, I link mine with his.

"Now, let's go get my baby sister and my best friend hitched."

Chapter Forty-Eight

Jack

"Uurrghhhh, it's wrong again," I growl, yanking my bow tie off and throwing it to the ground in frustration.

Fuck, I'm sweating.

"It was fine the first sixteen times you did it. Stop stressing. It's your wedding day. Have a whiskey and calm the fuck down," Harry says, scooping up the bow tie and turning me to face him as he starts to tie it for me.

"Why am I so nervous? This is ridiculous," I huff, running a frustrated hand through my hair.

"It is ridiculous. Pull yourself together. What do you think's gonna happen? She walks in the church, realize she could do better and walk back out?" Brad says casually from the chair in the corner of our hotel room.

I glare over at him. "Don't even fucking joke."

"Ignore Mr. doomsday over there. Ria isn't going to walk out. She loves you, and you love her, so quit your stressing, and breathe because I don't fancy giving you the kiss of life today."

I wrinkle my nose.

"Now that's perfect, don't fucking touch it," he says, tapping my face and walking away.

I reach for my tux jacket and pin the white rose to it. I smile because in the next hour, Ria's going to become my wife and I will officially become a stepdad. I've been as good as over the past two years but today makes it official and knowing that not only Ria will have my last name, but the girls' last name will be double-barreled with the blessing of Alex's parents floods me with emotion.

It's been a hard year, particularly for Anne and Steve, but they are good people. It wasn't their fault how their son turned out and they have welcomed me into their lives with open arms and they will always have my unwavering respect and appreciation for the way they are for the girls and for Ria and I'm happy they were able to make today. Being with Ria has shown me that family doesn't mean blood. It's people who show up for one another and love one another despite everything and anything and that's what we are, one big blended, chaotic, messy, perfectly unperfect family.

"Right, fuckers, have these," Brads says pouring four shots of bourbon into glasses.

"Brad, I can't," I say, pleading. "And why four?"

"Unless you have become a complete pussy, one shot isn't gonna make you drunk, plus it's tradition, remember?" I give him a knowing nod. Before any major event, tour, wedding or funeral, we have always done a toast and today it'll be no different.

The door opens and both Brad and Harry don't seem shocked to see Noah, standing in the doorway, dressed in the same uniform we used to wear and an overwhelming surge of emotion courses through me. He made it back in time, for her, for us.

"I've got to be quick; I need to get to Ria, but I wanted to see you all before the main event," he says, walking towards us.

"Right on time, my brother, come join us," Harry says, waving him over. The guys hug and greet each other. It's been a long time since the four of us stood in the same room. The last time was at the funeral of our friend, Scotty..

I hug and pat him on the back, and we give a knowing nod. No words needed. We've spoken many times before today and the night I called him telling him I wanted to marry his sister was the most nerve-wracking day of my life. But it didn't feel right to do it without his blessing.

Brad hands us all a shot and we raise the in the in the air as Brad says, "To Jack and Ria. May your life be full of good health, wealth and love. To the friends we wish were here but aren't. May they watch over us and protect us and may we always look out for each other no matter what paths life takes us on."

Harry continues with our tradition, adding something we would say before we left for patrol.

"No bullet, no shell, no demon in hell shall break this bond called brothers."

We raise our glasses a little higher and clink them together, saying together, "Semper fi."

I stand at the altar facing the man who will be marrying us, anxiously anticipating the music. The only thing Ria asked for was a quartet at the ceremony and I'll be damned if she didn't get it.

The violinist begins to play "Until I Found You" and the guests rise. I know Lexi and Elle, along with Ali and Gabby, will be walking down first. I turn to see the girls throwing rose petals perfectly, the biggest grins on their faces. A little giggle escapes Lexi's mouth as she throws the petals a little too high and they fall onto Elle. I let out a little chuckle. Ali and Gabby walk behind them a few steps apart, looking beautiful.

I turn back around to take a deep breath; I need a moment to just get it together before she appears. The music changes pace and gets louder and Harry leans in to whisper, "You're gonna wanna turn around, my man."

As my eyes land on her, the wind is knocked out of me. Ria glides down the aisle, arm linked with her brother, looking utterly breathtaking. No worry or nerves show on her face. Just pure happiness. Our eyes lock and the smile that beams across her face has me doing the same.

This incredible, strong, beautiful woman is about to become my wife, and I feel like the luckiest man alive.

Chapter Forty-Nine

Ria

We reach the altar, Noah kissing me on my cheek and then reaching over to place my hand in Jack's. When asked who gives this woman, my brother proudly answers, "I do".

Ali takes my bouquet and I blow a kiss to the girls who are standing so nicely, holding Gabby's hands. Hand in hand, Jack and I walk up the few steps to the top of the altar.

The minister welcomes our guests and talks about the meaning of love and marriage, but I hear none of it. All I can do is hold Jack's hands, feeling his thumbs caress the palms of my hands as we stare into each other's eyes with what most would describe as love-sick looks on our faces.

It's announced that we have prepared our own vows and Jack is asked to go first. My stomach somersault at the thought of the words he may say.

"Ria, two years ago today you came back into my life so unexpectedly, bringing with you all your beautiful chaos. You were everything I didn't know I needed but secretly longed for in the quiet for so many years. Once in a lifetime, if you are truly lucky, we get to meet someone who ignites a fire within us. Someone who makes us smile, someone who makes us love harder and makes us want to be better. Someone that captures your heart and you know in that moment they are your person and that's exactly who you are for me. You are my person, my once in a lifetime love, and I will spend the rest of my life showing you Lexi and Elle and any other children we may be blessed with, just how lucky I am to have you all. Ria, you are worth loving, worth saving, worth staying for. I waited so long to be loved by you, to call you mine, and I thank the universe every day for finding a way to bring you back to me. You are everything to me and I will spend forever loving you."

I take a deep breath, knowing I need to find the strength to say my vows.

"Jack, when you came back into my life, I had no idea how much my life was about to change. You are right, a love like ours only happens once in a lifetime. You were a constant amongst my chaos. It takes a special person to fix a heart they didn't break and love children they didn't make, but you, Jack, did just that. You are the most selfless and incredible man I have ever known. I always thought it would be difficult to love someone like me, but you showed me love can exist and thrive in the broken and the lost. You helped piece my broken parts back together. You walked into my life like you were always meant to be there and I'm forever thankful for that night we met again because it was the beginning of our love story and I didn't even know it. Thank you for loving me, for loving us. My heart has waited so long to be loved by you, but it was worth the wait. You are everything to me and I will spend forever loving you."

I know we are meant to wait but to hell with tradition and Jack is thankfully on the same page because he pulls me to him and plants a kiss on my lips and the room erupts.

We break the kiss, and the minister informs us that we need to exchange rings. We repeat after the minister and exchange simple platinum bands.

"I now pronounce you husband and wife. You may kiss the bride... again."

"Hell, yeah, I will." Jack laughs, crashing his lips to mine and dipping me. The room erupts again, cheering and clapping, but they fade into the distance as he kisses me like the world around us disappears and we are the only ones left. We break the kiss, linking hands as the violinist starts, we raise our adjoining hands in the air, earning whistles and clapping from our friends and family. The girls rush over to us and Jack leans down to pick Elle up and Lexi places her hand in mine. The four of us walk through the church hand in hand, united together as one perfectly imperfect family.

Jack came into our lives so unexpectedly, picking up all our broken pieces, and put us back together in a way that made us unbreakable, and now I get to spend the rest of my life loving, and being loved by him.

Epilogue

Ria

Five years later

"Girls, dinner is ready," I call from the bottom of the staircase. Faint sounds of music and laughter filter down from their bedrooms. We moved to the lake house three years ago, wanting more space for the girls to run around and knowing it was my dream house, Jack left the ball in my court as to when we made it official and moved. I love the hustle and bustle of New York, but the small-town vibe is where my heart is.

I plate the pasta dish I've cooked and glance up at the clock, knowing Jack will be arriving back anytime. He commutes a few days a week to check in at the clubs. The guys opened a third club a couple of years ago and they have ventured across the pond to England.

Once we finish popping out little Lawsons, we plan to spend a summer over there. I started volunteering at a local support group for women and children who are victims of domestic violence. It was incredibly eye opening how many suffer and I'd love to open up my own facility in the future when I have some more free time. I am very lucky that Anne and Steve still help out and Jack's parents are the most incredible grandparents. Between Anne and Jayne, the girls always have a grandma over helping with baking, diaper changes and giving me ten minutes to put my feet up. We are surrounded by so much love and support it took me a little time to adjust to all the offers of help, but now I couldn't be without them all.

I rub my heavily pregnant belly, feeling our baby girl kick. I am due in six weeks, and I am not sure how I am going to make it to my due date. I am huge! But hey, a fifth, yes fifth pregnancy will do that to you. A month after our wedding, I found out I was pregnant. We were so excited, and the girls were buzzing to be big sisters. We welcomed baby Aubrey, followed by her sister, Maddison, just eighteen months later. Two under two was not for the faint hearted. I don't think we slept for nearly three years and just as we came out of that baby and toddler haze and content with our four beautiful girls, when our world was rocked when two lines appeared on a pregnancy test. I was anxious, but Jack was elated. I swear the man has a breeding kink.

It was no surprise our gender reveal party revealed we were having another girl; Jack says he was destined to be surrounded by beautiful women and I think he's right. Baby girl number five who we are yet to name will be joining us very soon and whilst we keep saying this is our last, I've accepted that we are more never say never people. Watch me be the star of a Hulu special, fifteen kids and counting.

The sound of a car comes from our drive and Nugget barks. In his old age, he slowly makes his way to the front door to greet Jack.

"Girls, Daddy's home," he calls, stepping into the entryway. Within seconds, four sets of feet come bounding down the stairs, all fighting for his affection.

They all come in together, taking their chosen seats around the large wooden dining table that sits in front of the floor-length windows that overlook the lake. Jack balances Maddison on his hip and comes over to press a kiss to my lips and gives my belly a rub.

"How are my girls" he asks, reaching for a breadstick off the table to hand to Maddison.

"Your daughter has decided my bladder is her own personal trampoline park and your wife has swollen feet after making twenty-nine trips to the bathroom."

"Sweetheart, I'm sorry this part is rough. Does it help that you look beautiful doing it?" he says with the most charming smile on his face.

"Not really, but I appreciate the support," I deadpan.

"Eat and I'll run you a bath and then I'll clear up and get this sass squad bathed and ready for bed."

I feel my shoulders relax instantly at the thought of escaping to my favorite part of our home; our bathroom, my sanctuary. I love nothing more than being a mom. It's all I ever wanted, but by the end of the day I am touched out and exhausted and I've learned over the years you can't pour from an empty cup. When I take care of myself, I can take better care of them. Happy mum means happy kids.

"I knew I married you for a reason," I say, pressing a kiss to his cheek.

"Must be my good looks and big... charm, right?" he says with a wink.

I laugh, loving that our playful banter has never faltered, no matter how many babies come along or how many sleepless nights we have. We are still us. He's still as caring and loving as he has been from day one and not once has he broken his promise to never leave. He shows up every day for us and I couldn't do life without him.

"Okay, girls, eat up," he says, clipping Maddison into her booster and then walking round the table to help Aubrey with hers. Lexi tells us about her day at school and Elle has come out of her shell the older she's got and isn't afraid to speak her mind. I often feel overwhelmed at the thought of raising five girls to become strong independent women who know their worth, but I know with a dad like Jack, we'll figure it out together.

I eat my pasta, looking round the table at my beautiful girls, stroking a hand over my swollen belly. A pang of emotion hits me out of nowhere and I feel tears prick my eyes. Jack notices and gives me a questioning look. "Hormones," I mouth, dabbing my eyes with a napkin. Maybe it is my hormones, the lack of sleep, or maybe it's me having a moment where it hits me just how lucky I am. I wake up every day, grateful for the life I live and the man I have by my side sharing it all with.

When you come from nothing it takes time to believe you are worth something and Jack has made it his mission to make sure not a day goes by where he doesn't show me I am worth loving, worth saving, worth fighting for, but above all else I am worth staying for, because unlike most people in my life Jack has never made me question his love or his intentions, he's just simply loved me for me and proved to me that good men do exist, and god did I get the best one. Being Loved by Jack did turn out to be everything I hoped for and so much more.

Thank you

Thank you for reading Loved By You, if you enjoyed this world and want to find out more about Ali and Harry, You can pre order their story, Tamed By You here
https://mybook.to/tamedbyyou

'Alice Hart could not be tamed, but why would I want to, when it's the very reason I was falling for her'

Releasing Fall 2024

Acknowledgements

Thank you to...

I have so many people to thank, people who made this story possible, but firstly I want to thank you, the reader for reading and believing in me enough to dive into Jack and Ria's story.

To my Alpha readers Tash and Meghan...

Tash- Without you encouraging me, believing in me and giving me the push I so desperately needed to bring their story to life, this book would not exist. That prologue would still be sat in my drafts, never to see the light of day. Thank you for reading as I wrote and giving me incredible advice. Thank you for listening to my voice notes and giving me a pep talk on the days I wanted to quit. Thank you for loving Jack, Ria and the gang as much as I do but most of all, thank you for being an incredible friend. Forever grateful for you.

Meghan (Meghan Hollie Author)- Where to start? You have held my hand through this entire process. No words could express how truly grateful I am to you for your help, support and friendship. The endless voice notes, facetimes, our late-night writing sessions watching Fifty Shades of Grey, Samba Jack and Ria with her beaver, plotting storylines and blurb writing in little cafes in London, are all moments that made this journey unforgettable. Not only did you pick me up on the days I wanted to quit, but you cheered me on and celebrated every little milestone with me. My spiral sister for life. The universe knew we needed each other.

My amazing BETA readers, Emma, Lynsey and Kayleigh. Thank you for taking a chance on me, for loving Jack and Ria and reading them when they were still rough around the edges, I am so grateful to you all.

To my book bestie Kayleigh, When I met you all those years ago I finally found someone who loved books the same way I did. Bonding over books, being military wives and mothers, I don't think there has been a day that's gone by where we haven't chatted, discussed books or sent a silly meme. Setting up our book page and making the decision to go to RARE LONDON, changed everything for me. I am so lucky to have you in my life, I couldn't do life without.

To TL Swan and the cygnet authors, meeting you all in London was so inspiring. You gave me the confidence that made me believe I could do this! Tee, thank you for your words of encouragement and support. Picking up The Stopover during lockdown changed my life and took me in a direction I didn't think would ever be possible. Thank you for your endless support.

To my family, my mum, Jason, my brothers, their partners, my dad, my nan, my cousin, my best friends (you all know who you are) Thank you for always supporting me in whatever I do.

To the rare group chat girlies/authors. Thank you for all the laughs and your support. This wouldn't be happening without you all.

My editor, Sarah and my proof reader, Jo. You both did an amazing job and were a pleasure to work with.

And finally, Thank you to my husband and children.

To my three beautiful children, my little tribe. I did this for you, to show you can achieve anything you set your mind too and give you a mummy you can be proud of. I love you all to the moon and back, to the moon and back.

Rich- Thank you for supporting me, for believing in me and encouraging me to pursue something I have dreamed of for so long. I would have given up months ago had you not talked sense into me and told me to keep going. Thank you for never giving up on me, I love you, always and forever.

About the author

Natasha is a military wife, mother of three children and a Labrador, living in the South west of England. You will find her either juggling, work, mum life or tapping away at her laptop creating characters and worlds for you to fall in love with and get lost in.

Follow Author NL Amore on Instagram, Tik Tok and Facebook

If you enjoyed Loved By You, I would be incredibly grateful if you left a review on Amazon. Sending love and hugs to each of you.

Printed in Great Britain
by Amazon